SITE 123

by

James H. Summers

Gotham Books

30 N Gould St.
Ste. 20820, Sheridan, WY 82801
https://gothambooksinc.com/

Phone: 1 (307) 464-7800

© 2024 *James H. Summers*. All rights reserved.

No part of this book may be reproduced, stored in a retrieval system, or transmitted by any means without the written permission of the author.

Published by Gotham Books (April 1, 2024)

ISBN: 979-8-88775-459-8 (P)
ISBN: 979-8-88775-460-4 (E)

Because of the dynamic nature of the Internet, any web addresses or links contained in this book may have changed since publication and may no longer be valid.

The views expressed in this work are solely those of the author and do not necessarily reflect the views of the publisher, and the publisher hereby disclaims any responsibility for them.

Table of Contents

Monday
    Who Wants Pizza?... 1
Tuesday
    Time to Replenish Body and Mind... 26
Wednesday
    Preparation - P R E P A R A T I O N – Preparation 50
Thursday
    Strawberries? Yes please!... 66
Friday
    Introductions are in order 115
Saturday
    It's full! It's full!... 157
Sunday
    The unwritten rules of psychological horror 222
Epilogue 248
Author biography 249
Other works by James H. Summers.. 250

INTRODUCTION

This book was fun to write. The initial outline was finished one camping trip back in 2020. It was an open-ended story that followed a group of friends into the woods on a weekend camping trip that was anything but typical. When I thought about what could happen to them, added some personal camping experiences, and threw in a smidge of darkness and horror, Site 123 was born.

Although we all grow older, get busy, take different paths in life, and even eventually retire, memories and friendships prevail. We all need to catch up with our friends and get back into the woods, hopefully sooner than later; I'm missing my camping buddies more than you'll ever know.

MONDAY

Who Wants Pizza?

There was not much time left for her now, she knew that. She had not eaten in two, possibly three days. Kelly had stopped counting after the second, so she was not actually sure. One long, hot summer afternoon while hiking, she became the victim. Kelly was not going anywhere soon. She was injured and unable to escape her predicament. Most hunting traps were not, by definition, malicious. Those were generally defined by trappers who used them as being set and not checked with frequency. Looking around, Kelly saw raw nature. Looking around, she concluded that she was definitely in a bad place.

    Kelly's current situation came about from her need to provide for her family. She had started off hiking earlier in the afternoon so she could cover the ground necessary to get deep enough into the woods. Her goal was a ridge several miles from the road she had crossed earlier in the day. To be successful, she had to get there and hide in cover as the sun began to fall.

    That would have been all she needed to do; she was sure of it. Kelly had come this way before, multiple times. Each trip she took a slightly different route to keep herself as hidden as possible. She could not remember the last time she had taken this exact path, but she was sure someone knew she'd return eventually.

    Looking back down at her leg, Kelly winced in pain as she tried yet again to escape. Each time she struggled to free herself, cold metal dug deeper, and she began bleeding all over again. There must have been four different shades of red that now adorned her leg to varying degrees of wetness. Each color had originally travelled down her leg an equally bright red, and as it dried it became darker. It would not take long for her to stop bleeding again, but the pain would last for quite some time. There was nothing she could do about the pain; it was an inevitable part of her attempts at freedom. Even if she could figure out how to release the trap and escape, would she have the strength? The pain would still be an after effect, along with her injury and the possibility of having to crawl home instead of walking. If only her mother were here, she would know what to do.

    The sun was setting on another long, uneventful day. Each one came and went with her becoming weaker than the last. Kelly made herself as comfortable as she could and tried to stay warm. There was just enough room to pull her body into the nearby bushes. Although still unable to get free, there was a bit of comfort and warmth to be had there. Closing her eyes, she yawned softly and tried to rest for as long as she could.

    Kelly awoke to anxiety and panic, but she dare not move or breathe. Looking around by only moving her eyes, she took in her surroundings. The canopy of leaves overhead offered a small amount of protection from the elements and helped to hide her from most of the moonlight. Single raindrops fell infrequently around her, initially making the only noise she could hear. There was an occasional rustling sound of leaves above, something small playing around a tree up ahead, and more raindrops. They came more frequently now, and Kelly fought the urge to look in the direction of the noise made from each and every single one. Something was not right; it was still too quiet.

    Control your breathing, you must control your breathing, she thought, as she blinked her eyes a few times. It appeared that she was not as protected from the rain as she thought. Laughing inside, she fought off the urge to turn her head and more thoroughly search the area. She heard it first from her left. A single twig broke under foot, she was sure of it, but whose foot. If someone was going through this much trouble to approach slowly, cautiously, she was probably already compromised. Slowly she raised her head and turned to get a better look.

    The moonlight worked against someone stalking prey on nights like this. It was bright enough for a normal person's eyes to provide clarity, but it was even more beneficial for someone like Kelly. From about fifteen feet away, hiding behind an exceptionally large tree, she closed her eyes and reset her vision. Opening them slowly, she saw hot breath escape into the air and climb upwards. Slowly the mist travelled to the left as it went higher, before disappearing out of sight, having been scattered from a light breeze.

It was several feet from the ground when she had first seen it. Again, the creature exhaled into the moonlit air, but other than its breath, it remained unseen. *The height was too tall for it to be from a wolf; what could it be,* she thought. Watching the creature exhale she began thinking of her family. She wondered if she would ever see them again. She had to get free, she just had to. Again, the creature exhaled, continuing to remain hidden. *It was too tall for it to be a bear.* Her mind raced, thinking only of her family; Kelly's two girls, her son, she missed them all.

The rain fell steadily, and quickly began soaking her coat. It would not take much longer for her to be chilled straight down to the bone. The noise the rain made now as it hit the newly moistened leaves and rolled off onto the ground made it more difficult for Kelly to listen to her surroundings, but there was always the breath, she could still look for the breath. It was in the same spot, it came regularly, and it seemed to be escaping something that was patiently waiting. Again, the creature exhaled, its warm breath floating softly upwards. The fact that it remained hidden was driving Kelly mad. She knew not to call out. *What if it was resting? What if it was not sure she was in the area? What if it was not looking for her at all?* Her mind ran through all those thoughts several times before concentrating again on the escaping breath.

The wind began howling through the trees. It moved quicker now, and with more strength. The lower branches swung back and forth, bending to the will of the upcoming storm. Rain sometimes flew through the air sideways, taking with it any loose leaves it could find. Occasionally one would come through low enough to smack into Kelly's face, stinging her cheek. It was not welcomed, but she would not acknowledge it. The sheer strength of the wind made it impossible to see the breath of the one nearby now, she could no longer rely on that visual aid. At this point, she was not sure it was even there anymore. *Maybe, just maybe she was hallucinating?* Kelly was, after all, thirsty and hungry.

Thirsty, she thought again, as she lowered her head for a drink. The rain on the leaves around her gave her an opportunity to quench her thirst; Mother Nature had provided once again. Kelly took in as much rainwater as she could from what was available. It would not be enough, but it offered hope. Maybe the creature coming for her, if it were a creature, if it were still present, would be small enough for her to kill. Maybe she could gain nourishment from it. *Maybe, just maybe, she could be the predator,* she thought, frantically scanning the trees with her eyes. *Well, food and water in the same day, how wonderful,* she thought.

A smile crossed her lips, but quickly faded when she turned to her right to follow something walking into her peripheral vision. He was a tall man, dressed from head to toe in varying shades of green and black. It was if the storm itself had ended its tumultuous reign in his presence, becoming quieter the closer he came. The wind stopped blowing all together, sending the last of the leaves cascading down in front of him at his feet. The rain ceased, offering only an occasional drop that fell to the ground, regretting having ever done so.

"Kelly is that you?" the conservation officer whispered, still staring at her bright red hair.

Kelly looked up and threw half a smile in his direction. She managed a weak nod and closed her eyes; lowering her head in defeat, she half smiled.

"Why, you are miles from home. Here, let us have a look at you," he said taking a knee beside her.

Reaching for Kelly, the CO slowly extended his hand to comfort her. She recoiled and jerked backwards, leaving the safety of the bushes, which he sort of expected. She did not want him going anywhere near her leg. Looking down at Kelly, he saw the blood on her glistening in the moonlight. She looked pretty bad off, he needed to act quickly, and with purpose. He did not often walk through the woods at night looking for poachers with his first aid kit in hand, but it was never too far away.

Kelly saw a wonderful man in front of her, a peaceful, kind, and wonderful man. She remembered seeing him before, and he was as helpful now as he had been then. The CO was very tall, towering over her at a height approximately six foot three inches; he might as well have been a giant! He was a thin, chiseled man of men. He had exactly what he needed to be successful, no more, no less. His muscles, she imagined, were exactly as they needed to be. They were smaller, more defined, perhaps more so than most, but pound for pound, she had no concerns of him being able to take care of himself.

He had a calm, matter of fact demeaner that was only truly revealed by his actions, not his words. From their past conversations, which were brief albeit informative, he could physically exert himself without true exertion; he had a high tolerance for pain. He could do more with less, and he brimmed with pride and confidence at having completed all three phases of ranger training; his body was as physically fit as his mind was sharp.

The CO would not speak openly about his experiences in Afghanistan, Iraq, or other places, but he spoke highly, and often about his accomplishments when it involved his specialty training. He absolutely loved the physical aspect of pushing oneself until you couldn't be pushed any further, and then being pushed some more; *one could always be pushed more*, he said to those he spoke to. That was about as much as she could get from him. From time to time a new detail would emerge, but for the most part, he was a simple, quiet man; *a wonderful, simple, quiet, and kind man*, she thought.

She watched him walk away until he disappeared into the woods; one by one the trees ate him; first his left side, then his right, until he was no more. Kelly continued looking on, except, he wasn't walking away, no, he was walking towards her. Kelly was confused. A warm feeling passed through her, a feeling of foreboding, of dread. Kelly looked forward and concentrated to verify that she actually saw two men standing in front of her.

"Don't you go running off on me, you hear?" he cautioned as he turned to walk to his vehicle.

The CO took one step and froze in place. Standing not two feet away in front of an old tree was a man holding a shotgun.

"That's close enough," the man chided as he steadied his weapon.

Kelly put more distance between the arguing men and

herself. Sliding backwards with her good leg, she went as far as she could go, half hiding behind the furthest tree she could reach.

"You've seen enough movies to know what comes next. Slowly loosen your belt with your left hand and let it slide to your ankles. SLOWLY!" he shot out.

Kelly jerked backwards when the man yelled. Had she any extra room on her chain she could have possibly pulled her stake out. It would not have been anything she would have tried outright, but if surprised, it might have happened. The CO loosened his belt and waited. It slid down to his ankles, still offering a chance out of this situation, if he were to drop to the ground. He was not sure he could make it before the man brandishing the shotgun fired both barrels, so he stayed put.

"You don't really want to do this. It's not too late for you, just surrender and-"

"Shut up! Slowly step out of that belt and come forward."

The CO slowly stepped to the front and towards the left of his belt, as instructed. Looking around he assessed his chances of getting behind a tree for cover, grabbing his belt as he went.

"That's good right there. Now sit down on the ground," the man in control demanded.

The CO sat on the wet ground and again spoke.

"I've been taking your traps now for over a month, I knew we would meet sooner or later," the CO stated calmly.

"Get naked."

The CO could not hide his shock as he looked up at the man without speaking.

"I said get naked. I need you out of those clothes. Right now!" he snapped.

The man was somewhat quieter in his demeanor, but the weapon he had leveled at the CO spoke volumes.

"Alright!" he shouted as the man jerked the shotgun in his direction and widened his eyes.

He looked on as the CO took off his uniform shirt and T-shirt, placing them to his right, only a foot away from his pistol in his belt. Kelly continued watching the events unfolding in front of her while managing to tug feverishly on her chain. From the first jerk when the man had yelled, she noticed the stake loosening.

The pain in her leg was numbing her senses. Tears filled

her eyes as she continued pulling backward to free herself. Something told her this was the time. She had to go now if she were to go at all, if she were to live. There was no way to minimize the pain she felt when she jerked the chain. She could not pull on it without feeling excruciating pain in her leg, but she had to get free.

"Take all your clothes off. Hurry up."

The CO knew he was quickly losing his options. Soon he would be totally naked deep in the woods, right in the path of an oncoming thunderstorm. He was at least a mile from his vehicle, and miles further from town. He was not sure he was going to make it out of this. *What was Scott doing? How could he think he could get away with this,* the CO thought.

"Look, I understand this is not where you want to be. There's still no harm done here. Put down your shotgun and surrender and I'll put in a good word for you. At this point, all you were doing was some illegal trapping. The fines for that aren't really that bad," he pleaded, as he continued taking his pants down to his ankles.

Getting no response from the man, the CO slid them all the way off and raised up slightly to place them underneath.

"I know its cold out here, put these on," he said, throwing a pair of handcuffs.

They bounced off his knee and landed in front of the CO's shirt. Looking at the man towering above him, he slowly picked them up and paused, making eye contact. The man holding the shotgun continued staring at the naked CO and waited.

"If I see you look over to your right one more time, or if you even think about going for your belt, I'll finish you right here."

The CO felt all hope leave as he opened the handcuffs and tightened them around his wrists. Walking up slowly, the man stood in front of his prisoner and told him to close his eyes.

"I'm not going to look away. If you are going to do this, then you'll have to look me in the eyes," the CO blurted out excitedly.

Watching the man move around him made his heart race. To say it nearly pounded out his chest was cliché, but he definitely felt anxious and on edge. Moving behind the CO he kicked the belt out of reach and pushed him forward into the mud. The CO was cold before, but now he was really cold. Water will take it right out of you, and now he had been pushed into the wet, muddy ground. With one eye looking at Kelly trying to free herself and the other on the man down in the mud, he took the butt of the shotgun and hit the CO in the back of his head, knocking him out.

Kelly watched as the man on the ground stopped moving. The one standing looked over at her, and when their eyes met, she once again started feverously jerking on her chain. He took a few steps and stood in front of her stake. Stepping on it with his boot he pushed it in as far as it would go, deep down into the muddy ground. Flight was no longer an option, so she chose to fight instead. Readying herself to respond to his next move, she prepared as best she could.

Taking hold of his end of the chain, the man started pulling. His sole purpose was to remove her from the bushes and from behind that tree, and then get her out into the open. He applied constant and even pressure as he moved her close. When she was almost there, he began jerking on the chain. This sent pain deep into Kelly's core, making her cry out. A few times more and Kelly found herself out in the open with her leg once again bleeding. It added to the moisture on the ground, making the mud appear to resemble red clay. Another jerk and Kelly no longer fought back. She stopped resisting in an attempt to have the man stop pulling on her leg. Again, she cried out, tears filling her eyes.

The man stepped on the chain to keep her close. Kelly was no more than an arm's-reach away now, and without any hope of escaping. She grew frantic. Although she had not eaten in days, she felt the urge to vomit. Again, she started tugging, ignoring her pain. Saliva and stomach acid slowly dripped down her chin as the last of the contents of her stomach fell onto the ground between her legs. She sank deeper into the mud as she tried to leverage her body and remove her stake.

Kelly turned over onto her stomach and tried to pull free, but she was too small, too weak. She had always been small for her age, but she was fit and trim. This had worked for most things during her young adult life, but it would do nothing to save her now. Sliding forward in her attempt to escape, she found no traction and fell face first into the mud. Turning over again onto her back, she frantically continued jerking and tugging on her chain.

"That's right, struggle" the man said laughing as he retrieved a knife from his waist.

It was not the man's voice that caught her attention, that distracted her. What made her stop struggling was the gleam of the moonlight reflecting down from the knife blade. Kelly pleaded with the man to let her go. She did not know if it was possible to convince him, or even if her request would be considered, but she tried one more time. The man never responded. The smile on his face when he reached for her said enough to answer her question.

Kelly sighed in relief. He placed his hand on her shoulder and patted her on the back a few times. A quick blink allowed her to see his true intentions. Had it lasted any longer, she might have missed it completely. His eyes narrowed, and the smile left his face. His hand tightened into a fist, taking as much of her hair as he could to restrain her. Kelly's heart skipped a beat. He immediately shook her violently, raising her high into the air.

The man appeared to be holding his breath as he ran his knife across Kelly's leg. As if there was not enough pain shooting through it already, he had just added more. She jumped and jerked with all her might to free herself, but it was no use, she just wasn't that strong. Kelly sure as hell did not want to die without a struggle. She started scratching and clawing wherever she could. She even resorted to biting, but she was held far enough away from his body for that to be successful. Try as she may, all Kelly managed to constructively do was bleed.

She did not know how much longer the man could hold her up and away from his body, but she looked for that opportunity. When she hit the ground, whether it would be on her feet or thrown on her back, she would hit the ground running. The man had loosened the stake enough for her to jerk it out on her next attempt, she was certain. This would be her escape. If he wanted her after that, he would have to follow her blood trail as she ran through the woods.

Thinking of what to do next, she planned to head toward the nearby creek. That would help to hide her and slow or stop her bleeding all together. It would definitely throw him off, he might even lose track of her. Shaking her again he turned his hand to the side, positioning her body away from him. This was done mainly to prevent her from causing harm, but it had the secondary benefit of allowing the man to tighten his grip and control her as he saw fit.

Gone were Kelly's chances to scratch and bite. Gone were her chances for escape. Kelly looked at the creek's reflection in the moonlight as an artist would to preserve the image in their mind. In the blink of an eye, she saw the creek disappear. The man slammed her onto the wet ground and held her in place, pressing her firmly into the mud. He used a knee to push down on her back, sliding in close against her. His hand never released its fistful of red hair from the back of her neck.

The man pressed harder and harder against her. Kelly tried to scream out, but she could not easily breathe from the pressure. Her cheek was held against a rock with all the force the man could muster. It was impossible for Kelly to open her left eye, lest mud come in and cloud her vision, blinding her. With her one good eye she looked into the forest as far as the moonlight would allow and awaited her fate.

The muddy ground pressed against Kelly, sucking the life from her. Between the cold mud and the pressure from the man above, Kelly knew her life would soon be extinguished. She thought of her family. *What would they do without her? How would they survive?* Kelly struggled against the weight of the man, jerking upward several times, but she didn't make progress. She did little more than sink deeper into the mud; Kelly cleared her head from her thoughts of failure, of pain. She was forced to close her mouth and breathe only through her nose. The anguish Kelly felt was debilitating.

It was no longer a challenge at this point. He had trapped his prey, he had secured it, and now it would be dispatched. Taking his knife, he ran it along the side of Kelly's face and down her neck. He went slowly at first, and with little pressure, letting the knife do all the work. Once started, he went harder and pressed until he ran the blade alongside bone. Kelly's one eye that he could see went lifeless and cold. He pulled the knife from Kelly's body and stuck it in the muddy ground beside her head. Kelly spasmed a few times, stretching her feet out as far as they would go. This he thought was due to reflex, or possibly a last attempt to gain her freedom.

The man moved off and rolled her over onto her back. A flash of light preceded a deafening clap of thunder, and then the rain began to fall. It came slowly at first, and then it came in buckets. Looking around the man listened to his surroundings. The rain that had earlier stopped for the CO seemingly out of respect, had started anew unleashing its fury in apparent disgust of the other.

He looked on trying to determine if the rain was here to stay, or if it would pass on through; when it continued to make a mess of things, he had his answer. Clouds rolled in and hid the moonlight, masking it behind shades of gray and black. The wind picked up and howled around him.

Everything in nature displayed disapproval for the life he had taken. In one quick motion he picked up his knife and plunged it deep inside Kelly's stomach, telling Mother Nature she had no control over him. Maneuvering the knife aggressively, he made an incision from her groin to the bottom of her rib cage.

Placing the knife back into the mud, he took his hands and pulled apart the skin to expose her insides. Feeling around he searched for her stomach. Using as much light as was available, he slit it open and moved it around to see what was inside. He quickly rummaged through the contents of her empty stomach.

"Nuts," he mumbled under his breath, there was nothing for him to base his decision on what she had recently eaten.

Having found nothing, and with her held in the trap, he guessed she had been here for a couple, possibly several days. He stood up and took hold of the chain and raised it up. Pulling the stake out of the ground, he raised Kelly high into the air. He followed the chain down to where it met the trap and opened the steel jaws to release her. Kelly fell to the ground and hit the soft mud with a squish. The rain had been moving the blood downhill all this time, but there was still plenty below him. Kelly's blood went into the air and splattered the man as high up as his knees, although it would only be visible in daylight, she had left her mark upon him.

Looking left to check his surroundings, he reached down and picked up his knife. The clouds were still rolling in and the rain was coming down as hard as it could. He held out the blade and rinsed it off. Placing it back in his sheath, he reached down and picked her up. Looking one last time, he threw her body towards the creek bed and began walking back to the truck. Kelly landed face down on nearby rocks, with both of her feet in the water. The creek washed over Kelly's legs, sending what little blood that still escaped downstream. The red-tailed fox, who's life had been cut short, forfeited by the cruel man, was discarded in reckless abandon, true to his form.

"Who's hungry for pizza?" Scott asked.

"This guy!" he laughed loudly, pointing a finger at himself as he continued walking out of the forest, a bloody trap in one hand, and his new uniform in the other.

Looking down at his watch, he guessed he had about an hour to meet everyone. He was very hungry, and no matter how bad the weather was, Scott was going to meet them for some pizza.

Across the creek and miles away, Brian watched from the safety of his car as the thunder and lightning played havoc with his nerves. The flashes came in pairs as they lit up the sky. Before the last one had dissipated, and his vision returned, thunder announced its intentions anew. The sky was once again dark as clouds rolled in, followed closely by rain, catching him off guard. The irony was that he had arrived in plenty of time to have safely made it inside, but he found himself easily distracted. Brian had looked in the rear-view mirror and noticed his hair to be a mess. As he was fussing with it, the wind picked up and the first flashes of lightning lit up the early evening sky. He ignored the light show and began fighting with his windblown hair. Before he knew it, the rain was coming down in torrents and he was stuck in his car.

He waited several minutes more, watching as others were soaked before they even made it halfway to the front door. He watched on as at least three couples were thoroughly drenched before disappearing safely inside. One couple decided to forgo tonight's activities altogether and turned around before even making it halfway. Brian could wait no longer. If he was going to go, he had to make his move now. Looking around in the back seat, he rummaged for an umbrella for a few moments before giving up. Making a run for it, he jumped out and dodged as many of the puddles of standing water as he could, locking his car door with his remote as he ran.

    Opening the front door, he stepped inside onto the rug and waited until the dripping slowed. He breathed in deeply and enjoyed the smells. Looking around the large open room, he examined the pizza joint and searched for his friends. It was not unusually dark, but the lighting was soft. Double brass sconces hung around five feet high, adorning the walls about every twenty feet or so. Other than those, the only other source of lighting was from small globes that hung below the fans mounted irregularly from the ceiling.

    The walls contained assorted picture frames in various sizes and colors, sporting images of cowboys, old city buildings, and depictions of days long since gone. In all actuality, there was not much available space for new pictures at all; the walls were as busy as the business was. Maroon painted paneling reached upward from the floor to the height of four feet. From there, beige painted cinder blocks took over, and climbed up to the dark colored, stained wooden ceiling.

    Every week for the last three years, Brian had enjoyed coming here for pizza, beer, and a good time. It was not always a Friday, or Saturday that they visited, sometimes his friends would come earlier in the week. He can remember this place being smaller years ago. The building was twice as big now to accommodate the growing business. Additional square tables were added, as necessary, to allow for adequate seating. Each table had napkin holders, salt, and pepper shakers within reach. Parmigiana cheese and crushed red pepper shakers were visibly missing, but available upon request where you placed your order.

    Other than the pizzas and sports bar games available to patrons, they provided a nice collection of beers on tap. Other varieties were in bottles, but the six that came from kegs were by far the major draw. This place was successful for many reasons, but one might say it was mainly due to their simple business model. They sold pizza, subs, and oh yes, beer; and they've done so for over forty-five years.

The best thing about this place was their emphasis on accommodation. The plethora of small tables were easily put together to seat any amount of people. Each table was big enough to hold multiple plates, pizzas, and pitchers of beer, or the three Ps, as his friends called it. Scanning the busy room for the third time he gave up and ordered a Blue Moon on tap to occupy his time until his friends showed, or at least until he found them; he still wasn't sure he hadn't missed them.

Finding a few empty tables next to each other, he pulled them together and sat down to watch professional basketball; it was after all, Monday. He looked at the score that flashed on the screen and realized he did not have a dog in that fight, Brian did not care for either team; although he was enjoying his beer, he soon came to a sad conclusion: all that was left now was to eat his orange slice and walk back up to order another.

Standing up he noticed how unusually cold it was tonight. The room was colder inside than it was outdoors, which was unseasonably cold, but inside it was almost too cold. This was possibly due to a few weeks of unusually below normal temperature weather. Now that he thought about it, the sun had barely been seen on a single day over the last two weeks. He could not help wondering how next week's weather would turn out. *I could do with a little less rain, and more sunlight,* Brian thought.

Walking back to his left he passed several tables on the way to the small bar and paid for his beer. Nodding to the bartender he smiled and turned around to walk back to his table in front of the large screen TV, and that's where he found his friends. They had pulled three tables together and were looking at menus and drinking beer without him!

"Hey! Put that beer down!" he yelled as he approached their table.

When looking at the group for a hookup, Brian did not see someone as male or female, he saw someone as whether he would sleep with them or not. Looking at the sorry lot he could not help but be amazed at their similarities and subtle differences. Most of them were blonde, some with long straight hair to their mid backs, some short and curly, some with shoulder length, full body hair. Most had blue, but some had brown eyes. Their builds were from petite frail and athletic to big boned; it was obvious to everyone that God made all sizes and shapes.

There were three white, equally semi-pale blonde girls sitting side by side. A few seats down were the newlyweds, and on the end was another blonde. It was humorous to see them all the same side of the long table; it was as if half of the apostles were missing from their last supper. Another difference in that painting that would have stood out would have of course been their appearance. The girls were drinking beer, the newlyweds were making out, and the one on the end was playing with the orange slice on his empty glass.

His eyes went back to dwell on the newlyweds. Nick was a Latino-proud man in his mid-twenties with his ever-powerful piercing hazel eyes. Teena was a beautiful mixed light-skinned black woman with brown eyes and curly black hair. They made a wonderful couple, and yes, everybody knew that they were newlyweds! They wore matching white T-shirts with the words HIS on hers, and HERS on his, in stereotypical sexual orientation colors: pink letters on his shirt, and dark blue on hers, classic! Both wore blue jeans, and worn, nothing-fancy white sneakers. He could not really have given anyone a decent description of their faces, as they were mashing their lips together since before he had walked inside.

Brian took the last few steps with exaggerated bounds, making his brown curls bounce up and down, seemingly all by themselves. He was greeted with hoots and hollers from one and all, except the newlyweds who were still preoccupied. Those who noticed, toasted him, and took sips of their beer in his honor.

Looking at Brian there was nothing overly attractive about him; he wore his small, short, thin, frail build with pride. For tonight's relaxation, he chose a blue button up shirt, beige pants, a brown belt, and slightly darker brown shoes. It was his standards that were high. He hoped others would be forgiving, or just fall in love with his Grand Canyon-sized smile and good looks. Brian was lucky most of the time. He had won the lottery with the one on the far end; an attractive blonde-haired, blue-eyed sex goddess of a man.

"You all suck!" Brian smiled.

"We've been waiting for you for like thirty minutes. We had to start without you," laughed Linda between sips, with Christy smiling beside her.

"Whatever. You know you were the one that said '*hurry up. Let's get beer before Brian gets here, you know how much he drinks.*' I'm just saying," Brian smartly remarked, staring at Christy.

"Sure. Sure," Christy smiled.

It was funny to Brian when he walked up to a table full of mostly women and received that sort of welcome, particularly with him being gay. The only one he wanted to see tonight was sitting on the end, fully engrossed with his newly refilled Blue Moon.

"Hey Joseph. Save me some will yah, geeze," Brian said laughing.

Joseph nodded as another inch of his frothy beverage disappeared.

"Here. Let me help you all out," Brian said as he took the two empty pitchers back to the bar for more.

More cheers erupted when Brian maneuvered past tables with both pitchers held high above his head.

"Two more Blue Moon please. Oh. Can I get a small cup of extra orange slices?" Brian asked brandishing his two empty pitchers and a large smile.

"I'm sorry, but we're all out of oranges, man. Do you still want the pitchers?" the tall bartender questioned.

Looking back at his friends, he thought it was better to drink without the orange slices than to return without beer.

"Yes please. Two."

Brian paid, and on his way back he saw Joseph waving the Queen of Hearts playing card.

"How it suits you," Brian laughed at him.

Looking back at Joseph, Brian thought of himself as one of the luckiest men in the entire world; except for Joseph, who was luckier for being loved by him. They were supposed to have matched tonight, but Joseph wasn't too far off. He too wore a dress shirt, with a loose collar and no tie, but it was white. He had beige pants, brown dress shoes, too. Where he did stand out was his medium build, his slightly more-than-a-handful belly, and his thick, full brown beard. Although he was older than Brian, and everyone in their group of friends, actually, he was still a catch. Brian absolutely loved him.

They reached the table at the same time, announcing both their success and failure.

"They ran out of oranges, so re-use what you've got!" Brian said excitedly.

"I've the Queen of Hearts! It won't be much longer now!" Joseph told everyone.

Nobody cared for any of that; Brian doubted that anyone heard anything at all. It was obvious to him that beer seemed to be their focus. *Soon I would be eating pizza, that's what I want,* Brian thought, as he worked on downing his newest beer.

Christy reached out to Linda and gently cupped her breast, before squeezing. Mid-drink, Linda tightly held her lips shut so she wouldn't spew beer across the table.

"Just the way I like them," Christy remarked, swallowing.

She found herself actually staring, although briefly, at Linda's cleavage. Her white dress had about a million bright red polka dots in various sizes. This she found distracting, but not as much as her cleavage. Linda's hair was short, but not overly so. It hugged her face, and both sides curled under slightly, resting against her neck. Christy always told her that if she ever needed any, she had plenty; her hair was long and straight, reaching to the middle of her back and beyond. Looking up to smile at Linda, she thought about another sip of beer, and then glanced down at what *she* was wearing.

Christy had on one of her go-tos, an orange Sunkist brand T-shirt; it was one of her favorites! That, coupled with a moderately tight-fitting pair of blue jean shorts that were pre-faded on the thighs, were relaxation at its finest. She made a weird, half smile, half pucker face and turning her head slightly to one side, she stared at Linda.

"Time to play darts then, is it?" Linda snarked.

With one last squeeze before letting go, Christy nodded. Both women stood up, sipped more of their beer, and then went to play darts. This left the newlywed couple, Brian and Joseph, and Robin to wait for the pizza. The newlyweds were totally oblivious to anything other than themselves anyway; having hardly even touched their first beers. Brian and Joseph were carrying on their own conversation, and Robin was sitting facing towards the door, appearing to be waiting for someone.

To anyone coming in for pizza and beer, it would have looked like your woman was waiting for you. Robin was facing the door, infrequently sipping her beer. She wore a loose-fitting white blouse gathered at the waist, black slacks with matching short pumps. Her blonde hair was mildly curly and hung full to her shoulders. She had a slim, athletic build, and even from the door, her bright blue eyes could easily be seen. She didn't seem to be smiling much, but who knows what could happen after more beer.

"Queen of Hearts. Queen of hearts, your order is ready," a woman's voice cried out.

Brian and Joseph took the initiative to go and claim their pizzas.

"Thanks guys," Robin said softly smiling.

Joseph returned her smile as Brian, in the process of nodding, turned to the right and grabbed an empty pitcher for another refill. All the while the couple making out were still hard at it. Brian looked at Joseph, shook his head in disbelief, and thought, *man, you sure are lucky!*

As if on cue, the moment Robin was by herself, her eyes caught the front door opening. Her soon to be ex-boyfriend slipped inside and the door closed behind him.

"Don't want to waste a trip, we'll be right back," Brian blurted out, waving his empty pitcher.

Stepping inside, the CO's eyes shot around the large open room. Immediately off to his left was the kitchen. There was an open window where you placed your order, and further down to the right was the bar. He read the sign in front of him. *Order your pizza, move forward, order your drinks.*

It was organized, if he said so himself. As he was reading the sign and taking his first look around the place, several tables of customers, and even a few cooks shot him glances. It might have been the uniform, it might have been the way he stood just inside the doorway, but he drew stares, nonetheless. A couple of people did double takes over their shoulders, before going back to drinking their beer and enjoying their pizza. Scott stood still long enough to ensure everyone had time to finish staring at him before moving on.

Out of the corner of his eye, he kept taking in the man. He was unusually tall, with thin, chiseled facial features. His military look seemed to fit him, and because he was in a uniform, he had a sort of militaristic demeaner about him. His short sandy-brown hair, his clean-shaven face, even the way his hat fit, it all looked like he belonged. Although out of place here at the pizza joint, this nature-loving outdoorsy-type looked the part, drawing the man's respect. He turned his head and nodded to the man in green. Scott paid the man no attention, nor did he acknowledge his sentiment.

While the dark green uniform tended to blend in nicely within the confines of nature, it was in stark contrast to the urban environment where he now stood. Scott liked being out in the woods, he did not enjoy being in public, and he most assuredly didn't care for undue attention. He paused for the looks to subside, then continued his exploration. All the way forward was a large TV screen. To the left of that were the bathrooms, and everywhere else were tables.

There were so many tables of various sizes scattered around that they somewhat resembled a giant game of Tetris, except they were not moving, unless you already had too much to drink! Other than that, there was the fact that some tables had pizza and beer on them, surrounded by humans, and some were empty.

Focusing on the ones that had people, he continued scanning the room, he continued searching for Robin. She was meeting her friends here tonight, that's all he knew. He did not have to look too long before he saw her waving at him. Robin was seated with some of her friends, it looked like they had pulled several tables together. *Great. I wonder who was here tonight,* he mumbled with a frown. This did not go unnoticed by Robin, who quickly lost her smile and briefly turned away before looking back at him.

He watched Robin as he approached, ignoring the others around her. It made her somewhat uncomfortable, with him navigating the obstacles between them without seeming to look away. Moving through the maze of tables he sat down next to Robin. Before he even spoke, he looked to the right at the couple that were making out heavily. A small sigh escaped him as he turned back to her.

Looking at Robin for a few seconds before speaking, he again examined the room. Turning back to her, he took her in. Yes, she was pleasing to the eyes; the color and length of her hair was most appealing to him. After that, a close second, was her thin, petite, athletic look. Her electric baby blue eyes came in a close third. *Who had much time to look at eyes when your woman was facing the other way,* he thought; *oh, and she was young, too.* There wasn't much more he required physically from a woman, but it was her inner beauty that intrigued him the most.

Robin's beauty, her smile, he drank them in, everyone who met her did. Robin was wonderfully polite, kind, and an overall good person. It was her appearance that first caught your eye, it was her inner beauty that kept you coming back. *Hell, it would not allow you to leave,* he thought, as he found himself daydreaming about her.

"How was your day at work?" he asked quietly.

"Not too bad. Glad you could make it tonight. I thought you were too busy to come?" Robin managed to fake a smile.

No sooner had they exchanged greetings than everyone returned. Christy and Linda sauntered up. Flirting with each other in an attempt to get someone to buy their next drink. They sat to her right, with Linda making a big scene complaining about Christy cheating on her.

"Fine. Whatever. I saw you looking at her," Linda said to Christy, angrily turning away.

Shortly after that Brian and Joseph returned with two large pizzas and a pitcher of beer.

"They are out of oranges. Oh, hello Scott," Brian said with little interest if any towards him.

Joseph nodded his way as he slid the pizzas on the table down to Robin.

"Cheating? Again Christy? I would drop you in a heartbeat, but I'm not buying either of you a drink," Brian said loudly, turning from her back to Linda smiling, before breaking into laughter.

Both women flipped him the bird before turning away in disbelief.

"Yes, hi Scott," Linda sputtered half-heartedly, as Christy

just looked away.

Scott looked directly at Linda and paused. She too was attractive, but although he wanted to spend some quality time with her, he found her disappointing. Her hair was too short; it hugged her face, that was *his* job. Her medium, thick, big-boned build intrigued him though; he wondered how rough she liked it. *All those damn polka-dots,* he thought; *too distracting.* She too was young, but it was her inner beauty, or lack-thereof, that concerned him. He found her a bit offensive and racist too, and from time to time she was known to comment about '*all those damn illegals that were taking local jobs.*' He never understood that comment, nor did he agree with it; he just remembered her saying it, and from that day on, he no longer cared to get to know her.

"Hello all," Scott smiled, turning back to Robin.

Robin looked at the others and then back to Scott, trying very hard to be sociable.

"Come on everyone, dig in before it's all gone. I'm hungry!" Robin said excitedly.

Scott looked at them all in turn, acknowledging their dissatisfaction before turning back to face Robin.

"What are your plans this weekend? Are you all still going camping?" he softly asked.

Robin finished her small bite of pizza slowly, as if to delay her ability to respond.

"Yes. We've been planning this trip for some time now. We're here tonight to finish getting organized; we should be going out this Friday afternoon," Robin replied.

After hearing her response, her friends stopped mid-bite, mid-sip; the table grew unusually quiet as they awaited his response.

"I have to work. Why should I be punished for having to work?" Scott said defensively.

With everyone seeming somewhat pleased with his response and realizing that he might not be able to make it, the table's occupants happily returned to their eating and drinking, all except Robin and Scott.

"You don't. We are still going out this Thursday for dinner. We could even go out next weekend, instead. There's a new Italian place I've been wanting to check out that's open now," she continued.

"Just cancel this weekend, they can go without you," Scott fired out loud enough for all to hear.

The more Robin and Scott talked, the more uncomfortable things became, until everyone gave up and focused on eating and drinking, choosing not to be a part of the discussion. The more Robin thought about him, the more she wanted out; often she questioned if he was right for her. Her friends knew he was not. They had no doubts, not since the first time they met him.

"I'm sorry, Scott. I'm going camping this weekend," Robin declared as she took a larger bite of pizza, stalling her next response.

Getting up, Scott looked at everyone one last time. Taking the beer closest to Brian, he finished it and slammed the glass on the table. He took a piece of sausage and pepperoni pizza and shoved it inside his mouth, biting it in two. Dropping the half-eaten piece on top of the other slices, he turned and walked toward the front door. Robin's friends did not want him to come camping with them this weekend, they did not want him around at all. If they had anything to do with it, he wouldn't be welcome for a single meal, not unless Robin wanted him there.

Robin was relieved when he left, and although she tried to get back to a relaxing dinner with friends, that time had passed.

"Well, let's finish planning this trip," Brian said, refilling his beer.

Shortly after Scott left, the comments about how long they had been dating, did she love him, and would she consider seeing him again arose. The conversation quickly changed to what they were all bringing camping, when they worked, and what time they would arrive; gone were the comments or questions about changing her mind about Scott or what they thought she should do.

It was awkward at first, but after a few minutes more of eating pizza and finishing their drinks, things returned to normal. The friends soon found themselves tiring and in need of rest. Going over their plans one more time, they thought everything was in order. After saying their initial goodbyes, the group followed each other to the parking lot. Standing just outside the front door, and after a few more lengthy goodbyes, they agreed to meet at the campground sometime late Friday afternoon. With the evening ending on a high note for all except the CO, and with it looking like the only ones going camping were all friends, they headed to their vehicles.

Scott was sitting in his new company car watching everyone leave. *That group did almost everything together,* he thought, as he watched them talking before getting into their separate vehicles and driving off. Robin left by herself, that made him feel good, although he wasn't happy with her camping all weekend long with them. *Playing games, drinking, swimming naked together, who knows what could happen in a campground when it gets dark,* he thought. He was the CO. He was the one in charge, especially when he was at that campsite. As Robin turned left at the stop sign, he turned right and kept going. He had no place to be, he just found it easier to think as he drove. Driving helped him to clear his mind, to relax him. *Being me is stressful,* he would tell anyone who would listen.

All the friends would be home within the hour. Their favorite pizza watering hole was central to their lives and located nearby. Everyone made it safely, with most going immediately to bed for a good night's sleep. There were a few that went to bed for other reasons, and after a short while, they would be sweaty and exhausted, and they too would be sleeping shortly afterward. Robin and all her friends had to work tomorrow at some time or another, and their day would be filled with thoughts on their upcoming camping trip.

Within a couple hours, all were settled in and recharging their bodies and minds for the next day's activities, all except Scott. *I'm the CO; I'll go to the campground and see what I can find out about the reservations,* he thought, as he put on his emergency lights and made a U-turn. Thinking more about that decision, he determined that a little sleep would do him a lot of good; the CO was too tired to investigate tonight. *Tomorrow he'll go and check out the campground and see what he can find out.*

A yawn escaped him as he took the first of several roads to get him back home. Scott followed it around to the right, taking the dark country road to the corner at a good speed. Everything would have been fine; except he squinted a few times before closing his eyes hard in pain. Instead of the turn he needed to take, he continued straight and left the road.

*S*cott saw himself walking down an empty school hallway. He was young, maybe eight, nine years at the oldest. He had blond hair, and his blue eyes gave him a traditional, expected look. Scott even had freckles! He remembered only small pieces of his early education, probably due to being bullied, he guessed. He really had no good memories of this time whatsoever. He found himself holding a hall pass, which gave him permission to use the restroom in the middle of class. Although he had the right to be there, he still had to make haste. Looking around as he made his way to the restroom, he farted loudly and kept going, confident that no one would hear nor smell what he had done.

    He was a few steps away from the boy's restroom door when he saw it open. Tommy Jones and Johnny Tucket stepped out, dragging their feet on the poorly waxed floor. It was something they did throughout their school day, each time they thought about it. Their goals were to make as many scuff marks as possible, with an added bonus of bragging rights for the longest one. Scott hesitated mid step when he saw them, before starting again. He nodded at the two as he walked between them and into the restroom. The door closed with some delay to a loud thud, and the laughing of Tommy and Johnny. Walking in further, Scott listened as the laughing stopped to make sure the door didn't open again before entering the second stall.

    Scott listened for a few additional seconds before starting to pee; he had waited as long as he could, and he really had to go. The minute Tommy heard him start, he stepped in front of the stall and bent down. Scott's eyes popped wide open as he saw a pair of hands reach under and take hold of his legs. In one quick action his feet were pulled out from under him, and he was dragged out into the middle of the restroom on his back. His head hit the tiled floor with enough force to have split it open. He was still going at this point, and as he acknowledged his pain and tried to stop, he looked at Tommy.

    Johnny was standing by the door keeping it closed in case someone tried to come in. Scott flailed and shook, trying to escape. He tried to kick Tommy, and to push him off, but with his pants around his knees, he was limited in what he could do. At this point, *his pants were wet with urine and stuck to his legs. Scott's last attempt to kick him resulted in Tommy standing up and turning him over.*

"Come on Tommy, we got to go," Johnny said with urgency as he left guard duty and walked out.

"We'll catch you later," Tommy laughed, quickly following Johnny back to class.

Scott got up crying. He would not cry in front of them though, that would have been so much worse. Scott would spend fifteen minutes or so standing in front of the hand dryer with his pants slightly pulled down to allow the inside and outside to dry as quickly as possible. Lucky for him no one else was given permission to come and witness this event! The rest of the day Scott walked from class to class leaving a steady, strong smell of urine behind him. After a half a day of this, he actually preferred the smell of his farts…

The CO came through covered in sweat in the middle of a corn field with his vehicle in neutral, the engine revving loudly. Although it was mid-August, the corn was not as tall as local farmers needed it to be. Letting off the gas he took the first of several quick breaths to calm himself before putting it in reverse. Looking over his shoulder, he cleared the tears from his eyes and left the way he came. Glancing back in his rear-view mirror, he was pleased; *brown, I look better in brown,* he said, checking out his hair.

Shaking his head to jog his memory, he felt somewhat calmer now, but still did not remember how he got in the middle of that field, or when he had left the road. Minutes later he would be home, gathering his pillows against him and settling in for a few hours of what he hoped would be restful sleep. He never slept more than a few hours at a time, but tonight he felt unusually calm, unusually relaxed. *Maybe nature does help one sleep*, he thought, as he closed his eyes smiling.

TUESDAY

Time to Replenish Body and Mind

It was six in the morning on the dot. James stretched to the right and turned off the alarm on his cell phone. Raising his hand above his head, he searched the top of the headboard for his universal remote. Feeling for the buttons in the dark, and with his eyes still closed, he lightly ran his thumb over them. Towards the top right he felt the TV button, selected it, and pushed the button above it to the right and turned it on. Moving back to the TV button he went one over to the right and did the same for the cable box. Just like that, his eyes began adjusting to the light of the TV picture as the cable box loaded channel six.

  The morning news was starting, and a few minutes would go by before he had heard his preview of today's headlines. *Nothing stupid done by the president today, nothing yet,* he thought, as he yawned and got out of bed. Heading to the kitchen for his morning coffee he shuffled his feet sleepily over the wood-like laminate flooring. As he passed the thermostat, the furnace came to life. A faint whining noise began, and cold air started coming from the floor registers. *Why yes, I am hot, baby*, he said laughing.

  James thought of himself as a cross between Jack Nicholson and Jim Carrey. After meeting him, if he had to explain it to you, then you were already lost, and would never understand. Friends of James saw those similarities and laughed when it came up in conversation. Although a learned man might say that the vibrations from walking were enough to move the mercury in the thermostat, to complete the circuit, and start to heat or cool the house, James dismissed that and stuck with his hotness.

  After pushing the button to turn on the electric coffee maker and spending what he might say was an eternity waiting for it to turn on and heat up, James grabbed his hazelnut cartridge and began the process. *I really do have to take some time to find out how to make that coffee maker turn on by itself each morning,* he thought. The aroma was intoxicating; simply put, at times it was ranked higher on his list than sex itself. Unlike sex, the coffee maker never said no, stated that it was not ready, or that it did not want to make coffee. Not unlike sex, all you had to do was wait for it to heat up and give it a little time for it to start.

Next to the coffee machine was a small container of assorted sweeteners. Selecting a few green packs, he opened them and emptied their contents into the cup. A few steps to the right and he reached for the refrigerator door. Without looking, he opened it up, and then took another step closer to search for the cream in the door. He removed the pressurized can of goodness and shook it rather violently. A few sprays into the coffee cup and then he quickly stirred it with a spoon. Another shaking of the can and a few more sprays in a circular motion left cream evenly floating on top. It was that creamy goodness that first greeted him as the hot coffee underneath gently slid into his waiting mouth.

Taking the large cup of coffee, he made his way back through the hallway, and onto the bed to finish the morning news. James would not get those seven minutes back. Yes, he could use the DVR feature and rewind the morning news, but, if what he missed was important, the earlier headlines would have already warned him not to leave, so no biggie, he smiled. Sitting on the bed he pushed up against the headboard, supported by five pillows of various sizes and thickness. Sliding under the blanket, he covered just enough to stay comfortable while drinking his coffee and finishing the morning news.

Just about 20 minutes, no more-no less. That's what it took to get the gist and start your morning. During that time James would finish his coffee, catch up on recent events, and check out the weather for the day and the rest of the week. This would bring him peace of mind and help him make today's decision to go camping or cancel his reservation. Camping was wonderful. Camping was relaxing. Camping brought happiness and helped to replenish body and mind; and based on today's *Goode* weather report from his favorite local meteorologist Brian, it was game on!

James smiled, stretched, and then turned off the TV. No sense jumping straight into the shower before getting ready for camping, because after all that prep and work, after all was said and done, you would have to shower again before going to bed. Loose-fitting shorts and a T-shirt, white ankle socks and camping sneakers were the standard outfit. *One needs to stay comfortable and cool during this setup process,* he thought.

Once dressed, it would take about forty-five minutes to get to the site, and another half hour or so to get initially setup. Most of the preparation for having a wonderful camping week had already been completed. The camper was plugged in to power and the air conditioner turned on. The slide was extended, so the camper could be easily packed up and organized. Groceries, for the most part, had already been purchased and loaded into the camper. Even the truck was backed into the driveway and hitched to it the night before.

The remaining steps would be removing the wheel blocks on the camper, turning on the propane gas tanks, placing the refrigerator on the auto setting to use gas or electricity, closing the slide out, removing the power from the house receptacle, and connecting the camper's wiring harness to the truck. That list was extensive, and it was a series of steps that James had done many times before. *This isn't my first rodeo;* James would tell others*; get as much done as possible in advance and hook up the truck to your camper the night before,* he thought those words to be as true now as when he had first thought them. That splits up the workload and allows you to begin your journey on a positive note. You don't want to spend your first three hours getting everything loaded where you are exhausted before you even get your camper on the road; *words to live by,* he thought, feeling comfortably ahead of the game.

Before his camping trip, James usually spent one day planning food and getting groceries loaded, and another for electronic luxuries. He did not actually have a list that he referenced, he just went over things in his head and tried to review what he needed to compliment the purpose of his camping trip, what he needed to focus on. *Will I be fishing, hiking, traveling around the campground area, staying put, writing, relaxing with friends?* Those were most of his initial concerns, the main components of his mental checklist. Some of his friends might say that James included plastic wrap, tarps, Duct tape, shovels, and some sharp knives, but that was mainly said while joking around, mainly.

T hinking back, James thought about how uneventful last Sunday was. He spent a few hours puttering with the camper, while his chili cooked in the crock pot inside the house. It did not take long to test the air conditioner, the fridge, and all interior and exterior lighting of the camper. Taking one last look around, he ensured the fridge was on its coldest setting and headed back inside the house.

It was a cool and cloudy day, which made it fairly comfortable for today's trips in and out of the camper. Walking through the garage, he grabbed two reusable grocery bags, big blues, he called them. *These will reduce my trips many times over,* he thought, making himself and his legs equally happy!

Dodging his dogs down the hallway, he laughed. It was the sound of food, of wrestling plastic that attracted them. Like sharks drawn to blood, they came; wagging tails followed by utter disappointment when they saw nothing come out of the bag that they could either kill, consume, or both. If they had been sharks, they could have taken what they wanted from him, or demanded more, or something specific; good thing for James they weren't much larger and gray.

Placing the two bags on the kitchen counter, he looked down at them.

"Who wants a cookie? James said in puppy-talk.

He watched in amazement as both dogs ran for their bedroom cages.

"Best trick ever!" he exclaimed.

Following them into the bedroom, he closed their doors after giving each several. This he did to keep them out from underfoot as he finished his trips to the camper. It would also be a good way to keep them from seeing what he was doing, as both dogs recognized when he was packing up to leave, because they know, they always know.

Closing their bedroom door and turning around, he took one step and was hit in the face with the spicy aroma of chili. It made it hard for him to keep going. A small sample would tell him what he already knew; he needed more cumin. A few minor adjustments and it was back to packing. The way he loaded the camper involved several steps, but it generally started with one large blue bag of refrigerated and frozen foods, followed by another full of dry goods. He would load each up where they would not be too heavy to manage going down the stairs that led to the garage. He would carry them into the camper and then check individual items off his master list that resided in his mind; ensuring, without a doubt, that nothing thought of on the list would be left behind.

 Camping alone presented unique challenges when it came to setup, tear-down, and meals. With only a slim chance of having a visitor for any given meal, he reduced each by two. Cooking for one would easily produce enough leftovers for another meal or a guest. Although he wanted a campfire for each day, he did not want to cook that much, he wanted to enjoy said campfire with a strong spirit or bubbly, frothy beverage.

 Taking a quick moment to think about what he needed to bring, he went back for another load of camping goodies. This would be his last trip, and then he could focus on electronics and miscellaneous gear. His master list consisted of mainly foods and medicines, except for a single out of place thought that he always focused on, *don't forget your electronics!*

 James had brought everything he could think of on his initial attempt to comply with that last statement and make it proud. He stood in front of his camper freezer/refrigerator unit, opened the door to the refrigerator section, and pulled out an iced tea. Taking a sip, he closed the door and turned around, placing it on his dinette table. He thought about the things he had quickly displayed to inventory. It seemed to be picture-worthy, and with a few tweaks here and there, it framed up nicely. A few different angles taken from his cell phone, and he put things back where he needed them to be. Sitting down afterwards, he opened the pictures on his phone and laughed before posting them online to social media for rebuke.

 Starting front and center, he began describing what he saw,

taking notes for all posterity so he could include it in his new novel. Toilet paper, front and center, a roll of thick, *'bear-approved'* toilet paper that was 3/4s full, or thereabouts. Behind it was a six-inch-tall blue cylindrical object with drilled holes all around it, toward the top, two inches deep. It was his favorite water-proof blue tooth audio speaker, which he took everywhere outdoors, camping or not. To the right of that, was a large replacement desktop with a 21-inch screen. It was what he used to do all things computer, and sporting a full-size keyboard and that large monitor, that laptop weighed as much as a desktop did, he often joked.

    Looking back to the left of the toilet paper was a coffee mug, an open plastic bottle of flavored iced tea, a small glass bowl, a bag of beef jerky, a knife, the keys to the camper, and his game system controller. To the right, were a pair of speakers for the laptop, and immediately in front of that was another plastic case of flavored iced tea; one could never have enough flavored iced tea…

    Off to the side were a few things temporarily positioned on the cushioned bench seats, on the shelf underneath where the TV would mount, and a few things underneath the dinette table on the floor, but something was missing. There was a hole, a large square section of the table that was empty. It was about a foot in size, and there were things around it, but there was obviously something missing.

    Shaking that thought off for now, he moved some of his electronics together for review. Surveying his collection of goodies requiring electricity, he mouthed their names as he inspected them from left to right. A laptop, digital camera, a couple different models of GoPros, and an audio speaker system with a separate bass box; these were all followed by assorted cables, cords, and an extra power strip to run them all.

    Moving his eyes across the table and the benches around it, he followed through all the way from left to right and again noticed that empty space; it was blatantly empty, something was definitely missing! It was too small to be left for the TVs; besides, they were already placed side by side on the bed, totally surrounded and protected by blankets. James thought about what it could be, what is should be, but nothing came to mind.

    Several minutes later he was still staring at the dinette

table. James took off for the house again, after finally giving up. Just as he placed his left foot on the second step, a vision of his video game system popped into his head. It took him a few minutes to move things around and clean off the table for the trip. He made a mental note to grab that later, as he checked everything present one last time.

"Well, that's going to be loaded last," he laughed, and then closed the garage door for the night.

Today's work constituted the majority of his packing, he thought; the other parts of his list covered things outside of food and electronics, such as water, adult beverages, fishing equipment, survival gear, etc., *oh, and the game system,* he again thought of that game system.

There were some additional things that he packed either in the back seat of the truck, the bed of the truck, or underneath the storage area below the bed compartment of the camper itself. James had a solution for every scenario that could threaten to hinder or ruin his camping trips. He packed a sawzaw, corded and rechargeable drills, a hand axe, power jump boxes (plural), an air compressor, and much, much more. Those were in the back seat of his truck, on the floorboards as they should be used less often, or not at all. Resting on the seats and on top of the other gear were things like bungee cables, rope, lighting, canvas tarps, etc.

Packing was done approximately one to two days before he needed to finish his last-minute checks, before traveling to the campground. All this was possible due to James being a proud Boy Scout, and an even prouder Capricorn. One of the things that amused him the most was the saying '*if you ever need a screw, find a Capricorn.*' The meaning behind those words was that they collect all manner of items, and if you were looking for something, a Capricorn would have it. James played with those words by adding a little of his dry humor, giving it an alternate meaning. That thought sent him into a fit of laughter as he walked down the hallway to release the girls.

J ames stopped thinking about the past and jumped forward to the now. *This was going to be an awesome camping trip. What a wonderful Tuesday,* he thought. Getting to the campground on a Tuesday afternoon, after 2 p.m. or so was ideal. Around that time the campground resembled a graveyard. It was totally relaxing, quiet, and easy to navigate. Friday, on the other hand, was total chaos. When sites became available at 2 p.m., every sort of person with every sort of experience driving and parking campers would be assaulting the campground with extreme prejudice. If you've never seen it before, you should actually check it out one time (unless you are one of those arriving on a Friday or the weekend.)

An equally crazy experience was the fun of pulling your camper behind your truck or driving your RV, for that matter. Reaching the campground was challenging enough without vehicles passing you on the left and right, cutting you off, and pulling in front of you and immediately breaking, all at the same time. An abundance of patience and vigilance was a prerequisite. Each and every time James went camping was a unique driving experience, each one ending with the same result: the swift enjoyment of a refreshing golden beverage.

James examined the campground as he pulled in. It was basically empty, save for a few sites that were already set up the week prior, and that of the campground hosts. Filling up the water tank would be a breeze. There was no waiting line, so he could just pull up. But, even better, James could work his way over to site 123 and stop a few sites short to use the local potable spicket. Looking around one more time before he stopped to ensure he would not block another driver, he put on his flashers and turned the truck off.

Dirty, white, small, brown, these were all good words to describe the edges of the campsite. Small rocks, pebbles actually, ranging from white to dirty colors were scattered all around the edges of the road. Mixed with the brown soil underneath and assorted leaves and twigs, the rocks offered protection for those who walked and drove around the campground. They helped to keep vehicles from sinking down into the earth, getting stuck, and causing ruts and ruining the periphery of the camper's oasis. They also stopped excess water from pooling, mud from forming, and kept one's footing as stable as it could when feet were off the roughly paved road.

    James looked on to the left at the nearest potable water faucet. These were equally spaced, approximately four sites apart, and were definitely needed. Made from metal pipes affixed to treated 4x6s, the structures protruded from the earth in an unnatural, man-made way. Held in place by concrete hidden by a mound of dirt and rock, they were sturdy enough to be functional, and placed deep enough for one to wish they had not hit one, if accidentally backed in to.

    A single three-foot section erupted from the ground and stood straight up, supporting the pipe that carried the water. On top of that, was another section of 4x6, approximately two-foot long that attached to the end of the main piece, and with another one attached and angled to support them both, the structure resembled a crude letter P from the alphabet. The spicket was on top at the end opposite the base, mainly for drinking, with another one below that you could attach a hose to. Both had a crude handle that had to be held open to allow the water to run. It was the best way to conserve water; this meant that one had to be present to use it, and the minute you left and let go of the round handle, it automatically shut off.

    Around the potable water structure were three partially buried 4x6s that attached to each other, partially sectioning off the sides of a large square and blocking off the area surrounding the faucet. Inside that was a slightly raised gravel surface, with the purpose of keeping the area neat and devoid of mud, no matter how much water hit the ground. It was a perfect design, and one idea that was well planned and implemented. Although that was something simple and natural looking when campers enjoyed their settings, it was highly functional, and leant to a cleaner camping experience. The last thing you wanted to do was to track mud throughout your camper, your vehicle, or to be waiting in a comfort station full of people queued, all needing to remove the mess.

Filling up your clean tank for your camper at one of those local water stations required a special tool; one that had to be crafted to particular specifications. Taking a few steps through the grass he quickly found one. James bent over and picked up a small stick. He approached the station and turned the handle to ensure that it fit. He let go of the small wheel and it quickly went back to lock in place, effectively shutting off the water, conservation at its finest.

That's where the stick came in. It had to be just long enough to function as a wedge and lock the round four-spoke handle in place to keep the water coming. This was important due to the fact that it took quite some time to fill the tank with the amount of pressure that was available. Further complicating things was the height of the water station, which was much lower than any adult cared to bend over for any given amount of time.

Measuring the stick, James found it was too short, so he had to throw it away and find another. The next one he picked up was longer, which was ideal. He bent over to the road and rubbed an end over the surface to file off a small amount. Once it fit, he tested it to ensure it would stay on. Success! He removed his stick and went to set up his hose to connect the water station to the camper. Several minutes later he pulled up a small folding camper chair and sat patiently watching until he noticed water slowly escaping the tank's overflow.

He removed the tool and placed it in his pocket, turning off the station. A few moments after that the water stopped coming out. Replacing the cap to the tank, he then gathered up the hose and drained out the excess water before placing it in the bed of the truck. James got in and drove to site 123. It took him several times to back into the site and position the camper just the way he wanted it. This process was much easier with an outside helper, but this week he was by himself, which made some things more difficult.

A half hour later James was sitting on a camping chair overlooking his little piece of heaven. He sat there enjoying a cold beer, the warm evening, and all manner of nighttime creature; all without a human in sight. The only lights on his entire end were his, and a single light bulb on the outside wall of a distant comfort station. It was a little more than half a football field away, nestled on an oval grass island between him and the road that circled the sites.

There was not much more that needed to be done tonight. James was getting tired, but it was more than that; it was probably more accurate to state that he was totally relaxed. He had unplugged from social media because the bars on his cell phone went from one to three whenever they felt like it. Sure, he still had a laptop, a Playstation 4 game system, and a couple of other random electronic devices, but his need to like, share, and tweet were curtailed. James could quit those things anytime he wanted to, he just didn't want to, not unless he was forced!

He stood up, took his beer, and walked across the road to stand inside the center grassy island, and turned around to look at his camper. He always did this to see how his campsite looked. It wasn't so much as to see how others would perceive him, it was to see what he was missing, or what he had forgotten. Taking in all his handiwork; this is what he saw.

The 2013 Heartland Trail Runner was backed in far enough to allow for the truck towing it to be connected and still be clear of the road. The awning was extended, with the section above the rear door a bit lower to allow the rain to flow down and away from the main entrance. A string of lights was held in place on the edge of the awning with clips every three feet or so, allowing them to be draped.

The slide out extended from the driver's side, or what you would call the outside wall. The inside was stationary, and where the two doors were placed to allow access into the camper. Slide outs were awesome, and they really gave one additional comfort and the feeling that you were home, a home away from home. With the slide out retracted, it allowed for limited access from one end of the camper to the other, segmenting the living quarters and the two captains' chairs and couch from the opposite front end where the bedroom was. When the slide out was extended, you were in heaven.

There was an outdoor camping mat between the two doors that helped stop debris from being tracked into the camper. Two picnic tables were touching end to end, tucked in against the side, totally protected from the elements by the awning. There were a couple of collapsed folding camping chairs just inside of the main door. The campground was neat and organized, although some things were not completely set up.

An orange extension cord provided the power for the exterior lighting and was connected directly to the outside power post. A collapsible spring-loaded trash can sat on the edge of the second picnic table. The two outside yellow lights that were adjacent to each door, front and back, were lit. The fire pit was about thirty feet away to the rear of the site. Around it were a few chairs and a handful or two of twigs to get a fire going. All the seasoned wood was stacked neatly on the second picnic table, protecting it from the rain, along with a few extra handfuls of kindling. *Time to replenish body and mind,* James thought, as he walked back to the camper dragging the two camping chairs from the fire pit and headed inside for the night.

Soon he would be relaxing out in nature, with as many electronics as he cared to have by his side. Sitting in one of his captain's chairs, he closed his eyes and took a relaxing breath. Lynn was camping with him this week. She would arrive closer to the weekend because of her work schedule, which gave him time to get setup and do a few things before she arrived. He looked forward to fishing, writing a few chapters for his current project, and playing some video games, that's what he called *total relaxation*. James wondered what she was doing now, and that led to one of his most favorite memories of all.

He thought back about what she said to him on their second date, before she was his girlfriend. It was the description that she gave him that was most memorable. It was her reply when asked about what she was doing the following weekend.

"Well, I am hanging out with one of my friends," Lynn told him.

"Oh, well, that's OK," he replied, hiding his disappointment behind a natural smile.

He sipped on his wine, looked away and then back at her, noticing her smiling.

"Hmm. What's she like then?" he said, returning her smile.

"I never said it was *a 'she'*. He's bald by choice, and kind-hearted, with quick wit. He has a long torso with short legs. He is a rotund 6-foot 1-inch-tall man, about 240 pounds, and mildly quirky, with large brown eyes. You know the type, a cross between

Jack Nicholson and Jim Carey," she said seriously.

"Oh," he replied.

"Let's not forget the *hooded doe eyes*," she said before breaking out in laughter.

"Doe eyes?" he questioned.

"Yeah, they are hooded. His top eyelids are a bit hooded," Lynn could barely get out, before laughing harder.

Only slightly less memorable was when she told him of her dream job. Lynn wanted the title Chief Chipmunk Counter. She desired this because she always wanted to wear an outdoor camping uniform of some sort and travel the Indiana State Parks counting chipmunks. She thought she would be good at it. *I have plenty of experience*, she told him. *I even had two at my mom and dad's cottage that I fed, Chippy and Dippy. They would come up and eat out of my hand. How wonderful*, he would reply. He loved those memories; she was indeed someone special. James really liked her, and he couldn't wait to see her again.

Hours later, and miles across town, the CO was driving towards the campground. *Maybe arriving during the off hours would provide him with some leeway for his investigations,* he thought. He was not sure what he could discover about their camping trip, but he hoped to get a lead on the area they were staying in, what campers they were using, or even their campground site numbers. He would find them. He would use any resource he had access to; he was after all, a CO.

Time to replenish body and mind, Scott thought as he pulled up to the stop sign. Looking right he saw the lights turning on in the convenience store. The large sign read *Snacks, Beer and Bait inside.* The CO took notice of the missing comma and moved on. He put on his right turn signal and pulled into the parking lot, stopping parallel to the building. He turned off his vehicle and finding the parking lot empty and dark, he quickly walked to the door.

Looking through the window he saw her. Behind the counter was a petite young woman with dull blonde hair. She had acne, she was short, about 5'2", and she wore a black ball cap. The woman was packing a blacked-out pistol on her right hip, locked and holstered.

Upon first glance, although slightly unattractive and moderately homely, she became a woman of interest when she radiated a *'hands off, I can take care of myself'* attitude by moving around sporting her weapon at her side. It drew his attention away from her face and down to her body. All he wanted to know was, *could she?*

The CO walked in and turned over their business sign to closed, before locking the door. Looking around at the distracted woman, he smiled and greeted her.

"Sodas and snacks?" he questioned, pointing to the left.

"All along the back wall, actually." she replied to the CO.

Smiling still, he nodded and walked straight ahead. Grabbing an energy drink from a nearby shelf, he quickly turned on his heel to watch her. He had to make sure no one else had come in, and that she had not noticed the fact that he had turned her sign over and locked her door. Seeing that she was still wiping down her counter and organizing what was there, he quickly made his way back to her. He extended his left hand holding a twenty and waited. She smiled and rang him up.

"One sixty-nine. Out of twenty," she stated, looking up to reach out for his bill.

"Yes please," he replied, finding her offer of a 69 acceptable.

He took hold of her wrist and tightened his grip, causing shooting pain to radiate through her small hand. Smiling still, he was looking at her face when he pulled her over the counter and onto her stomach. This was all done very quickly, and without pause, catching the usually vigilant woman totally off guard. All the hard work that she had done organizing the contents of the countertop had been in vain as everything followed her over the edge. Tiny eyeglass repair kits, lighters that looked like a small mouth bass, packs of toothpicks, colored flashlights, everything landed on top or around her, scattering across the aged white tiled floor. When she finally realized what was happening, and struggled to free her pistol from its holster, she hit the floor with an unbalanced thud, breaking her concentration.

The CO leaned backwards, stretching her out by her hands and pulling her further away from the edge of the counter. Stepping over, he sat down on her small backside. Keeping her hands outstretched from her head, he removed her pistol. Placing it behind his back he tucked it inside his pants and glanced down at the woman who was beginning to shout for help.

"Shut up and stop squirming or I'll shoot you in the face," he yelled as he continued to control both of her hands.

She screamed several times before his message became clear. He bounced on her back twice, and then grabbed a fist full of her short, dirty blonde hair, slamming her headfirst into the floor. He felt the fight leave her; the young woman's arms loosened, no longer trying to pull away from his grip. He bounced on her one more time for good measure. This sent the air racing out of her lungs in a large exhale, fully granting him the confidence he needed to proceed.

He checked the small shop to ensure they were still alone. Once certain of that, he stood up and dragged her across the floor and into the back room by her hair. Keeping hold of her head, he again lowered himself to her. This time she found herself on her back, still struggling to breathe. With the situation even more unmanageable because of her trouble breathing, it was difficult for her to concentrate and struggle on getting free. She was looking to the side inhaling deeply when the CO started pistol whipping her. He used her own weapon against her repeatedly, until she succumbed.

Dazed and beaten senseless by this point, the woman was looking aimlessly away when the CO again secured her weapon. Scott pulled down her shorts to her ankles and she began to struggle anew. She was attempting to crawl backwards away from him when he moved close to sit on her stomach. With the woman held down in place, he slid up to her navel. Scott easily sequestered her arms, holding them together above her head by her wrists. They were small enough for him to grip with one hand, so with his other he took hold of her chin, and positioned her head towards his face, getting her full attention.

He squeezed harder, shaking her head until she began

crying, before violently pushing her head backwards and letting go. Feeling overcome with fear and somewhat overwhelmed, she started crying uncontrollably. She turned her head from him and while continuing to cry and sob, she closed her eyes against his abuse. She found it difficult to catch her breath. Her back hurt, her face felt beat up, caved in. Looking up at him for a brief moment, she looked away lest she show her attacker the fear he so wanted.

    He took her by her waist and flipped her over. He sat on top of her lower back and again fished her wrists out in front of her. She screamed as he pulled her arms up toward the ceiling. Raising them higher into the air while sitting on her lower back sent pain throughout her body, her mind. She did not see herself living through this; the man on top of her was systematically tearing her apart.

    "Shut up!" he spat, as he lowered her back onto the floor.

    She continued crying but ceased her screaming. She did not struggle, she did not cry out in pain; whimpers did escape her lips, but only reluctantly, and with reservation.

    "I said SHUT UP. DO nothing. Say NOTHING!" he finished as he jerked her around and over on to her back, slamming her down again like a child's doll.

    He let go of her wrists and pushed against her breasts; they were two of her redeeming qualities. Without having gotten to know her personality, her mind, he judged her by her breasts, her ass; her body would have to communicate to him what she could not. She closed her eyes against his advances and tried not to upset him by gasping or recoiling against his touch.

    She held her breath as he mashed them together and pushed them how he saw fit. Pinching them caused distracting pain, and her eyes and head jerked up making her look at him. He was staring at her. Smiling, he let them go and told her to turn over. He moved to the side, and she went to her knees and followed his instructions, turning over hesitantly.

    The floor was cold on her breasts, her rounded stomach, her thighs. Her breathing was irregular, as between breaths she waited to be punched or kicked. She was conscious of the pain in her face caused by the swelling, it was getting worse now. It hurt for her to cry. Her lungs hurt. Her eyes hurt. Her cheeks hurt. She imagined how bruised she must look. In the back of her mind, she wondered if anything was broken. Resting her injured face on the cold floor, she waited.

Would I live through this? Is he going to kill me? Am I going to walk out of this, or will it take an ambulance, or a Hearse? These thoughts flooded her head as he again lowered his body on top of hers. Looking down he saw her sky-blue panties. It was not what your mother would wear, but it was not lingerie, either. *Average*, he thought. There she was, a young woman with an attractive body, with a slightly messed up face, and wearing the clothes of a twelve-year-old girl.

"Why?" he asked her.

She said nothing.

"WHY?" the CO asked louder.

The woman jerked at that word. She whimpered and fought back sniffling and responded.

"Why what?"

"Why do you dress the way you do? You are exceptionally beautiful. Why do you dress like a twelve-year-old?" he questioned as he started to gently rub her shoulders.

This confused her and she continued whimpering and sniffling as he pressed down harder. He took hold of her hair again and pulled her head backwards as he used his other to firmly massage the front of her left shoulder. She closed her eyes against what she was feeling. He tugged on her hair, forcing her to open them, and once again witness him staring at her.

The man started to push down even harder on her left shoulder as he tightened his grip. This turned her body towards him, exposing her right breast. Letting go of her head she again lowered it to the cold tile and closed her eyes. His hand slid underneath and fondled her. In his mind, he was trying to warm her up, having noticed earlier the coldness of the floor. Moving his hand from the left of her body to her right, she raised and lowered in response. Stopping on her right side, he slid his hand upward, holding her breast tightly.

Squeezing harder, he stretched his hand out towards her head, trying to pull it off. The CO was looking down at the woman when she screamed; he didn't let that distract him though, he continued mashing her breasts with an ever-present smile across his lips.

"Shut UP!" he yelled as he took hold of her nipple.

The woman bit her lip as he twisted it between his forefinger and thumb. Letting go he again went to her shoulders. Sliding up to her dirty blonde hair, he ran his fingers through and grabbed a handful. Moving her headfirst to the left and then right, he rolled her cheeks across the cold floor.

She tried to block what was happening from her mind, she was all over the place; the more she tried, the more frantic she became. She thought about what she had to do later to get the shop closed. She thought about having already mopped the floor this morning with lemon scented bleach.

Would he use the same bleach to clean up her blood when he finished raping and killing her, she wondered. The young woman tried to calm herself and stop thinking about what she could not control.

Inside, she continued whimpering and crying, but she went to great lengths to keep her noises to a minimum. Her breathing slowed, becoming more normal. Trying to breathe only through her nose, she kept as quiet as she could. She looked for a way to get in control, to fight back, she just didn't see an opportunity. She took the CO's body on top of her as an attack; it didn't matter if he wore a uniform, or if he was in a position of authority. She wasn't being arrested; she hadn't been given her rights. With a snap in judgement or reality, the thought of what he would say popped into her head.

You have the right to remain motionless, beneath me. Anything you say can and will be used against you, by me. You have the right to receive bruises from slaps and punches, from me. You may choose to speak, as long as you are spoken to first, by me. Crying, shaking, and whimpering will not be tolerated, and may result in additional personal injury, from me. You have the right to my penis inside you. With those last thoughts she came through staring at the ceiling and being violently groped. She didn't know when it happened, or how long she had been out, but he had turned her over, and he continued to inflict pain.

"Wait. Wait. No! Stop!" she screamed and slurred her words between crying.

"I told you no crying," the CO said, holding onto her waist with both hands, he leaned forward.

The CO looked on as the woman protesting beneath him tried to squirm away. She shook her body on the floor and pushed with her legs. She tried to free her hands by twisting and turning them. She even attempted to push him away by raising her head and chin into his chest. All those things did little in the way of gaining her freedom, he was still on top pressing down, asserting himself upon her. His weight, his attitude, the way he held her bundled up, everything seemed to work against her. A piercing scream of frustration billowed forth from inside the woman, but from where the CO did not know. If asked, she would not know either, it just came. The moment it started she knew she was in trouble; the moment it started, he knew it too.

Scott noticed her second wind, her fight or flight reflex, he called it. The woman beneath him just made her choice to fight. He acknowledged it but gave it no credence, it didn't carry any weight with him. The CO knew who was in control here. Although she saw despair running straight at her, she would not give in, she would not stop struggling. With as much force as he pushed down against her to keep her body motionless beneath him, she pushed back. The young woman was definitely smaller and didn't have the strength to raise her body high enough to slide out from under him. She scanned the area looking for anything she could use as a weapon, all the while attempting to wiggle free.

The CO continued pressing his body against her. She was conscious of all his weight bearing down, her shoulders became one with the floor. He would call it massaging, but to her he was just pressing her onto the floor, keeping her from escaping. He watched her relax. Her breathing seemed normal; so much so that he could not tell if she was still crying. Moving more against her shoulders he stopped at her thin neck and closed his hand around it. Tightening until he saw her hold her breath, he slowly raised her up before letting her go. Again, he massaged her shoulders.

The CO was watching the woman beneath him when she started breathing normally again and slowly, seductively raised herself. Her bottom moved first. She rolled over and then went to her knees, before placing her body and her thighs back down on the cold floor. This she did a few times before he slid his hand slowly down. She was offering herself to him, although she didn't understand why. *She was accepting her fate*, he thought, looking on, somewhat puzzled, somewhat curious.

Scott caressed and rubbed her shoulders, pulling on her hair when he wanted to, when he saw fit. She followed him with her head, soft moans escaped, then she closed her eyes. Turning her head further, she opened them slowly and their eyes met, and as if on cue, her lips quivered. She closed her eyes to him, and slowly moved her head away to face forward. She could not believe she was doing this. It seemed to be initiated in an attempt to end this situation, no matter what the outcome. She didn't know where it came from, and she didn't know if it would be enough, or even accepted, but she followed through, even attempting to smile. It was found lacking, and truly less than half a smile, she judged, as anger overtook him.

He raised himself slightly above her and rubbed his body against hers. He moved his hand passionately down to her back side. Pressing his thumb deeper the lower he went he slid it between her cheeks. Pushing in her sky-blue panties as far as they would go; she softly moaned as he palmed and squeezed her firmly. Removing his hand, he quickly reached to his pistol for his release.

She saw what she was doing caused the man to no longer hurt her, to no longer yell. She writhed slowly a couple of times before letting out a few long and drawn-out moans. She was raising and lowering her bottom towards him one more time when he hit her in the back of the head knocking her unconscious. This he did several times, and purely out of anger, although she would not know that, when she awoke, if she awoke, she would have a powerful headache, but she would not know the true violence that he had unleashed.

He looked at her lifeless body spread out over the floor and watched her breathing. Noticing she wasn't moving or trying to escape, he looked at her body more closely, as only a man who desired a woman could. With her no longer struggling, no longer putting up a fight, she was no longer interesting. The CO did not even have an erection at this point; like her crying, her whimpering, that too had passed. In his eyes, she had lost; all he thought about was his girlfriend; he wanted his sexual release, but on his terms, and with Robin. The eternal struggle between a helpless woman and the hunter, the man; the fight, a rough release, that's what turned him on. He stared on at the woman in front of him.

He stood up and placed his foot under her hip and raised her enough to roll her over on her back. Her body flipped over slowly, and he stared on as her breasts moved back and forth before settling flat towards the sides of her small body. He stayed put a few moments, just to verify that he was no longer aroused. *Nope*.

Scott looked down at the woman who he had controlled. He sat down beside her and played with her hair, moving it around her face. He brushed the back of his hand against her breasts. He reached down and took a handful of ass, raising her up he looked on, but nothing. Squeezing her one last time he again noticed how cold the white tiled floor was, and how clean. *Good thing I did not have to kill her,* he thought. *It would be a shame to have to bloody up the clean lemon-scented floor.*

He took a knee and kissed her. Pulling away he looked at her face, at her mouth, her lips; he found them uninviting, unattractive. The CO stood up and walked to the front of the store. Taking a candy bar from the side of the counter he read the wrapper. *Snarky*, he mumbled. The CO looked one last time, before taking the energy drink, his candy bar, and his twenty-dollar bill and left, closing the door behind him.

*S*cott reached for the door handle and paused as images of his mom flooded his brain. Bringing tears to his eyes, he stood motionless as his mind raced. Maybe brought on by him remembering that he was on his way to the campground in search of his girlfriend, or possibly for what had just happened inside. He saw himself with his family at a campground one cool weekend afternoon. It was sunny-no, partly cloudy, but a slight wind made it appear cooler than it actually was.

Mom and dad were fighting again. It seemed to happen more and more nowadays. He was eleven or so, and it was Father's Day. He and his brother were playing among the trees when the volume of their parents arguing grew louder. It was enough for them to start making their way back to their picnic table. Mom was setting everything up for their lunch and dad was grilling. He had just put all the meats on, and shortly after, small areas of flame erupted around the drippings from homemade burgers.

She smiled at them as they sat down on opposite sides of the table. The traditional red and white checkered plastic tablecloth must have had a hundred holes of various sizes; soon it would need to be replaced, maybe before their next trip, Scott thought. Looking at dad and then back to mom, Scott shifted his concentration back to the table. Mom and dad were not talking to each other unless they argued; as a family rule, there was no yelling or arguing at the table, so for the moment things seemed calmer.

The picnic table had a center area of mustard and ketchup, salt and pepper and other things necessary for burgers and hot dogs. Looking around, Scott grew concerned when he did not see any buns. This quickly passed when he found a loaf of thin-sliced bread that was just placed on the end by his brother. Scott remarked that it seemed to be clearing up, which his brother reminded him that he still would not catch more fish than he would. Scott smiled at his brother. His brother smiled back.

Scott remembered the smile on his mom's face when she asked dad for the keys to the truck.

"I need the napkins and ties from the back seat, honey," she said smiling.

Looking over at her, he motioned to the camper.

"Inside, hanging by the door," he replied.

With the smile never leaving her face, she slowly walked into the camper and came out with her purse. Scott froze on this image, and in slow motion she walked to the truck, got inside, and started it up. And that was it, that was the last time he ever saw his mother. He remembered his dad taking off running after her, trying to get her to stop; again, he yelled, but this time Mom did not say a thing, she just kept on driving.

Scott blinked a few times and oriented himself. He was not sure how long he had been standing by his vehicle holding the handle, but when he pulled on it to get in, upon releasing it, he found it was covered in sweat. Again, he looked over his shoulder into the shop, but there was nothing stirring. With a sense of urgency, he got in and took off in the direction of the campground.

Somewhere back in the middle of the woods, far off the posted hiking trails sat Kevin, with his back against a tree. He was naked, his hands behind his back were handcuffed, and he was tied to the tree with the type of snare wire that was typically used for trapping wild animals; he wasn't going anywhere soon.

"185 pounds of shit, that's what you are. That's all you'll ever be," the instructor told him, pressing his boot down on Kevin's head and leaning forward.

The CO heard those words as if they had just been spoken, although nobody was present. His eyes were closed and hearing them sparked his resolve. Those words were what molded him, those words were the reason for his being; those words were responsible for turning him into the man he was today. Although they were powerful and held great meaning, by themselves, they were not enough to set him free; he was going to die here unless someone came to rescue him. He wasn't sure if that was going to happen; he was off the beaten path, he had not reported his most recent position to his department, and his vehicle, if that man hadn't taken it, was at least a mile away.

Kevin fidgeted and struggled with his handcuffs out of not wanting to give up, not out of an attempt to get free; the metal around his wrists would not afford Kevin his freedom so easily, he would have to work for that. The tree was too large to try to climb up, and if he could manage to get some leverage and stand up, there were many branches to overcome. He didn't want to make noise and shout for help unless he heard humans, he didn't want to attract the wrong type of attention. Around these parts, foxes were about as bad as it got, but there were rumors of coyotes and even coywolves. He had never seen one, nor any signs of them moving through the state, but this didn't mean they weren't present.

With his new position within the DNR, Kevin didn't have direct supervision, he didn't really have direct reports either, he was the TOP. Since he didn't have these things, he was free to come and go as he pleased, although he did have executive responsibilities. Kevin rotated throughout the parks reviewing and reporting on daily operations, ensuring policies and procedures were being followed, performing audits of assets, and basically anything else that needed to be done. This month he was scouring Hearty Lake.

He always started off with nature, preferring animals to people, nine times out of ten. Taking the trails where normal people travelled was generally done first. After those, he would move off them, and basically pick a direction and perform sort of a walk-about. He would sometimes rough it, sometimes take supplies, but it was always light hiking and survival. It was those skills that he learned in the military that helped him with his career, it was his career that helped him use the skills that he enjoyed.

Iraq, Afghanistan, now those were dangerous places, Kevin thought, as he struggled again with the metal around his wrists. Although he had been shot at, he had been too close to unexpected explosions, and even had to retreat while running full speed while being shot at, he had never been handcuffed to a tree and left for dead; he welcomed this challenge and looked forward to finding a way to escape. This place wasn't supposed to be dangerous; he didn't ever think he would wind up naked, tied to a tree, not in a national park in the good ole state of Indiana, USA, not anywhere.

He thought back to how all this happened. He could have fought harder, he could have pushed back, and normally he would have, but there was something about that man. He seemed unstable, on-edge, Kevin could not know if his normal training, his survival instincts would have helped him, or caused a desperate man to behave in a non-standard way. *This would never happen again,* he thought, *next time; next time would be different.* Kevin fell asleep out of boredom; there wasn't much at this point he could do, anyway.

WEDNESDAY

Preparation - P R E P A R A T I O N – Preparation

James woke up when his body told him to wake up, not when his phone told him to. The camper was comfortably cool as he stretched and yawned. Getting up, he put socks on so he wouldn't walk on the cold floor. The lovely blue lights inside the camper called to him. He walked past his cell phone, his Blu-ray player, and his PS4; stopping abruptly in front of the coffee machine which he pet lovingly while rummaging for a coffee cup.

"Later my friends; I'll play with you later," he smiled and passionately looked into the eyes of his coffee machine.

"Hazelnut, two days in a row, unheard of," he murmured, inserting the cup into the machine.

Looking through the blinds of the window above his kitchen sink he saw a few birds hopping around, but nothing else. While the coffee finished brewing, he put on his blue T-shirt, shorts, and shoes. Taking the coffee outside he grabbed a camping chair from underneath the awning and took it with him to the firepit. A gentle breeze occasionally found its way through the trees, helping to keep the temperature comfortable. Although it was early in the morning, the campground had retained a high seventies temperature overnight.

Enjoying some peace and quiet with his coffee, he thought about today's schedule. He did not have one. He wanted to go fishing today, maybe catch something for dinner. Some time tonight he would start a fire. He would do this no matter if he caught fish or not; fires while camping were really relaxing. Possibly a movie after dinner on his forty-inch HD TV, followed by Final Fantasy XV! This he would do until the late evening. He loved having a bourbon outside by the fire, no matter how many neighbors were around. James would be the first to declare that the bourbon would taste better with less distractions, although it would still be enjoyable with company; tonight he would have some, with company or not.

When James finished his coffee, he stood up, stretched, and walked into the camper to cook breakfast. The air inside was comfortable as always, no matter what temperature it was outside. This morning he would cook his breakfast inside the camper, so it was necessary to keep the air at a low setting. Reaching up to the register in the center of his camper he closed the end that blew over the stove, leaving the other three alone. He opened the refrigerator and took out a few eggs, some spicy pork sausage, and all the extras that he would require, hot sauce, cheese, and some more cream for another cup of coffee.

Reaching into the microwave which he used for additional storage, he took out the bread and marshmallows to finally be able to reach the tortilla shells. Placing the other items back inside, he closed the door. *Today would be breakfast burritos!* It did not take long to get everything ready, and before he knew it, he was back outside with his second cup of coffee, enjoying two tightly rolled breakfast burritos, with all the toppings!

While James was enjoying his morning rituals and breakfast, miles away into town, his soon-to-be neighbors were either shopping, packing their campers, or thinking about doing those things whilst they were working. He had no idea if his entire end would be filled this week or not, nor when it would be, but with James being a betting man, he would have said that the chaos would start some time on or after two P.M this Friday, like clockwork. Not everyone was able to take off during the week, and truth be told, most people needed the money of a full work week. James had made his arrangements ahead of time, saving over the last several months for his annual camping blowout, so no financial hardships were in his immediate future.

I f James was an early riser who loved the camping experience in the woods, finding it relaxing, Scott was his opposite. Scott looked towards the woods as a trapper and a hunter did. He found it sometimes to be a chore or a job. As far as the camping components, James looked at those times as a necessary thing to do; and time spent there was to be considered like staying at home. Scott did not have any good memories of camping from his childhood anyway; after all, his mom did leave his dad on that fateful day.

      It was afternoon when Scott rolled over and started to wake up. Today was going to be a busy day for him. Today he was going for a walk in the woods, and as a bonus, he would be scouting out some campground sites. From what Scott knew about the group's weekend plans, they all worked until Thursday, with everyone taking off at least Friday, Saturday, Sunday, and possibly even Monday. Scott was not sure how busy the campground would be, but he hoped his search would go easier due to his recon. What he needed was to narrow it by excluding areas that were already occupied. Anyone he found in sites now could be overlooked, saving him time.

      Scott had to wake up, but he did not like the taste of coffee; the flavor did not matter to him at all, but he liked the effect. Energy drinks did not agree with him, and he never took those pills; just coffee, black please, he would say. After he juiced up, Scott got dressed and gathered some belongings for today's trip. The last thing he grabbed before leaving his house was a few bottled waters from his fridge; the more he thought about it, he packed rather light, taking only what he needed for a few hours, and not all day. *I can get anything else I need when I'm out and about,* he thought, but he doubted he would need to do that. The hike itself was initially four miles, after that he would take a break for lunch and then scout out the campground.

      Scott was in his new vehicle and now on his way to the local convenience store; it appeared it needed to be juiced up too. It would not take him long at all to get started. Pulling up to the pump, he jumped out, leaving the vehicle running and began pushing buttons. After he started pumping the gas, he turned around and looked at others filling up around him. There he saw a woman who looked like Robin, but upon closer examination, the hair was too long, and she was a bit heavier. He saw her everywhere he looked, in some shape or form. Shit. He had almost forgotten to confirm their date for tomorrow evening. He grabbed his cell phone and selected her name, waiting for her to answer.

"This is Robin." She said into her phone.

"Hey, this is Scott. I was wondering if we were still on for tomorrow evening. We have dinner plans." he said cautiously.

"Oh, hi. I'm busy now, can't talk much here at work, but yes, sounds fun."

"Well, I'll pick you up around seven then?" Scott asked.

"No need. I'm going to be in the area doing some errands after work. I'll just meet you there," Robin said quickly.

There was no response from Scott, or it did not come quick enough, and Robin had to get back to work.

"I'll see you there then. Have a good day, Scott." She said, quickly ending the call.

He pulled the phone away from his head and looked at it, wondering if she was still there, or if the call had ended. He was not sure if she hung up or if it dropped, but he had his answer. He'll be there tomorrow night and see if he can talk her out of camping so they can spend the weekend together. Just as he finished that thought, the gas pump fill warning clicked and shut off. Draining the last of the fuel from the hose, he put it back and pressed *no,* when asked if he wanted a receipt.

Winding road after winding road. It was almost painful for him to take the turns on his way to his trailhead. It was not unlike switchbacks for hiking, but for your vehicle. Finding a good place to put two wheels off the road, he pulled over. Getting out he adjusted his utility belt, ensured he had what he needed, and locked up his vehicle. With an old burlap bag in one hand, and a bottled water in the other, he headed off downhill.

There was some things Scott excelled at, and some he did not. Four months ago, he spent his last two hundred dollars on traps from an online company located somewhere in Nebraska. He practiced setting them up, tearing them down, and setting them up again. Once he was sure they would function properly, and he was using them correctly, he went to set them in the wild. Some people would need to use a map or their GPS from a cell phone or hiking device to keep up with them all, but not Scott. He required no map, not for this area. He grew up here with his family on camping trips. He and his brother would be released into the woods for hours at a time. The only thing his dad asked was for them to return a few times a day and check in. It was during this time that his mom would bird watch, and his dad fish.

The placement of traps and remembering their individual locations was not the problem for Scott. The problem was that he didn't have permission to place them. Two times since then he had to re-order traps. It appeared that someone had issues with him trapping, and they were being stolen. He would hike down to check them, and they would be gone. He never truly knew if he had caught anything at all, because when he went for the big reveal, everything was missing. This time would be different. This time, he was checking for the person or people who were stealing from him. *This time, he would be trapping them!*

Three in a row! Three!!!' he mumbled as he walked closer. Anger welled up inside him. He remembered what the CO had told him earlier this week; *I've been taking your traps now for over a month, I knew we would meet sooner or later.* What Scott didn't know, was if the CO had already found his traps, or if there was someone else still out there. He kept walking and took a sharp left from where he was now in the direction of his fourth trap.

It took about ten minutes of hiking before he arrived. Passing an old tree with a familiar knot, Scott walked up to his marker and straight toward his trap. After a few steps he knew something was there. A few steps more and he saw the chain. It was pulled taut, disappearing behind the tree and out of sight. His anticipation grew. He found himself holding his breath as he rounded the tree. His steps slowed as he walked as softly as he could to keep his element of surprise. With a small exhale and a sigh, he viewed his prize. It was a dog. Scott looked on intently, trying to determine what had happened to it. It looked like it had been eaten by wild animals.

The smell of death hung strong in the air immediately surrounding the dead dog; it was a wonder that it hadn't been eaten entirely. Upon closer examination, it was a Golden Retriever, possibly six or seven years old. Moving closer he removed the trap and pulled it free. Picking up the dog by the head he rotated it until he could read the tags on the collar, *Property of Hearty Lake Campground.*

The dog's name was Parker, and on the back side of the tag was a phone number. Scott had no intention of calling it to inform his owner. He did however, plan on taking Parker deeper into the woods and discarding him.

Placing the dog on the ground at his feet, he took a knee and pulled out his knife. Poking the dog a few times he determined that the opportunity to investigate the contents of his stomach had long passed. Putting his knife back in his sheaf, he stood up and listened. He took a mouthful of water and thought about the dog tags. *Property of Hearty Lake Campground, i*t looked as if he was meant to visit that place; his fate demanded it…

*D**ogs had always been associated with bad memories,* Scott thought; *painful, sad memories from his childhood,* and right now he was experiencing one of the earliest, one of his most painful.

One day in school he was being picked on at lunch. It was a daily routine for a few boys to pester Scott. It usually involved one of them pushing him around while the other took his lunch. Today was a little different. Just as the boys were working him over, a fight broke out on the other side of the room.

The larger one took this as a sign and seeing his opportunity, picked Scott up. Placing him over his shoulder, he quickly left the cafeteria. Going down the hallway, being bounced up and down with every step, Scott screamed out for help. The two boys kept going, and with everyone being on lunch, they had nearly made it down the entire hallway before being noticed. An old lady, known to the students as Mrs. Johnson was walking her service dog Jonesey by a short leash, and when she saw the boys, she smiled, asking them to put the smaller boy down. The older boy agreed, and upon doing so, noticed the fear pasted over Scott's face. He was shaking so hard that the woman thought he could barely breathe.

"Are you alright, young man?" she asked with great concern.

Scott did not answer. The two boys stood motionless, they were sure they were in trouble. Mrs. Johnson looked at the three, struggling to remember their names. There were so many kids here at school that she had no idea who they were; not my job to know you all, she thought.

"Well, run along you two. Go back to your rooms," she told them.

The two boys turned around and started back off to the cafeteria. As they passed the door to the boy's restroom, they went inside. After a few minutes, they came out and looked around, the coast was clear. They started walking back down the hallway, they had no plans to go back to the cafeteria.

Stopping in their tracks as they turned the corner, they waited until the woman went into the classroom, closing the door behind her. Scott was left standing in the hallway holding the dog by his leash. After a few moments the woman would come out, take the service animal from Scott and they would walk to the next classroom. Several times she would enter one classroom leaving Scott with the dog, before coming out, taking Jonesey, and heading off to another. The boys watched as the woman came out, gave the leash to Scott, and walked into the last classroom on this end of the hallway.

Scott was watching the boys looking back at him when the woman entered the classroom. Soon lunch would be over and then it would be back to class; oh, if he could only make it to that time, Scott thought. The boys started walking to him the minute the woman disappeared.

Moving from a brisk walk to an outright run, the larger boy took the leash from Scott, pushing him backwards. Handing it over to his partner in crime, he again pushed Scott against the wall and held him there. The other boy tied the leash to Scott's right leg and then took a step backwards. The first boy laughed, pushing Scott again for good measure, and then kicked the dog.

The boys watched as it took off running, knocking Scott to the ground on his back. He presented little difficulty to the large dog's attempt to escape, which proceeded to drag him down the hallway kicking and screaming. The school bell signaling lunch was over rang out and kids soon flooded the hallway. Everyone laughed as the dog dragged Scott past them bouncing and *screaming. It seemed like an eternity to him, but it was all over in a matter of moments. Scott was still screaming when a teacher reached out and took hold of the dog, freeing the crying child on the floor in front of them. Scott stood up and took off running. He didn't stop until he had reached the main entrance, and then left school.*

He would spend the rest of the day hiding in his backyard until it was his normal time to come home. This was but one of the memories Scott had towards dogs, Golden Retrievers, to be more specific. He cared little for dogs in general. He cared nothing for this one. Picking the dog back up he continued into the woods to check the last of his traps. Out of the remaining ones, only two were missed by the CO; of those, both were empty. Looking around, he found a bushy area full of thorns and thistles. *This would do,* he thought, as he tossed the dog over to the right side of those bushes. *We wouldn't want anyone to not find you, Parker,* he laughed.

Scott found a good size rock and sat down for a water break. He took in his surroundings. He finished the water bottle and closed his eyes as the last mouthful went down. The water was warm, soothing. He would have preferred a cold beer, but water would do for now. He slowly opened his eyes and enjoyed his view. The sights, the smells, he really did love nature. He considered it his only true friend. Be that as it may, there were still times where he distrusted it. Scott put his empty water bottle back in his burlap bag, setting it on the ground beside him. He placed his hands on the leaf covered dirt and slid down off the rock. Getting comfortable he stretched out and laid back, taking in the fresh, nature-purified air, and closed his eyes for a nap.

The campsite was peaceful and quiet, he was still alone. Not a single camper came in overnight, it looked the same now as it did when James had gone to bed. Gathering up a few things, he walked to the camper door and reached to the right, taking the keys off a hook. *Wallet, keys, coffee, he had everything he needed,* he thought as he hit the steps on a mission. He was in dire need of some bait for fishing and some additional ice, one always needed additional ice when camping.

      Taking the steps carefully, and one at a time, James finished the last of his coffee as he left the toasty warmth that was his camper. By the time his left foot hit the ground, the door was closed, and he looked at the emptiness around him. He thought about going back inside for another cup but decided to look around instead. Walking to the road, he placed his cup on the nearby picnic table and continued through the gravel to the roughly paved edge, taking it all in.

      On the other side that belonged to the island was a deep rut where it rounded and curved. It was full of water from last night's torrential downpour. Although it hadn't kept him awake, it looked like it had rained quite heavily. The large puddle looked like an over-sized comma, with the lower round part to the left side and curving up the road to the right was the thin upper portion. The grass in the center section was riddled with twigs and branches that had come down in the wind while he peacefully slept.

      There were small puddles scattered throughout the grass that reflected the sky above, but it was not overall muddy. *There was no need to walk through that anyway,* he thought. The road curved around to the right and the left of the island; that took anyone wherever they needed to go.

      If one did walk up the road, inside the middle, about four sites away and a small distance off center sat the comfort station. Each site between here and there had two picnic tables positioned end to end, adjacent to a graveled parking spot for a camper, their own electric box, and a fire pit with a sliding grate. Some sites had more trees than others, some had none at all, but all had those basic features. Looking left to right, both sides of the center island had enough room to hold campers at each end, with plenty of space between them; again, nicely thought of, designed, and implemented.

      Walking back to the camper, he locked the doors and raised the stairs before jumping into his truck and heading down the road. After leaving the main gated area and waving at where the volunteer should be, it was only a few miles away before he would pull into the closest convenience store. Thinking about what he knew about the park system, he really didn't expect to see anyone there this time of the week. The gate was not staffed one hundred percent of the time during non-peak days; come weekend, James was sure that the place would show more activity.

At various times he had run into and carried on conversations with the property manager, an asset manager, and a handful of volunteers. Other Park officials and DNR employees too numerous to count had also talked to him, even if they hadn't wanted to. From what he could tell, from all the positions that he could think of the best duty was working with all things Raptor! The worst, or the positions that seemed to have the most unhappy, unsmiling faces were office and concessions.

The volunteers were just that, volunteers. They were not paid, and about ten were maintained at all times. The workers that operated the gates were paid employees, no volunteers were staffed there; well, not normally anyway.

Approaching the store James pulled into an empty spot to the right of the front door. There were a few trucks parked by the building, with another fueling up. He nodded at the old man wearing overalls and went inside. Taking a step, he froze when he saw a woman draw down on him, holding her pistol tightly in hand.

"Apology. I'm a bit nervous, is all. Sorry. You startled me," the woman said timidly, rambling on.

"That's quite alright," James replied,

And understandable, he thought, from the way her face looked. She was badly bruised, and as she turned to walk away, he noticed she had a bit of a limp. After a few steps, James watched as she holstered her pistol and removed her hand without securing it; she was definitely on guard and awaited someone's return.

James knew exactly where he was going, and what he was looking for. As always, he found a couple of things that he would like to try, or that would be useful for this week's fishing. With full hands he made his way back to the front counter.

"I need a large bag of ice also, please," he said politely.

"No need to be that formal, I said I was sorry," she half smiled.

James smiled back and paid with a credit card, due to the sign that stated credit card only please, no cash. Thanking the woman, he left to get his ice from the chest outside.

"Thanks again," he said smiling as the door closed shut behind him.

Placing the ice into the cooler, and the live bait into a small, insulated bag, he quickly jumped in the truck and took off for the campsite. Checking left, right, and left again, he pulled out. Looking around upon leaving, he noticed there were still two trucks parked by the building, but he had only seen one employee. *Weird.*

With James getting ready for fishing, and getting a late, lazy start to his day, it grew closer to the afternoon than it was the morning. By the time he was all sorted out to go fishing, it was time to make a small sandwich to take with him. *A salami and cheese on rye would hit the spot,* he thought, as he threw everything into a plastic baggy and added it to his tackle.

Locking up the camper yet again, he started walking down the trail behind his camp site. It was one of the reasons that he chose site 123 in the first place, that and the trail that led to the camp site itself. James walked for a few minutes dodging tree branches and rotting logs. He reached the bank and sat his things down to take a look. A few swells came and went, a turtle flopped into the water and disappeared into the murky darkness, and a few dragon flies buzzed around his head; not a bad start to his day, and those experiences were all his, it was nature at its finest!

James would try crickets, night crawlers, meal worms and all manner of size, shape, and color of Rooster tails, to no avail. It would always be the next cast; he would catch one on the next cast. He changed to a slightly larger red one with a metallic finish, and cast in. He waited to eat his sandwich until after the next cast; there was always a next cast. An hour later, James accepted his fate this fine afternoon and ate his sandwich with no pole in the water, he didn't think it mattered anyway. Closing his eyes after a bite, he looked out onto the peaceful lake; he enjoyed being outdoors.

With his lunch eaten, albeit late, he packed up his gear and headed to the camper. He would have to set out some Polish sausages from the freezer so they could thaw, there would be no fish tonight, unfortunately.

    Looking around to make sure he was taking everything back with him, he made his way up the trail. James returned to his campsite, iced down his live bait, and placed it next to the tackle boxes in the back of his truck, feeling slightly sad that he didn't catch fish today. Those steps would keep his bait safe, and off the ground from the critters overnight. He would not make the same mistake of placing the bait in the camper's refrigerator, or on the dinette table, not this trip.

    Settling down, he reviewed his tackle to prepare for tomorrow's fishing, and put in a movie to half watch, half listen to: *The Princess Bride,* by S. Morgenstern, it was a true classic. It would take hours to plan and sort out his lures and tackle, during which he would start the movie over, twice. *What a relaxing way to spend an afternoon.*

Miles away and still tied to a tree, Kevin awoke to the sound of a single breaking twig off to his left. All he did was open the eye that faced the direction the noise originated from. It appeared to be getting darker around him as he looked on and tried to focus. Gauging by the lack of daylight present, it was early evening, or late afternoon, at best. He was cold, but not overly so. He was a little hungry, but mainly thirsty. He breathed in slowly and exhaled through his nose so he would make less noise.

    Looking around he saw nothing. A few minutes went by before he felt comfortable that it wasn't a carnivore, or worse, the man returning. Kevin managed to stretch his body out as far as he could and allowed a yawn to interrupt the calm environment, before settling into his current situation and thinking about how he was going to escape.

    He found himself becoming one with his environment. Kevin wouldn't go so far as to say he was being assimilated; it was as if he was becoming more attuned. *Nature would provide,* he told himself, *nature would provide*. He looked for proof of this but found nothing. Looking again, just off to his left he saw something that made him equally happy and sad. Mushrooms had recently popped up, just out of reach of his legs; the problem was that they were either chanterelles or jack o' lanterns. The first was safe, and edible, the second was poisonous. Even if he could use his feet to move them closer to him, he wasn't sure if he could, or should eat them.

It wasn't so much the issues with his hunger, he could overcome those urges, it was the lack of water. If Kevin had counted correctly, today was Wednesday, meaning he had been here for a couple of days. He also knew that he was a few miles southwest of the southernmost end of the Outward Bound trail, known to hikers as Old Number 2. He was outside the oak-hickory and the beech-maple climax forest. Where Kevin was the oaks were sparse, at best. The tree he was tied to was hickory.

This put him several miles due west of the main gate, and easily lost to all except those off the beaten trail. Kevin could not predict when or if he would be spotted, and if it would be by a hiker, a hunter, or someone who knew him from the DNR.

"I really gotta make it a point to try and find more time to study our local mushrooms," Kevin said, shaking his head in disappointment.

That's when he saw it. Towards the edge of the tree line in the distance, he saw the gray mass that he had just noticed stop as if it heard him. Wolves were not native to Indiana, although there were rumors. Up north, outside of Indianapolis, was a n54ew rescue center for wolves. Ever since that was established, there had been rumors.

Some say they have seen them at a distance, others heard them, but no one ever saw them out in the wild close enough to positively identify one, not in the state of Indiana, not until now. Slowly turning to the left, Kevin's right, the coywolf snaked in and out of his vision through the trees. Rumored to be a hybrid cross between a coyote and a wolf, they have never been captured, or had their picture taken, so officially they did not exist. It was too far away for him to even entertain that thought, to him it was a wolf. The only weapon Kevin had was his feet, and possibly his voice. He would use them both if it came at him; Kevin always thought ahead in survival situations, this would be no different, as he thought about how to posture himself for success. The wolf stayed on the periphery, and although it was circling him, it never came closer. The next time it moved between the trees, it disappeared as easily as it had come.

He thought long and hard about his encounter, and how it had turned out. There was another possible explanation for today's visit, it could have been Charles. He had first encountered Charles when he was a young boy. It was during a cross country race at his middle school when he had taken a tumble and broke his left ankle. He was stuck in a ditch until late in the evening before he was found; he had been crying so hard that he had no tears left.

The large wolf that crept up the opposite edge of the ditch towered over him, sending chills through his body. He jumped backwards against the dirt wall and attempted to crab walk out before pain shot through his foot and up his leg, causing him to pass out. Kevin awoke to a series of jerks from the wolf pulling him from the ditch and dragging him to the side of the trail. The wolf looked at him long and hard, before lowering its head, turning, and disappearing into the woods.

Kevin was found not ten minutes later by an assistant coach who was retracing the course and searching for him. Those memories were clear in his mind, he would never forget that first encounter. Charles was his spirit animal, a member of the wolf totem. He came to him during his hour of need, returning a few times throughout his life to assist, as necessary. After his initial visit on that fateful run, he had appeared next while in his Mountain Phase of Ranger training, and again now.

Kevin remembered most of what he read when he first searched the internet for understanding. It mentioned the symbolism, how the Native American Indians modeled themselves after the traits of the pack's efficiency, cooperation, and loyalty. After reading about him and determining what he was, he named his new friend Charles. The wolf was thought of as a spiritual pathfinder, displaying leadership along with intelligence to the members of their pack; a great benefactor to have indeed, he thought, pondering what to do next.

Back home, outside of Floyds Knobs, Jeffersonville, and Clarksville, Indiana, the friends were just now getting off work. They had been texting all day, on and off again, and had finally agreed to going shopping at their favorite local Chinese goods importer. It would be open all day, and it was also close to a few places to grab a bite to eat, if they had time. It was almost 7:30 p.m. when the last person to show, Brian, drove up sporting his 32 foot pull behind Grey Wolf, which he bought new within the last year. Lowering his window, smiling from ear to ear, he waited for a response.

"Let me guess," Christy said, "shitter was full?"

"No. Laundry day. Nothing clean, right?" said Linda.

"Why is Joseph hiding in the back? Was he burned by acid or something?" Robin added.

"Funny. Funny. Three of my favorite movies, but funny.

We are buying camping stuff, why pack it up twice? Joseph and I agreed to load it up here and get it ready to go. A head start, if you will. What do you all think?" Brian asked.

"Brilliant!" the newlyweds said, with simultaneous laughter.

"Do you have to do *everything together*?" Brian said, starting to raise his window.

"Shop. Shop. Shop shop, shop," Linda said with sarcasm.

"Shop, shop. Shop. Shop shop," Christy replied, then laughed.

"YES!" Robin said as their posse made for the main entrance.

Brian and Joseph just shook their heads. The newlyweds nodded their approval between stopping for a few small kisses.

"This is going to be fun!" Brian shouted excitedly.

Approximately four hours later, and with much bickering, they all had what they thought they needed for their weekend camping trip. The only person to buy ice was Brian, and that's because they were all set up for it. Everyone else would be using their ice, until the following day after setting up, when they would buy their own. *No biggie,* Brian thought.

"Well, no time for dinner tonight, not for us, anyway,"

Joseph stated.

"Yeah, we all have to get organized and pack what we can tonight and tomorrow, so we are out, too," Robin said for the girls.

Smooch. Smooch. Suck, lick, smooch came from the newlyweds.

"Yeah, yeah, we get it-you're in love," Brian laughed, and everyone parted ways.

"Hey Brian," Christy shouted from her passenger side window. Give us a ten-minute head start before you start killing everyone with your driving, mkay?"

More laughs erupted, and everyone drove off.

By the time they had made it back to their homes and appropriately stored their frozen and refrigerated goods, over at the campsite, James was already grilling his sausages and frying his potatoes. Thinking of one of his favorite movies, he loved the way his little friend said 'po ta toes', he wished he had brought that trilogy.

James was enjoying his dinner by the fireside, as it grew darker around him. Still, not a sole in sight, he was the only one at this end. Once again, he looked forward, and to the left to the single outside light that marked the comfort station building. Listening to the nature around him come to life, he chose not to watch another movie tonight, nor play his PS4-he would just stay outside and enjoy a few cold beers.

THURSDAY

Strawberries? Yes please!

Today was James' EFD, as he would call it. The phone alarm went off and awaited his response. It came when he reached for it and it dropped to the floor. It continued to annoy him, so he had to finally open his eyes and search it out. EFD was code for early fish day, and yes, it was early. *A little past 4 a.m. now, and with any luck, a snooze or two more to come*, he thought.

Reaching for the phone he finally found it and swiped left to snooze the alarm. Five minutes later, lying in bed underneath a single sheet, his eyes popped open. He took the phone and turned it off, it was time to get up. When it was this early, James usually preferred cereal over a cooked breakfast. It could be warm or cold, but something quick, something he could not mess up with sleepy eyes, so Captain Crunch it was. After one large bowl with just enough cold milk to have it turn bright yellow, he made a cup of coffee. This he placed into a metallic pre-heated, insulated cup, screwed on the spill-proof lid, and started to get dressed. Supposedly the cup would keep your beverage hot for over ten hours, like his coffee would last that long.

Walking to the other side of the couch he picked up his laid-out clothes and prepared for his day. Old blue jean shorts, a T-shirt of days long gone, and shoes he no longer cared about, he was ready in no time. Taking his coffee, keys, and wallet with him he left the camper. Locking the door, he walked over to the picnic table to get organized. He grabbed his fishing poles from the compartment below the bed of the camper and stood them up against the table. All he had to do now would be to grab his bait and he was on his way.

He walked up and lowered the tail gate. There were opened bags and containers of bait strewn all over the bed of the truck. There were half- dried night crawlers frozen in various positions of death across the end of the molded bed protector. All three different types of catfish bait packages were either torn open or missing. A large bag of strawberry flavored catfish chunks was draped over the passenger side of the bed. The top of the package was ripped open, its contents entirely eaten. The carnage left behind looked a bloody mess with the drippings sliding down to the wheel well and drying.

It had to have been a raccoon, James was sure of it, but there was no proof. There were no paw prints in blood, no fur left behind; no sick animal in the bed of the truck from having eaten almost three pounds of bait, nothing. There was no time to go out now and purchase more. Although the convenience store would have been open, it was more of an issue with time. He would use the two spare bags of shad in his tackle box; they would do in a pinch.

It was his Boy Scout conditioning, his backup plan, if you will. He was going to go fishing this morning, no matter what. He would get more bait later for the next EFD. Walking with his tackle box and two fishing poles in one hand, and coffee in the other, he used the light on his ball cap to show him the way. Within minutes he was all settled in. Resting with his back against a tree, and his butt on a rock, he watched his floats meander ever so slowly from right to left. He loved his lighted ball cap!

Soon it would be daylight, and it would be time to go back and clean all of the fish. They had a few nice screened in fish cleaning stations strategically placed around the park. They had running water, napkins, hand sanitizer, and electricity! They could be used any time, day, or night. He laughed when he thought about them, he had never actually used one. Not that James never caught fish, he just never caught a lot of fish. His day would come, he knew that. It would not be today though, today he caught none at all.

After several hours he called it. It was time to make his way back and get cleaned up, replace his bait, and try again another time. The saying *a bad day fishing is better than a good day at work* was totally true, but it was more enjoyable catching fish, for sure. James spent an hour setting up his poles for lures instead of bait, then came inside the camper for another cup of coffee. He reflected on his recent fishing endeavors but came up with nothing he was doing was wrong. *The more you go, the better your odds are,* he thought while sipping his coffee.

Not too far off, Scott sat in his DNR vehicle watching traffic on their way into the campground. He didn't need to break out any tools, or to sit with a clip board, he benefitted from just having his vehicle spotted. He was up the hill, and about a half mile away from the gatehouse. What he was waiting for was for the attendant to leave. Soon it would be lunch, and being Thursday, and not the weekend, who knows when she would come back. Drivers that passed him noticed he was looking through binoculars. Right after seeing that, they applied their brakes and started obeying the posted legal speed limit.

Soon it would be locked, and unattended. Soon he would be able to look around with no one over his shoulder. That time was closer than he knew. Scott was watching the most recent car pass through the gate when the side door opened. The employee waved the driver through and then placed the closed sign telling the park visitors to drive around. Shortly afterwards, she walked to her car and left the park, waving to him as she passed.

Scott had been up for hours now, and to be honest, his back was a bit stiff from laying on the ground. He had taken a nap and slept a bit too long. He woke up hours later, and after driving home and trying to sleep in a comfortable bed, he could not fall back asleep. He stayed up watching a little news and having a few cups of plain, black coffee. He was waiting for lunch so he could review the records and find Robin's site.

This was his chance. He waited for her to pass around the corner and then placed his vehicle in drive. Stopping at the gatehouse he parked and got out. Fiddling with his key ring he found the duplicate door key and let himself in. Looking around, and taking another peek outside, he closed the door. Moving towards the computer he marveled at how archaic their equipment was. There was an old, corded phone adjacent to an even older calculator. Both devices were beige colored, showing their age by fading from time and being exposed to sunlight. The computer next to them was equally old, but in all honesty, they probably didn't need much computing power just to access a camping database anyway.

Looking around the room he found paper reservation receipts sorted in numbered slots. They were organized on a wooden board with vertical compartments. It was a basic setup, and efficient; all the person needed was the number of the site rented, or a last name to lookup in the computer. He moved the mouse and a password screen popped up. He took a few guesses and then started looking around for the password. He checked behind the monitor, on the computer, underneath the phone and calculator, without success.

He was still holding the calculator when a pickup truck with a smiling face slightly higher than the steering wheel drove up. A woman was waving with one hand, sipping on a coffee with the other. Scott returned her smile and waved her on. With a nod, the woman pulled off and he went back to work. Looking through the papers on the wall he did not find Robin's name. He didn't remember her last name, only her first, but there were no Robins on the wall.

"Shit! Shit! Shit!" he shouted as he left the building and locked the door.

He would come back tonight when he had more time, he didn't want to overstay his welcome. Scott drove past the nearby convenience store and into town. His goal was beer, and some fast food, it wasn't to run into his old friend. Stopping at the local burger joint, he replaced his stockpile.

"Welcome to Blue's Burgers. How can I make your day better?" the pleasant voice asked.

"Yes. I'll take two number fours, extra cheese, no tomato, large, with fries for one, and onion rings the other," he replied.

"Alright. That will be two Big Blue combos, fries, and onion rings, hold the tomatoes. What do you want to drink with those? She said with a smile.

"Keep the drinks. Well, I'll take one large coffee, if you can do that. Black please," he found himself speaking as nicely to her as he was being spoken to.

"I can do that! Please pull to the second window," she told

him. Driving forward, he stopped at the first window and waited.

Looking inside, he saw two young girls arguing, but with the window closed, he could not make anything out. A young girl smiled and pointed in the direction of the second window. He smiled at her and pulled forward.

"That will be twelve sixteen," the woman said, obviously hiding her frustration.

He handed the woman a twenty and waited. She smiled and went to make change. Seconds later she handed it to him, and then his drink.

"It will be a minute on your fries, can you pull forward to the door and I'll bring it out?" she said nicely.

Scott nodded and pulled up to the door to wait. Looking back in anticipation, he saw the two girls arguing again. His server was holding his bag of burgers, but she was arguing with the other taller woman. Scott noticed for the first time how attractive she was. He guessed she was about five feet tall, five foot one at the most. Her blonde hair was pulled up in a ponytail and half hidden under her cap. She wore a blue uniform, blouse, and jeans, with a name tag that informed everyone her name was Susan.

She wore just enough makeup to be noticed, not to be seen as plain or simple, nor too much to be mistaken as a woman of the night. Her colors were spring, and although her cheeks did not pop, her eyes did. Her build was skinny, almost too much so. If it weren't for her breasts that he was trying not to stare directly at, he would not have noticed her at all. She was a distraction for him. He forgot about Robin. He forgot about his upcoming visit to the gatehouse. He even forgot about being hungry. He watched on as the two continued bickering. A few hand gestures and they both looked at him through the glass.

He wasn't sure if she was standing her ground, or if she was the victim. The young girl looked at him and then opened the door. Smiling, she came out and handed him his food. Through a broken smile, she thanked him and turned away.

"I'm sorry you have to work tonight. Is it a double?" he asked her.

Turning back around, she smiled again, wiping her tears.

"Have a good day. Thank you for your visit to Blues!" she

said and went inside.

Scott would spend the rest of his day parked across the street and in view of the building's main entrance. He had eaten both burgers, all the fries, and half the onion rings before he saw their shift change. Both women promptly left at four thirty and got into different cars. Through the binoculars he wrote down her plates. Accessing the vehicle's onboard computer, he ran them and wrote down her address. She lived only two streets east of here; he would visit her right away.

Scott parked around the corner from Susan and walked to the apartment building. He looked for unit 6 A and knocked on her door. He waited before knocking a second time; still no answer.

"DNR. Open up," he said with authority.

The door clicked and slowly swung halfway open. "Yes?" the girl asked.

Scott looked at her. He took in the fact that she had already changed into a matching gray sweat suit, but she still smelled of burgers and fries.

"You have the right to remain silent," he said.

Taking hold of her shoulders he turned her to the door and slid behind her. Pushing her against it he secured her hands behind her back.

"What have I done?" the girl asked, deciding not to put up a struggle.

He slid his right foot between her legs and pushed them apart, immediately the girl lost a foot in height. Placing his left hand on her shoulder, he held on tightly. His right hand interrupted her next words by covering her mouth. She began actively struggling now, thinking something was definitely wrong with all of this. He moved into her apartment and closed the door.

Taking hold of her arm, he took her along with him as he checked out her living room. There wasn't much value to be had here, but he wasn't robbing her, he was taking her against her will. After a quick check of the bedroom, he tossed her onto the bed. If her mind wasn't racing before, it was now. Susan was terrified and could not scream out or move; all she did was produce tears and dart her eyes around the room in panic. He took hold of her feet and pulled her onto the floor. Susan looked at the

CO with pleading eyes. He secured her to the bed by handcuffing her to the frame and told her to be quiet. Taking his pistol out, he paused for dramatic effect before he explained it to her by slamming it against the left side of her face.

She stopped moving and fell over to her side, her head resting against the mattress. He took this time to look at her and take her in. Curly blonde hair to her shoulders, her blue eyes were closed, her face was thin, gaunt. He took hold of her head and turned her to the left and right, examining all her features. The sweat suit was baggy, comfortable; it did nothing to show off her body. He knew what he would find underneath, he could wait a little longer before exploring her.

Scott left the apartment dragging behind him a medium piece of black luggage with a bright yellow tag that had her name and address on it.

"Susan," he said out loud; "what a pretty name."

Placing the luggage in the back of his SUV, he shut the hatch and drove away.

Dinner tonight would be at La Bottiglia Operta, which loosely translated from Italian to English was *The Open Bottle*. Scott doubted he would have anything fancy, it would probably be a plate of spaghetti and meatballs, with a glass of red wine. The purpose of his meal with Robin was to iron things out. He wanted to exert his control over her. He wanted her to cancel her camping trip and spend time with him; he wanted to test her loyalty, his power.

He wasn't sure how things would turn out, but he was hoping to have sex change her mind. He thought that if they could have sex, it would somehow cement their relationship, his control. Sitting in his vehicle he thought more on the subject. It wasn't so much as an issue of control, as it was the process itself.
Everything came down to control. Kissing, dating, love, death; all were components of control, he thought. Without control, nothing can happen to finality.

Smiling in the middle of a thought, he looked up and pictured Susan, hand cuffed, gagged, and stuffed into a zippered piece of her own travel luggage. The words that popped into his head were *backup plan.* Tonight, would go as he expected; one way or the other, he was going to have control. One way or the other, he would have sex. Turning his head to the left he saw Robin get out of her extended bed, quad cab truck. It was white in color, with black accents above the wheel wells. The headlights and taillights on it were blacked out, too. Were it not for the purple neon lights that were underneath for an accent, it would have been a sweet ride. He cared nothing for neon lighting, loving instead standard factory defaults, but he agreed with her decision to black out her lights.

He exited his vehicle and locked the doors with his remote. He called out her name, but he was either too late, or she didn't hear him; he watched her walk inside and the door close shut. Maybe she heard him and chose to keep going, maybe she didn't, he wasn't sure. It was not a good sign for him. The more he thought on it, the more he thought it did not bode well for her. Reaching the door at a brisk pace, he swung it open and followed her to the table. Robin had just sat down when he walked up.

"Let me get that for you," said the server.

Scott looked on as the man slid the chair underneath her. He looked at Scott, who turned down his offer.

"Very well. My name is Rhoelphels, and I'll be your server. I'll be right back with tonight's specials and your water," he informed them.

After a short pause, Rhoelphels left, and Scott took his seat. A few minutes after that, their server returned.

"Tonight, we have an appetizer, salad, and a choice of two main courses for ninety-nine dollars. With this you will enjoy a complimentary bottle of our finest champagne. We have Carciofini Marini, baked artichoke bottoms filled with crabmeat and scallops, glazed with lime hollandaise, Insalata Di Cesare, our take on the classic Caesar tossed with romaine lettuce, herbed croutons and freshly- grated Parmesan cheese, and your choice of Salmone Allo Champagne, grilled North Atlantic salmon with a champagne dill cream sauce, garnished with mushrooms or Spaghetti Con Aragosta and Pomodoro E Arugula, spaghetti with

South African lobster tail, petite shrimp, sun-dried tomatoes and arugula sautéed with extra virgin olive oil, garlic and Italian parsley. How does that sound, signora? Signore?" he politely asked them.

Robin looked at Scott, awaiting his response. Scott smiled and looked at the server.

"That sounds lovely. Thank you for that. The lady will have the salmon, and instead of all that seafood nonsense, can you bring me out spaghetti and meatballs please?" he said softly.

She looked at her server and said she would just have the salad. When Rhoelphels looked at her, she mouthed the words separate checks. He nodded at Robin, and then the gentleman dressed in the army uniform, filling their waters before leaving. Had Scott taken the time to notice, he would have commented on Robin's new dress.

It was a lovely print, and it was picked out to represent a new beginning. It offered up to the man, or woman who desired her, a glimpse of what they would never have. It hung low for her cleavage, displaying way too much, her mother would say; the length, the length, she heard her mother's voice. The shortness of her dress hung dangerously high above her knees; again, acting out girl tested, mother not approved, she laughed, exposing the largest smile he had seen from her all night. Her smile could not have been released at a more detrimental time: It was immediately after a comment that he had made about not caring if her friends missed her, he wanted her close this weekend. He did not approve of her smile at that time, not at all.

The small talk was painful to listen to, just ask anyone ten feet or so from their table. Those watching would say that the woman nodded, a lot, and the gentleman talked with his hands the entire time. The conversation never became heated, as Robin just gave up trying to work with this man. Scott spent his entire time discussing the top ten reasons why she should cancel her camping trip, between mouthfuls of spaghetti. Robin ate her salad slow enough, timing her bites where she could not talk or respond, save a nod of her head and a half smile.

Scott thought all was going well, up to his last comment with her large smile of defiance. Robin prayed for a fanatical shooting spree to come in and intervene to save her; she was willing to take a spare bullet just to stop this madness.

"Well, it's obvious that we are not meant to be together. We just don't have the same feelings and thoughts," Robin said softly.

He looked on, pausing for effect. He wanted to hear more from her.

"So, I think I'll be leaving now. I think some time apart would be exactly what we need. Who knows, maybe we'll see how things go after the trip?" Robin continued.

Still, Scott sat motionless, silent.

"OK We are in agreement then. Have a wonderful evening, I'll pay for mine on the way out. Good night," Robin said as she stood up and wiped her face with her napkin.

There wasn't anyone within earshot who wasn't staring at them, awaiting a negative response from the man. Onlookers expected anger, sadness, compassion, any emotion at all, but he did nothing. He said nothing. Finishing his water, he sat thinking about what had transpired. His server came back and asked him if he wanted dessert.

"No thanks," he managed. "I'll be having mine later," he said smiling as he stood up to leave.

Those around him that heard his comments doubted that, and if it were to happen, it wouldn't be with that fine lady who had already left. Scott paid for his meal and left the establishment without incident, something his server thought would never have happened.

S cott searched for his key fob and unlocked his doors. Reaching out, he placed his hand on the cold metal and paused. *Scott was a senior in high school, approximately seventeen, he guessed. Gone were his freckles and blonde hair. Most to all of them had disappeared and his hair gradually turned browner, seemingly overnight. He was still at home, but his brother was in the process of moving into an apartment. The only real times they talked recently were at family functions and holidays. Although seventeen, he had not spent any significant time with a girl, no one he liked, anyway. He went to last year's prom as a favor to a friend, but not with anyone that he had asked out. Scott didn't spend much time with friends growing up, he didn't have many. Of the friends he did have, none were girls.*

There was a girl that he did like, and everyone seemed to know it, even his brother. Suzi was her name. Her classmates picked on her, telling her she could not spell, and that her mother did not like her due to the fact that the 'e' was missing at the end of her name, but Suzi didn't care. A fun and friendly blonde-haired little girl, in the most literal sense; Suzi was physically small for her age. Throughout school their paths crossed from having the same classes, and the same school clubs, but they never talked or sat near each other. One of the reasons he didn't talk to her was that he didn't want to be joked on for being friends with someone that short. It was something that the older he was, the less it meant to him. Not that he was being less picky, he just didn't care what others thought as much as he used to, not anymore.

One day his brother knocked on the front door just in time for dinner. He often came to see their stepmom and dad, or 'mom', as their dad wanted them to call her, on occasional weekends. With today being Tuesday, tonight's visit was unexpected. Whenever dad saw his brother, he would usually make him take a box or two with him, in the hope that one day soon, all the stuff in his old bedroom would finally disappear. Scott was always amused by this, and he made a point to be there when his brother was confronted. Most of the things his brother cared about were already moved out, so it really didn't matter to him. Scott's brother could care less if dad threw what remained into the trash. One weekend in particular, his brother packed up the last of his camping gear. Scott found that interesting, and out of curiosity asked him about why he was taking it now.

"Well, I wanted to talk to you about that," his brother told him.

"Me and Gretchen ran into Suzi the other day," he continued.

Scott had not seen her in months. With it being summer, he was spending a lot of his time in the woods, with and without his family.

"Oh yeah?" Scott replied.

"Yeah. She asked about you, what you were up to," his brother said with concern.

Scott tried not to seem interested. He wasn't sure if he cared or not, but he wanted to hear what his brother was going to say next.

"How's she doing, anyway," Scott asked matter-of-factly.

"Well, she's coming off of a bad break up. You know how she likes to go to the woods to clear her head, we've all done that before, it's calming out in nature," Scott's brother stated.

Scott paused but looked away as he thought about how he could get ahold of her.

"So, Gretchen had the idea of the four of us going camping together, just us four," he said excitedly.

Scott did not hide his feelings on that, his brother noticed he was interested, very interested.

"I'm interested. Sounds like fun," Scott said quickly.

"Well, it's not for a few weeks, but we are driving out on a Friday evening, and we'll be staying the weekend. Get your gear packed up, grab enough clothes for a few days, and we'll swing by and pick you up then?" his brother said to Scott.

"Sure. Alright," Scott replied.

That night's dinner went off uneventfully, and both parents noticed that their sons were getting along rather well. Weird, they were both thinking, but anything, just as long as they were not fighting. And as an added bonus, his oldest took two more boxes home. Yay!

Scott told his brother good night as he drove away with the majority of his camping gear. Had his brother's windows not been up, Scott would have heard him laughing as he sped off. It would be a few weeks before Scott spoke to him again. He would have forgotten about his camping date with Suzi, were it not for the phone call from his brother reminding him the day before. It was a short call, it came in after dinner, and when his brother thought he had the best chances of reaching Scott at home.

"I'll be ready around 6 p.m., would that work?" Scott asked.

"Great! We'll pick you up then," his brother said,

abruptly hanging up the phone.

Although school was out and he didn't have a job at present, Scott still found it difficult to sleep; all he thought about was his camping trip with Suzi. He hoped everything went well, and that he could get along with his brother long enough to enjoy her. He wondered what Suzi looked like now. He thought of a thousand excuses to cancel on his brother, but none of them stuck. Scott really wanted to see her and catch up. He finally fell asleep around four in the morning, the Friday of. He wouldn't get much rest, but he would be fine, he thought, closing his eyes for a few more winks.

Friday afternoon passed quick enough for him, and before he knew it, his brother pulled up with Gretchen and Suzi. The back of his Chevy truck was full of totes and bags containing camping gear, food, and supplies, he imagined. His brother was good at packing for trips; there wasn't much, if anything, that was forgotten or left at home when the family went camping and he was in charge.

"Hey guys!" Scott said as the truck came to a complete stop.

"Get in. Put your stuff in back," his brother said.

Gretchen and Suzi called out and smiled when he entered. Gretchen was up front with his brother; Suzi was in the middle of the back seat. No matter which door he got in to, he would be sitting dangerously close to her. Scott threw his black duffle bag into the bed of the truck and chose the closest door. Smiling, he put his seat belt on and cuddled in.

The ride to Hearty Lake was quiet and seemed to take forever. Suzi smiled often when Scott looked over, and he returned the gesture. Most of the talking was up front, with his brother asking Gretchen about her day, her work, or how her writing was going. Small talk ensued, and every once in a while, he initiated with Suzi. Her responses were polite and adequate, but she never initiated any conversation herself.

Pulling into the park his brother made it to the primitive section and slowly entered their reserved spot. Within an hour the tents were all set up by him and his brother, while the girls worked on getting a fire started. It was a good thing everyone wore T-shirts and shorts; it was summer after all, and outdoor work did tend to heat one up. It was a wonderful afternoon for Scott, relaxing by the fire with hotdogs, s'mores, beer, and Suzi. After a few beers, Suzi was more talkative, Gretchen too, but his brother was the same.

Scott wanted to go fishing soon; he loved to fish, but he didn't know if he was expected to spend time with them all the while, or if he could slip away to the lake. It would have been wonderful to have caught some fresh fish for dinner, he thought, if he wasn't already full of all those hotdogs. He tested the waters anyway.

"Anyone want to go fishing?" Scott asked between sips of beer.

At the same time, both his brother and Gretchen said no, with Suzi not saying anything. Scott paused before commenting further.

"Here is fine," he said as he moved his chair a little further from the fire.

Suzi picked up hers and placed it near Scott. Gretchen and his brother passed glances to each other, but neither moved nor said anything. It was getting closer to dinner, and it was getting darker, too. With everyone full of campfire hotdogs, s'mores, and beer, no one really wanted dinner.

The darker it became, the more his brother and Gretchen whispered sweet nothings to each other, and the more Suzi talked to him. The small talk became even smaller, if that was even possible. The roles of Scott and Suzi were reversed, with Suzi the talkative one, and Scott now growing silent.

"So, what have you been doing this summer then, Scott?" Suzi managed.

"I've not been doing much, really. I find time to hike in the woods. Oh, and I fish a lot, as often as I can," Scott said smiling.

Immediately after that comment, Gretchen announced they were going for a walk, and to not wait up. Suzi told them goodbye. Scott watched them leave; he felt uncomfortable the minute they disappeared down the road.

"Would you like to go for a walk, too?" Scott asked out of feeling obligated.

"No, I prefer our time here alone," Suzi smiled.

Standing up, with an outstretched hand, Suzi looked over

at him. Her large breasts hung level in front of his face. He had not really looked at her much when everyone was around. Examining her in the light of the fire he saw for the first time that she had red hair, it used to be blonde! Her eyebrows were light colored, blonde, but not red, that was his tell. He was amazed and embarrassed that he had not noticed earlier. Although he tried not to stare, it was initially hard to pull away. Suzi looked on, waiting with her outstretched hand. She noticed him looking at her hair.

"There's another way to remember, another way to tell," Suzi said smiling.

She looked down at her hand again and paused. Scott stood up and took it, waiting for her to make the first move. Suzi smiled and led him to their tent, entering first. He followed her and sat down to her side. Suzi was still standing at this point. A large smile crossed her lips.

"No one's here except us," Suzi said as she sat down beside him.

It was much darker in the tent than by the fire. Scott saw even less of Suzi's detail now; he wished they were still by that fire; he wasn't done taking her in.

"I've always wondered what it would be like to kiss you, Scott. We never had that chance. Why have you never asked me out?" she said as she removed her T-shirt.

Half looking at her, half away, he did not reply.

"Well, I know why, it's scary," Suzi said, leaning in.

Scott found himself pulling away. He was touching the side of the tent now and could not move any further from her. Placing a hand on his shoulder, she went in quickly to seal the deal. Their lips met, and unbeknownst to him, she thought he kissed rather well. Scott had forgotten to close his eyes and was watching her closely as they kissed a second time. Her eyes opened, and she smacked him on his shoulder, pulling away.

"Perv," she said laughing.

Suzi went in for another kiss. Placing her hands on his chest, she slowly moved them down to his shorts. A few more kisses and Scott was all in. He was enjoying this, and Suzi could tell. Lower her hands went. It was the most powerful sexual experience he had ever felt. Of course, he had been hard before, someone had to take care of his needs, but no one had ever done *anything for him, or to him.*

Scott's hard on was her main focus now. One of her hands controlled him with a fist full of his hair, and the other had a fist full of him down below. Scott grew more and more excited; his kisses became more passionate. His breathing quickened; he knew this feeling, it's happened to him before. Suzi's next kiss was shorter, more passionate. She pushed his head to the side and held it there. She let go of his hard on.

Pulling away she smiled and let go of him. Both of her hands ran their fingers through her hair, and then down the front of her body, stopping at her breasts. Taking off her bra she squeezed them and then let them fall back into place. She stood up and again held out her hand. He took it and she pulled him to his feet. Letting go, she lowered her hands and took hold of his shorts. Digging her fingers inside the waist band, she grabbed both underpants and shorts, and slowly slid them to the ground. Looking at him for a second, she moved in close for another kiss.

A few more, and she slid her hands back down to him. Even more kisses came, faster, more passion escaped Suzi, her hands running over his shoulders, his chest. Taking a step backwards, she left the tent laughing quietly. Scott followed and ran straight into his brother, almost knocking him over. He too was laughing and could barely manage to hold his flashlight still. Illuminating Scott's penis was his job, Gretchen's was to take the pictures; Suzi had already done hers. Everyone burst out in laughter, jeering, and pointing to Scott's erection.

Scott reached down and pulled up his shorts. Walking into the tent he looked for his T-shirt to finish getting dressed. He was crying when he started walking up the road. It took him about thirty minutes before he saw the front entrance through red, teary eyes. Upon reaching the gate, he was approached by a park official who promptly called his parents to come pick him up.

Scott awoke from this living nightmare sweating and twitching anxiously. Scott would never camp with others again. He never saw or ran into Suzi, either. Things haven't been the same with his brother since. As far as Gretchen, no one's seen her in years, the rumors are that they broke up after what happened that night. Feelings flooded over him. He came to reality when he finished thinking about the ending of that night. He liked to camp, hike, fish; he was self-described as outdoorsy, but he did not like spending time outside with anyone other than Mother Nature.

Releasing the door handle, Scott left sweat marks where his fingers once were. He stared at them until they disappeared. Moments later he opened the door, got in and drove away. Scott drove angry. The more he thought about that night, the angrier he became. He was sitting at a red light in front of the intersection by the convenience store. It wasn't worth the risk to him to stop there for dessert. Tonight, he would have his dessert at home. Looking both ways, ensuring it was safe, he started down the road to the main gate. *I'll have to look them up one day,* Scott thought, as images of Suzi and Gretchen popped into his head.

The CO loved living at the campground. It was as close to being off the grid as he wanted to be. Now, before he was a CO, his life was noticeably different, sure, but donning the DNR uniform and riding around in a marked vehicle did have its advantages. He was basically allowed to come and go all throughout the campground at all hours of the day or night, a free pass, if you will.

He took this time to run around and look for Robin and her friends. He doubted that they would be here this early, but it was worth a shot. There really wasn't anything else to do this time of day. It was getting dark; what campers that were here have probably come back or would be back soon.

Scott made a mental reminder to return after dark, when it was easier to check for lights, occupancy, and to move about without being so easily seen. The evening also allowed him to use his night goggles. *They must have been a recent addition to their tools,* he thought, he'd not seen a DNR CO, or park ranger use one yet. Tonight would be his first time playing with them, and to be honest, he was looking forward to trying them out.

Driving slow around the park, he focused on the electric campground sites. There were a few campers in that section for the moment. He knew this would change after 2 p.m. tomorrow, and into the weekend.

That was the check-in time, and it was when most campers came to get set up. It would be total chaos then, for sure. A few more turns and then he would loop back to the main campground road. Still not many campers out, he would probably not need to come back out tonight. Although, it would be a good dry run for him to get used to those night goggles. *It was agreed*, he thought. He would come out tonight, walk through the woods and check out some sites.

Nothing makes one hungrier for dessert more than driving around looking for women. That statement was partially true, Scott thought, because some of Robin's friends were guys, and he would be happy to find any of them out camping. He thought back about Robin and tonight's dinner. It didn't go well. It did let him know where he stood with her; he expected something to be wrong, she had acted strange all week. Scott had seen everything he needed to see by now, so he hurried home. If he planned properly, and his calculations were correct, he should have a few hours with Suzi. If things went the way he expected, he could spend a little more quality time with her, but he had to go back out and test those goggles.

Scott pulled in beside his camper and backed up to clear the road. He was on an end close to the amphitheater. It sometimes drew walking traffic as movies, events, and even raptor nature releases took place there. His site was off the beaten path, and for someone to visit him by accident, one would have to follow lights at night (if he had them on), or to be really drunk and walk randomly through the woods instead of following the road around.

Exiting the SUV, he stopped to listen to his surroundings. It was quiet, all was well. Unlocking his camper, he went up the steps and closed the door behind him. Looking out the nearby window, he noticed how dark it already was; *perfect*, he thought. Again, he stopped and listened. He didn't hear a peep. Placing his keys on the hook by the door, he locked the camper from the inside and walked down the hallway to the fridge. Taking a beer, he closed the door and enjoyed a sip before walking into the bedroom.

At the foot of the bed was that piece of black luggage. It was zippered up, and zip tied in lieu of a lock, but it looked secure. The room seemed to grow quieter the closer he walked to her. Stopping a hand-reach from the luggage, he listened closely.

"Are you alright?" he softly asked. No response.

"Suzi, you awake?" he asked again.

Still no response.

"Well, if you're dead, you're of no use to me. I'll have to

throw you in the lake. If you don't give me a sign, you're going swimming," he said loudly.

Susan flailed and bounced as much as she could. Looking on, Scott saw the smallest of movements, but he could tell she was alive. Still, no sounds escaped the luggage.

"That was good of you," he said as he cut the zip tie and opened his present.

"Well look at that, and it's not even Christmas!" he joked.

He reached over, and taking the edge of the luggage, he upended it. He continued watching as Suzi rolled out and hit her knees on the floor before stretching as far as she could. Looking down at Suzi, he wondered how she even fit in that thing. Taking a step back, he looked down at her and paused. It was not Suzi he was looking at, it was Susan. Scott wondered if he was acting out of anger, out of rage. He wondered if he had been rash in taking this woman. Scott wondered how things would turn out.

Susan panicked. She was in a bad place, and she felt the cold, icy grip of despair take hold. She was willing to do anything to escape, to get free, literally anything. She could not tell him that, not now anyway. Susan had been in bad relationships before, many times, but never where her life depended on maintaining it. She was always able to leave, and she was generally quick to break up with anyone who turned into a loser. Susan was stretched out on the floor looking straight at a loser, but he was the one in control.

Scott reached for her and picked her up. She was easy for him to hold on to, she didn't struggle or try to get loose; Susan waited patiently to be placed back down. Turning to his left, he tossed her on the bed. Climbing up beside her, he turned her over and began rubbing his hands over her bottom. Susan did not respond at all; she did not jump, jerk, or recoil. Susan did nothing in response to him, she just lay there thinking on what to do next.

He mashed her cheeks in his hands, often sliding his fingers just inside between them, but no further. This he felt made her uncomfortable, or aroused, he could not tell which. She was still gagged, and although she was not yelling or screaming, she was not moaning, either. Scott squeezed harder. He pushed her down firmly onto the bed. A few times he pressed his fingers deeper, further, touching and rubbing her anus. This made Susan respond, where first she tried not to do anything, she now found herself trying to slide away from his attention.

"It's OK, you'll like it, you'll see," Scott said in a quiet, seductive voice.

None of that mattered to Susan. She didn't expect to live through this unless she participated, unless she played along. While she pondered that last thought, she jerked uncontrollably upward when two fingers were thrust inside her. It made his attempt to tease her more forceful than it was meant to be when she pushed up towards his hand, making him go deeper than he had intended. *He was already there, so what the hell,* he thought. Pushing his fingers in further and further, he pulled them nearly out each time before repeatedly pushing in deeper again. This he did until she nearly found herself jumping off the bed.

Scott rolled over on top, removing his fingers. He placed both hands on the sides of her head and firmly squeezed. Susan stopped jerking. He slid his hands down the sides of her neck and applied more pressure. Susan would be able to breathe, but he was cutting off the oxygen to her brain. He raised her head upwards and shook her. Her hair moved back and forth before returning to lay down flat against her shoulders and back. More pressure, and then he shook her again.

Control, it was all about control. He let go of her and flipped her over, looking into her eyes. She was still lucid, he saw panic, but she was still in control. Sliding up further, he again placed his hands on the sides of her face, squeezing hard. Her eyes widened. They grew even larger when he slid them down to her neck. It was as if he were trying to remove her head. *She needed that,* she thought irrationally, she had to keep her head.

Her eyes pleaded. She began to cry. Shaking and looking directly at him, she made her passionate plea. Blinking her eyes repeatedly, she jerked her body up from the bed as high as she could, but his weight kept her exactly where she was meant to be. Susan felt lightheaded, and before she could think any further, she blacked out. Her eyes closed slowly, and with one additional shake, he let go of her. Scott was totally hard now, and he felt uncomfortable, restricted by his uniform.

He slid off the bed and began undressing. Taking everything off he stood over the side and took hold of his hard on.

A few strokes and he knew he was ready. Scott let go and walked out of the room. Stopping in front of the air conditioner, he dropped it to fifty degrees, set the fan on high, and went back to give Suzi the attention she desired.

Back in the woods, and far, far away, Kevin was breathing out of his mouth, taking slow, deep breaths. Every two or three he would close his mouth, swallow involuntarily a few times, and then return it to an open, relaxed position. He had been doing this for an hour or two while he slept. To Kevin it seemed the middle of the night, and the rain that was coming down slowly at first, now came at a good pace and was coating his tongue, causing Kevin to swallow reflexively. Watching this man from a distance, one would not go as far as to say he snored, but he wasn't quiet, neither.

Nature will provide, he thought, as he woke up, opened his eyes, and stretched, swallowing again. He scanned the tree line, moving his eyes instead of his head. The only movement Kevin did was to swallow from time to time, and then slowly open his mouth to catch more. It was the only moisture he had received in days, and he wasn't about to miss any of it. Kevin continued scanning the woods using the light provided by the moon. Using his eyes as best he could, and with the rain coming down as hard as it was, he continued scanning the forest. A nearby crack of lightning disrupted his thoughts, followed shortly after by thunder off in the distance.

Kevin found himself back in ranger training, the memories were as vivid, as fresh now as they were back then. The Mountain Phase, as it was affectionately known, was orchestrated in a little place called Camp Merrill, located in the remote mountains near Dahlonega, Georgia. Thinking back on this, there wasn't a more perfect time and place for his spirit animal to pay him a visit. It was here where he began to doubt his resolve; it was here where for the first time, he found himself tested beyond his strength. Not that he hadn't thought about quitting, recruits think on this at the beginning and end of each training day, it's just that today was different.

Knowing what he knew now, he thought back to the notes he took in training, and his thoughts. Right from the beginning, one had a guide for what to bring to your training; requirements, recommendations, etc.; a guide full of rules, and rules mattered.

There was a list to help you get started for your training, all recruits received it. Aside from regular, expected, common sense gear such as your military BDUs, gloves, boots, socks, multiple copies of your orders, which would disqualify you if you didn't have the proper amount or didn't have the requirements on that first portion of your list, one was expected to bring some other non-standard helpful items, such as black electrical tape, nylon cordage, a compass, extra bootlaces, a sewing kit, batteries, and other assorted items.

Outside of both of those two previous categories, there was another section of items, such as large trash bags, a folding knife no larger than 4 inches, waterproof bags, alcohol-free baby wipes, alcohol erasers, chemlights and other optional, but recommended items. You were set up for success, or at least you were given a guide to assist you in achieving success, all you had to do was apply yourself.

The training focused on a balance of overcoming mental and physical barriers; it stressed the enemy within as either one's physical or mental state. It trained you to recognize your ever-present enemy within, and to overcome it. You worked together as a team to challenge yourself, displaying your strengths and weaknesses to one and all. With your training, and the help from your buddies, you were taught to succeed, and to recognize and embrace your failures. The enemies that you were training against were always close, but you were safe within your group.

Along the way, you were presented with opportunities to

succeed in various roles, such as one of four squad leaders, a platoon leader, or a platoon sergeant. At any time, in any situation those roles could be reassigned, and your name chosen to lead. The first four days were introduction to training skills and some practicals, the remainder of the two weeks were ambushes, patrols, OPORDS (Operations and Orders), and all things combat. You were up against an organized and highly skilled enemy; for ten days you were to match wits against them. They were not referred to as a superior foe or force, as rangers, you were superior to the enemy; but you were trained to respect them, their abilities, and skills.

  On this day, his squad drew security. Other squads were assigned their individual assignments and sent out north by northwest in half hour increments to achieve those goals. No one squad knew which one had been given which assignment; even the one for security would march off, and then circle back around only to arrive back at camp to be given that mission. It was as mental as it was physical, and it was a daily occurrence that change occurred, leaving them to embrace the suck. Sometimes, two squads were given the same assignment, the same goals, pitched against themselves as much as the enemy that was around them. Today was one of those days.

  Keven led his group up the boot trodden path and after an hour of maneuvers they left it, turned due west, and started straight up the hill. Another hour and they were ordered to return to basecamp and set up a perimeter; they had been assigned to security today, and time was running out. In many ways, it was the most stressful of the assignments you could draw, at least for the beginning portion. You were to lock down the camp, and treat all those that approached as enemies, until proven otherwise. You wouldn't know who was approaching, the true enemy, or one of your squads, who until verified and allowed to pass, were also the enemy.

  To make matters worse, security detail lasted longer than most of the others, and when your brothers returned for resupply, to discuss their day, and to receive their debriefing, settling in as much as they could, you were still hard at it, keeping the camp secured from the enemy. Making matters even more challenging was the fact that Telford, Smith 3, Montgomery, and Sulley were all told they were sick today. Telford and Sulley went with another squad, probably to burden them with wounded, leaving Montgomery and Smith 3 resting here inside a tent; they would be in their shelters on their backs the entire scenario; Kevin was hamstrung right from the beginning. That left him responsible for a total of nine rangers, including himself.

Looking at what he had to work with, he noted that they were all soldiers; everyone looked like soldiers. All had painted faces in the traditional local foliage and rock colors; no two looked alike when he thought about it that way. All their faces were skinny and attached to those skinny faces were various-sized bodies, all dressed in the same BDUs. Other than that, there weren't any notable differences between them, except their personality, the sound of their voices perhaps, oh, and their names.

He assigned his team into pairs and set up light security at the main entrance. He went with a heavier presence on his right flank, which he thought offered the highest possibility for the enemy to sneak in; it was the best he could come up with in such short notice, so he went with his gut and sent his men out to prepare.

"Jonesy and Michaels, take the south, Neidermeyer and Sanchez, the East," Kevin said, then turned to his right.

"Lewis, you go west; that leaves you the front gate," Kevin finished looking directly at Paulson.

Kevin walked off to the headquarters' tent and wrote down his plan, drew a basic camp diagram, assigned names to locations, then left the tent to assess; paperwork wasn't his strong point, he hoped that his implementation would suffice and carry him through to a successful grade for today's training. He started at the center of camp and walked in each direction in turn, reviewing and taking notes. Kevin would need those notes later for his debriefing, so he did take the time to ensure everything was complete.

Paulson used his left thumb to open his 551. A single click was the only sound heard as he continued walking up to Neidermeyer.

"All set here, boss?" he asked him.

Neidermeyer nodded, catching a brief smile from Paulson before he turned back to scan his surroundings. *He had missed Paulson's approach, but he was a ranger; hell, we're all rangers,*

Neidermeyer thought, as he scolded himself for not noticing. Taking a small breath, he looked to his left and leaned against a tree to scan his surroundings once again. *No one else is going to get that close without being noticed, not on my watch, not again,* he finished that thought and then looked over his right shoulder to watch Paulson walking away into the woods. Turning back around, he again went about his duty.

Paulson kept walking towards the direction of where he thought Sanchez would post. He closed his knife and placed it back in his pocket. Moving in a straight line, he headed directly to the largest tree at the base of the hill. *The red cedar stood proud, majestic; it would make a lovely grave marker,* he thought as he laid eyes on Sanchez.

"¿Qué tal una barra de pan?" Paulson asked in what Sanchez would call piss-poor Spanish.

"Una barra de pan cuesta ochenta y siete pesos, demonio blanco," was always Sanchez' reply.

It was quite comical to Paulson, and offensive to Sanchez, but they used that greeting, none the less. *How much for a loaf of bread*, was the question, followed by the response, a *loaf of bread costs eighty-seven pesos, white demon.*

"You know, I looked that up the other day, white demon? Cute," Paulson told him, smiling widely.

"Well, you can be taught; sort of," Sanchez replied, smiling back, and turned away to check his field of view.

His fleeting smile was met with a single Judo chop to his neck. It damn near killed Sanchez, leaving him effectively stunned and debilitated, he dropped lifelessly to his knees. Paulson helped him back up on his feet by placing him in a headlock and walking backwards raising him against his chest. Sanchez resisted by lowering his chin into Paulson's arm, grasping for an opening.

"You see, I've decided to drop. This thing here isn't right for me," Paulson said as he took Sanchez up into the air, twisting him around, slamming him down onto a nearby protruding rock.

Paulson leaned over Sanchez, tucked his knees into his side and rolled him over on his stomach. Sanchez was bleeding now from his left ear and lying motionless when Paulson took the back of his neck in his left hand and pulled out his 551 with his right. A quick thumb action and the blade swung open, making a soft click as it locked in place.

"How does that go again," he asked Sanchez before remembering.

"For it's one, two, three strikes you're out, at the old ball game," he sung, as Paulson repeatedly stuck the blade into Sanchez.

When enough blood was pouring out onto the forest floor, he placed his knee in Sanchez' back and reaching forward, sliced his throat.

Instead of continuing his quest, Paulson decided to go back and take care of his unfinished business, lest he leave a man behind. He moved along the opposite side of the creek bed that he had left, coming at Neidermeyer from the other side. He was able to get close enough for him to close the distance in a run, and hopefully take him by surprise. He doubted that he could sneak all the way up unnoticed, he didn't even want to try that. Keeping to the larger trees, Paulson did the best he could to stay hidden, it wasn't the noise he made that was going to alert his prey, he didn't make noise, it would be sight; there were only so many trees now that he could use to hide himself, and although stealthy, they would not be enough to hide him, not anymore.

Before stepping out from the last tree that could provide him sanctuary, he dug a foot-long piece of paracord out of his pocket. Breaking into an all-out run, Paulson stayed to the right of Neidermeyer. It took six steps for him to get close enough to launch his body into the air and attempt a tackle; *five steps too many,* he thought. He had made contact with his right shoulder before Neidermeyer had turned to see what was coming, and with a short grunt from the two men, combat had begun.

Most fights went to the ground, eventually. He was trained to do this when he took martial arts as a youngster, and his military training had been no different. The two men grappled and threw punches, rolling around like a couple of teenagers before Paulson found himself on the bottom, the recipient of several blows to his face and chest. A well-placed knee from Neidermeyer had enabled that to happen, it wouldn't happen again.

Flailing around and jumping his body to the left, he threw off his attacker and now he was on top. Paulson didn't use a knee to get the advantage, he slid off to the left and rolled Neidermeyer over, falling on top of him. Taking a risk and stopping his punches and grappling, he managed to wrap the paracord around his neck and pulled back hard. Paulson twisted and turned him around, dragging him closer to a log about four feet away, jerking wildly as he went. Neidermeyer could no longer speak, all he could do was to try to overpower the stronger man, which is something that Paulson would not allow to happen.

Paulson continued dragging him, albeit laboriously, until he was close enough to throw over the log, Deliverance-style. Sitting on his waist, Paulson pulled back, and pulled back hard. Neidermeyer could not believe what was happening. He was being held face-down, ass-up, over a log by a psychopath who was trying to saw off his head with a piece of cordage.

Paulson shook his victim violently back and forth, while pressing down on him with all his strength. It would never saw off his head, but it did help to disorient and control him, while performing its main function of killing, by cutting off his oxygen.

He was pulling with every muscle he had at his disposal. The position of his arms resembled that of a chicken, or a rooster crowing. Paulson's hands were close together, as were his arms. His elbows were tucked into the sides of his body and pushed back behind his sides as far as they could go; Paulson wanted to deliver as much leverage to his cause as necessary; he took no chances. Neidermeyer fought less and less, until he made the last gasps that he would ever make and ceased struggling all together.

He let go of his left hand and pulled the paracord free. Neidermeyer's head fell forward and hit the log with a thud. Placing the paracord back into his pocket he reached for his 551 and slid the blade open. Paulson stuck with his fascination with the number three and cut him several times before rolling him off the log, his body bouncing to the bottom of the dry creek bed. *One, two, three, let's call it three then,* he thought, as he lost track of the bounces. Looking around for something to wipe his knife clean, he walked down the hill and used Neidermeyer's shirt. Kicking him one time for good measure, he headed south.

"Have to clean the knife after every use," Paulson said as he closed the blade and returned the knife to its home.

He didn't know if he would run into Jonesy or Michaels first, it didn't matter much to him. Thinking on the lay of the land, he focused on the southern end of their basecamp. The first feature he would reach would be the creek, followed by a small new forest area. *So, the first one that I run into will die in the creek, and the other among the saplings*, he thought, letting a few evil snickers escape into the woods.

It took a little longer than he would have liked to reach basecamp. It wasn't like he could take the shortest distance between two points and walk through the middle, he had to move around the periphery, keeping to the shadows, the edge. He ran into the creek early on and stayed on the eastern side as he travelled closer. Up ahead he saw some movement that concerned him; there were two soldiers! He didn't want to get closer, but he had to move around a little so he could hear better.

Listening to their conversation would help him determine who he was looking at, and it would tell him if another was close, or if there were only two. If Kevin was here, that made things more difficult; if Kevin was here, he might have to change his plan entirely. Paulson listened as best he could while standing motionless partially hidden behind an oak tree. It wasn't enough, he was too far. Sure, he could not be seen, and had not been heard, but it was still too far for him to hear. The way he saw it, he could just walk straight up, taking his chances. He could get as close as he could before showing his hand, or he could walk closer, moving cautiously to allow him to stop when he could hear well enough to make that determination.

Paulson started moving to his left, their right, one tree at a time. Each time he was protected by a newer, closer tree, he paused to see what he could hear. *Still too far away, shit*, he would have to do something more. *Patience, you killer; all killers have patience,* he thought, as he paused longer and continued listening.

"You guys are a little close, I'm going to need you to move west 10 or so meters. I'll ask the same of Michaels, but east," Kevin said, pointing his arm towards the west and awaiting acknowledgement.

Paulson still could not make them out, nor hear, but when one nodded to the other and headed off in the direction of basecamp, he had his answer. *Jonesy or Michaels, you're gonna pay,* he found himself whispering softly as he moved around the trees and Kevin left.

He was much closer now, and it was easy to tell who he was going to drown in the creek. *And today's next contestant in You're Dead, is Jonesy.* Approaching him from the same direction he was already walking, Paulson stepped out from behind a tree, taking his first steps in the shallow creek. Jonesy was caught off guard, and jumped back a step, not expecting to run into anyone on today's boring assignment.

"Hey, not cool man," Jonesy said smirking.

"I was told to let you know you guys were too close, but it looks like Kevin beat me here," Paulson told him.

"Yeah, I'm on my way now," Jonesy said as he walked past him.

Making a hammerfist strike, Paulson swung as hard as he could, hitting Jonesy in the back of his head, behind his left ear. He followed through, then as Jonesy fell forward, he moved closer and took hold of his BDUs, helping to introduce him to the water. Before he collapsed into the creek and blackness overtook him, Jonesy heard an all-too-familiar click and felt excruciating pain. His screams came out, but instead of being heard, water flowed into his mouth and down his throat.

Paulson pressed his advantage. Continuing to push down on his body, he gathered his arms to his sides, keeping them in place with his knees. Straddling Jonesy, he used his left hand to keep his head below the water, and his right to finish the third of his strikes with his 551.

"I planned on drowning you in the creek, which will probably happen before you bleed out, probably," Paulson joked as he pushed Jonesy's face deeper into the creek.

Jonesy would never know the answer, nor would Paulson. One moment Jonesy was struggling, the next he was one with darkness. The blood slowly turning the creek water downstream crimson, had something to say about Jonesy's death, too. This time Paulson submerged his 551 in the creek and let the water clean it, before taking off for Michaels.

By a freak chance of fate, Michaels was looking in the direction that Paulson was moving, and at a distance, he witnessed him sliding in and out among the trees. If Paulson were walking normal to him, or straight at him even, that would have been OK, but he wasn't, he was taking great pains to keep hidden, except he wasn't, Michaels had easily noticed his movements. *You're not messing with me today, not today, Paulson,* he said looking directly at him. Paulson was easy to identify from a distance, he was a bit large for a ranger. The guys joked that training would eat his muscles up, and he would just fade away; that was a joke about him not being as smart as the others. Paulson relied more on his strength, whereas strength generally came to one in training. You didn't bring your strength with you, you found it, the instructors would say.

When he knew he was noticed, Paulson started walking normally, and stepped more into the open, avoiding the existing cover. Watching Michaels closely, he smiled when he walked deeper inside a small open clearing, leaving the protection of the large oak. *Well, it wasn't open, it just didn't have any trees, they were all small, young saplings; perfect,* Paulson mumbled as he threw his arms outward to his sides, greeting Michaels.

Michaels was on guard, he was alert; *this would not go well,* Paulson thought. Paulson kept walking closer, wearing his smile as well as he did his BDUs.

"You're not going to get me negatives today, Paulson. Kevin just came by and told me to move more to the east, and I've already done that. Go and check your own position out, mkay?" Michaels said sarcastically.

"Yeah. Cute. Kevin's changed his mind; you were fine where you were before. He's chosen to move Jonesy further west, so you're good." Paulson said as he started to walk past him.

Michaels followed him as he went, turning his entire head. He didn't use just his eyes, he didn't try to be tricky or coy, it was obvious that he wanted Paulson to know he wasn't taking any of his shit. Stopping one step after passing him, Paulson turned and opened his 551.

"No need to hide my love for you," Michaels said crouching and stepping off to the left.

"But I want to show you mine," Paulson replied.

Both men were brandishing their knives and moving slowly around each other with only a few saplings between them.

"So, we'll handle this then, just us, just our knives then?" Michaels asked. Paulson replied with a nod, slashed a few times in his direction and then smiled.

They lunged forward and swung wildly, Paulson with his 551, and Michaels with a battle tested favorite, his grandfather's Ka-Bar. The knives were completely different; the Griptilian 551 was a folding blade only 3.5 inches long, whereas the Ka-Bar had a straight edge with a 7-inch blade. Both lunged and swung, and then lunged and jabbed; they did nothing but parry each other's attacks. They kept their eyes on what they needed to focus on, each other's knives.

Paulson would look at Michael's face from time to time, but he focused mainly on the knife he used. Designed back in World War II to serve our United States troops, the Ka-Bar has been a strong combat and utility knife ever since. With an overall length just shy of a foot, this straight blade knife knew exactly how to make its user happy. Parrying definitely gave Michaelson the advantage, even if one blade slid against another, it still had more to work with. He had to change his tactics.

Sporting a black blade with an alternating black and gray colored handle, Paulson's 551 folding knife was a formidable combat tool. Paulson remembered what the site said about his knife when he read the reviews: *If you use your knife a lot or tackle a large number of heavy tasks, the Griptilian 551 could be for you.* What Paulson liked best about the knife was its physicality, or thickness, he would say; it was a stable, sturdy knife. But of all the features, of all the specifications, some of which he understood, some of which he cared nothing about, his most favorite was the end of the handle where he could tie a rope around it. He used a tether made of paracord, and he found that a piece about a foot long was perfect. Things got lost, the ability to have a rope on the end was immeasurable. This fight was by far, the hardest task it had ever started; he hoped it would fare well in today's endeavors, as he scanned for an advantage.

From time to time, Michaels did the same; he looked from Paulson's eyes to his blade, and back again. Like him, Michaels used a non-standard knife; no one else in their squad used a 551 or a Ka-Bar. More parries and then a slash; the parries complained to various volumes, sending their disappointment into the surrounding area with metallic clanks. At times, it sounded like a B-grade Chinese Kung Fu movie; with all that noise, they were making no progress at all. It was time to use Paulson's weight and size against him, with some feints and jabs; then a possible lunge or grapple, he wasn't sure what would work, but he had to try something different.

Three times in a row, he swung wildly to slash, keeping Paulson at a distance, then jabbed to a parry. Metal hit metal. Again, he did this, and again Paulson parried. On the third time, Michaels decided to send a roundhouse toward Paulson's head immediately after the first slash. *Nothing else was working, it might work,* he thought, as Paulson repeatedly jabbed and lunged, changing what he was doing. That's just what he needed, he would do the same, he would change his attack, and then he would see if Paulson would bite.

This was just what the doctor ordered, a few series of two to three slashes that filled the forest floor with metallic clanks again came and went. On the fourth, Michaels followed up with a roundhouse that went high.

Paulson ducked under, and raised up, and turning to his left, he sent Michaels to the ground. Paulson took an opportunity to slice along Michael's leg, from thigh to knee, allowing his blood to pour out and anger him. He didn't land on the ground; Michaels was sliding down a limber sapling. He was partially bent over one that was about two inches thick, standing barely taller than he was, when Paulson came at him again. While Michaels was about a foot off the ground Paulson jabbed him in his good thigh and twisted. Michaels returned the favor, and swung his Ka-Bar blindly backwards, meaning to slice him, but he rammed it in so hard that he hit bone.

Paulson jumped off his victim, with his 551 in one hand, and Michaels' Ka-Bar sticking out of his thigh, gripped tightly in the other. No scream came from him when he wiggled the knife and pulled it free. He dropped them to the ground and closed on his enemy, placing him in a headlock. He pulled him over the length of the sapling until he fell off, landing hard with all his weight on his wounded side. Michaels was to catch no break today with him mashing his bad leg beneath him onto the hard ground. He bled even more, all the while being held in Paulson's death grip, finding it harder to breathe. Squeezing him tighter and tighter, he twisted Michaels over on his back and then raised up sharply, breaking his neck.

He walked back to the knives and picked his up to clean it. Moving over to Michaels, he left his Ka-Bar on the ground. When he reached him, he wiped his 551 against his BDUs until it was again clean. Paulson then cut through his uniform to make a cloth tourniquet. Taking all of a minute, his external bleeding was stopped, but his pain, and the damage done to his thigh was going to be an issue. *What do I care about that,* he thought? *I'm going to be dead at the end of the day anyway, but not before Kevin!*

From where he was now, it was closer to sneak into camp from the south, dispatch the two sick men, and then leave to find Lewis. Heading due west, he would leave the edge of the basecamp, circle around to reach him, then he could walk straight in and call out Kevin; *man, what a day,* he mumbled as he played with his 551, opening and closing it while walking. Paulson had worked through his plan in his head, finishing it a few steps before he approached the southern side of their tent.

Taking his knife, he slit a hole big enough for him to enter and slid inside. Knifing the closest ranger as he slept, he silenced him with a hand over his mouth, until he stopped fighting; he already knew the other was gone. Pulling the body outside the hole he had made, he dragged him to a nearby bush and fussed with the body to hide it before returning to the tent. Listening before he looked inside, he saw the other sick person sit down and start taking off his boots. *Rather cocky, aren't we?* Paulson thought, as he paused a few seconds before entering. Catching him laying down, he ran the knife over his throat as he bent his head forward, silencing the dying man.

Leaving him where he was, he covered his face with a blanket and left the tent, heading due west. *It was end game for him,* Paulson thought, so wiping his knife off across his chest to clean the blood caused him no concern; he wore it as a badge of honor. Not just any person can kill 9 rangers without raising an alarm; it reminded him of the Otorten Nine. He had first been exposed to them watching a documentary-like show about aliens on his cable television. It had not happened yet actually, he was on his way to run into number 8, with number 9 not too far away.

"*Oh, that was incorrect,*" he said out loud, as he crept around trees.

I am on 7; Lewis was 7, Kevin is 8, and I am, I am 9, he

thought, as he drifted away on his squirrel. From what he remembered, it all happened on a cold mountain in Russia, many, many years ago. This happening occurred towards the end of the fifties, maybe 1959, he didn't remember exactly. The name of the mountain was Death Mountain, or Mountain of Death, and its local name, Gora Otorten, literally meant 'Do NOT go there!' There were supposed to have been ten for their trek, but one fell ill and never made that fateful trip, so hence the Otorten Nine.

    On their way, the group ran into inclement weather, which forced them to a crucial decision, camp up on a pass, or go back to safety. Going back would cost them time, it was over 1.5 kilometers back from whence they came, but staying put would allow them to shelter in place in a large tent. If they made camp where they were, all could huddle inside until the bad weather cleared out, or at least the next day when they could continue their hike up the mountain, or they could turn around all together. This was an important decision for right now, as today they were losing light.

    Bizarre behavior, inexplicable injuries, strangely colored skin, missing tongues, radiation, lights in the sky? He remembered that much, as they said that sentence several times during the recaps, after commercials, etc.; it was a powerful sentence that sparked lots of interesting conversations. From that statement, saying it two or three times, you know something bad had happened. He made a mental note to check that special out again, when he got home, *if* he got home; it was stored safely on one of his three cable boxes. *Who knows,* he thought, *maybe I'll look it up online.*

    Paulson rounded the next saddle, keeping to the trees and here came Lewis. He was running up to him making haste, and stopped just feet away, struggling to articulate his thoughts; he wasn't out of breath, he just couldn't explain what was wrong.

    "The others. They're dead," Lewis managed.

    "What are you talking about, Lewis," Paulson asked him, placing a calming hand on his shoulder.

    "Well, I think Kevin's snapped," Lewis stated as he turned around to ensure they were still safe.

    "What do you mean?" he asked Lewis, shaking him a little; *that was fun*, Paulson thought.

"He's the only one not accounted for," Lewis said as he looked down from Paulson's eyes to his chest.

There was a dried blood smear that went from left to right, starting off larger than it ended, and Lewis' eyes seemed to linger on it.

"Wasn't he over at basecamp? He was there earlier," Paulson said as he shifted his weight from his bleeding leg to that of his better one.

His movement brought Lewis' eyes down even lower, and to the bloody tourniquet around Paulson's thigh. It was in the same BDU material, but the pattern went the wrong way, and oh yeah, there was the issue of the excessive amount of blood. Moving his eyes back up to Paulson's face, he had barely glanced away when he heard the small click. Paulson pushed into the ranger's stomach burying the blade deep inside before moving the knife away from him, and to the other side of Lewis.

"Sorry my friend, of all the others, I liked you the most," he said, as he removed his knife and kicked Lewis' dead body over to the side.

He wiped his knife against his shirt underneath the other blood smear. Looking down at his chest, he knelt beside Lewis and bloodied his 551 again with enough blood to make 7 individual streaks. *Soon it would be nine,* he smiled, *soon it would be nine.*

Kevin wasn't sure what he was or was not allowed to do with his sick men. Screw it, he thought, they are sick, they can still do some things, and that decision's final. He started walking over to the tent to ready his rangers, they were going to assist with the front gate, both together, each one watching the next, whether they wanted to or not. It was unusually quiet as he approached the tent. Daylight was wasting, it seemed to be getting darker the closer he walked to the tent; it was as if a dark cloud of ill will hovered, as if a strange feeling of foreboding loomed overhead.

Kevin rehearsed what he was to say to the men as he walked closer. Upon sticking his head into the tent, he would give his orders, and not truly wait for any disappointment or frustration to appear, he would pause for dramatic effect, then leave as quickly as he had come; that wasn't necessary though, he was only two steps away when he turned to hear Paulson more clearly.

"I'm quitting," Paulson said again.

Now fully facing him, Kevin looked at Paulson, who was waving his so-called stress card violently in the air, his hand high above his head. Looking on, he didn't say a word as Paulson started walking closer. He had started shouting at him when he had stepped inside the gate; he was still several yards away. No sense in shouting back, he would wait to get closer before addressing him. Looking down at his watch he noted the time.

Taking out his notebook he wrote down *Paulson - carded out*, then added the time. Placing it back into his BDU pocket, he looked up in time to sidestep Paulson, taking his arm and throwing him off balance to his left. Paulson hit the ground and rolled forward, springing to his feet.

He made his movement of pulling out his blade and clicking it open slow and obvious to Kevin.

"All that work for you, and all I have to do is pull out mine. Look, it's already opened," Kevin said, trying to get under Paulson's skin.

This went back to the ongoing joke where most of the rangers' used knives that were easily pulled out, ready to work, they didn't require opening.

Kevin sized up the threat in front of him. He hoped for a soldier, an instructor, or anyone who was close enough to be a witness or provide help to appear, all the while keeping his eyes on Paulson. He was alone, that was both good and bad. The knife fight that ensued took both men through every bit of an hour in their minds, but in all actuality, it lasted a mere two minutes. It left the men bleeding from multiple sticks and slashes, their bodies on the ground in one tangled heap, surrounded by a pool of their blood. Neither man moved. Neither man made a sound.

Charles approached from downhill. Moving slowly, he took deliberate steps looking around as he moved towards them. One paw raised as another lowered, this again, was done slowly, stealthily, quietly. The two men had fought for the high ground, and of all the land inside their base camp, the spot they found themselves fighting on was a small area only a few inches higher than the ground surrounding it.

Charles stopped abruptly and listened, with one paw raised in the air held motionless. Nothing. Lowering his head to the ground he lapped at a small stream of blood. Looking back up at a pair of legs that twisted to the left, he licked his lips and continued moving towards the men. He looked at the two and assessed the danger. Nudging the pair of legs in front of him, he whined a few times and nipped at the closest ankle. Again, he nudged, and the feet moved. A harder nudge was met with a downward strike from Paulson. The knife stuck in the wolf's shoulder, its tip buried deep inside him.

Charles jumped to the side, pulling the blade from the man's grip. Baring teeth, Charles snapped a few times before taking a menacing position towards him. Paulson pushed himself backward, seeming to hop into the air several times before turning to his side to crawl away on all fours. Charles thought that ironic, and half smiled before turning his attention to Kevin. This time the wolf nudged the right man, and again whined a few times to help wake him. Kevin didn't respond.

The wolf took hold of Kevin's boot, taking it in his mouth to the ankle and began pulling him off the mound, and over to the nearest tree. This he did by jerking and pulling Kevin in small movements. Soon he would be at the edge of the trees, and then a small incline would help to add distance between the two men. Charles let go of Kevin's foot and thrust his head into the air to listen and look around. He didn't see the other man, but he had heard him. Looking around a little longer, he thought it safe to continue.

More jerking and then Charles let go of Kevin's foot. He watched as his body rolled down the hill, striking a few trees as he went. Stopping against a small rock, Charles glanced away from

Kevin and again looked for the other man. He neither saw nor heard anything else. Turning to move down the hill he saw a green tree come to life and fall on top of him.

Paulson launched himself through the air in an attempt to tackle the large wolf.

"I'll be taking this back, if you don't mind," Paulson said out loud, reaching for the knife.

Charles moved to the side, easily keeping the man from reaching him, and his objective. Paulson had missed his mark, and being off balance, he began rolling down the hill, straight to Kevin! Charles watched at a distance as the man landed off to the side and began crawling. He headed down the hill to intercept him, but he wouldn't make it in time. Paulson was climbing up on Kevin's legs and was now taking hold of his waist. Pulling himself up higher, he searched for Kevin's knife, it wasn't there.

Paulson continued to search the ground surrounding Kevin for the knife, but he could not find it. He slid off and rolled him over to see if he had landed on it, but still it could not be found. Paulson went to his knees to ponder when the thought popped into his head, *it must be back where they fought!* He stood up and turned to face the hill. Charles was in mid-jump by this point, landing squarely on his chest. He leaned forward and buried his face into Paulson's neck, biting and clawing violently.

The impact sent Paulson to his back, with the wolf still attached to the front of his body. He landed on his upper shoulders, slamming his head and neck backwards to the hard ground. He would have died immediately from the impact were he not already dead, his throat torn out. Charles made quick work of the man and bounded off him seconds after his body hit the ground.

Moving over to Kevin, he pushed his head into his chest a few times before snapping and growling to wake him. Kevin opened his eyes groggily to a gray shadow only inches away from his face. The blur became clearer, and as he focused, and his eyes began to work, he found himself staring back at the large wolf. This was the second time that he had seen him, and it was the second time he had come to his rescue.

Reaching to his waist for his knife, it was soon clear to him that he had dropped it while fighting. *Fighting. While he was fighting*. He thought about Paulson, and where he was last; he had no idea how he had arrived at this location, nor where he was. He paused as the wolf sized him up, but did not move, neither one moved. Kevin's eyes went to the animal's shoulder and the knife that was sticking out of it. He knew who that knife belonged to. Talking calmly to the wolf, he slowly reached to pull it out. The wolf growled and almost bared teeth, then Kevin froze, his arm nearly fully extended out in front of him, exposed to the wolf.

    The wolf lost its threatening posture, lowered his head slightly in an act of non-aggression, and took one step closer. Kevin slowly moved forward and reached again for the knife. Placing his hand around it, he cautiously tightened his grip and pulled it out with one swift motion. The wolf moved away and watched Kevin from a distance.

    Kevin no longer felt threatened, sitting motionless for a few minutes before thinking about walking back up the hill. He wanted to do this to get back to base camp, to warn the others and report what had happened. But another reason was to secure his knife, a ranger was never to be without his knife. Slowly turning his back on the wolf, he took a single step before finding the need to thank him for what he had done. Looking over his shoulder he turned his head slowly, in a peaceful gesture, but Charles was gone.

Kevin came through feeling somewhat calm and with an inner warmth of peace deep down inside; although it was a wonderful feeling, and an awesome way to wake up, he quickly realized that he was freezing cold and soaking wet. He continued looking around, occasionally squinting and shook his head to remove the rain that was dripping into his eyes. The next time he blinked, he saw the silhouette of Charles appear. Kevin watched as the wolf took his time and moved directly at him, stopping about twenty feet or so away. The wolf lowered his head as if bowing, turned to look to his left, and then bounded off into the woods and out of sight. Kevin didn't understand this, not at all.

He didn't know how the wolf would be able to help him anyway, but he didn't question the fine animal; he cherished any time with Charles, especially nowadays.

It had been several minutes since he last swallowed rainwater. Kevin tried a few times with little to show for his hard work, before he looked up and noticed that the rain was slowing, if not stopping completely. Another crack of lightning, and timed perfectly with that, in true dramatic fashion, the silhouette of Charles appeared again, off to his right. Somewhat closer than his last visit and further off to the side, he watched as Charles slowly circled and moved in closer between the trees.

The closer Charles came, the less he looked like Charles. His coat, the size of his head; no, his body, his body was smaller. Charles seemed to be angry and bared his teeth between growling. Kevin never knew Charles had teeth; he had never seen them before. This wolf was definitely more vocal, angrier, and definitely not Charles. He recognized the animal for what it was, a coywolf. *So, the rumors are true then*, he thought. Kevin postured himself as best he could, moving his feet to the animal; as the predator moved to his right, so did Kevin's legs. This he did several times before the coywolf growled and lunged. Jumping forward about six feet, he shook his head and again bared his teeth, growling, his hairs bristling in the wind.

Kevin would have jumped straight up in the air had he not been held in place with snare wire. He wasn't shouting at the animal, he wasn't displaying anger, not yet. The coywolf moved to his left, growling, and snapping, disappearing behind one tree and reappearing in front of another. Continuing to growl and hunt his prey, the coywolf turned to face him and lunged again. Kevin was taken aback, and kicked his legs upward in the wolf's direction, solely out of reflex. Every time it lunged it covered a good chunk of ground. He thought that one, maybe two more lunges and it would be on top of him.

That's that then, Kevin thought. Charles had come to say goodbye; he had literally bowed out. Throughout his life, Kevin had seen Charles take care of him by leading him to a path for success; helping him to make a good decision, or to choose the correct course of action, or inaction. He wondered if Charles saw no way out. Kevin thought those words as he stared at the animal in front of him, making purposeful eye contact. This seemed to unnerve the coywolf, and although it was close enough for him to see the animal's lips curl and quiver, he was not close enough to count teeth, not yet.

    Kevin continued staring at the coywolf while slowly moving his feet to keep them between the animal and himself. It was obvious to the beast he was moving, but he didn't see the man in front of him as a threat. That feeling was totally reversed when Kevin thought about the coywolf moving slowly to his right. Not only was the animal disappearing from Kevin's sight, but he was also closing the distance between the two. This was not evident to Kevin until he started counting; one, two, three.

    By the time he raised his feet in the air, the coywolf was mid-lunge. Kevin caught him in his chest when he kicked his heels out in front of him. The animal made a short whine like a dog, then it switched to snapping and baring its teeth. Kevin's feet slid outward from the center of the coywolf's chest and against the inside of both the animal's front legs, half out of fear, half out of necessity. Kevin tensed as the animal continued pushing forward against him, only to be kept at bay by his feet pushing uncomfortably outward on his two front legs.

    A couple times, Kevin bent his knees, allowing the animal to get closer, to get enough strength and leverage to push it away and again land blows against the coywolf's chest, but it wasn't going to be enough. He wanted to kick it in the head, or against the nose, like one might do a shark, but he could not manage to push it far enough away to kick it there. Kevin knew he would tire first, before the coywolf would, and then he would become prey, for the first time in his life; that would not do, he thought, as he pushed the animal enough to kick it with his right foot.

    His right heel scraped against the left side of its face, pushing past his eye and glancing off the animal's ear, it was not amused. His strike was high enough to not put his foot into the coywolf's mouth, but he just didn't have enough strength to do any real damage; he was going to die here. What remains that would be found, if he were ever found, remained to be seen; he laughed at that thought, at his choice of words, as he pushed the animal back far enough to allow his right leg to resume its defensive position.

The coywolf's jaws snapped open and shut repeatedly, its maw getting ever closer to Kevin's stomach. The sounds that escaped it were brutal, primal, belonging to a raw predator; it would not stop. The noise it made sounded like the din of a thousand souls screaming for attention, for food, for nourishment. A wolf went for the underbelly or throat as they were generally softer, easier targets to grab on to and tear apart; it was that instinct that afforded little comfort for their prey, more often than not being fatal.

Kevin was supported with his back against the tree; it was the only thing keeping the coywolf from knocking him over and killing him outright. Lunge after lunge, the animal used his back legs to propel itself forward, throwing his weight into each and every attempt, but its food stayed put, resolute. Each time its progress was met with Kevin pushing back with his feet. Had the coywolf tried to attack his legs, instead of trying to eat him whole, things might have been different. It was this desire to inflict pain, to kill at any cost, that was its downfall. Out of the corner of his eye, Kevin saw him.

Charles was slinking towards Kevin and the coywolf, maintaining a low profile as he moved ever closer. He was on Kevin's right, and he could not have arrived at a better time. Kevin pushed and kicked at his attacker with all his strength that remained. He found it more difficult to keep pressure on the animal, each time it lunged it managed to get a little closer. It did not stop, and the closer it got to Kevin, the more it threw its body into him, the more it tried to win. It seemed to be jumping forward and making progress as it continued thrusting; in its mind, the coywolf was winning, it was going to eat today.

You came back! You came back! Kevin thought, as tears moistened his eyes. It was clear to him now that he was apologizing earlier for having to lead the animal to him. It was time for Kevin to do his part, time for him to distract the coywolf enough for Charles to attack. Kevin tried to push the animal back far enough to get in a kick, but he couldn't. Anger took over. Kevin rallied, turning his frustration and despair into newfound strength in his heart, if not his mind. Fully extending his legs amidst snaps and snarls, he let go and again threw his right foot into his attacker.

His blow was not as high as he would have liked, but he managed to hit the coywolf squarely in the creature's left eye. The first of several dog-like noises, stuck somewhat between whimpering and howls, came from the beast, filling the forest with pathetic sounds of pain. They were quickly silenced as Charles took that distraction as an opportunity, and lunged. Charles took hold of the coywolf's throat, and with all fours he dug in, pulling backwards with quick jerks. He tugged and pulled and when the coywolf decided to channel his anger from Kevin to Charles, it was too late.

Charles shook his body violently to the sides, ripping the coywolf's flesh from its throat. The animal flailed wildly, spurting blood through the air as it rolled on the ground. Its screams and growling were silent now, only blood came when it cried out in pain. Kevin kept trying to stand up, pushing his legs firmly into the ground for leverage, again and again.

Charles circled the coywolf, placing himself between it and Kevin, and waited for another need to defend, but it never came. The coywolf had bled out, and lay there lifeless on the cold, wet, blood-soaked ground.

Kevin was full of emotion, of adrenaline, squirming about as if he was dancing. More to the truth, Kevin was trying with every ounce of strength to get free. It might have been survival mode, his body's attempt at superhuman strength, or just shock setting in, but his efforts fell short. He hung his head in defeat, somewhat exhausted from flailing around and throwing his legs at his attacker and his attempts to get free. Charles turned to look over his shoulder, and walked up to Kevin, licking him about the face. He did this until Kevin calmed down, took a better attitude, and smiled.

"OK I get it, buck up little camper," he said to Charles.

Another lick and then Charles moved to the dead animal. Taking hold of the fur around its neck, he began dragging the coywolf over to Kevin. Charles looked at him and nudged the animal's head forward as if asking him to take it. He could not oblige. Charles took hold of the animal and dragged him past the tree. He again nudged the coywolf's head toward Kevin, this time pushing it against his hands.

He understood what Charles was offering, and he was

going to try. Kevin felt around the head and opened its mouth. He was going to use the teeth as a saw to cut the wires. His range of motion was restricted, and he had little to work with, as he moved the head up and down against the tree. Kevin could not know exactly where he was trying to cut, and more than likely, he was rubbing those teeth against different tracks, but nonetheless, he was making progress, or so he thought.

He had been at it for quite some time now, and he was still tied to the tree; this wasn't working, he couldn't help thinking. As he moved the animal's open jaw up and down against the tree, he sometimes found himself staring off into the woods, or closing his eyes, or thinking of food; Kevin was having issues concentrating. When he focused and thought to search his surroundings to reassess, Charles was gone. He didn't know when he had left, or if he had moved somewhere out of sight, but he was gone. *How long had he been trying to cut himself free,* he wondered; that he did not know, but he kept at it, this Ranger would not quit.

Kevin was once again cold and alone in the dark woods. He was still tied to that damn tree. Growing more frustrated, he tried to distract himself by looking up at the night-time sky, and not forward into the forest. He kept pushing the coywolf's head up and down against the tree, hoping to cut through those wires, looking off into the darkness, his mind wandered.

F eeling totally relaxed, refreshed, and relieved, Scott looked to his coffee maker. Making a cup of strong black coffee, he took in the aroma and briefly closed his eyes. He inhaled deeply before opening them and taking a sip. It was almost too hot to drink, almost. A small sip and he placed the cup on the dinette. He walked back into the bedroom. Looking over at Suzi, Susan he corrected, he slapped her on the ass. She did not move. Her body was warm to the touch, although the room felt cold. He rubbed his hands over her backside a few times before inserting two fingers, nothing; there was no response from her. Pushing deeper, a couple of times he tried to wake her, to no avail. With each thrust, he pushed her down further into the bed than the last, but still nothing. It was anger's time to take control. *Everyone had control except him,* he thought. Again, he thrust his fingers inside, but Suzi did not respond.

Scott removed his hand and again slapped her across her ass. Each time he received no response, he slapped her again. Again. Again, he slapped her. He found himself breathing heavy, and now perched on her lower legs at the bend of her knees, slapping her ass, but still no response. Stopping more due to exhaustion than out of a lack of response, he looked down at her redness; *Suzi had an apple bottom shape before, but now she was as red as one, literally,* he remarked. Smiling at his last thought, he rolled her over and positioned her back on the center of the bed.

Looking down at Suzi, he was unaware of his attempt at pleasuring himself. He was hard again, and before he knew it, he was coming. Half squirting forward onto the bed, half dropping to the floor, he made his mess, continuing until he finished. Angry thoughts filled his head, which lingered until the point of exhaustion. Upon doing so, he felt the last few spasms complete before he again felt calm, at peace. *That was her fault,* he thought, as he used his underpants to clean up the mess.

He climbed on the bed with his underpants in his hand. Flipping her over on her stomach he sat on her back. Sliding up and placing his knees against the sides of her breasts, he reached for her face. Removing the pink and purple striped Duct tape from her mouth, he jammed his underpants into a ball and pushed them inside. Susan was still unconscious and offered no resistance. Scott retaped her mouth shut and let her face fall forward onto the bed. Taking her hands behind her back, he Duct taped them, too.

Rolling her over, he pulled her to the foot of the bed. Her legs were hanging off the edge, bent at a perfect ninety-degree angle. He looked for some way to secure her feet, keeping her in place, and at that angle, but it was not to be. He was unwilling to tape her to the bed frame, and there was nothing to tie or secure her to, not in the bedroom, anyway. He knelt beside her feet and Duct taped them together at the ankles, taking the tape around her a few more times before cutting it.

Scott stood up, admired his handiwork, and then taped her

wrists to her ankles behind her back. This left Susan in an uncomfortable, circular position, but she didn't care; Susan wasn't feeling anything right now. Reaching for a pillow, he removed the cover and placed it over Suzi's head like a hood. Looking around the bedroom he found nothing to secure it.

Going back into the living room he took a brown extension cord from underneath his dinette and wrapped it around her neck until he was able to plug the ends into itself. It was loosely wrapped around her neck, and its only purpose was to help keep her hood in place; Suzi was going nowhere. He covered her up with a few blankets to keep her warm, put on his uniform, and then left the camper, locking it from the outside. He took a bottle of water and his night goggles and walked down to the amphitheater.

Scott placed the water bottle in his pocket and played with the goggles as he continued walking. He moved closer towards the water, stopping just shy of it at the last set of benches. He sat down and continued playing with them. He looked for the power button, pressed it and then placed them onto his closed eyes. After a few seconds, he opened them to darkness. Toggling the on/off button, he waited for them to turn on. *Nope*, he thought. He stood up and walked back to his camper for batteries.

He opened the door to a young blonde-haired woman who started crying when she looked up at him. She was bent forward, leaning against the kitchen cabinet, only inches from a possible escape. Scott doubted she could have raised herself high enough to pull the latch, but she could have slammed her body into it, repeatedly, drawing unwanted attention; he shook his head smiling.

"You almost made it," he told her, dragging her further inside against her struggles and muffled screams.

Stopping at the foot of the bed, he dropped her and went back to close the door. Locking it, he started undressing. By the time he reached her, he was totally naked. Tonight, Scott would spend the remainder of his time with Suzi, Susan, he corrected. Placing his hands on her head, he walked beside her, climbed onto the bed, and pulled her close. Susan helped as much as she could, but for the most part, she was pulled onto the bed by her hair.

Scott laid down on the right side to block the outside door

and slid in close against her. He was on his left, with his back to her. Susan's stomach rested against him; her irregular half crying, half breathing made it touch and recoil, almost tickling him. Turning over, he placed a hand on her to pull her in tight and held on until he saw Suzi calm down.

When Susan's breathing became more relaxed and normal, he slid his hand down between her legs and made a fist around her pubic hair. Pulling up as far as he could, he raised her body from the bed to Suzi's muffled screams. He let go and she fell backward, again laboriously breathing between her crying. He moved to the foot of the bed and went into the kitchen for a knife. He cut the tape that kept her wrists bound to her feet. Susan was thankful, although she could not communicate that.

Putting the knife back in the drawer, he stopped at the fridge and pulled out a six pack and took them to Suzi. He moved in beside her and sat up with his back against the headboard. Reaching over, he placed his hand around her neck and pulled her on top. This time Susan was able to help and used her knees to move closer as he tugged on her.

"I'm taking your tape off now. I'm going to remove your gag, and then you are going to drink with me. Do you understand?" he asked, before removing her tape.

Scott watched as Suzi nodded and blinked her eyes. A second after that, he ripped the tape off in one jerk. Susan did not scream, she just continued waiting for him to take the gag out.

"Do you understand?" he asked again.

Suzi nodded and Scott removed her gag. The first thing Susan did was breathe in through her mouth. A large deep breath, then an exhale. She sat motionless, staring at him, awaiting her part of the deal.

"Beer?" she quietly asked.

Reaching over without speaking, he opened the first and held it in front of her face. She parted her lips and he poured. Susan kept going until he paused to let her catch up. It was cold, it was carbonated, and it was the closest thing to food that she had in she didn't know how many days. It was wonderfully refreshing. He started pouring again, and soon it was gone. He opened another. Scott watched Suzi open her mouth again, and they both repeated their actions. Susan didn't want to tell him how many she could have without being impaired; *it was about ten*, she thought, but she planned on appearing drunk way before then.

    He turned to his right to open the third. Stopping what he was doing, he looked back over to her. She was still waiting. He turned away to finish, and then presented it to her face. Suzi opened her mouth, and he poured it in. This time he kept going, without a pause. It was a surprise to Susan to have to keep swallowing without a break, and although she finished without spilling, and without a smile on her face, she did smile when she let out a long, deep belch.

    Susan finished her fourth and fifth beers on a full stomach.

    "I have to pee," Suzi said, looking directly at him.

    Scott leaned in to kiss her. She stayed motionless and returned it. He took her tongue in his mouth, kissing and holding on to it gently. He licked her teeth as she paused between kisses. He tasted her beer, her sweetness. Scott slid her a smile and nodded for her trip to the bathroom. He stood up first and moved her around the bed and over to the bathroom door. He placed her on the toilet, and she relieved herself. He waited for her to finish and stand up.

    Susan got up, turned to the side, leaned backwards against the sink for balance and immediately felt dizzy. The room started to spin, she felt light-headed. He held on tightly as he guided her back into the bedroom.

    She made a few noises, with some undiscernible words escaping her. Susan tried to finish a sentence, but everything came out wrong, slow, slurred, wrong. He pulled her over against him and held on as her high took effect. He had put the pills in her third beer, and after about ten minutes, they had started to take effect.

    He doubted he needed to keep her taped at this point, but it was all about control. He rolled over on top of her and lowered his face to her breasts. Squeezing, kissing, pinching, pulling, he enjoyed them both. The moans were the only sounds that came normal for Susan. Scott understood those clearly, paying attention to what she liked the most by what actions drew her loudest, most passionate responses. Finishing the last beer in the bedroom, he leaned in to kiss her. Suzi's eyes were already closed, although her lips moved and trembled as she continued mumbling. She did those things more when he rubbed his fingers over her gently shaved vagina. Susan was confused, tired, light-headed. Looking around the room as he touched her, she didn't focus on him, she just drank in the way she felt.

    She was almost where he wanted her to be. He was building her trust, he hoped. He had not truly broken her, which he was trying to do with each and every breath she took. Inserting a single finger, he swung it around wildly to moans and a single, clearly uttered word: *YES*. He removed his finger and did it again. After receiving another positive response, he climbed on top and entered her for the first time, the way God intended.

    Scott didn't pretend to cater to her needs, to her protection, her safety. He pressed down upon her, not trying to lessen or support his weight. He thrust any way he wanted to, the sides, balls deep, just the tip; he spent his time on his needs, he knew she would get hers; he was incredible! One minute later, to his amusement, he came inside her. Susan was oblivious to time, or to what was happening, she just liked the way she felt. Had she been in control of her faculties, she would have been left utterly disappointed by Scott's quickness.

    He rolled Suzi over and sat on top. Pulling her body slightly up by cupping her breasts, he moved her back further to cause her some discomfort. Moans and groans escaped Susan. Taking her hair with his left, he held her at that angle while his free right hand probed her from behind. More moans. He removed his hand and rubbed his fingers over her lips. When she went to moan again, he inserted them and rubbed over her gums, her teeth. Susan unknowingly sucked on his fingers, from the tip to where it met the hand.

    This she did several times, as if it were his penis. He thought about it for a moment before positioning himself in front of her, but Susan had passed to the last stages of her high; she slowly leaned forward, and with her head sliding to the bed, she silently gave in to sleep. With Suzi being still taped and drugged, Scott felt confident that all was well. He fell asleep beside her and together they both had the best night sleep they had in months.

FRIDAY

Introductions are in order

A couple of hours later Scott woke up. He was cuddled into Suzi hard. Not with a hard on, he wasn't hard, he was cuddled in against her. He thought about that and smiled, then yawned. Rolling out of bed, he made himself a coffee. Taking it with him, he sat beside her and turned on the television. The reception wasn't the best, but he did get all those free local stations over the air. After a few minutes of channel surfing, he looked over and tried to wake her, but she was still out; she would be out for hours, probably all day long. Taking another sip, he leaned over and grabbed a breast. Pulling on it, he rolled her over and slid beneath.

Kissing her several times, he ran his hands over her breasts, cupping and grabbing them, he slid his kisses up to her neck. Susan would not know any of this, she was still unconscious. Taking her ear into his mouth, he bit it and sucked on it. Scott found himself growing hard. He buried his face into her neck, he took hold of her waist and pulled her down tightly. He loved feeling her breasts pressed against him, her body, her warmth. More kisses came, and then he entered her. Holding on to her tightly, he rolled her over while thrusting.

Not missing a beat, he was now on top pumping away. A minute later he came inside her. Scott found it easy to get hard, easy to get aroused, when he was forcing himself upon a woman, and equally disappointing when he quickly came. If he were to have any success at all at finding a woman for the long term, to love, to marry, he would have to find other redeeming qualities in her, and probably compromise way too much for his liking. *Why do all of that*, he thought, when he could take what he wanted, and stay true to himself. The sad truth was that Scott didn't see he had a problem, he didn't see any flaws with himself, none at all.

Taking hold of her shoulders, he shook Suzi in an attempt

to wake her, but she would not have it. Rolling off, he lie back down beside her and closed his eyes to think. He practiced what he would say to her when she awoke, saying the words in his mind repeatedly. Before he knew it, he was talking to her. Susan heard nothing. From time to time, he opened his eyes to see if she was awake, but shortly afterwards he closed them; looking over at her, Suzi was still out cold. Again, he did this, several times actually, before closing them and keeping them closed; Scott had lost track of time and although he thought he was waiting a few minutes more before he would check again, he had finally fallen asleep. He jerked and jumped beside a passed-out Susan. His eyes rolled beneath his closed eyelids, his breathing became irregular, his legs spasmed, appearing restless; he was in a nightmare.

Scott was thirteen years old. Like most weekend days, he was in the woods with his brother. Kids normally wore shorts and a T-shirt during summer, but he and his brother wore blue jeans. Fishing, hiking, running through the woods, that kind of stuff would tear up and ruin shorts, let alone one's legs. It was one of the things both boys took away from their father.

Everything the boys did together was competitive. The amount of chicken wings eaten at the dinner table trophy went to his brother. The most money after destroying the other at Monopoly trophy went to his brother. The most beers chugged at one time without using the bathroom when his parents were not around trophy, again, his brother. Tree climbing, well that was the one thing Scott excelled at. Today was tree climbing day, and today would be no different, Scott would destroy his brother.

The rules were simple, one brother would pick a tree and climb up as high as they were willing to go and stop. The other would then pick an adjacent tree and climb up to the height of their brother, and then go a little higher. This would go on to one yielded. This would go on and Scott would win; that's what normally happened, this day would be different, if his brother had anything to say about it. Scott's brother looked at the trees in front of him and chose the shorter of the two. It was actually the thicker, stronger one; today, he liked his odds of winning.

"Scott!" his brother yelled.

Drawing Scott's attention, he started up the tree. Scott watched as he made a great attempt to climb up. His brother stopped halfway and looked down at him, smiling. Scott nodded and jumped onto the neighboring tree. He made quick work of it, and as he passed his brother, he laughed.

Scott looked down at him and saw a frown come and leave his brother's face. He started climbing again, keeping a steady pace. Slower and slower he went, until he was even with Scott. His brother looked like he was really struggling. It seemed that it took everything he could do to reach him. Scott didn't know if he could, or if he should pass him up again. With a look of great concern, their eyes met. A sigh escaped Scott's brother, as he started climbing again. Scott watched as his brother went to town. Hand over hand flew above the other, his legs pushed him, supported him. He kept going.

Unknown to Scott, his brother had always let him win at trees. He had never felt safe climbing any height, let alone anything over twenty feet. Today he guessed they were about thirty. He wasn't sure how Scott would react when he looked all the way down. Would he pass him, would he go higher to beat him, he wondered, he didn't know. Scott's brother stopped climbing, he was done, he would climb no further.

"Well? Let's go little brother," he said, egging Scott on.

He didn't look down; he didn't care about that, he cared about beating his brother. The climb was easy enough, the diameter of the tree was gradually getting thinner, and therefore easier to hold on to. It wasn't the height that bothered him when he climbed, it was generally the thickness of the trunk. Within no time he had reached his brother, and stopping about a foot above, he was ready for his 'victory laugh', as he called it. His brother looked up at Scott and climbed to barely a head past his height. Stopping right there, he made sure Scott saw him.

"I hope you realize you've lost. Oh! Don't you look down now," he said as he started descending.

Scott could not ignore his brother's comment. His brother told him not to do it, so therefore he must. Looking down, Scott felt nauseous. A pit in his stomach, pain, lightheaded, panic; he felt panic. He had never climbed this high before, never. Scott froze, he tried not to look down any longer, not to move, but he was already facing that way. He watched as his brother made it to the last three feet or so and jumped down to the ground.

"Come on, hurry up," Scott heard his brother yell out.

Scott didn't move, he didn't blink, he almost forgot to breathe. Scott always found it easier to climb up than down. It was more natural for him to look up, than to tilt his head down and navigate backwards. Now he had to do both things he hated, tilt his head downward and lose to his brother. There was no way he was going higher, he was done. Scott worried exclusively about climbing down.

Again, he tried lowering himself down the tree, but he could not move, he was frozen with fear. Trying to distract himself about how high up in the air he was, his eyes left the tree trunk and branches and he focused on his brother. He was pacing back and forth, trying to rush Scott to climb down the tree.

"Hurry up, it's time for you to lose, and it's time for us to leave. Come on Scott, geeze," he said loudly.

Scott closed his eyes for a second, which was a big mistake. He immediately reopened them, his heart raced, his lungs expanded and contracted several times before he appeared to subconsciously hold his breath. An exhale and another breath and he tried to climb down one branch, just one branch; baby steps, he thought. No dice. Scott hung on for dear life. His brother looked up one last time, and if Scott were looking down, he would have seen him shake his head and take off, smiling. His brother looked ahead to orientate himself in the direction of the camper and left Scott stuck up in the tree.

Scott clung to the tree and did not move. He no longer heard his brother down below. He must be gone, he thought. He was angry that he let his brother make him climb higher. He was angry that his brother left him. He was angry that he could not climb down. Scott had to start climbing, fear, pain, anger or not, *he had to. It was getting darker; he had no choice by this point.*

He didn't fear coming down anymore, he feared arriving back at the campsite after dark, his dad would kill him! Scott went as fast as he could, he was motivated by impending darkness, he was motivated by not being killed by his parents. Scott no longer competed directly with his brother, he no longer cared for him. He never climbed another tree. He took a big hit on humanity, on friends, on family; from this point on, he trusted only in himself. If he were unsure whether he could rely on himself, he might still try it, but he would not ask for any help, he would not trust in others, not anymore.

Scott never forgot the way he felt that fateful day. Although it was a dream, he awoke upset and angry, shaking and sweating. He was upright on all fours, his head lowered to the bed, and his eyes were closed. Opening them and taking a moment to look around, his eyes began to see. Most of the time when he relived bad memories from his past, he was awake, and it was more of a memory, more of a daydream, not a feeling. This one brought back pain, frustration, anger. Scott squeezed his eyes closed and reopened them, shaking his head to clear his thoughts; this wasn't a dream, it was a nightmare.

He awoke to find himself leaning over Suzi with his hands tightly gripping her neck, his thumbs pushing against her throat. Her eyes were large and wide, staring motionless back at him in an empty, horrid gaze of death. The tears that had travelled down the sides of her cheeks left their salty trails, there was no more moisture to be had. It was obvious that she was awake when he was strangling her. When he realized what he was doing he loosened his grip, but it was too late. *Suzi was dead, and had been so for quite some time,* he thought.

It was official now, the jury was in; Scott was destined, no, doomed to live a life of despair, of loneliness, of pain. He sat beside Suzi, Susan, he shook his head, and thought of what to do. He got up and finished getting dressed. Bringing her luggage back into the bedroom, he folded her into it and zipped it back up. He searched the room for his cell phone. Finding it on the nearby counter, he took it, partially unzipped the luggage, and took a few pictures of her head just inside the opening before he closed it again and locked it with a zip tie. He pulled it to the living room and left it standing by the side of his camper door. Feeling overwhelmed and panicked, Scott grabbed his things and left, locking the door behind him.

It was a little after 10 a.m. when Robin, Christy, and Linda pulled up in three different vehicles to the same place they had already been earlier in the week. It turns out they needed to purchase more food and some additional items for their camping trip. Within minutes of arriving, the girls were on their way inside, and they were already bickering over the contents of their list.

"Three women enter, one woman leaves," Robin joked.

"Sure, sure. Laugh about it, but shootings happen in these stores all the time," Christy stated, shaking her head several times, looking like she was answering a question.

"Nope. Not here, not in this neighborhood, maybe in yours, Christy." Linda said with a tinge of racism.

An older couple pushing a half-full cart of diet sodas and tortilla chips turned towards them, as did a young woman with a baby, and a family with a few kids who seemed to be fighting over cookies. Everyone immediately around them stopped and stared. They weren't looking because they were offended, they were annoyed at the second woman's voice, at her laughter. Christy rolled her eyes and moved on, the other two followed, laughing quietly.

They went through the part of the store that had softline and hardline goods first, and towards the end of their trip, they went for the food.

"All of this trouble and pain for marshmallows?" Robin asked.

"Not just any marshmallows, the large ones, and they are strawberry! They are pink!" Christy annoyingly laughed.

"Why can't we just get the white ones?" Linda asked.

"White ones? Seriously Linda? Coming from anyone but you," Christy said laughing.

Everyone laughed as they made their way through the store. The sum of their efforts was two pair of blue ankle socks for Christy, a brand-new outfit for Robin consisting of blue jean shorts, a yellow blouse, a pair of high ankle cow skin hiking boots, six large bags of ice, and a bag of large non-white, racist strawberry marshmallows. The girls had forgotten to get ice the first time, Robin made a point to get it on this trip; *it's better to get the ice closer to when they were to camp, the boys would be so surprised,* she thought. Try as she may, Christy could not find any T-shirts that she either liked or didn't have already; it was a sad day for her.

The women went through the self-scan and headed out. Throwing everything in the backseat except the ice, Robin got the girls' attention.

"Well give me a hand, will you?" she asked, lowering the tailgate.

The three worked together to put the ice into coolers and then secured them with bungee cords; those were the only things outside the cab of her truck; *there just wasn't enough room for three hot women and their coolers,* Robin smiled inside. Technically, it was still daylight, and with everything checked off their list, they thought about breakfast.

"Hey all, why don't you park your cars towards the back, and we'll all take my truck. No sense taking extra vehicles, there's not a lot of room at the campground anyway," Robin said.

They looked at each other and agreed.

"Three sexy women showing up at the campground in a pimped-out, redneck truck pulling a camper, I love it!" Christy shrieked excitedly.

Robin waited for Linda to buckle up before pulling off and heading to their favorite place for waffles.

It was 2 p.m. now, and James had pulled his blue camping chair from the fire pit closer to the road for a better view. He had been up for hours by this time. James had already made breakfast and walked down to the lake for some early catfishing and to enjoy his second cup of coffee. After several hours with not a single bite, he packed up and prepared his poles for his next trip. After this he opened a can of tamales, splashed on some hot sauce and had his lunch. The morning had been uneventful up to this point. He grabbed several beers from the cooler and placed them in a small bucket of ice to his right, opened a bag of Cheesy Poofs, and then sat down to enjoy the show.

This is gonna be great, he thought, as he opened the first beer. Everything happened in threes, it was the way. James looked forward to seeing what would happen today when people came to set up their campers. No sooner had he thought that, a small blue truck pulling a large white camper slowly drove by. A man was arguing with a woman, and as they tried to read the painted numbers in front of the driveways, they passed up their spot. Stopping exactly where they were when they determined that, they continued arguing.

"And so it begins," James said, finishing his beer.

A few minutes later, the couple finished their third attempt to back up and pull into their spot off to the right of his camper, before giving up. They would drive around two more times before getting the proper angle. They had finally agreed to pull through, instead of back in, like the man wanted to do; she had won the argument and gotten her way. The couple would start setting up about thirty minutes later, after they finished arguing about how far in to place their camper.

James opened his second beer and took a sip. Placing it down in the holder, he stuck his hand in the bag for another handful of cheesy goodness and waited for the next act.

"Ah," he said, as a large diesel pusher rounded the bend.

He watched as it stopped in front of him, and a middle-aged woman got out. She closed the door and walked around to the front of their vehicle to determine where they should set up. After watching her for a few minutes, he decided that these guys would get it right. James was almost bored when the couple methodically, and with great ease, backed in their RV on their first try. He watched with excitement as the man used his auto-levelers, balancing their RV; *he didn't have those,* he thought, sipping his beer. No sooner after that happened, the woman disappeared inside.

Moments later she came out with a few beers. They were a surgical team, and he made a mental note to run in to them later and have a chat. Raising his beer and nodding at the couple who were now setting up across from him on the center island, he took another sip.

"This one doesn't count," he said, swallowing another mouthful; he would have to wait for another camper-he demanded a redo.

The next performers were driving too fast down the empty road to his left. They hit their brakes as they rounded the corner and their camper made horrible metal scraping sounds, announcing to the entire campground, 'watch out, here we come'. From his guess, James thought it was their anti-sway bar doing its job. They too had passed up their spot. A large diesel quad truck, bright red in color, was pulling an older white Coachman.

Poor bastard, he thought. James sipped on his beer and continued watching as the man got out of his truck, looked at the angle, and backed into his site. He was by himself, and this was probably a starter camper for him. People often did that to see if they would like camping, or if they cared for it at all. He must have gotten out ten times before he started backing into that site. James continued watching as he turned his steering wheel to the left, instead of the right, backing directly into the only tree on his site.

James had been there. James had done that. Why, on his last camping trip, his friend Jay gave him directions and waved him backwards into their spot, where he hit the only tree on his. *So it happens, to the best of us,* he thought smiling.

"Cheers!" James said, waving his beer to the man shaking his head; "need a hand?"

"Nah, I'm good here, but thanks," the man said as he pulled forward to try again.

"Stee-rike two," James whispered, finishing his beer.

OK, James thought as he opened his third beer. This would be the last of his three for now. After that, he would go about his business; maybe he would run in to town for a few things before it got too crazy here.

Another pull behind came in. A black truck was connected to a small vintage, shiny silver camper. Sometimes, as weird as this sounded, a smaller camper was harder to back in than a larger one. This was a true statement for what he was witnessing now. The man pulled forward, then back, forward, then back, forward. Back. Forward, then back, about ten times before he again, pulled forward, and back. James didn't talk to the man who was sticking his head totally out of his window, looking backward instead of using his mirror; he just finished his entire beer and walked into his camper to use the restroom.

"And here's your sign," James said as he closed the door behind him.

J‍ames was in the bathroom when the girls pulled in. Before Robin unlocked her doors to allow Christy and Linda to get out, she asked them for their cell phones. They were to be turned off and placed into her glove box for the entire trip.

"Let's have 'em. Cell phones. Now." Robin demanded.

The girls followed those instructions. They knew they had to surrender them, they just found it difficult. Robin started whistling the theme of Jeopardy while the girls turned their phones off and handed them over. Placing them in the glove box, Robin released the child locks on her doors. Christy and Linda got out, holding beers in one hand, and directing her backwards with the other; Robin ignored them. Using only her mirror, she backed her older model 30-foot Sunline pull behind camper deep into their site on her first attempt.

"Boom, bitches!" Robin yelled out to the women.

"Yes!" shouted a man from a few sites down, throwing a fist up into the air.

The women all laughed. James walked to his chair and pulled it back to his fire pit. Shortly after that he locked the camper and headed into town. In their cheerleader's absence, Robin and the girls would start setting up their camper and personalizing their site. Robin had already assigned duties to the girls. *A leader can't lead from behind,* she thought as she started working on her part. Robin positioned her blocks under the scissor jacks and levelled her camper. Walking past the girls, she went inside after connecting the power post. Turning on the air and adjusting the thermostat, she extended the awning and turned on the exterior lighting.

Outside, Christy and Linda placed chairs by the fire pit, covered their picnic tables with tablecloths, connected strings of lights to the awning; all things outside were being done by them, while Robin was inside, and had already opened her first beer.

"Hurry up, bitches!" Robin shouted as she walked over to their fire pit and sat down to watch.

"Aren't you gonna help?" Christy asked with a smile.

"Hey. I used my brain, you use your brawn," Robin laughed.

"We should be using our bras," Linda commented.

The others laughed. That was what they referred to as using their smiles, their bodies as a woman to get a man, or in today's social environment, a woman, to do their work for them.

"Girl power!" Christy said, cupping her breasts and letting them go.

The women finished adding some additional lighting and moving their coolers close to their main door before sitting down by the fire pit and drinking. Soon they would get their party on, soon they would be relaxing on a wonderful weekend of camping. The girls didn't have any plans tonight with their friends, it was just for them. Sometime tomorrow they would all meet up, it would probably be early afternoon, they guessed.

Two campsites to their left, a newer model 32 foot pull behind Grey Wolf camper stopped exactly where it should have. A pair of matching bookends jumped out and examined their initial surroundings. There was no bickering, no yelling, or frustration of any kind, they worked together as a team. One man walked to the back of the site while the other got back into their truck. Both of them looked around without talking to each other, taking everything in. Guided by the one at the back of the site, the driver checked both ways before proceeding to back the camper onto the dirt and gravel pad.

Joseph looked at the trees on the site, and having no concerns, he waved him on. Brian looked at the trees on the site, and not having any concerns, he kept backing up, continuing to follow Joseph's guidance.

Everyone who laid eyes on the duo paused what they were doing and watched on in amazement. A couple walking a dog slowed, left the road, walked onto the center grassy island, and stopped to watch. A little boy on his bike locked his brakes and slid to a stop in the grass and continued watching. An RV pulled safely past them, cleared their drive, and stopped to finish watching the men's handiwork.

Brian put the truck into park and closed his window. Shutting off the engine, he put on his emergency brake and jumped out. He was met by a firm handshake from Joseph, cheers from several people standing around them, and a thumbs up sign from a man in a nearby RV. The men took a bow and thanked them for watching.

"We'll be here all weekend long, thank you, thank you," Brian said laughing.

Joseph shook his head in disbelief, waved at their new friends, and turned to begin setting up their camper. Although they were a stone's throw away from the girls, they didn't visit or say hello. Tonight, the first night of their camping weekend always belonged to the individual parties; it was their time away, their me-time, they would agree.

It was close to 5 p.m. before the newlyweds showed up. Their friends all saw them arrive, mainly due to the fact that they had to drive around twice before they could find and back into their site. The girls laughed at this. The boys laughed at this too, but their reasons for laughing were different. The girls just thought it was funny, amusing, and well, possibly due to their beer and wine, possibly due to them being overly fun, Christy would say it was just good entertainment.

The boys laughed because it was always the same issues. They were not good at parking their camper, and because their site 127 was the same site they always reserved, Brian found it particularly amusing. *Too funny*, he thought, as Brian laughed again, remarking that they were trying to back in-an older 14-foot Jayco popup. In his defense, Joseph would say, *sometimes the shorter campers were more difficult to maneuver...*

Instead of watching the show outside, he decided to watch one inside. James microwaved a bag of popcorn and added the required amount of extra salt and butter before pressing play. He had set the air to seventy, pulled out a few green teas from the refrigerator, and buried himself beneath the three blankets on his bed. Taking the remote, he changed the input to HDMI 1, and waited. The bedroom came alive with yelling, gunfire, and explosions as space marines took to clearing aliens out of their corridor, right where he left off. *That feature was annoying at times, and helpful at others,* he thought, as he pressed the back button.

Taking a fistful of popcorn, James never took a single piece or two, he jammed what he could into his mouth. It was a race to finish his second handful before pressing play on his remote. *Perfect timing,* he thought, wiping off his fingers so he could use it without adding extra butter and salt to it. The movie had just started when he heard a loud, metallic clank. Pausing the marines, he lowered his eyebrows, turning his head to face the bedroom's camper door. After hearing nothing, his eyebrows returned to normal, he faced the television, and again pressed play. Clank. Again, he paused the movie and came out of the blankets. Opening his bedroom camper door, he walked out and sat down on the steps to listen.

Clank, he heard again, followed by a few expletives and the easily recognizable, all-too-familiar sound of beer bottles.

"Horseshoes and beer!" James exclaimed.

They were playing horseshoes. *Better now than later*, he thought. The couple on the island who set up their diesel pusher, they were the ones playing horseshoes, he was sure of it. Looking around at his neighbors, the sites around him were filling up nicely. By this weekend, it would be more than halfway full. This would be an interesting trip, he remarked. Looking back at his camper, he got up and spent a few minutes reviewing his tackle and checking his lines, the clanking would not interfere with that.

James would have a date this weekend. She hailed from Louisville, Kentucky, just over the bridge. He wasn't sure when she would arrive, but they had dinner plans tonight, so he expected her around 6 to 7 p.m., no later. There was no time to go fishing now, nor would there be time later.

He thought that Lynn would be spending the night, possibly the weekend, but she would be leaving Sunday afternoon or evening; he would be staying all the way to next Friday. He would have plenty of time to waste waiting on fish to jump on his hooks!

Yes, it was true that he didn't have time to go fishing, he did, however, have time to walk around and check out his neighbors. Grabbing a bottle of water from his cooler by the door, James took off down the road. He would pass the comfort station on his left, keep going, and then make another left to circle back around, passing a power transformer and the trash receptacles; everything was placed on the center island, it was spaced out, but it was all organized. James walked slow enough to be nosy, but quick enough to effectively stretch his legs and not draw undue attention.

About two months ago, while camping at site 123, he ran into a young girl sporting a vintage 1966 Avion Silver Bullet camper being pulled by a 1970's era Volkswagen bus; they were all things of beauty. He's never seen one in person since, the silver bullet, that is. He wouldn't see one here this weekend, either; most of the camp sites were already full, and he hadn't seen one yet. He continued walking as he checked out various camper models and the humans that hauled them.

There were big campers, small campers, slide outs, pull behinds, hybrids, fifth wheels, all sorts of campers littered the campground. And just like there were numerous models, sizes, and types of campers, they were parked equally diverse. Straight close to the road, crooked far away, crooked close to the road, straight faraway, and any combination in between. This was 2 p.m. chaos at its finest. James finished his walk and looked down at his empty water bottle. *Water wasn't cutting* it, he thought.

"Beer. I need beer!" he muttered, heading back inside the camper.

Bringing several outside, he walked over to his fire pit and sat in his soft, blue camping chair. Thinking about what he had seen, he reviewed the models that he recognized. Some were common or popular and some were rare. A few of the more notable ones were an older, 30-foot Sunline, a new model Grey Wolf, probably 32 feet long, an older Jayco popup, and several Highland Trail Runners of various lengths and years. He generally didn't pay attention to RVs, the ones you drove didn't interest him. However, the one parked across the road from him in the center island looked solid; a bit older perhaps, but solid, and well taken care of. He would have to look that one up later, the name on the side said Neptune Holiday Rambler. James made a point of running into them sometime this weekend to talk about the differences, the likes and dislikes of an RV opposed to a pull behind, as he finished his beer and continued staring.

The friends went about their business from when they finished setting up, to way into the evening. With them all being within a few hundred feet of each other, it was unusual for their group to keep to themselves, but that was by design. The three women got their party on, drinking more beer and wine than everyone around them combined. Brian and Joseph spent their time together focusing on the environment and food.

Brian set up the fire pit, started and maintained the fire, basically preparing everything outside, while Joseph did the prep-work and was to cook their meal. Between the boys, not a single alcoholic beverage disappeared.

For the newlyweds it was status quo. They had barely finished setting up when they went inside and never came out. Their friends knew they would spend most of their time together this weekend without them, but they made it a point to pull them away from each other, as much as necessary, for all to have a good time.

Brian and Joseph finished their dinner outside around their fire pit. Instead of setting up camping chairs to eat on, they moved one of their two picnic tables close enough to receive some light, but upwind so no embers would hit it. Looking down at the carnage, Brian noticed that Joseph did the same here that he did for any dinner, he only ate half. Looking down at his empty plate, Brian acknowledged his weakness for food. He always finished his plate. Now this was a little misleading for those onlookers who judged; he never filled his plate all the way up, he always took smaller servings. So, if you thought about it, eating all of half your food was the same as half of a larger portion.

"I'll put this in the fridge, and I'll be back in a few," Joseph said as he took his leftovers.

"Keep it out here for the bears," Brian joked.

"You wouldn't know what to do with a bear," Joseph laughed.

"Try me!" Brian snorted.

"Been there, done that," Joseph said as he took the steps into the camper smiling and closed the screen door to keep the pests outside.

Brian laughed again as he put some wood on the fire.

"What a waste," he said snickering.

From inside the camper Joseph heard him and couldn't help to pause and stare out the window. He did love him, very much so. He found him attractive, yes indeed. He wanted him, daily, every minute of every day. What Joseph wanted the most was a ring. He wanted to be married, not just living together. The topic had come up several times, but no progress was ever made, not enough for his liking, anyway.

"Hurry up, it's getting daylight out here," Brian shouted towards the camper.

"I hope not, lest you explode and burst into flame," Joseph said seriously.

The truth in that was disturbing, Brian thought. With his schedule, his sleep habits, or lack thereof, it did tend to keep him up to all hours of the night. This left him somewhat grumpy, tired, frustrated, and often fatigued during the day or early evenings. This did not bode well for his love life, but it did not bode well for Brian, either. Tonight would be like most nights, Joseph thought;

Brian would charm and initiate, and he would push back, gently, with a headache. Joseph wondered how much longer it would take, how many more headaches would be required before a serious, productive conversation would be had. He really wanted to have that conversation, and he, deep down, deep inside his heart, believed this weekend would make that happen. He hoped as much, anyway.

Brian grew tired of waiting, literally and figuratively, and began walking to the camper. Halfway there he saw him coming down the stairs. Smiles and pleasantries were exchanged, and in mocking fashion, Brian pointed to the fire pit. He bounded and spun and jumped like Puck, all the time pointing to Joseph to join him. Seconds later, James saw the second man hop and bounce to the first, who was half dancing, half having seizures around their fire in large, counterclockwise circles. James finished his beer, shook his head, and went for another. *It was going to be an unusual weekend,* he thought, as he checked the time.

L ate. *Lynn would be late tonight,* he thought. It wasn't a big deal, he half-expected it. She worked way too hard, and often was required to spend extra time on projects that she was responsible for, and some that she wasn't. Tonight's menu would change from dinner to apps, no problem. James would settle in and play his game system until she arrived, mainly out of an attempt to remove the recent memories of his new neighbor, Puck.

James didn't look out his window, nor listened too closely to the goings-on outside. Brian and Joseph grew weary sitting in their chairs, totally relaxed, until the flames died down, then they retired inside. Both men found a good night's sleep as their evening came to an early close; *setting up one's campsite can be exhausting,* Brian thought.

A few sites over, the girls were enjoying their first evening camping with a light dinner and heavy drinking. There wasn't a piece of meat to be had in tonight's campfire snacks. What one might find lacking in their meat selection, they would find most impressive with their vegetables and drinks. On one picnic table were tapas-style plates full of various non- meat selections. There were assorted baked apps consisting of baby quiches, spanakopita, three cheese pizza rolls, a bowl of spinach and artichoke dip with yellow tortilla chips, and a vegetable and cheese tray to die for. On the other picnic table were three bottles of Pinot Grigio, six Chardonnay, and four unusually bright, golden-colored Rieslings. Off to the side there were a variety of assorted liquors, most notably Cabo Wabo tequila, Knob Creek bourbon, and Tanqueray gin; and finally, beside those were assorted mixers, garnishes, and a large cooler of ice.

The three found peace and quiet here in the woods. They enjoyed some nice food and drink and some small talk sitting next to good friends, all the while enjoying their campfire. Robin liked the comfort in having the company of her friends the most, their good, quiet company. She found the level of relaxation satisfying; there were no worries with them nearby.

Robin was comfortable, she felt safe. Christy was actually the most drunk of the three, and therefore the quietest. She was a calm drunk, a relaxed drunk, and somewhat emotional. She loved her friends, and she would do anything for them, especially right now. That left Linda. Now Linda was a hot mess without her friends. With her friends though, she flourished. She was drinking a little less than the other two, but it was for relaxation purposes, for taste; she wasn't drinking to get drunk, that would happen with the others present.

The girls sat outside until they grew too comfortable, too tired. The fire was on its way out, and soon it would be totally dark around them. The girls had talked about making s'mores tonight, but all were full of veggies and drinks; *there was no more room*, Robin thought, so she would not mention it tonight. *The s'mores would be rescheduled,* she thought, *management has spoken!*

Each girl was tasked with taking two plates inside, and

Robin would come back out to lock up their alcohol. Like normal, Robin had additional responsibilities, but it was her camper, she was kind of the host of their glorious weekend's endeavors. Even when the friends all met, they would meet over here; Robin was, inevitably, the center of their universe.

"It's good to be the queen," she exclaimed, as she made the last of four trips carrying in the alcohol.

"Next time I'm bringing a box for all of this, and possibly a servant," she mumbled under her breath.

Of all the friends here for camping, the three women were the first to arrive, and the last to enter their camper for what they hoped would be restful, relaxing sleep. The girls crawled inside and disappeared in their usual pecking order. Robin walked in first, it was her camper, after all.

Christy followed her, and Linda took up the rear. The girls often joked that of all of them, Linda's rear was the largest, thus it always arrived late, approximately 5 minutes after everyone else did. Robin thought about that as Linda closed the door and walked over to the couch to claim her spot.

Robin sighed as she opened the door and walked outside to look for anything they might have forgotten to bring in. Looking around and seeing nothing that required immediate attention, she perused their sleepy campground. Checking the nearby campers for any signs of activity, and seeing nobody outside, she took a chance. Robin removed her T-shirt and bra and placed them on a nearby chair. She was lit only by red, fading embers.

Slowly she danced around the fire, bouncing, and twisting her body, her breasts flying this way and that. *If one can't catch a man after all of this, then there were none to be had,* she thought, completing her circle.

"No one, really? Shit!" Robin spoke her disappointment to the surrounding trees.

Smiling from ear to ear, she grabbed her clothes and headed for the camper. Locking her door, she quietly walked down the hallway to her bed. Moving around the edge to the right, she slid the covers back and jumped onto the bed. Sliding more toward the center, it didn't take her long to realize both Christy and Linda were already lying under the covers, fast asleep. *Passed out, more like it,* Robin thought. She found them comforting, and they were good friends. Robin smiled as she pushed in beside them and buried herself beneath the covers, hoping she could fall asleep so easily.

A way from the campsites and back at the main gate, Mary was awoken out of a deep sleep by an approaching vehicle. The first thing to run through her mind was the now all too evident fact that her daytime job was interfering with what she loved to do.

"I'm too young for this," she chuckled.

Mary awoke staring at a wall in the small shack, shaking the cobwebs from her head. Sniffing a few times, she turned to face the coffee maker that was nearly as old as she was. The smell of burnt coffee was not too far from that of burnt toast. Looking at the cameras she checked both directions before peeking through her side window, but there was no vehicle. *It's coffee, not toast, so it's not a stroke,* Mary thought, shaking her head laughing. The CO had parked his SUV in front of the wood pile and stepped out without closing his door, leaving his vehicle running like an ambulance.

Mary reached for the coffee maker and turned it off. The first of several yawns escaped her, killing the cacophony of crickets too numerous to count. It would be several minutes before the coffee pot would be cool enough to be cleaned. Several minutes after that she could make another pot; Mary needed another pot.

Shuffling her feet across the floor she made her way to her chair in front of the cameras and got back to work. She had no sooner sat down and spun around to view the video screens when someone stuck their head in her window. Mary fell out of her chair screaming. Looking back up from her new angle on the floor, she noticed the man's smiling face sticking out of a DNR uniform.

The CO had been watching the volunteer from the edge of the window, just outside of her view. Looking close, he saw a middle-aged woman with thin shoulder-length, straight blonde hair. She had an attractive body, so she had to be widowed a few times by now, possibly due to killing her partners during sex. It wasn't the diminutive hourglass shape of her body. It wasn't the way that one's eyes focused on her, passing over all others present, as if she was the only one standing in a police lineup. It was her small, perfectly rounded head. *Stunningly beautiful for her age,* he thought, smiling at the woman through the window.

"I'm sorry. I thought you had seen me pull up. I did not mean to startle you," The CO replied through a crooked smile.

"No biggie. I saw lights coming in, just lost track of them. How can I help you?" Mary stood up and awaited his response.

"Inspection. I need to inspect your," Scott said with a pause as he stared at her breasts.

"I'll need to inspect your weekly report and review your surveillance tapes, I mean," Scott said to a blank look on the woman's face.

Without hesitating she opened the door and moved off to the side.

"I've never had one before, so you'll have to let me know what you need," Mary smiled.

"Sure. It won't take long," he said, closing the door behind him and locking it.

Turning around a few times quickly and scanning the room as if looking for something specific, his question was answered before he even asked.

"Burned coffee. It's one of those things that sometimes gets away from me," she acknowledged embarrassingly.

"Ah. Well, my name's Scott. I need you to show me that the surveillance works," he stated as he produced his small clipboard and pen.

"Well, here's the inbound traffic, and this one's for leaving."

"Nice," he whispered, checking off a box before looking back up to her.

"It can be paused, restarted, fast forwarded," she quickly demonstrated.

"OK," he replied, checking more boxes.

He thanked her by nodding and continued checking boxes and taking notes. Making sure to look directly at her, he softly spoke.

"Mary, is it?"

"Yes," she replied, feeling like she was in trouble.

"Mary, ever been robbed at gunpoint before?" he asked, pulling his service weapon from his side.

Mary's heart sank. Her breathing seemed to stop. The CO watched as she slowly turned white from head to toe. Becoming overly nervous, she scanned the room frantically before finally remembering to breathe.

"Open the safe."

"It doesn't open until 9 a.m.," Mary responded without thinking.

"Use the override. I won't ask you again," he said smartly.

Mary entered the sequence 911 and the small brown door clicked before opening an inch and stopping.

"Put it all on the floor."

She took hold of the door to open it wider. Slightly bending forward, she reached both hands inside and slid the contents onto the floor. She slowly raised up and looked away from the man.

"Get on your knees," he commanded.

"Please. Don't. There's no need for this, take your money," Mary pleaded.

"Knees," he sternly said by raising his pistol to her chest.

She went down to the floor and again lowered her head to the side. Other than noticing the floor was uncomfortably hard, she saw only his shoes. They were old, cracked leather boots covered in places with dried red clay.

"Been hiking around Cemetery Trail looking for mushrooms?" she asked anxiously.

"Remove your blouse."

Mary paused, moving her head slightly towards him as if trying to say no, or to protest. The courage never came.

"Now. Off. NOW!" he yelled, pointing at her.

This was the first time he had acted towards her with hate, with malice. Mary did as asked. The man in the CO uniform watched her closely, removing his eyes only occasionally to check the video feed.

"Lean forward so you can remove your trousers," he whispered.

Mary did not move a muscle.

"Your pants! NOW!" he demanded.

Mary jumped at his words. His voice sounded different, crazed. She had a bad feeling about how things were going to go now. One does not make a victim get naked during a common robbery. She began crying as she loosened her pants, leaning forward only as far as she needed to slide them down to her ankles.

"Nice. Good," he told her, pushing her forward.

He sat on her lower back, service weapon in hand. Squeezing his knees together against her sides, he rendered her arms useless; those steps were the first he did when gaining control over a woman, Scott referred to them as foreplay.

"I'm sorry it has to be this way. I need you to stay put while I look around. I'm going to get up now. Keep your eyes closed, and you'll live through this. Understood?" he questioned.

A single word, *yes*, was all she managed to get out through all her shaking and crying. Steady whimpering came from Mary as she shook uncontrollably. The CO ran his fingers through the reservation cards looking for his girlfriend's name but found nothing. Occasionally he looked down at the park official. Each time he laid eyes on her she was exactly where he left her, even with all of her shaking and whimpering.

"Be quiet!"

Her whimpering lessened, but she could not stop it. Looking back at the vertical reservation board he picked up random cards and moved them up or down four to six spots, mixing them up. Looking at Mary, and then back to the board, he admired his organized chaos and continued searching the room. Moving the old, corded mouse attached to an aging computer, he was prompted to log in. Turning back around he reached down and grabbed hold of her neck. Pulling her up, he maneuvered the woman in front of the monochrome monitor.

"Log in." he shouted.

Mary did not struggle. He moved her around as one would a child. Her crying and whimpering grew louder as she typed in S3xYMahMA23 and hit enter.

"Quiet please. Stop crying, it's OK."

Mary turned to the left and looked sincerely at him, pausing only a few seconds before looking back down at the floor.

"Seriously? That's your password?"

Mary nodded yes, between whimpers.

"Get back on the floor now. On your stomach. Move!"

More whimpering followed Mary as she shook herself down to the floor. The CO kept watch on her as he continued to search the computer for anything on his girlfriend. There was a scheduling program, a park official database, and a couple of calendar spreadsheets. The only thing interesting he found was an announcement for Raptor Days. It was dated a week from today. He was glad that they all went camping now, before it was even more crowded. It would definitely be easier to move around now than it would be then. *What a lovely idea,* he thought, as a smile crept onto his face.

"Get up please," he said softly.

Mary took a knee, rested for a moment and then stood up. She was not wobbly, but she did show her fear. It was hard for Mary to hide the way she felt when she was still crying and whimpering uncontrollably.

Looking around the office, Mary was shocked at the amount of damage and chaos the man had caused. For the most part, he had opened everything closed and closed everything open; the place was a mess. The only thing he had not done yet was murder her outright and set the entire place on fire. Taking one more look, she turned to him and raised her head.

"I need you to find her. I've looked through everything, but I can't find her reservation," he said calmly.

It was the nicest thing he had said to her since he introduced himself; Mary was caught off guard. Looking around the room again she spoke.

"Well, what is her name? Maybe I can cross reference-"

Mary did not have time to finish. Realizing Mary was no good to him anymore, he walked to her and took hold of her shoulders. Mary jumped at this.

"Oh God. Don't do this. Please. No!" she managed, before being turned around and pushed forward to a nearby table.

Leaning against her he pressed down on her shoulders, placing her chest flatly on the table. Her head was pushed up at a slight angle, leaving her right cheek leaning against the wall. Mary looked at him through a steady flood of tears from her left eye.

"Please. Plea-" she cried as the man brought his pistol

down against her head.

    Between the CO's physical blows, Mary struggled to get free, but she didn't have a chance. Every time he slammed the pistol down seemed to take the fight right out of her, until there was nothing left. Each time he made contact, her eyes closed a little further, until all at once they went dark; it was lights out for Mary, her body relaxed. She stopped struggling and her face lost all expression of pain. Her eyes started to close. Her lips parted slightly before her eyes had totally shut. He moved away and Mary's body slid quietly to the ground. She would have considered herself lucky being still alive; Mary was always ever the optimist, but those thoughts were never formed.

    There was a little blood from her ear but upon closer examination, it did not look like a murder scene. The place looked robbed, pillaged if you will; there was a body, but no excess blood, and she was still breathing. The CO stepped over his unconscious Mary and started closing the cabinet doors. He moved some furniture around, placing chairs behind desks. A quick look at the chaos around them and he gathered up loose, unorganized papers, stacking them to the right of the mouse. He logged out of the computer and then turned off the monitor.

    Looking back at Mary he found a small pool of blood by her head. It was the size of a quarter and was easily cleaned up. He looked over at the half naked woman lying prone on the floor beside him. Reaching down he stroked her hair. Taking some between his fingers, he pulled upward. Mary's head moved to the side and rolled towards him. She would have made an effort to pay him attention were she not half dead and unconscious.

    Moving his hands lower he brushed against her breasts before taking both hands and squeezing them. He smiled and let go. Moving them lower, he took hold of her waist band and pulling it upward, let her underpants snap back into place. Taking another look at her body it enticed him. She was available, she was willing, she wanted him, he was sure of that, but she was not his.

    It was not Mary's fault his girlfriend did not put her name on the reservation for this weekend. *Hell, it might have been done purposefully; for all he knew, she was probably going to dump him anyway.* It was done to spite him; he was sure of it. It would not matter if she were breaking up.

"Shit!" The CO muttered as he picked Mary up by her waist and carried her outside to his still running SUV.

He placed her face down on the floorboard in the back, with her head behind his seat. The CO went back inside and gathered up all the belongings he recognized as being hers; her clothes, cell phone, keys, her purse. Looking down at her phone he saw the screen with a low battery warning of 5% remaining. Thinking about this, he flipped the phone around and removed the battery and then jammed everything into her purse. Taking a step towards the door his eyes moved past the surveillance monitors.

"That ought to do it. Oh, I can't forget these."

The CO reached for the surveillance boxes and rewound the tapes to their beginnings and pressed record. Waiting a few minutes longer, he let them continue to capture empty, night-time footage. Looking around the walls he finally found what he was looking for. The CO opened the breaker box and flipped the main switch, killing the power to the building. One final look around and he placed the closed sign on the window and left.

It did not take him long before he had reached the main park road. Driving for a few minutes he took a right and started down the unpaved service road to the raptor house. Frequently, he found himself staring at the woman in his back seat. He couldn't see much, but her round backside seemed to be calling his name. Every once in a while, he swore he saw it move. He knew she should still be out cold. Turning his lights off and pulling over into the grass he stopped and turned off his engine.

He twisted to face the back seat, placing his hands on her waist. She felt warm. She felt firm. *Too bad we met this way, perhaps things would have been different?* he thought. Raising her up he turned her body where her feet were on the seat cushion and her knees were against the back.

Sliding his hands down her hips to her ankles he took hold and began pulling Mary to the front. He stopped just short of pulling her all the way, leaving her stomach straddling the center console, with a leg dangling on either side.

Mary's head hung lifeless in the back seat down to the floorboard, but he cared nothing for that. Reaching towards her head, he passed it up and started massaging her shoulders, her back. Once he was sure she was still unconscious, he closed his eyes pretending she was Robin. More caressing of her shoulders, her back, only filled him with rage. Removing his hand, he took his pistol out from his pants and slammed it down against her calf. *Can't lose this one, not this time,* he thought.

Reaching into the back seat he took a handful of hair and pulled her backward far enough to do the same to her right arm, just above her elbow. *Now you need me. You need me more than I need you.* Grabbing her bad arm, he pulled her all the way into the front seat. He pushed her down to the passenger side floorboard headfirst, folding her legs over on top of her. Securing his pistol, he positioned himself behind the wheel, started the engine and continued driving to the raptor center.

The man drove under the pale moonlight for several minutes before thinking to turn on his headlights. Making a slight bend off the road to the left, he hit the brakes to pause briefly and take another look at Mary. A few more seconds went by before he turned back on to the road and again continued driving. After a few minutes more, the building came into view. He pulled into the closest parking spot out front.

There were no vehicles at all in the parking lot, and the outside security flood lamp was angled to the far side of the right most door, providing little if any efficient lighting. Turning off the engine, he smacked Mary on her ass, to no response. Opening his door, he got out and stretched. Leaning into the SUV he took Mary by her waist and pulled her out the door and onto the ground. He let her land on the gravel as he checked the darkness around them. No movement or sounds other than Mother Nature were heard. It was as if she cared little for what he was about to do. Moments later, and without notice, everything around him grew quiet. It was as if she knew his cruel plan after all and wanted nothing to do with it.

Mary sat motionless on the gravel, naked down to her bra and panties. She was leaning forward with her head resting against the seat and her chin off to the side of the seat belt strap. Moving closer, he placed his boot against her shoulder and pushed her over. Closing the door, he reached for the ankle of her injured right leg and started for the gate. He dragged her on her back and dropped her at the foot of the locked, fenced-in gate.

The CO fiddled with his key ring and on his third try the

gate was unlocked. Again, he took hold of her ankle and dragged her body inside, and then dropped her. Stopping to lock the gate behind them, he paused briefly to again take in the sights and sounds around him. It was the dead of night, although the moon made it clear that it would betray him to anyone who cared to gaze upon him or look in his direction. It was, however, unusually quiet. *Quiet is good,* he thought.

If before Mary was a looker, someone to keep close and treasure, now she was disposable. He was only keeping her around while he investigated further. Scott wasn't sure if she would be of use anymore, or if she ever had been. The last time he had paid her attention was before he had undressed her; seeing her naked and realizing she wasn't Robin changed everything.

Another dim flood lamp did its best to illuminate the side entrance. This time he had nearly exhausted his key ring before the door gave in to his request. A loud metal click was the only sound heard for miles as he turned the key and the lock opened. Reaching down to grab Mary he felt nothing. Moving his hand to the left and then the right resulted in the same emptiness. He glanced down and noticed he had forgotten to bring her; he had left her back at the gate.

Turning his head, he saw her looking over her shoulder at him as she pulled on the door handle, trying to escape. When Mary's eyes met his, she began screaming for help. She managed to pull herself up and place her good hand towards the top of the gate before he caught up to her. Kicking Mary in the small of her back, she felt the coldness of the fence against her body and then came the pain. It was hard enough for her to hold herself upright with one good arm, let alone stand.

Mary understood he had hurt her, but she did not know when he did it, or why. It was apparently his goal to kill her slowly. The CO leaned into her and placed his hands on her shoulders before pushing her to the ground. Mary was again crying and begging to be set free. Her right shoulder and arm hurt her, her right leg hurt her too, but most of all her back. No matter what she did, how she turned, what she moved, her back was killing her. It even hurt her to breathe. *Not like she had broken ribs,* she thought, but more like a thousand cuts and bruises. The CO made Mary stand up and walk beside him; they were side by side when he stopped her short of the entrance, where she promptly fell over.

"Move it. Get up. We're going inside," he snapped, shoving her forward.

Mary half walked, half hopped to the door. Looking up overhead she saw the caged ceiling, and for the first time recognized where she was. The CO pushed it open and led her inside. When they were far enough into the room, he shoved her to the ground. He kicked the door for effect, pushing it backwards to close it. Mary stayed put and tried to gather strength, having landed on her good side with the help from her left arm. The CO examined the room in the dim light. He did not want to advertise his presence by turning on the main overhead lighting, so he did what he could with what light he had.

He checked his surroundings and was overcome with raw emotion. He briefly closed his eyes to it, enjoying the moment. When he was younger, his mom had taken him and his older brother here for a nature tour. They came one weekend afternoon to see the wildlife, similar to the upcoming Raptor Days festival, he surmised. It was different back then from what they were allowed to witness, what they were allowed to do.

In the dim light he walked forward and looked into a large display. From left to right there were four large cages, approximately twelve feet deep and tall, and twenty feet wide. Each one was similar to the next with vertical pine boards for the sides and ceiling, and chicken wire stretched over the front. The center of each display had an opaque plexiglass section approximately a third of the entire ceiling. It was meant to simulate a cloudy sky during the day by providing some natural lighting.

Moving to his right, he looked at the displays in great detail. They were different from when he was here; more modern, larger, and built like a natural home away from home for the healing raptors. Some had partial wooden fence sections, trees, and perches. All had natural dirt and grass for the ground, with some having hay bales or an old barrel for additional dressing. It was as much for us as it was for them, but it did lend to an aesthetic, peaceful recovery. A few of the displays had ladders that went up a wall for climbing and jumping; most of what was present was to help the raptor regain strength and promote healing.

Looking at them from the door onward, there was a bald

eagle, a red-tailed hawk, a large eastern screech owl, and a very menacing looking great horned owl, if his memory served him. In the dim light the animals seemed surreal, mysterious, majestic. The red-tailed hawk had a cast on his left leg, and the screech owl seemed to be missing part of its right wing, but the others looked fully healed, or at least physically they looked alright. He started to walk away, and the great horned owl seemed to follow him. A few aggressive squawks came from the angry bird, telling the CO how it felt. He could not determine if it were a male or female, but it looked large enough to be the latter.

    The CO exhaled and turned to his left, as if contemplating his next move, or reminiscing on that day from long ago. Two long stainless-steel tables held at least two dozen glass aquarium tanks. Glancing at them briefly they all had metal exercise wheels, water bottles, and were full of mice hidden under various depths of pine chips, empty toilet tissue rolls, and miscellaneous pieces of cardboard and wood. Looking at all of the cages he was certain that they provided an almost never-ending supply of pinkies and jumpers for a living, natural food source. That's one of the memories that hit him in the face when he first walked in, the smell of pine chips and urine. Those smells were hard to get rid of when it came to breeding rodents. It can be masked, it can be lessened, but it could never be fully removed from the room.

    Looking at the opposite wall he saw a large section of separated cages, from the floor up to about five feet high. Each individual cage looked to be about two to three-foot cube-like compartments. The metal front had about an inch between each, which was barely enough to hold the hinge for each cage. It was sea foam green in color, with some sections discolored with rust. Now this was just as he remembered it being when he had seen it years ago.

    Peeking inside some cages he saw various animals. Several small screech owls, various small birds such as ruffed grouses, and several ducks. Walking further to the right he saw a canvasback, a wood duck, an American black duck, and an American coot. *Apparently, the center had expanded to include other wildlife, instead of only raptors*, he thought.

    Although ducks are omnivores, and they are able to fly, they didn't catch their food with their talons, they used their beaks, which if he remembered correctly, was a deal breaker for being considered a raptor.

All were quiet, content, or possibly just trying to sleep. The canvasback had a cast on its left leg, the wood duck it's right. Others were harder to tell why they were still here. Looking back one more time at the stainless-steel tables he remembered playing with the pinkies and jumpers, right before he fed a pair of baby barn owls. These experiences were memorable for him and his brother for different reasons. His brother was interested in animals, forests, nature, but this CO was fascinated by pain, death, and the frailty of life.

That day long ago shaped both of their lives. He thought about it often; he wished his brother were still around. Another happy thought came and went, turning quickly from happiness to that of anger, of hate.

"I'm afraid we seem to have run out of time, Mary," Scott said matter-of-factly.

The CO turned to take her by the hand, but she was gone. Looking around the room he noticed the open back door. Scott didn't know how long he walked around remembering the past, it didn't matter though, he knew she could not escape. Quietly he approached the open door and looked through a narrow sliver into the fenced enclosure. Mary was leaning against the gate, using her good arm to pull herself up to the top. Looking around the room he thought of what to do. Taking a leather glove and an old towel, he approached the cage cautiously, slowly. He glanced at the red card beside the door. *Luna, Great Horned Owl; nice to meet you, Luna,* he said calmly, but it did not matter; the winged creature was watching him closely and appeared to already be agitated.

With a loud screech the raptor flew straight into the stranger coming towards her. Throwing the towel in the air to blind it, he used his gloved hand to force it to the ground. Once it could not see it was easier to handle. It was several minutes before Scott could safely hold it against his body. He managed to wrap it in the towel, covering its head and held the raptor's feet tightly in his gloved hand.

Mary used this time to attempt her escape, but she was so severely injured that the CO was not overly concerned. Everything he had done to her seemed to be in an effort to postpone or delay her death, to torture her. She came to that conclusion by the way he acted. His mannerisms, the words he chose, the sickest of looks that came and went across his face when he watched her; this monster was no CO, he was definitely an imposter. Considering how she felt, she was confident that all her efforts to escape were in vain, although she had to try.

Taking baby steps toward the door, the CO stuck out his leg and pushed it open. Slowly he walked out, holding the towel close to his chest. A few steps more and he was almost there. Before he could call out to get her attention, his surprise let out the first of several long and drawn-out screeches, betraying his intent.

Mary looked around to him and knew he was hiding something awful. With a look of hate on his face, he took another step toward her and threw the towel and its contents in her direction. He was already walking backwards through the door when she flapped her wings and tried to fly. Landing in the middle of the fenced-in yard, Mary yelled for help while turning her back against the gate to face it.

On the ground in front of Mary stood a fully feathered, foot and a half tall pointy-beaked monster. Although a mature adult female could stand taller than 2 feet, this Great Horned Owl was notably shorter for her age. What she lacked in height though, she more than made up for in ferocity. With one wing held slightly higher than the other, she knew immediately who it was. Some popular names that were provided to recovering raptors were Mr. Haney, Elmo, Moonshine, Digby, Taklamakan, Mowgli, Bougie, Grendel, Obi, and Tickle or Tinkle; she wasn't sure on the last one. This one was different, she was both loving and angry, caring, and indifferent; her name was as special as she was temperamental, her name was Luna.

Mary knew she could not fly, not far anyway; her wings were unable to support her. Some of her bones in her left wing were missing, and some in her right were malformed. Luna kept hopping forward, and when she was close enough, she launched her big bottom into the air towards Mary's midsection. A horrific scream drew his attention from the door frame out to the yard. The owl had landed on Mary's stomach and was trying to crawl up to her face, Scott struggled not to turn away, and continued watching.

Mary thought about what was happening, and how it

wasn't Luna's fault. She remembered when the injured owl first came to their center. There were a few ways this happened, but normally it was either a drop off directly to them or a referral from another wildlife agency. In Luna's case, she came to them wrapped up in a beach towel, held gently by a young woman. She arrived unconscious, but she was thought to be dead. A quick once-over determined she was alive, and after a more detailed examination, they rushed the raptor into surgery.

When a raptor arrived, it went straight to the intensive care unit for a thorough examination from head to tail, literally. There were lots of rules to working with raptors, and although she was allowed to assist in their recovery, it was always under the direct supervision of a state licensed veterinarian. There are numerous reasons why a raptor would require medical assistance and supervision. Those that receive any medical attention were housed indoors until their recovery could be reassessed. If no medical attention was required, or the raptor was healing properly, it was moved to an outside enclosure.

If the raptors were inside the building, facility ambassadors were more hands on, and they were hand fed during their recovery; if outside though, if the raptor was housed outside, it was a step closer to what they called graduation, which also meant they were able to eat on their own. As the raptors were closer to being released, their human ambassadors backed off and became more distant, in preparation of transitioning them back into nature.

This was a raptor rehab center, and above everything else, it focused on healing. Recovering raptors had their needs attended to, and they were given everything to be successful and fully heal, with the mutual goal of being released back into the wild as soon as possible. Luna's injuries were extensive, and she underwent two surgeries to correct her wings before it was determined that nothing further could be done. Luna would never fully heal, and therefore she could not provide for herself out in the wild. If the animal had injuries that prevented it from being released, it was taught to be a part of the center's educational program or shipped off to another facility to tend to the raptor's needs.

As far as why most raptors required the center's healing and rehab, well, the most common injury was due to being hit by a vehicle; that was Luna's reason for being here, as well. For Luna, the words *road* and *kill* were both what she was doing, and what she almost became, before she was gathered up and brought in for recovery. Once the center's help was required, the raptor went through an extensive process. It was assigned a number, and everything was documented; its genus and species were recorded, the sex determined, who found it, where it was located, known injuries, where the raptor was to be housed (an inside or outside enclosure), and any pertinent medical veterinary information, such as diagnosis, weight, height, dietary requirements; everything was recorded into their database on their computers, and on a colored card that was placed on the left of their cage's door.

    Once carded, the raptors were taken care of and loved from the beginning of the recovery process to the end. The main goal of the center was recovery and release, and although it was human nature to be involved and touch, the raptors were off limits to all but a few. All had yellow cards next to their names, all were to be treated equally with caution and respect, all except one. The only red card ever assigned in the facility went to Luna.

    She was the one who went through the most extensive surgery to repair her wings after being hit by a truck. She was the one who spent the longest time recovering. While in casts and bandages, she required extra human tender love and care. And above all, she was the one who resented being captive for the rest of her life. Her wings never fully healed to bear her weight during flight; with one never healing enough to provide normal, natural movement. This was what kept her in captivity, and this was what made Luna a permanent member of their educational program. Humans thought her lucky to be alive after all she went through, Luna thought herself unlucky to have not been killed.

    When the raptor was being rehabbed and healed, only a select few were allowed to handle them. It was only after detailed training that one could do that role; Mary was not lucky enough to be able to do those kinds of things, she was simply the one who helped prepare the food and clean the enclosures. She made it a point to be a part of as much as she could in anything she was allowed and qualified to do. She participated in education, helped to maintain a professional appearance for the center, she volunteered for Raptor Days breakfast and activities, and basically took care of anything that needed to be done around the buildings, inside and out.

These things held special memories for Mary, they were things she cared about dearly, but they paled in comparison to her current situation; her focus right now had to be on survival. The face of the great horned owl was as high as Mary's chin and seemed to be somewhat perched on her breasts. Mary found it difficult to remove Luna from her death grip due to her eyes either being closed, or her vision blocked by protecting her face with her hands. While struggling against her foe, Mary made poor choices; several times she attempted to cover her eyes and face, only to have the Luna go for her neck, her shoulders, her breasts, basically anything exposed.

The CO witnessed attack after attack, with most going towards Mary's face. It was almost too much for him to take. Mary's screams turned into pleading, into begging. They were not meant for Luna; They were meant for him. One time, Mary managed to turn her head sharply to her right and take hold of Luna's neck. It stopped her attacks to her face, but it's talons grabbed repeatedly at her soft flesh. Mary tried to pull Luna off of her body, but every time she pulled, the great horned owl's talons dug deeper into her supple breasts. When Mary finally let go, Luna loosened her grip.

The CO was right on top of them when Mary shrieked again, causing the great horned owl to flap its wings in anger. Scott was reaching for the feathered monster when it cut away a piece of flesh from Mary's left breast and threw its head backward, appearing to swallow it. *Nothing hit the ground,* Scott thought in horror; *nothing hit the ground!* Finally able to grab it, he took hold of her wings and began pulling. In his attempts to remove the owl from Mary, Scott had not thought about how she was attached.

Luna was dug in hard, and held on ferociously, causing Mary a great deal of pain. As her talons were pulled free from her breasts, pieces of flesh came along with them. Excruciating pain overtook Mary, and she promptly passed out. Her body hit the ground and rolled over on her side. She bounced in slow motion two times before settling on the gravel, her blood glistening in the moonlight.

Turning around cautiously, Scott started making his way back inside. He walked through the doorway carefully holding

Luna out in front of him, his arms fully extended. He took Luna back to her display and tossed her inside. Backing out quickly, he closed the door with his foot, as he still felt the urge to protect his body from the winged beast. Locking the cage door, Scott read the card on the side of the cage again. *Luna, Great Horned Owl, handle with caution!* He already knew her name, he missed the *'handle with caution'* warning; *well, no shit*, he said, w*ell played, killer.* The owl looked back at him, fully satisfied that it was now back in its home.

It was not until he walked up to Mary to take her away that he noticed all the scratches, all the tearing, the multiple holes where Luna had beaked her. There were small folds of skin that were separated, bleeding small torrents of blood onto the ground beside her. Scott had a few things he could do with Mary. He had not really thought all of this through, he admitted to himself. He could take her with him, he could leave her out in the external caged area on her back with the owl, or he could take Mary and place her in Luna's cage, leaving the door slightly ajar; those were the three things he thought of initially.

The cage it is, he decided, as he picked Mary up and carried her back inside. He opened the door very carefully, only a few inches at first. Slowly he opened it further, stopping every few inches as he went. When he was sure he could place her safely into the cage, he picked her up and using Mary as a human shield, he walked inside. Luna squawked and squeaked, her wings flapped angrily, but she never came at him.

Laying Mary on her back, he spread her legs, slightly bending her left knee. Keeping one eye on Luna, and one on Mary, he reached for her hands. One at a time he placed them palms up, as if protecting her face. Taking her right arm, he pulled it back to him, and toward the gate door. He wanted to make sure that she was seen to have *nearly made it,* meaning that just before she reached the exit, she had been overcome.

Once determined that she was properly positioned, he again placed her hand palm up, over her face. Backing up slowly, he closed the gate door shut, but did not lock it. Scott took several pictures on his cell phone of Mary posed with her hands protecting her as best they could, from various angles, positions, and with the perspective from the picture being taken from both sides of the gate. Reviewing them before he exited, he smiled; *what a way to go, if you were a nature lover.*

Scott had been busy today, he thought as he left for the campground. Busy, yes, but he still had time for coffee. Driving off slowly, following all posted speed limits, and staying between the lines, he pulled into his campsite. Turning off his lights, he drove towards the back, then stopped his engine. Getting out, he reviewed the area surrounding his camper as he always did when he returned. Everything looked good, so he entered to unwind and make some fresh coffee.

    He finished one cup, then poured another for his trip. Testing his goggles for power, he turned them off, and took a spare set of batteries with him, just in case. Smiling for a brief moment, he thought of what was to come. *Busy indeed,* he thought as he left his camper and walked into the woods.

    Scott slowly walked around the outside edge of the campsites, keeping out of the light as much as possible. With a coffee in one hand, and his goggles in the other, he navigated the bushes and trees like an Eagle Scout. He would maneuver close enough to use his night goggles, keeping enough distance to not be heard. Scott methodically scouted each and every campsite he came across, scouring them for any signs of Robin or her friends. It was a slow process, and there was no guarantee he wouldn't run out of time, but he kept going.

    He was doing it all wrong, he realized. He was going from site to site, looking for knowledge, searching individually, looking individually; he needed to go to a central point. *He needed to stake out the entrance to the campground, the local campground convenience store, or a comfort station, perhaps?* Right in the middle of that thought, Scott turned to his right, and at a brisk pace, made his way to the closest of the three buildings nearest him; Scott had chosen the comfort station.

    Scott wasn't sure which door he wanted to focus on, so he positioned himself inside a small clump of bushes, facing the most populated side. From this angle, he would be able to watch someone approach and enter either door, men or women. *From this angle,* he thought, he would be successful. Scott settled in, getting as comfortable as he could, and waited. Nothing doing. No one was out and about, it was just not going to work, so Scott gave up. Maybe it was due to his lack of patience? Maybe because he could not relax? Maybe it was due to him being out of coffee, again; he didn't know, but Scott knew it was time to try something different. Taking a knee, he started looking at nearby campers.

It turned out to be pure dumb luck. It was luck that made him stop concentrating on the comfort station and switch back to individual campers, instead of giving up. It was luck that the first camper he trained his goggles on caught a man closing a camper door, and it was luck that he recognized his face.

"Well hello Nick," he quietly mumbled.

Scott watched as the man seemed to be walking down the road coming straight for him. He went from a knee to all the way down to the ground. Thinking that was not enough, he slid backward further into the bushes. Not knowing if he was adequately hidden, he lay there holding his breath as Nick passed him by and turned to enter the comfort station. Nick was wearing dark shorts and a white T-shirt. Scott wasn't sure why he was here and not using his camper, but he didn't care.

Scott felt confident that no one else was inside except Nick; he had watched the doors for hours. He waited a few seconds after the door closed behind him before committing himself to action. He jumped forward and at a small jog, made quick work of the distance between the bushes and Nick's camper. Passing a plastic trash bag that was gently blowing in the wind, he reached down to pick it up. Stopping at their picnic table, he took off his uniform shirt and pants, stripping down to his underwear and a white T-shirt. Placing the bag over his head, he poked two holes for eyes and slowly entered the camper.

This was a small popup, the man had left to clean up, or shower after sex, he thought, *or maybe to use the restroom?* Since it was a small camper, upon entering and closing the door, he immediately saw Teena to his right, stretched out on the bed. She was lying on her stomach, her backside glistening with sweat, bathed in the light provided from a single candle. The air conditioner, continuously running, placed a chill in the air, almost drowning out the country music coming through their camper speakers. Teena told him to hurry up, turning over on her back to look at him. With a large smile on her face, she looked on. Noticing he didn't move, she flipped back over, smacking her butt with her hand. In the dim candlelight, she didn't notice anything out of the ordinary about the man standing in the darkness wearing just a T-shirt, underpants, and a trash bag over his head.

"Come on baby. Hurry up, get back in bed," Teena said softly; "and take off that ridiculous bag," she laughed.

Scott took off the trash bag and slid in beside her. Placing a hand on her shoulder, he turned Teena over. Before she opened her eyes, he pushed the plastic trash bag over her face. Instead of struggling, she called out Nick's name and told him to stop screwing around. Scott finished climbing on, and when he controlled her, he punched Teena in the face several times, one right after the other. Any noises that might have escaped Teena were now quieted from John Michael Montgomery's failed competition with the air conditioner.

Teena had no idea of what was coming, and from the very first blow, she was effectively subdued. Dazed, confused, she didn't have any thoughts about anything at this point. There was no registering of danger, no fight or flight response, she just lay there. Taking off the trash bag Scott looked at Teena's bloody face. Her nose was moved over to the right side, and obviously broken. Her right eye was closing, bruised, and changing color in front of him as he watched. She wasn't crying, or struggling, she was totally out of it.

Continuing to look at her body, her moderately muscular, athletic build found itself lacking to compete with her breasts and her lovely, light skinned complexion. Her brown eyes and short, curly hair finished off her look of beauty. Second only to Robin, she would have been his next choice. Scott didn't have much time now, soon Nick would be coming back. He handcuffed her wrists behind her. Taking the trash bag, he pushed as much as he could into her mouth, and then rolled her over on her stomach. Pulling the blanket over her, he quickly left the camper.

Looking around, he didn't see Nick yet. He grabbed his clothes and moved behind a tree close the to the main door to finish getting dressed. He had just pulled up his pants and tucked in his shirt when Nick approached. Stepping out from the side of the tree, Scott shined his flashlight in Nick's face.

"Stop right there. Is this your site?" the CO asked.

Nick was surprised and had jumped backwards when the CO popped out.

"Yes. Just got here today," Nick replied.

"We are looking for an escaped inmate. He's rumored to be in this area. Do you mind if I look around here, and check your camper? We gotta be sure," The CO asked.

"No worries. My wife's inside," Nick told him.

Scott made sure to talk quietly, and to stay slightly outside of the light of the camper. With him shining the flashlight towards Nick, that also helped to hide his appearance, it was obvious he wasn't recognized.

"Lead the way then," the CO said.

Nick took the steps and opened the door. Climbing in, he saw his wife sleeping under the blankets. The CO followed him inside and closed the door behind him. Nick called out to his wife. When she didn't answer, he took another step. Scott hit him from behind with the flashlight, knocking him out. Nick fell forward, face first, on the floor between Teena and their small kitchen sink. Rummaging through the cabinet doors underneath, he found a set of steak knives and dinnerware; it wasn't what he was looking for. Checking the stove and then the top of the sink, he found the knife block. It was a small one, and only held four of the main knives one would use.

"No one ever has a boning knife nowadays, nobody," Scott said passionately.

Taking the smallest one, he knelt over Nick and slit his throat, before turning his attention to Teena. Raising the bloody knife out in front of him, he pulled back the blanket, exposing her light skinned, voluptuous body. Standing at the foot of the bed, he reached down and rolled her over on her back, taking in her beauty. With her vision impaired, her eye left the bloody knife and slowly followed him as he crawled onto the bed before she looked away. Teena closed her one good eye and began crying. The trash bag was still inside her mouth, one eye was completely swollen shut, and blood slowly dripped from her nose; he took it all in as she shook and made sniffling noises. Scott called out to her, and when she opened her eye, he looked at her face and paused. Scott opened his mouth wide in an exaggerated movement and nodded his head twice. She blinked in acknowledgement, clearing away tears and opened her mouth, like he asked. Scott removed the trash bag and placed the flat of his knife across her lips.

    Teena slowly closed her eye and reopened it, trying not to shake. Scott reached above her head and turned up the radio. Now the music was drowning out the air conditioner. Looking back down at her, he removed his knife and motioned for her to get up. Scott slid to the side and waited for her to stand next to him. He positioned himself toward the center of the wall, resting his back against the window. Leaning forward, he took a handful of her hair and pushed her down to a kneeling position before letting go and then stared at her. Teena cried harder now, as Robin's boyfriend removed his pants. He exposed his penis and motioned for her to approach by shaking his head slightly to the left. Teena didn't move to him. He opened his mouth and stuck out his tongue, flicking it a few times in her direction, and again nodded.

    Teena, actively crying now, shook heavily and moved over to him hesitantly, unwillingly. Reaching to her, he grabbed her curly hair and helped move things along. Pushing her down closer, he waited for her to open her mouth wide enough. When she did, he shook her violently and pulled her around where her back faced him, to her screaming and shaking. He let go of her hair, and hugging her tightly, he entered her from behind. This was unexpected, and although slightly less traumatizing then being forced to please him with her mouth, she found herself struggling to please him another way; both were unacceptable to Teena, as she continued to fight, and let out a couple long grunts of frustration.

    Teena's efforts to dislodge Scott only helped him to get where he wanted to go. The knife he held to the left of her face was easily seen and kept her from screaming further, although she still struggled against him. She moaned and twisted and turned, moving her body away from him as best she could, while his penis thrusting inside her kept Teena jumping. This was perfect for him, and although it would only last a minute, it was equally exciting for him, and horrible for her. As he started coming, he leaned forward, bending her down to face the floor. Finishing, he ran the knife against the side of her neck. Holding her head bent over with all his strength, Scott found it somewhat unnecessary as she immediately stopped fighting. The last thing she saw was her dead husband on the floor in front of her, only a foot away.

Only one thing left to do here, Scott thought. He took the knife he used and ran it underwater in their kitchen sink, wiped off the handle and threw it in their trash. Reaching for his belt, he flipped the leather snap and took out his 4-inch Allagash folding hunting knife. He opened it and locked it in place. *There was nothing more special than this knife*, he thought as he rotated it for a closer inspection.

Setting it down on the foot of the bed, he picked up the woman and placed her dead center with the back of her knees resting against the edge of the bed and her feet dangling near the floor. Taking his Allagash, he inserted it as deep as he could, slightly above her pubic bone, twisted the blade, then slid it upward several inches. Pushing his hand inside, he felt around until he found what he was looking for. A few more cuts and he pulled out her stomach, placing it slightly above her belly button. He examined the contents, and finding nothing noticeable, he placed it back inside. Moving Nick next to her, he did the same to him, to another disappointing result.

"Listen folks. Skipping dinner and going straight to the alcohol and sex is no way to feed your body," Scott spoke out loud.

Wiping his hunting knife on the man's T-shirt, he cleaned the blade from the excess blood. *A few seconds for some quick pictures*, he thought, and after checking them, he pulled the blanket up over their heads. He hid them from view as best he could, turned the radio up a little higher, and left. He locked the door and went back to continue searching for Robin and the rest of her friends. Scott walked around slowly, keeping just inside the darkness, but he saw no other activity to investigate. He decided to go back to his camper for some more coffee, and some left-over pizza. *Now where did I leave that coffee mug,* he thought.

SATURDAY

It's full! It's full!

Two sites away, three women were deciding one thing: whether or not to let their fire die out so they could go to bed, or if they should add wood and prepare for s'mores! Three times now, Robin, Christy, and Linda decided both ways. The only thing they *could* agree on was alcohol before vegetables before meat.

"I'm calling it," Robin said.

"We will honor the Carnea!" she said excitedly.

"Great. Wait-what?" Linda asked.

Christy knew what that meant. She got up, and taking the poker, pulled the main pieces of wood to the sides, and out of the embers. She meant to let the fire die out. *We would have s'mores another night, possibly Saturday night or Sunday*, Linda thought.

The three made their way inside to settle in for whatever sleep they could get. So, suffice it to say the women were sleeping in today due to EHO; the girls knew that acronym to mean *Everyone's Hung Over*. It would probably be noon before they even thought about getting up. Saturday would be a lake day. Everyone would be swimming, laying out, oh and yeah, drinking.

Later on, their plans were for the three to meet up with the newlyweds and the boys for dinner, s'mores, and a campfire game or two. *It was going to be fun,* Robin thought, *just as long as her soon-to-be ex-boyfriend didn't kill their weekend.* She was actually glad he worked.

Christy and Linda fell asleep, or passed out, rather quickly. Robin's mind lingered. As she drifted off to sleep, her last thought was that it would be easier for her to just rip the Band-Aid off.

Off to the side of the girl's camper were a man and a woman with an RV. It was hours after the women had gone to bed, and it was early in the morning, but some were already stirring. The man walked around the campsite looking this way and that, checking things out from the night before. He gathered some wood and started the first steps to building a fire.

As particular as Shanelle's scrunchies that tied up her hair were, Thomas had his hats; he really loved his cowboy hats! He often wore them out in public, and he had a different color for each day of the week. Although his hats were mainly different shades of brown, he did have an off white one or two, but his favorite by far was a large rimmed black one. It was well worn and showed its age, but it was a quality hat, which he wore as often as he could; that black hat had gone to more parties and had line danced more than he cared to confess.

When it came to fishing or boating though, he usually wore a ballcap. The bill was always bent in a rounded shape that hugged his face, with their colors being generally white. He did have a few darker colored ones that he wore later in the day, but in the heat of the sun, white was definitely preferred.

Slightly older looking than his wife Shanelle, Thomas wore his gray well. For the most part, he was well shaved, sporting only a gray mustache that gently curled downward on the sides. The ends were a lighter gray, looking as if the tips had been dipped in white paint, with the portion above the lips being somewhat darker. His balding head offered more gray hair on the sides than it did on the top, but it wasn't from wearing hats. Thomas was a bit thinner, not frail, just thinner. He had enough muscles to do what he needed to do. He was an excellent handyman, and an even better fisherman. Thomas was nothing if not outdoorsy; *putting me behind a desk would be a death sentence*, he would often tell others.

Shanelle had thick, wispy dirty blonde hair, usually pulled back loosely, allowing stragglers to spread out and move in the wind like the legs of a nervous spider. She was in her mid-forties and mildly heavy set; *not overly so, just hearty*, she would laughingly tell others. Shanelle looked like how one would picture a frontier woman to be. She also had the mentality and the skills to go along with that distinction; she was handy in the kitchen, she had a recipe for whatever you needed her to cook, and often improvised in such a manner that one would say, *that has an interesting taste, what's in it?*

Like Thomas, she too could fish. They were competitive at everything, but nothing more so than fishing. She baited her own hooks, she could captain the boat to where she wanted to go, she had her favorite fishing holes, just like Thomas; with the exception of maintaining the boat, which is what he did, Shanelle was an equal partner in all things outdoors.

Together they made a great couple. Watching them interact out in public, and listening to them speak, one could not help to notice their love for each other. Their similarities, their differences, and their passion were shared by both with equal importance; their passion was in everything that they did. Even when they fought, it was together, passionate, and even sometimes violent. Arguing seemed to be another subject that they were both equally competitive on; no one wanted to lose an argument, especially not to the other.

Before it was even daylight, Thomas and Shanelle were giving it hell. Like most mornings, Thomas was responsible for making coffee, and Shanelle would cook breakfast. Most of the time it was thick sliced bacon with a variation of eggs, with or without toast or fried potatoes. All this was done outside, either on a fire started by Thomas, or an electric griddle. This was both good and bad for nearby, or downwind campers. They would smell something incredible, and either be happy, or sad.

Whether or not they started their mornings early depended on if they were going fishing that morning, and if they were able to wake up after a late night of partying. Thomas and Shanelle's beverage of choice was alcohol; sometimes it was beer, sometimes margaritas, bourbon, or anything in between. Last night involved mainly beer, and it was an early night; this lent favorably towards an early day of fishing.

They sat at their nearby picnic table and enjoyed their fried bacon, eggs, and potatoes with each holding an oversized mug of hot strong black coffee. Shanelle always made enough to have some leftovers. This was to be reheated and prepared if visitors came, or to have something quick to add to another meal, today was no different. There were enough eggs to feed at least two additional campers. This would provide useful down the road when they met new camping friends.

Shanelle would clean up breakfast, while Thomas would do basic maintenance on the boat. He was supposed to have done it last night but had put it off. He thanked Shanelle for once again reminding him of that fact, as he drained the oil, changed the filters, and the spark plugs. After performing all those steps, he ensured that the new filters and plugs were firmly in place before starting to tidy things up. Shanelle finished putting away breakfast and started to plan for lunch. She whipped up chicken salad, cut up some fresh vegetables, and grabbed a half pint of ranch dressing, placing them all into an insulated bag, then added ice. In another bag she placed some bottles of beer and water; her part of prep was now done.

Stepping up to the screen door, she stuck her head out and assessed his progress; she didn't like what she saw. Thomas had moved a picnic table closer to the boat's engine and had several pieces of equipment and parts cluttered about, as he was poking something else inside the engine with the flat end of a long screwdriver. *Not good*, she thought. *Not good at all.*

"Is everything OK?" she asked.

"There's an O-ring that needs to be replaced. She's leaking fuel," he replied.

"So, what do we need to do then?" Shanelle asked, as her cell phone made the first of several notification sounds.

"I'm going to continue to clean this out, I need you to run into town and get a few of those rings. I'll replace it and have a spare for the next time this happens," he said to her.

Blah blah. Blah blaaaah, blah-blah, is what Shanelle heard from Thomas.

"So, no fishing this morning, got it," Shanelle replied as she left to get her purse, keys, and another coffee for her trip.

Thomas shook his head *yes* to her as she left. When she had driven out of sight, he shook it to the sides. It was late into the morning, almost afternoon when Shanelle returned to Thomas sitting in a chair by their fire pit. He was drinking a beer and taking a break. All of the cleaning had been done, it was close to lunch time, and he needed a break.

"I'll get lunch ready," Shanelle said grinning, as she tossed the small bag to him.

Finishing his beer, Thomas got up and started putting it all back together. He had just tightened the last bolt when the camper door opened, and Shanelle brought out a couple of plates.

"I'll get the beer," Thomas said, taking hurried steps to the cooler.

Lynn didn't arrive to close to 2 a.m. last night. She had driven about forty minutes to arrive at the campground when she did, and when she arrived the front gate would not let her through. They called for him to come and pick her up. It turned out that there was only one vehicle allowed at the site, so her car would be left in the parking lot adjacent to the main gate.

When the call came through, James was finishing alternate endings for Nier: Automata on his PS4 gaming platform. He saved his progress and wrote down some notes of where he was supposed to start, and what he was to do next, and left for the front gate. Picking Lynn up he gave her a hug and drove her to Site 123. Parking out front and off to the side, he backed in and shut 'er down, turning off the lights.

The site was illuminated by the lights hanging on the awning and his Beacon of Hope; they were her favorite parts of his campsite. The *Beacon of Hope*, as it was called, was a vertical cigar-shaped series of colored plastic interlocking pieces. It was in a series of six stripes in the gay pride flag colors. Starting at the top it went red, orange, yellow, green, blue, and then purple at the bottom. Suspended from a shepherd's hook and powered by a forty-watt light bulb, it could easily be seen from camp sites on opposite ends of the campground's main road.

He had done as much for Lynn ahead of time as he could. The camper heat was on (which he never used when by himself), extra blankets were on the bed, (he only required one), and he had a bottle of Tanqueray gin in the freezer (he preferred bourbon).

Those three things made her happy, them and James himself. Altogether, those things helped her to relax. *Camping trips are nothing if not relaxing*, Lynn smiled. Nothing bad ever happens while camping…

Lynn made herself a medium size glass of Sprite Zero and Tanqueray and went to the bedroom to burry herself beneath the blankets and enjoy the heat. It wasn't long before they fell asleep. On her side of the bed, Lynn was underneath three blankets, and on James' side, as normal, he only used one. The morning would be half gone before Lynn felt awake enough to rise from bed. James was up for hours by this point, playing his PS4, and drinking coffee when Lynn first started to stir. This wasn't until early afternoon, which didn't bother Lynn at all, after all, it was the weekend!

A couple of sites over, the three girls had not yet started breakfast, while their neighbors Thomas and Shanelle were nearly finished with their lunch. This was a prime example of the first rule of camping, there were no rules of camping. One camped when and how one wanted to camp. Breakfast could be had any time of the day, the same would be true for dinner.

Robin woke up fully rested and buried beneath two women. Christy's right breast was on her right forearm, and Robin's left hand partially palmed Linda's ass. Any man would consider himself unworthy of awaking in such a manner. Robin smiled as she had an idea. She began squeezing Linda's cheeks with her left hand. With her right, she slid her elbow out and took Christy's breast, assaulting her nipple. None of these actions had initiated reactions; the two were totally knocked out.

"Oh, come on!" Robin said loudly.

"Time to get it up, girls!"

Robin slapped Linda's ass, and then pinched Christy's nipple. Both girls jumped into the air, cursing. *There's my reaction*, Robin smiled.

"Wakey, wakey. There are two, possibly three soon-to-be

ex-boyfriends just waiting on the beach for each of us, let's go!" Robin shouted.

Both women turned over and tried to sneak in a snooze, as if Robin were their psychotic, human alarm clock. Reaching over to Linda, she pinched her waist.

"An energy bar for you," she said to her.

"And a meal replacement for you," Robin said, pinching Christy next.

On that note, Robin jumped to the floor with a thud and made her way into the kitchen to start their coffee. The three girls sat at their dinette with half-closed eyes, as the coffee finished brewing. There was a coffee machine that used pods not a foot away, sure, but making a single pot for multiple caffein-addicted patients made more sense. When it finished, each girl in turn filled their cups and walked outside to the fire pit to enjoy their morning. The girls' usual pecking order was not followed when it came to coffee, as evidenced by Linda making her way out the camper first. This time, Robin was last, although she didn't understand why.

Outside, the three girls sat around their fire pit with half-closed eyes and coffee mugs in hand. They sipped their coffees, and when their eyes finally worked properly, they looked at each other with the same revelation: *It's afternoon?* Laughter broke out, and when their coffee was finished, they went back inside to put their bathing suits on underneath the clothes they were wearing.

A quick trip to the newlyweds to capture Teena was in order, the boys were on their own today, they agreed. The girls would walk there, and then take Robin's truck to the nearby beach. When they were closer, there seemed to be something wrong. The girls looked at each other, before slowly approaching, and continued checking their site out as they moved even closer. Immediately opposite the newlywed's camper door, Robin went to knock, but stopped and looked at the others.

"I can't do it," Robin told them. "I just can't."

"I know, right. We *all know* what country music means, and when it's this loud, we should not be here, we should go," Christy said in a serious tone before snickering.

Linda smirked, and turned around to walk back, but waited for the others. She was quickly joined by them, then they all walked back to Robin's truck. The girls ran inside the camper to grab a few things, then they left for the beach.

She pulled in and parked as far away as she could, with no vehicles next to her truck. The girls knew Robin did this, they knew why she did this, so it didn't matter to them.

"You know the rule, Robin," Christy said smiling.

"You parketh at a distance, you carryeth at a distance," Linda finished. It didn't matter to Robin, either.

"Well, you know *my* rule: gas or ass, no one rides for free," Robin smiled.

"Besides, I have the keys?"

"Well, I'm not sleeping with you," Linda stated.

"I've slept with her; wasn't that good," Christy said matter-of-factly.

"You've both slept with me," Robin laughed.

"Yeah, yeah. Come on, give me a hand," Christy said as she took one side of the heavy cooler.

Linda took the other, and both followed Robin to the beach with absent smiles.

"It is the way," Robin said, looking over her shoulder.

Robin surveyed the sparsely populated beach and turned to move closer to a busier area. She didn't want them laying out all by themselves when they were there to meet boys.

"Over here," Robin said as she turned again.

A frisbee flew dangerously close, landing in front of Christy. A moderately tall, well-built man with blonde hair reached down and picked it up, exposing his back side to her. Turning slightly to his left, he gave her his *butt shot,* and walked a few steps away before stopping and turning around, laughing.

"It's me!" Brian said, still laughing hysterically.

"Eww!!! Oh my GOD! EWW!!!" Christy said, then laughed.

"We're over here guys," Robin told them; "move closer!"

"That will teach you!" Linda scolded.

The friends would spend the rest of the afternoon together, swimming, playing frisbee, attempting a pickup game of volleyball, and laying out. After determining they all sucked at volleyball, the girls finished the rest of their afternoon laying out, while the boys spent their time swimming, throwing frisbee, and sucking at volleyball.

The girls had gone through all their water bottles, and in secret, all the beer in the cooler. Having not brought food, they thought about going to the general store for snacks before they remembered they had s'mores.

"S'mores?" Robin asked the girls.

"Yes please!" they answered in unison.

Looking over at the boys, they were still sucking at volleyball. The girls looked at each other, and then to the boys. Again, they looked at each other, and back to the boys. Robin flailed her arms in the air like a sex crazed teenager waiting to be noticed. Half of the people between them and the boys turned and stared, just not the boys. Pointing to the water, she waited for someone to determine if she was trying to reach them.

"And that's how it's done," Robin said as Joseph looked her way and shrugged his shoulders to query.

Pointing to the cooler, and back at him, she waited for Joseph to agree. Shaking his head *yes*, Robin had her answer. With large smiles, the girls walked up to their truck to leave, notably lighter than when they had arrived.

Back over at the campsite, the girls walked inside somewhat hungry and relaxed. Linda asked if they would be able to shower one after the other in the camper without running out of hot water. Robin thought so but had some fun with her answer.

"Well, we should probably shower in pairs to conserve the heat," Robin said seriously and walked inside, turning on the water in the shower.

"Linda, are you coming, hon?" Robin asked.

Linda stood still, staring as Robin removed her shirt and

put her hands behind her to loosen the top of her bathing suit.

"Not yet I guess," Christy said, "But I am…"

Everyone burst into laughter.

"Go ahead Linda, you can shower first," Robin said.

Linda walked past her and into the bathroom. Robin followed her inside and paused, before again breaking out in laughter, and leaving. Linda quickly closed the door. Robin and Christy looked at each other, and more laughter filled the camper.

"Yeah, funny. Not," came from behind the bathroom door.

By the time the boys arrived, all the girls had finished showering, changed clothes, started the campfire, and pulled out all the ingredients for s'mores. Brian saw Robin hovering by the fire, poking it with a stick, and the other two girls sitting in chairs, drinking wine.

"I know," Brian said, "it appears we are not needed," as they carried the cooler to the picnic table and set it down.

"Maybe for one thing," Joseph laughed.

There really wasn't a need for small talk, jokes, serious conversation, or communication in general when s'mores were involved. This was the most relaxed they had been in months. Looking around, Brian turned his head in a large circle, before turning back to face Robin. She smiled and handed the boys the last two s'mores, promising to make more later.

"Anyone notice anything wrong with all of this?" Brian asked, between biting off a small chunk of graham cracker, dropping both chocolate and marshmallow onto his left shoe.

The girls looked at each other, at the boys, around the campsite; Robin looked further outside their initial circle, checking out her truck, the road, neighboring campers. *The neighboring campers. Where were the newlyweds*, she thought.

"The newlyweds," Linda blurted out, beating Robin to the punch.

"Yeah, wonder where they are?" Robin asked.

"You know where they are. We all know where they are. They could have just stayed at their place all weekend long. It would have saved them some money," Linda said sarcastically.

"Don't be hating on them because they are getting theirs, at least you have Robin," Christy said laughing.

The rest followed. Even Linda placed a smile on her face,

although short lived.

"Let them do what they want to do," Joseph said seriously; "they seem incredibly happy. Let's make a point to run into them tomorrow, we'll break down their door if we have to."

"Tomorrow it is," Christy cheered.

Brian put more wood on the fire. Joseph ran back to their camper to grab their chairs. Robin replenished everyone's drinks. The group finished another round of s'mores and being too full to plan dinner at the moment, decided to take in nature and enjoy their drinks. Within no time, everyone sat relaxing and enjoying each other's company this fine afternoon around a warm, roaring campfire.

While Robin and her friends were relaxing together at one end of the campground, over at the amphitheater, Scott was not. Although it was only afternoon, with all the work he was putting in searching for her at all hours of the day, he was exhausted. He found it hard to concentrate without knowing where she was. There wasn't enough coffee in the world to keep him going. No matter how many cups he made, no matter when he drank them, caffeine didn't seem to help, not anymore, so he tried to take a short nap.

Scott couldn't obtain any measurable amount of sleep, no matter how hard he tried. Every time he awoke, he would try to reach out and communicate with Robin. With all the girls' phones locked up in the glove box of her truck, the messages were never checked. They came in as texts, voicemails, and even a few video chats, none of which were answered. It's not communication unless a response to the initial message is received by the sender. Scott had no way of knowing that Robin never received those messages, so he thought the worst.

He grew furious that she would not talk to him. The anger he felt was a contributing factor that interfered with his sleep. For hours now, he tried and failed to get rest, he tried and failed to reach Robin; and because of those failures, he could not sleep.

Scott continued to toss and turn, and although he wanted to sleep, and his body demanded it, he could not rest.

J ames left the camper wearing an old white T-shirt, blue shorts, and six- year-old white sneakers; he never wore nice or new clothes for this process, nor did he shower before, he always showered *after* emptying the black and gray water from the camper. He produced a pair of gloves from his pocket and put them on. Walking over to his truck, he lowered the tailgate and pulled the gray container to him, removing the lid. Picking it up he carried it to the side of the camper. Lynn looked at the contents, which all looked strange to her.

"It's all the cables, hoses, and connectors for emptying the wastewater. I use them at the dump station when we leave, and times like today, when we are doing a partial," he said, answering the puzzled look on her face.

James connected his hose to the camper black water side of the Y adapter at one end, and the other to the Smurf. He pulled the black water lever on the side to release the tank's contents. The hose straightened, and liquid and solid material started to quickly flow. James was watching the waste hauler fill up when the black water hose disconnected. He slammed the lever closed and angrily looked away. Lynn was over his shoulder, about twelve feet away, biting her lip and trying not to laugh.

He was splashed with the black dirty water about his face, his shirt, shorts, and shoes. It was all he could do not to cuss or to act out in anger. Glancing over at Lynn, it was obvious she knew, she wouldn't even look at him. Continuing to stare at her, he noticed she was trying really hard not to laugh. Lynn looked on, still biting her lip. She did not laugh, nor did she say she was sorry, or offer to help; she could not speak at all, it was too dangerous. She started to shake, and after looking away, she burst into laughter.

James replaced the hose and wrapped an old towel over where it connected to the Smurf. Keeping a foot on it, he pressed down and stood up, leaning back as far as he could. He stretched forward with one hand, and slowly released the lever. Success! He watched until the liquid fill line was a little over ¾ full before pushing it closed.

"That's how it was supposed to have worked the first time," James said laughing.

By now, Lynn had finished shaking and laughing, almost.

"I'm sorry," she managed, before again biting her lip.

He attached the cod pin into the handle after connecting it to the Smurf. Gently pulling to the right, he turned the blue Smurf around and walked slowly to the truck, pulling it behind him. When he was close enough, he put the handle over the ball of the hitch, and searched for his second cod pin, he didn't have it. James checked inside the truck, the container that the hoses were in, and his pockets; it was nowhere to be found. *I'll have to drive slowly,* he thought, as he told Lynn he would be right back.

James disconnected the hose and placed it in the plastic container and loaded it on the truck. He closed the tailgate, got in, and looked around before pulling out onto the road and turning right. He would be going uphill, and as long as he drove slowly, all would be fine. He lowered his window and listened as he drove. He heard the noise from the plastic wheels rolling over the rough road. Occasionally a wheel would hit a rock or piece of gravel, making a bit more noise, but all was well. He raised his window, put his blinker on to turn right, and started to gently apply his brakes about a hundred or so feet before his turn.

He started to come to a stop, and that's when it happened. Lynn was watching James drive down the road, slowly hauling the blue Smurf behind him, when it separated from the white handle and started coming down the hill all by itself. The handle stayed on the truck, throwing metal sparks several feet behind him as it bounced against the road. As he came to a complete stop, a car passing him slowed and beeped their horn. Lowering his window, the woman excitedly told him he was dragging something.

Looking out his rear window he saw the blue Smurf rolling down the hill. He thanked them and turned around after it. Lynn watched in horror as the blue rectangle full of black water travelled down the gray road back to her, avoiding the green grass. It would move a little to the left, then a little to the right, but for the most part, it stayed on the road, as if it had a mind of its own. She saw James turn his truck around and speed up, but he would not make it in time; she doubted she could even catch it herself before it crashed. Looking at the campground across the road from her, Lynn saw a couple working together on their boat. The man would ask for a tool, and the woman would hand it to him; they were oblivious to what was going to happen.

"It's full! It's full! Watch out!!!" Lynn shouted at them.

The couple looked at her, and then down to where the noise was coming from. Heading straight for them, totally out of control and unmanned, came the blue rectangular waste hauler. Lynn crossed the road and tried to intercept it. She would not make it. James was going the maximum speed that he could, and he tried to intercept it. He would not make it. Just when Lynn thought it was over for them, it turned to the right and went into the grass. That slowed it down tremendously, and with a slight incline, it came to a complete stop, one foot from the couple's boat.

"Hi! I'm Lynn," she said to them, laughing.

James pulled up and got out, apologizing. He too introduced himself.

"This is Thomas and Shanelle. They'll be here all week long," Lynn said laughing.

"Well, I smell right now. Let me take care of this and we'll stop by later this afternoon, if that's OK," James said.

"Sounds good," Shanelle replied.

"Just so you know, I'm not shaking your hand," the man said laughing.

Lynn left to go back to the camper when James moved the waste hauler back to the truck and secured it with some wire. Taking off back up to the hill, he had no issues making it to the dump station and emptying the Smurf. Rinsing it out before he attached it back to the truck, he headed back, with his tail between his legs.

Parking the truck where it was before, he disconnected the Smurf and rolled it back underneath the camper. He placed the lid back on the plastic container and started walking to the door.

"Oh no you don't," Lynn told him.

James looked at her, stopping dead in his tracks. She was pointing to the picnic table, where she had piled up clean clothes for him to change into, and a trash bag for what he was wearing. She then pointed to the distant comfort station and laughed. James entered the building, walked up to the second shower stall, and stripped down to clean up.

Lynn didn't shower, she didn't need to. James had his in the comfort station, so he was good. They laid down for an hour and took a nap to refresh their batteries. It was Lynn's idea; something told her tonight would be a late evening with their new friends.

Their neighbors were slightly older, had an RV that they drove, and a truck that pulled a boat. James had lots of questions and couldn't wait to bend their ears. Lynn and James were on a different course at present, at a different point in their lives than the other couple were. James had rented pontoons before, which were awesome; but it was the only boating experience he had. James and Lynn had camped in a hybrid model camper, and after seeing how much they loved camping, and the limitations of the design, the following season they upgraded to a pull behind model with a slide out. The way he figured it, it was only a matter of time before they too had a center console, fish killing boat, and an RV they drove instead of pulling, to boot!

James and Lynn grabbed a few beers each and left the camper to spend time with their new friends. They wanted to come over for a few beers and talk a little before dinner, and then they would part ways. They didn't want to take up all their time, they just wanted to get to know them. Upon crossing the road and walking about twenty feet they saw Thomas setting up cornhole. James had been meaning to get one for some time now. It turns out that there are rules and specifications to be mindful of. He didn't know any of those, he just knew he like to play.

"Hello guys," James said as they walked between their RV and where the boat used to be.

"Had your shower then?" Thomas asked smirking.

James nodded, laughing. He tried to hide his disappointment when he looked to Thomas and asked about the boat.

"Thomas, did you guys launch your boat?" James asked.

"We just got back, actually. It's floating down by the amphitheater. It's closer than the boat ramp. It gets us on the lake quicker," Thomas said.

The guys went to the left, with Thomas setting up the boards, and James watching and talking about scoring; and Lynn going to the right, where Shanelle was standing with an unusually large teal sippy cup. It seemed natural, like good friends who haven't seen each other in a long time catching up. Shortly after clarifying some issues about scoring and the rules in general, James started asking questions about the boat, with Thomas only too happy to share his thoughts and opinions on that particular model.

The girls were talking while the guys were talking and were unaware that the game had already been set up. Thomas was starting to give the specifications on the boat when he was interrupted.

"Well, it's a 21-foot 6-inch Triumph, two thousand and, " Thomas managed, before a bag arced through the air and came down, slamming against the board.

"Guessing you guys are ready then?" Shanelle said laughing.

"Can you walk it out to see if the distance is good?" Thomas asked.

"I'll do it. How far should it be?" Lynn asked.

"Twenty-seven feet, inside to inside," was his reply.

"HB, that's twenty-seven *normal size feet*," James said laughing.

Shanelle looked over at Lynn, and then watched her count out the distance. It probably wasn't close because she had small feet, but Shanelle didn't care too much about that, she was curious about the '*HB*'… Lynn was all set; *it was close*, she thought, as she went back to Shanelle.

"HB?" Shanelle asked.

"James, what does HB stand for?" Lynn asked from twenty-something feet away.

"Honey Bear. It's our nickname," he replied.

"We have another nick name for you," Thomas said slyly.

James paused but didn't dwell too much on his statement. Thomas looked on and smiled. Looking back at him, James raised his beer and took a sip.

"Over here, try one of these," Thomas said pointing to the cooler by the camper.

James opened it and dug through the ice. He pulled out a Redds apple cider.

"Never had that before; any good?" James asked.

"Well, by God," Thomas replied.

James finished his beer and opened the Redds; he found it wonderful.

Shanelle wanted the boys versus girls for cornhole, but she also wanted to talk to Lynn and get to know her, so couples it was. As the couples played, the boys started off strong, with them winning most of the points for their teams, for the first two games, anyway. The more they played, the more they all drank. The girls played better as the afternoon progressed; it was now their turn to win the points.

"You know, they are going to be impossible to live with if they get on the same team," Thomas stated, as Lynn's bag slid past Shanelle's and fell into the hole, ending their fifth game.

"Yup," James said, finishing another Redds.

Everyone walked to Thomas and Shanelle's picnic table. With Lynn and James raising their beers to honor their new friends, they sat down.

"You know, we were going to take the boat out this afternoon to catch some fresh fish for dinner, would you like to come? We can have a fish fry afterwards?" Shanelle asked.

James and Lynn were talking things through when a golf cart pulled up. Everyone looked over and waved at the campground hosts as they worked on placing their sign.

"We need one of those." Lynn stated, as the golf cart turned the corner and disappeared.

"Maybe someday, getting a boat is a big decision, you know," James replied as he took another sip of his Redds and smiled.

"Yeah, right," Lynn laughed. "I was talking about the golf cart."

"Time to go all, let's clean up later. Hurry up. Let's get out on the water and fish!" James said excitedly, and without getting Lynn's buy-in.

Everyone looked at each other as he stood, drained his

Redds, and quickly placed the empty bottle on the table.

"We need fish! A man's gotta eat. Let's go!" James shouted as he headed for his camper to grab his tackle, a few poles, and some fresh bait.

"Well, that's it then," Thomas said as he threw his empty beer can into the trash and went to get ready.

Within minutes everyone was walking up to where James was already standing, small coolers in hand. Moments after that, they were on their way to the amphitheater. Thomas' boat was often left there overnight so they could quickly get back out on the lake. The walk would take a little longer than normal, as James was the weakest link. His left foot was still healing from a sore that seemed to hinder him at the most inopportune of times, making him walk significantly slower than the rest.

It was midafternoon when the CO was startled out of his latest attempt at sleep by what he referred to as a small army surrounding his camper and demanding his surrender. Half a dozen beer cans flew into the air when he sat straight up in bed. He was exhausted, his eyes would barely open, and his breath was foul. Turning to his left towards his bedroom door window he closed his eyes and listened. Laughing, joking, and bickering could be heard as they tromped along through the wooded trail. They made enough noise to wake the dead; although with as much experience as he had with the dead, Scott had never seen them come back to life for any reason.

He listened as they continued on, their voices and noise growing quiet in the distance. The CO turned his head to the foot of the bed and saw it covered with blood, beer cans and an open pizza box. He slid off the edge of the foam bed, so he would not make noise. Standing up he had taken one step when a piece of pizza that was stuck to the side of his face fell, splattering on the laminate floor at his feet. From the looks of the half-eaten piece, it was pepperoni and sausage, *my favorite!*

The CO reached out and grabbed a nearby blanket.

Searching for a clean spot he wiped off his face and threw it back on the bed. Making his way to the kitchen he started a pot of coffee. He was sure it was late afternoon by this point; it wouldn't be much longer before it was night again and he could continue his search. Taking a large cup of black goodness, he stood with his eyes again closed and finished the entire cup. Pouring himself another, he went to the bathroom to begin his daily ritual.

He felt himself starting to come alive. The coffee was definitely helping him jump-start his afternoon. His eyes were open now as he enjoyed his coffee and looked out through the open bathroom door to think. The last thing he remembered about Mary was that he had decided to leave her in the enclosure. *He did leave her in the enclosure,* he thought. It must have been some time after he came back to the camper, after he had his pizza and beer, that he had thought about bringing her back here. *Weird,* he thought. The CO stood and closed the toilet lid, pulling his underpants up. Walking out he turned and closed the bathroom door.

"What the hell do you think *YOU* are looking at?" he said loudly, slowly turning his head to the bedroom and smiling at the park official's naked body.

"Daddy's home," he mumbled as he walked in and shut the sliding door.

Looking down at Mary, he was once again distracted by all the noise outside. Peeking out the corner of the window, he searched for them. Down at the lagoon, he watched as the four made their way to the boat. One at a time they boarded the center console; *he had never seen so many fishing poles on a boat before,* Scott thought. The CO watched them from a curtained window in his bedroom until the boat made its way out into the lake and turned port side, disappearing out of sight. It was obvious to him that he was still safe, and that no one had known who was hiding here in the camper.

Scott didn't want to miss an opportunity to take a picture

with Mary here in the camper. He sleepily made his way to the main door and took his cell phone off charge. Walking back to the bedroom he stopped just inside the doorway and turned off the flash. He went to take her picture and he saw that he already had one of her on the bed in his camper. Opening the viewer, he pulled it up. It was taken with Mary posed just like she was, from almost the same exact spot where he was standing now, but it was taken around 3:30 a.m.! *That was hours ago,* he thought; thinking back, he had no memory of it.

Looking at his phone, he wondered, then swiped left. It was a picture of Mary sitting in a camping chair by a fire pit-his fire pit! Another swipe and Mary was leaning forward through the main gate office window, with her breasts hanging over the edge. Swiping left again and Mary was posed on the hood of the DNR vehicle, her butt in the air, on her tippy toes, with her hands reaching over her head holding the wiper blades. Again, and Mary was sitting in the front seat behind the wheel, with her hands at the correct 10 and 2 positions. He swiped again, he had to see the next one. Mary was in the back seat on her back, with her knees bent at a 45-degree angle, her hands over her eyes.

The earliest picture was time stamped 3:11 a.m.; Scott had been busy, very busy. He had started taking pictures outside the raptor center around 3:11 a.m. and had driven them to the front gate for a picture there, and then back to his site at his fire pit, before taking her inside for the final pose on the bed. *Wait,* he thought, was there an earlier picture than the back seat? Nope. Looking over at the bedroom's sliding door, he closed it, and with a grin, he shook his head, turned around and jumped back into bed beside Mary, cuddling in close.

James watched as the boat turned to the left and the distance between the banks broadened. It looked deep, wide, and with only a few boats in sight, he felt like they had the entire lake to themselves. Thomas wanted to show his new friends some of the aspects of boating, so he headed to a deep section before opening her up. Thomas was behind the center console with James beside him; the two girls were on the bench seat behind them, off to the sides of the Yamaha 150. Thomas was smiling ear to ear as he took them faster.

The wind ripped past them, plastering everyone firmly against the backs of their seats. Moving the boat slowly left and right, as if clearing pylons, Thomas slowly reduced speed before placing his girl in neutral. The boat slowed quickly, throwing everyone forward. James found himself using his feet for balance; by pushing down he kept himself from visiting the bow on all fours. Thomas took the next few minutes telling James what the different components were, what they did, how the boat did this and that. Basically, Thomas told James everything he needed to know about boating in one fell crash course.

Shanelle and Lynn looked on, enjoying the gentle swaying, the wind through their hair, the peace and quiet of the open water. Lynn breathed in deeply and closed her eyes to heighten her experience, she was in love. Shanelle took this time to move starboard side and then to the bow to open the ice cooler for some more beer.

"Lynn," Shanelle called out while holding her beer.

She smiled back at Shanelle, while everyone laughed. Thomas spent a few more minutes showing James the fish finder, telling him how to determine depth, and what the numbers on the side meant.

"Running out of daylight," Shanelle told the guys.

"Aye aye, Captain. Time to get to the fishing hole," Thomas said.

Moving the throttle forward, the boat came to life, and they were once again on their way, fighting the wind as they sliced through the water. Lynn smiled as she enjoyed the sun on her face, the wind in her hair. James loved the experience as well; except he really didn't have any hair for the wind to assault. Thomas wore a skull cap, with a fishing mask hanging loosely around his neck, while Shanelle sported her hat.

Thomas maneuvered his boat around stickups, and outside of the trees that were standing up through the water like rotting brown fingers trying to take them deep into the depths below. James looked at Thomas and waited for him to explain.

"Experience. Fish finders show you underground features, too. Also, there are maps that help you learn what areas to avoid," Thomas said loud enough to be heard past the rushing wind.

It took several minutes to navigate the wooden minefield before Thomas felt comfortable opening her up again. Minutes after that he hung a Louie that nearly sent everyone overboard, scrambling to stay on their feet.

"Woah!" Lynn managed as she hung on for dear life.

Shanelle had it easy, she just leaned in closer to Lynn, smiling. Thomas was smiling too, as he took her just above neutral, reducing her speed. They went in slowly and stopped just shy of the mouth of the inlet. He cut the engine and let her coast in.

"We'll get our tackle swapped out here, and then go in slowly, fishing as we drift," he told his new friends; Shanelle smiled, she already knew this.

Thomas reached over and picked up a pole from the port side and within seconds he was casting towards the bank, he was definitely organized. Looking at the boat, one could not help feeling both intimidated and in awe. Each side of the boat had four fishing rod holders, each sporting a fishing pole, each with a different configuration to accommodate various fishing situations. Two more holders were on the bow of the boat.

Additionally, there were six fishing poles on the canopy above the console pointing straight up to honor the fishing gods, along with three or four more lying down along the starboard walkway. Whereas James only had two fishing poles that he changed from various depths and lures as needed, Thomas just grabbed the appropriate pole. James would change the way he fished when more funds came in, he wanted to adopt this new philosophy, he just needed a few hundred dollars to make that happen. Now, from all the intense fishing that was happening, and James struggling to keep up, there was one place where James shone brightly, and Thomas saw him as the eternal Boy Scout.

James had two tackle boxes that were nearly complete, both of which were almost packed full. There was always something that he would add to them, but he did have a strong variety of tackle and items to get on with one's fishing day. He had assorted tools, tackle, gear, batteries, baits, assorted lures, hooks, floats, etc., if it had a possible use for fishing, he took it along, just in case. He would tell anyone who asked that he was a Capricorn, and he was proud of it. That, coupled with an intense Boy Scout mentality made him a strong resource for all things camping and fishing.

Both Thomas and Shanelle were fishing before James was even tackled up, but neither had caught any fish. That was, not until he looked over at Thomas. He was fighting with something, so James stopped what he was doing and watched. It was a small bass. The fish had chosen to go for a shiny golden spinner. James took note of that and changed to something similar on one pole, while setting the other one up for bottom fishing; it was the best he could do. He was sure they would bottom fish for catfish before going back to the campsite, they just had to!

While Shanelle fished to the side of Lynn, James was up by Thomas. While Lynn was relaxing, James was stressing; he still had not caught a single fish! This went on for what seemed like hours to James before Thomas had everyone pull in so they could try another spot.

"OK James, get set up for bottom fishing," Thomas said as he took off for another spot.

Thomas followed his usual protocols; he cut the engine, let her drift forward into the area they were to fish, and then he would look for a place to tie up, if applicable. It was applicable. James moved to the bow and extended his hand out to push back against the tree that protruded from the water, completely stopping the boat's forward progress. He tied a rope onto it to keep them in place. The boat changed position to the port side due to the current, then settled and stayed put.

James took the port side, and Thomas, the starboard. Lynn settled in and took in the sun, and Shanelle stayed aft. Everyone who was fishing bottom fished; and as before, both Thomas and Shanelle caught fish before James did.

"Well, that's just not right," Thomas said, looking over his shoulder at James.

"Looks like we are going to stay here until you catch a fish. Change sides with me," he told him, as Thomas placed his third catfish into the fish keeper.

He quietly moved around, swapping locations with Thomas, and cast towards the bank. No sooner did it hit the water and sink, than he was fighting with the only fish he would catch this day. Looking at Thomas and Shanelle, he excitedly said the two words that he'd been wanting to say all day.

"FISH ON!" James said with all the excitement of a six-year-old on Christmas day.

"There you go," Thomas said as he reeled in yet another catfish.

James had more water to pull his fish through than Thomas did, so before he had his in the boat, officially landing it, Thomas had already cast back out, and was awaiting his next bite.

"They are biting nicely now," Shanelle said as she pulled in another.

Thomas reached into the fish keeper and started counting.

"OK all, we have enough fish, let's go home and fry them up!" he said with a pause, as if not realizing that his crew would not dare disobey their captain's wishes.

James was sad to be leaving, he wanted to catch more fish. Lynn was sad to be leaving., she wanted more sun. Thomas and Shanelle were sad too, they wanted James to have caught more fish. Truer to the point, Lynn was sad that they all had caught fish. Although she liked to eat them, she didn't care for anyone killing them first. *I know, weird, right?* Lynn was happy though, she was happy that everyone stopped fishing when they did, providing enough food for a couple of meals, instead of fishing just to freeze an extra couple hundred pounds of cleaned fish. *Not that they could catch that much anyway*, Lynn smiled.

Everyone enjoyed the trip back to the amphitheater, the way the boat seemed at times to float effortlessly through the water, the way it cut through the wind, it was peaceful, majestic. The weather cooperated, too.

"What a lovely, sunny day," Lynn said to the agreement of all concerned parties.

Even with all of the good things that they experienced, especially firsts such as the way the boat glided to a stop or turned under the screaming power of their Yamaha 150, their trip back occurred too quickly for James and Lynn; they both wanted to stay out on the water, but for different reasons, of course.

It wasn't long before Thomas cut the engine and coasted towards the amphitheater. James and Thomas worked on locking down and closing the boat and emptying the contents that they had to take back to the camper, while the girls walked to the campsite and got Thomas' truck. The guys would then load it up and then they would take it all on one trip. Being on the lake tends to relax you or wipe your energy, depending on the person you asked. By the time the girls had come back, the contents of the boat were staged by the side of the road and the guys were sitting on a bench.

The girls backed in as far as they could and the guys loaded tackle boxes, some poles, all the coolers and some 5-gallon buckets full of catfish. The guys got in the back, between the coolers, and Shanelle drove them to their site. The girls started unloading, while the guys took to cleaning fish. They hadn't caught enough to warrant possibly waiting in line at one of the cleaning stations, so they decided to do them at the camper. Taking out a well-used cutting board and a trash bag, Thomas gave the bag to James, and kept the cutting board for himself. James told Thomas that he wasn't good or practiced at cleaning fish.

"You have to catch fish first, before you can learn how to clean them," Thomas joked.

"Hmm," was James' reply, "insightful."

Thomas told him that since they wanted to eat fish tonight, that he would filet them, and show him how to do it another time. Thomas made quick work of the catfish. After separating the filets, he cut some into nuggets, and placed everything in the metal bowl; it was James' job to gather the leftover, unused parts and place them in the bag. *This he accomplished with great skill,* James thought.

Inside, the two women sliced vegetables, peeled, and cut potatoes into slices, and refilled their drinks. They too, sat down after doing some prep work, enjoying some good conversation and cool air conditioning.

"So, you guys married yet, or just dating?" Shanelle bluntly asked.

"Dating, but we are engaged now," Lynn replied.

"Nice!" Shanelle said, sipping her drink.

"This is a great camper. How long have you had it?" Lynn asked her.

"It's new. To us, I mean," Shanelle clarified; "we're still making some repairs and tweaking it to fit our needs."

"You'll have to show me around sometime this weekend," Lynn said as she nosed through the cabin.

"Sure, we can do that," Shanelle replied, as she stood and started working on the dry mix for the fish.

The girls finished with a small tour of the camper, focusing on the washer and dryer for their clothes, and their dishwasher? *These were things that would not fit in their present camper,* Lynn thought, but down the road, if they upgraded to an RV, she would make sure they had them.

"Let's check on the guys to see how much longer on the fire," Shanelle said.

Shanelle poked her head out of their camper and saw that they had just finished cleaning the fish. She asked Lynn to go out and get the bowl while she continued on the dredge.

"I was told you had something for our dinner?" Lynn asked the guys, smiling.

Thomas handed her the bowl smiling back at her. James had finished putting the messy newspapers and the rest of the fish parts into the plastic bag.

It was at this point that everyone broke up to complete their individual tasks. Thomas worked on setting up the fire. Shanelle brought out the dredge and flour mixture for frying the fish. Lynn worked on the vegetables and placed the potatoes in foil after seasoning them with sea salt and olive oil. James took the unwanted parts of today's fishing trip to the dumpster out on the grassy island.

By the time he had returned, Shanelle was filling up a tall metal pan with peanut oil, and Lynn was positioning the potatoes on the metal grill rack on the side of the fire pit. They would take the longest, so she swung the metal rack to the center to check for proper coal placement. Soon she would position them over the coals for quicker cooking if the guys ever got the fire going.

James walked over to Thomas at the fire pit. The wood was already stacked several layers high, with kindling placed inside, and additional wood stacked vertically in a circle.

"What do you think we need now?" Thomas asked.

"Lighter fluid or gasoline," James said the first thing that entered his mind.

"A good woodsman needs not those things. A good

woodsman needs a fatty," Thomas said, sticking his hand into his pocket.

With a large smile on his face, Thomas produced one, laughing. James looked closely as Thomas explained.

"It's a section of pine tree root heavy with sap. It burns hard and ignites quickly with little effort. You can use one and if conditions are right, you won't need kindling or tinder," Thomas said, sharing one of his many camping secrets.

"Very nice!" James replied, as Thomas lit his fatty, and dropped it down to the center of the wood.

It wasn't long before the fire caught, and flames erupted dead center from inside the stacked pile.

"Shanelle knows this trick too, so don't let her fool you," he laughed.

James and Thomas sat down beside the fire, having done all the hard work that they could for the moment. The women left the camper with replenished drinks and walked over to a raging fire. Thomas was poking it and moving around the coals.

"Not much longer now," he told them.

"We just need more time to make coals. It's got to burn down a little more," James chimed in.

Perfect timing for a couple of questions on the boat, James thought.

"Hey HB. Thomas is gonna show me the boat. Can you tend the fire for a few moments?" James asked, taking a few steps towards Thomas.

Lynn grew silent. James already knew the answer; besides, they really didn't have enough time now anyway.

Several calls had come through to the gatehouse throughout the day, but none of them were answered. There was no voicemail feature available on that phone, so if no one picked up, the only other way to make contact was the volunteer's personal cell phone. Calls were made there too, but Mary did not answer that number either. With her voicemail full of multiple attempts to reach her, he was now unable to leave a message.

Herbert, the Hearty Lake asset manager, was running out of options. He was worried that Mary was unreachable, but his main concern was for the staffing of the front gate. He really didn't want to call Carmen; she was their second volunteer, she didn't have gatehouse experience, and as far as their facility went, she had only worked here a handful of times. What he did like was that she was much more technical. She was a more modern, younger, more technical volunteer, not someone who wanted to work at a campground after retiring; he saw her as someone who might want a full-time career. *Well, that's that then*, he thought, as he looked up her number and gave her a call.

"...What we need is for you to cover for Mary until she returns. You'll want to check the gatehouse to ensure everything is working properly, check the phone, reboot the computer, reload the reservation software," he rambled on before stopping.

"Just follow the steps on the sheet of paper in the file cabinet folder labelled *Instructions,* and you'll be fine. Oh, the campground hosts said Parker hasn't been seen in a few days. He's their Golden Retriever. Can you ask around for them, it would mean a lot to me," the man continued.

"If you are finished leaving your message, please press 1 to save," the voice on the phone told him.

Herbert was confident that his message was complete. *If she had questions, surely, she would call,* he thought, as he pushed 1 and hung up.

Back at Thomas and Shanelle's campsite, everyone chose to get their drink on, firepit-style, and wait for the wood to burn down to enough coals to cook their dinner. Thomas cornered James and critiqued his fishing skill, or lack thereof, while Lynn continued asking questions about what Thomas and Shanelle did for a living, where they lived, their favorite foods and colors; all things personal, Shanelle loved it. James was too busy taking notes from Thomas to fully enjoy his interaction, but the more Thomas spoke, the more James fell in love with his fishing skills, and the way he told stories and anecdotes.

It wasn't long before the fire was ready, with an ample amount of red-hot coals. Thomas put the oil on and let it start to heat up. Lynn placed the foil pack of potatoes on the coals and noted the time. The vegetables would go on last, probably after the potatoes were turned. James and Shanelle enjoyed their drinks and watched as their partners did their jobs. Thomas assessed the situation with the oil and decided to use an electric burner by the camper instead.

"It's going to be quicker, and we're all hungry!" Thomas told everyone as he put on some oven mitts and carried the pot over to the electric fryer on the picnic table.

Lynn took this opportunity to put the veggies on the edge of the grill, allowing them to cook slowly. James and Shanelle both nodded to Thomas, as they sipped their drinks, thinking about today's events. James loved spending time with Thomas, his stories, his knowledge. Shanelle loved spending time with their new friends, they seemed down-to-earth, easy to get along with, and fun. Thomas was too busy frying fish to think of anything other than that, he was laser focused. Later on, he would find a bit of time to reminisce on how fun today was.

"Everything should finish around the same time," Lynn announced as she flipped the potatoes over.

Ten minutes later fried fish was being drained on paper towels, the vegetables were being plated, and the potatoes were being given a few minutes more to finish.

"Come and get this fish before it starts getting cold," Thomas shouted over his shoulder.

Taking a piece, he tasted it for quality, before refilling the fryer with the last batch of filets and nuggets. Lynn plated the potatoes, added some extra butter, and went over to James to sit for a moment, before getting back up and grabbing a paper plate. James and Shanelle followed her lead, and by the time they got theirs, Thomas turned off the fryer and made his plate. Shanelle and Lynn went into the camper to refill their drinks.

When they sat back down by the fire pit, everyone was all situated with food and drink.

"To great friends, great food, and a great day out on the

lake!" Thomas said, as everyone raised their drinks in agreement.

Four new friends were eating today's catch, drinking cold beverages, and enjoying each other's company around the red glow of their fire pit. Not a foot away the light from the embers faded into total darkness. Thomas reached over to his side and put a few logs on the fire. He stacked them into a small pyramid and went back to his fish. When the wood caught, it threw just enough light and heat to keep their group's evening going. It was a very relaxing evening for them all.

A few sites over, the boys and girls were still relaxing around their campfire after their afternoon at the beach.

"If you work for a living, why do you kill yourself working?" Brian asked.

"Movie quotes, this late in the day, really Brian?" Joseph replied, "*The Good, the Bad and the Ugly,* 1966."

Brian smiled back at him, then turned to look at the girls. Robin was sitting on one of their matching camping chairs. They were all pink, they had a tray on the right side to hold a small plate, and a hole large enough for a single beer. They resembled a small director's chair, more than comfortable enough for camping.

The boys had brought their own. They too matched, but theirs were much larger, much more comfortable. They were oversized and bright red, with exaggerated arm rests and a high back that resembled a throne. Their arm rests didn't have an attached tray, so they each had a drink holder off to the side. They were metal rods that pushed into the ground, and the top was a spiral that hugged cups and bottles. Brian's was neon yellow, and Joseph's was neon red.

It was way past their normal dinner time, but everyone was choosing to drink instead.

"This fire is large enough to mask the bodies of three dancing naked blonde virgins," Joseph said.

"If we only knew where to find them," he finished laughing.

"Well, you're blonde, go and find two others," Christy smiled.

Between more smiles and drinking, everyone laughed, nodded, and otherwise agreed.

"I wish," Joseph remarked, taking another large sip, before he too broke out into laughter.

Brian looked away, unamused.

To the right of the fire, on a small cooler were all the leftover ingredients for s'mores. Everyone had been drinking away their dinner and had forgotten that they still had some left. Looking around, Brian saw everyone relaxing and having a good time. He absolutely loved his group of friends; *he would do anything for them, anything,* he thought, looking back at Joseph.

Taking his eyes away from him and to where the girls were sitting, he faced Christy and cleared his throat. On cue, as expected, everyone looked his way. Robin and Linda took new sips of their margaritas, Christy stopped drinking her beer, mid-sip and moved it to the side of her face to cool her down, and Joseph just laughed.

"I have a proposition," he said continuing to stare at Christy.

Joseph continued smiling, Robin and Linda drinking, Christy was indifferent.

"You had your chance, years ago," Christy laughed, sipping her beer.

Joseph was still smiling, although he was curious where this was going.

"How about we all skip dinner, make s'mores instead, and play some campfire games?" Brian proposed.

"Oh, how fun!" Robin said excitedly.

Christy finished her beer and got up to walk to the camper cooler for another, before she nodded and smiled.

"Awesome!" Linda and Joseph said at the same time.

"Then it's settled, s'mores it is!" Brian said, moving over to the pile of split wood.

The group would not have to wait long before they had a raging fire and enjoyed their s'mores. *It was good enough before it received the extra fuel, but more wood couldn't hurt,* Brian thought, smiling as he held the last log out in front of him.

"Uh huh, keep wishing buddy," Joseph said under his breath, returning his smile.

Everyone waited as the boys walked the tree line to find branches long enough to roast their marshmallows. Robin and the girls watched laughing as they continued to search. By the time they had found large enough sticks and came back, the girls had already eaten their first s'mores. Brian and Joseph stood still, attracting flies with their open mouths.

"What? You guys didn't bring your four-foot aluminum telescoping campfire marshmallow roasting poles?" Christy asked laughing.

"I've never seen you guys take so long to find your wood before, strange," Linda joked.

"I was going to go there, but I'm not touching their wood," Robin joined in.

The two boys stood there dejected, as the girls made more s'mores and started to eat in front of them.

"Oh, come now. You know these are for you guys," Robin smiled, holding hers out to Brian.

Christy did the same for Joseph. Brian took his and sat on his throne, thanking Robin, and shaking his head. Joseph reached for his and Christy pulled away laughing, as she bit his in two.

"Oh day-um!" Linda said, then extended hers out to Joseph.

"I'll take that thank you," Brian stated as he grabbed Joseph's s'mores and started enjoying his second.

"Now don't take this the wrong way, Joseph. No one is saying *you're* fat, okay?" Robin said, reaching for the bag of marshmallows to make him another.

"You guys are hilarious!" Joseph just smiled as he went to sit on his throne and await his turn.

"Not that we haven't been playing games already, but what's next?" Robin asked.

"OK, wait for it, wait for it; Never have I ever! Let's play that!" Brian blurted out, jumping up and out of his chair.

He moved closer to the fire to warm his hands before turning to the group.

"Let's arrange our chairs from youngest to oldest, fill our glasses, and the youngest goes first," Brian said in a single breath.

Everyone exploded into motion, as they moved their chairs to face the fire, placing their backs to the main road. It went Robin, Brian, Christy, Joseph, and then Linda.

"I'm not the oldest here; no fucking way am I the oldest here!" Linda said as she stood waiting.

Everyone laughed as Brian stood up and swapped chairs with her, hiding the fact that his Joseph was the oldest.

"Drink!" Robin said, pointing to him.

He obliged and took a sip before curtsying and assuming his position on his throne. Joseph was laughing so hard he spit some of his bourbon onto the ground, almost hitting Christy.

"Alcohol abuse! Drink!" Robin shouted, pointing to him.

"What are you, the Alcohol Czar?" Christy asked.

Robin stared at her until Christy laughed.

"I know, I know. Drink," Christy said, taking a mouthful of beer.

"OK Are we all ready to start?" Brian asked everyone.

The group looked on, no one objected, so Robin spoke up.

"Never have I ever trolled someone on social media," she said.

The girls all drank in turn, with Robin and Christy smiling larger than Linda.

"Conniving bitches! Girls are ruthless!" Brian laughed, drinking along with them.

"No explanations necessary," Joseph smiled.

"Never have I ever climbed out of a bedroom window," Linda said.

Crickets. No one drank, no one said anything; everyone looked at each other with puzzled expressions.

"Seriously Linda?" Christy asked, shaking her head.

"I'll do better next time?" she said laughing, unsure of her response.

"Never have I ever sent a sext," Christy said.

Everyone looked at each other with anticipation, but no one drank.

"Unfortunate," Christy said, taking her sip.

"Yes, I know," Robin said, sipping hers.

"Ah hell," Brian said, laughing, drinking.

"Why don't the rest of you just drink and get it over with," he said smiling.

Joseph and Linda took their sips, to the delight of the others.

"We'll all have to share our stories later," Joseph informed them.

Robin looked around at the group and nodded her approval.

"Never have I ever deleted a post on social media because it didn't get enough likes," Joseph said.

No one drank. Looking around for assurance, Brian turned back to Joseph and paused.

"No such thing as a bad post," he said.

"Never have I ever cursed in a church," Brian stated.

Nobody drank. *This was looking like one sad game*, Brian thought.

"OK, everyone just take a drink, we're not making any progress here and I'm losing my buzz," he laughed.

"Well, don't you have to go to church for this to be a valid statement? When's the last time anybody here was in a church? Geeze!" Robin said, as everyone finished their glasses and bottles before walking back for refills.

"Never have I ever gone down on a girl," Robin said.

"Now we're talking!" Christy yelled.

Robin paused for full effect, then drank, twice. Everyone looked at her, not judging at all… They were equally impressed when Joseph drank.

"Well? Explanations *are* in order, I'm afraid," Linda boasted.

"Nope," Robin simply replied.

"I was curious?" said Joseph, as Brian continued staring.

"It was a long time ago, way before I met you," Joseph expanded, while Brian didn't even blink.

"Way before us," Joseph continued.

Linda looked back at Robin and waited.

"Nope," she stated, smiling.

Laughter erupted from all, even Robin joined them.

"I know, right? But it's still a solid *nope,*" she told them.

The look of disappointment was obvious, but Robin did not stray from her response.

"Never have I ever gone 24 hours without showering," Linda said.

Everyone looked at Linda, paused, and took a long, deliberate drink.

"Filthy animals!" was Linda's reply.

"Never have I ever spent more than $200 on an outfit," Christy said, staring at Robin.

"Cute," Robin replied as Linda rolled her eyes to her response.

"It was cute, I meant," Robin said smiling and taking a sip.

"No one else then, Brian, maybe?" Linda asked.

"Nope, not me," he said drinking.

"Christy, then?" Linda was working her way through the group, *peer pressure's a bitch,* she thought, as she raised and lowered her eyebrows at her, before asking again.

"Christy?"

"Look at me Linda, aren't I always wearing some old T-shirt?" she said laughing.

Christy looked on, not drinking, and returned Linda's stare. Linda drank, smiling at the entire group.

"Cute," Brian said, again shaking his head.

"Never have I ever fallen asleep during sex," Joseph looked around, smiling.

Brian looked at Robin. Robin looked at Joseph. They all drank in total silence.

"Never have I ever taken the walk of shame," Brian said.

Joseph drank. The fact that he took two long sips was easily seen by most, but Brian and Robin seemed to pay particular attention. Linda watched the group for responses, and when it was close to the end, right before Robin spoke, she took hers.

"Never have I ever vacationed by myself," Robin said.

Linda took another drink, smiling.

"I was between boyfriends," she softly replied.

"That's sad. It's just sad," Brian mumbled.

"I missed the beach," Linda said laughing, and took another large sip.

"It's my turn again. Yay. Never have I ever worn someone else's underwear," Linda said.

Both Brian and Joseph drank as the girls looked on.

"Each other's doesn't count," Robin laughed hysterically. "Yous guys, I swear."

Friendly laughter erupted from all. Non-judgmental, friendly laughter; everyone was having a wonderful time. *Everyone was getting fucked up!* Christy thought.

"Never have I ever gone skinny-dipping," Christy said.

Everyone looked at each other laughing, and then all drank.

"Never have I ever cheated on someone," Joseph stated.

Crickets. He knew that Robin had cheated before but chose to say nothing when she didn't drink. Linda knew Christy had cheated, and said nothing when Christy didn't. Brian knew Linda had cheated before, twice, and he too said nothing when she chose not to drink. In short, no one who had cheated took sips, and those who knew differently didn't betray their friendships, choosing not to call them out. This was a truly caring, truly loving group of friends, without a doubt.

"Never have I ever used a fake ID," Brian said.

"Lame. We were all kids once," Christy smirked.

"So, drink," Robin said laughing.

Christy drank.

"Never have I ever kissed someone immediately after or during oral sex," Robin said.

"Whoa there, missy. You are going there?" Brian asked.

"Yup. And don't expect a kiss afterwards hon," she replied laughing.

Joseph shook his head. Christy shook hers. Linda just looked down and sipped her beer. After a sigh, Brian finished his bourbon. Out of sympathy, Joseph finished his too. As the night grew older, the group kept drinking and having fun. The girls were relaxed, and the boys were too.

Nobody was sloppy drunk, nobody had thrown up, nobody was obnoxious, they were just friends partying and having a wonderful s'mores and game night by the campfire.

"Hey, can we take a restroom break for a few?" Linda asked.

The group nodded positively, and the girls left to use their camper's bathroom, while the boys took off around the corner. As unusual as this might be, all parties concerned finished around the same time; the girls were coming out of the camper as Brian and

Joseph approached their thrones. Everyone was back in their seats within a few minutes, and it was soon time to start back up.

"I'm going to win," Christy said a little louder than usual.

"Right. Looks like you are already winning," Robin said smiling.

"Who's turn is it now," Joseph asked.

"It's Linda's. I had just finished my turn before we took a break," said Robin.

"Never have I ever had a one-night stand," Linda said, with a slight slur.

"OK, before anyone drinks, I think it's time for Linda to change to water for a bit," Joseph stated.

"I want to keep playing," she said clearly.

"Oh, you can play, you are just to drink water for your responses," Robin said as she handed Linda a bottled water.

"Now everyone on three. One. Two. Three," Brian chimed in as everyone drank.

Through all of this, one thing was apparent, Robin thought they had a lot in common. Everyone had some differences, but for the most part, everyone meshed nicely, they all just fit. It was clear to Brian that everyone was getting tired, sleepy, possibly drunk; and he wanted to end the night on a positive note.

"Hey all, let's end the game with a few more questions, and relax to enjoy our fire. What do you think, two more questions? I have one," Brian said.

Total buy-in, he thought, as he asked the last question he wanted to ask.

"Never have I ever lied to my friends about who I'm sleeping with," Brian said.

You could have heard a pin drop when Brian finished that question. It addressed the white elephant in the campground. Robin took one sip, then another, then kept going. She finished the rest of her margarita, and everyone grew sad.

"Sorry. I shouldn't have asked that," Brian stated with remorse.

"No, it's OK. I know that he's been a wedge between us all, and for that I'm truly sorry," Robin said.

Everyone registered acknowledgement of the issues between them and Scott, and for Robin's feelings. Her friends toasted Robin and then took turns hugging her.

"Well, I might as well tell you all now, Scott and I are finished. He's not who I thought he was, so I've ripped the Band-Aid off," Robin informed them.

If Robin only knew how far away from the truth that statement really was. Scott was totally obsessed with her, and he would stop at nothing to control her feelings.

"All right! And on that note, I'm afraid we must part ways. Earlier today Joseph challenged me to a game of horseshoes, so before it gets any later, we need to throw a few," Brian said to cheers from Joseph.

"You're going down, man," Joseph told him.

"Later, if you're lucky!" Brian joked as the two stood and folded their thrones.

The boys carried them off and told Robin they would help clean up tomorrow. The two walked away, each of them thinking on how they would beat the other. Moving out of the light of their campfire, they headed back to their site, disappearing into the darkness.

The girls moved their chairs a little closer to the fire, then went into the camper for a few snacks. Taking out a few small paper plates, they went back out to enjoy the nighttime and their campfire.

"Nothing helps to absorb the alcohol more than snacks!" Linda said as she jammed a spanakopita into her mouth smiling.

"Well, there might be one thing," Robin said as she bolted for the camper.

Back at the main gate to the campground, Carmen looked at the video surveillance and watched the small red Toyota move from the top left to the bottom right screens, disappearing from one, then reappearing on the next. It had taken all day for her to get them back working properly, and her daylight had long since disappeared. For whatever reason, on the last night Mary worked, the system took a header. The fuses were tripped, the tapes rewound. If she didn't know better, she would have suspected foul play, but she didn't know better, she wasn't trained to. The park was not a secure military installation, nor was it treated that way. When something broke, or didn't work as expected, the focus was on repair, resolution, not determining what foreign power or entity had acted inappropriately.

Petite, thin, frail, angry, manic, driven; all were words used to describe Carmen by some of her peers. Her friends would say she was helpful, resourceful, and darn handy to have around.

"I'm good enough, I'm smart enough-" Carmen began, although she would never finish that sentence.

The bright red hair and electric blue eyes complimented her and provided plenty of initial glances and second looks. It was her overly light complexion that threw most off, she was paler than 9 out of 10 Irish women. She laughed. The funny part of all of this, if there was one, was that Carmen would say that the carpet didn't match the drapery, or something like that, for she was not truly Irish. *No, the carpet doesn't match the drapes, and blondes don't have more fun,* she thought, nodding confidently.

Carmen was red by choice, and it was a bright red. It was bright enough to rival what one would see on a fire hydrant, a stop sign, or the brightest of stop lights. Her eyes were bright too, some referred to them as 'God's little gift of electricity.' She wore her uniform with pride. Although her small package was described by some as lacking, as far as she was concerned, she was complete, and wore her uniform just as well as the next guy.

She was called in with no notice to get the gatehouse organized, to repair the video surveillance system, and to cover for Mary. It appears that management wasn't sure if she would show up tonight. Carmen didn't mind helping out, she had been filling staffing holes state-wide for a few years now, and she was still referred to as *Volunteer #2*, or Carmy, by her friends. Not that she wanted to advance this way, but if Mary could no longer cut it, she would be happy to call Hearty Lake home.

From what Carmen understood, this campground was no different from the others she volunteered at. Normally, the officials who worked the gates were not volunteers, those positions were held by hourly employees. *There wasn't enough money in the budget*, or so the rumors said. *These are unusual times*;

management would say to her. *We are going to hire one additional person soon,* they would continue. Carmen didn't care, she would wait for her chance. *At least it wasn't totally an inside office duty assignment like clerical or concessions, those were the two worst areas to work*, she thought. The best ones were the gatehouse or the raptor center, anything in the raptor center actually; those two positions were what Carmen desired the most.

Looking at their rearview mirror, the park pass was in the right place. The date covered them until next Wednesday, so they were good. Carmen watched as they stopped in front of her window even though she had waved them on.

"Can I help you," the woman asked them with a smile.

Two young women smiled back as the driver lowered her window.

"Hi. Can we have another map of the park. Our last one went hiking and never returned," the first girl said laughing.

"Sure. One sec," Carmen replied.

Fishing one out from the left side of the desk, she circled a few areas of interest, made a larger red circle around the words '*You are here'*, and handed it to them.

"Thanks! Have a good night," they told her.

Carmen waived them through and turned her window sign around to read Closed. Taking her clipboard and a pen, she exited the gatehouse.

She locked the door and pulled the gate sign that was on rollers out far enough to block inbound vehicles from stopping and walked to the golf cart. '*Drive Through,*' it read, in large yellow letters. *There would still be someone that stopped and waited before backing up and driving around,* she laughed. The last thing she was asked to do was to reach out to campers and determine if anyone had seen Parker, the campground's Golden Retriever mascot. He was a mutt of a male, but their friend, and loyal to a fault. He'd been missing for days now, and the campground hosts were just now starting to get worried.

Scott continued to scour the campsites that had any activity whatsoever, from a distance, of course. He stayed in the shadows and relied on his nighttime goggles. He focused on a pair of couples who had finished cooking dinner and were now comfortably enjoying their fire. Looking through his goggles, he slowly panned left and right; he saw nobody he recognized. Scott watched and waited for others around them to stop by, to interact, but no one came. With the exception of their campsite, there weren't any others active. What a waste of my time. *There were better ways to spend two and a half hours, like sleeping,* he thought. Scott found searching for Robin exhausting, and his time spent thus far, totally unproductive.

He was on his way back to his camper when he was spotted by an older couple that was complaining about some kids.

"Clank. Clank. Clank," the old woman complained.

"They are throwing horseshoes, and it's too late at night. It's keeping us up. Clank, clank, clank is all we hear," the old man quickly chimed in.

"I'll take care of it. What site are they on?" the CO asked.

"Site 130, I think, across from our Highland Trail Runner with the large blue globes on the awning. You can't miss those guys, just listen for the clanks," she said excitedly.

Nodding to them, he kept walking to his camper. Scott would make more coffee, eat some leftover pizza, and then go check it out; *who knows, maybe he would run into his friends there?* Finishing his coffee and a piece of cold pizza, he quickly got back to it.

The CO drove to the nearby comfort station and parked. Getting out, he listened for the clanks and watched for movement. When he didn't hear anything out of the ordinary, he scanned the nearby sites for campers with large blue balls. He found them over to his left. Scott didn't notice those lights before, the kids must have woken them up, they turned them on, and probably went outside to investigate the commotion. He headed in that direction on foot, but this time he walked as a CO, with authority, not as someone needing to hide in the shadows.

Walking closer, he saw two men standing across the road

from the old couple. *Probably talking to each other*, he thought. They were definitely not playing horseshoes anymore. Moving closer, he noticed the two were younger than the couple he had met earlier. He saw one man laughing at the other, and after a hug, the second started walking in his direction. The CO continued walking forward, watching all present. When Joseph recognized the man in front of him as DNR, he averted his eyes and turned slightly away. Joseph was watching the CO at a distance, not looking directly at him as he kept walking to the comfort station. A pleasant '*hi*' came from him as he addressed the CO while still looking at the ground; he had been drinking and didn't want any trouble, not tonight.

  Joseph's half smile, half frown was recognized by the CO, but Joseph didn't recognize Robin's ex-boyfriend; possibly because they nodded and didn't speak, no eye contact was made by either man, or maybe due to the overall darkness present. Scott walked slower, allowing Joseph enough time to enter the building before he turned and followed him inside. Joseph walked straight up to the urinal and lowered his shorts enough to start.

  There were two kinds of *comfort stations* located throughout the campground. Some were centrally located, but most were on the periphery. If you wanted convenience, one would choose an older, less modern building, something close by. If one wanted luxuries, then you would have to work for it. The number three is a magical number. Throughout history it has leant itself to good and bad, power and weakness, holy and unholy. The larger, newer, centrally located comfort stations were based on that number.

  Not only were they newer, cleaner, and more frequently maintained, they had all been recently remodeled and filled with ever-changing modern conveniences. Built from cinder block, the building a were freshly painted and tiled. There were matching adjacent sides, one for men and the other for women; the campground had not yet taken the leap forward in supporting or offering unisex buildings. The two sections were identical, with the exception of the men's partition having toilets *and* urinals.

  Scott walked in and looked around. The porcelain was white and matched the clean tiles on the floor. Beige paint nicely coated the walls. Everything was spread out in threes. Three beige toilet areas with locking doors, three sinks suspended on the wall, with mounted mirrors above them, three hand sanitizer dispensers, and for the men's area, three matching urinals. The scents of lavender and bleach hung heavily in the air. Off to one end, past the bathroom section were the showers. Yes, there were three showers separated by beige cinder walls, each one tiled with white porcelain squares!

The main purpose of visiting this station was the man in front of him trying to urinate. Scott approached slowly, taking deliberate steps, one after the other. When he heard Joseph start, he lunged. Joseph had just begun when he was pushed forward against the wall. He immediately stopped mid-stream. He turned his head to the left in time to see a man behind him beginning to pull his T-shirt over his head. Joseph had started struggling when Scott punched him in the kidneys and kicked him in the back of his right thigh, taking Joseph down hard to his knees. Removing his service pistol from his holster, he slammed it against Joseph's head once, then again for good measure.

He felt disoriented and dizzy. White pain blinded his vision as the man behind him pushed his head into the urinal and hit him a third time. Joseph was kneed in the back before again being hit from behind with Scott's pistol. Falling forward lifeless, he ceased struggling. Scott looked down at Joseph; his head was half inside the urinal, his chin was resting on the deodorizer, and he had started peeing again. *Classic,* Scott thought, as he took pictures with his cell phone from different angles.

"You really have to work on your aim," Scott told him.

Taking hold of his feet, he pulled him backwards until his face left the urinal and fell onto the white tile.

"Sorry about that," Scott said as he dragged Joseph into the second shower stall.

Handcuffing the unconscious man to exposed copper pipe, he left for Brian. Getting in his vehicle, he drove straight up to his campsite and drew down on him.

"Hey! No need for that," Brian pleaded, throwing his hands up in the air.

"We've had complaints. Get down on the ground and cross your legs. Interlock your fingers behind your head," The CO issued those commands boldly, the words dripping with authority.

Brian dropped to his knees and leaned forward, following the CO's instructions. Scott approached from behind and off to Brian's right, before taking control of his hands and cuffing them behind his back.

"Cooperate and everything will be fine," he told Brian as he raised him to his feet and led him into the SUV.

The old couple watched quietly, cheering on in their own way, as the park official took away their troublemaker.

"About fucking time," the old woman said under her breath.

"Now Audrey, you know you get better results with sugar than salt," the old man told her.

"Whatever, Jimmy," the old woman said as she went back to finish her movie.

"You know you can't sleep anyway, keep it down," Jimmy joked.

He was met with a slap across the side of his face from a folded magazine. Audrey returned her instructional behavioral modification manual back to her table beside her for the next time she needed to use it, and pressed play on her remote.

Scott drove straight to the comfort station, parked around the side of the building, and got out. He opened the back door and climbed inside. Pushing Brian over so the men could see each other's faces, he removed his pistol and proceeded to beat the snot out of him. Brian recognized him easily when the men were up close. *I always knew you were violent,* Brian thought as Scott confirmed it by hitting him several more times.

"Miss me?" Scott asked as he turned out Brian's lights.

Leaving him unconscious in the back seat, he went to get Joseph. Taking off at a brisk pace and looking over his shoulder, he approached the men's side and confidently walked in. Scott had just rounded the corner and entered the shower to remove him when he heard a vehicle pull up. He immediately turned around and headed outside to assess.

Scott met the woman's gaze in passing as he exited. The attractive brunette smiled at the CO before walking past him and entering the woman's door. A quick glance toward her car told him she was alone. Scott promptly followed her inside and called out.

"Ma'am, I'm sorry, but this building is being closed, the plumbing is all bad. You'll have to use the other one up by the main gate," he said sadly.

"But I have to go really bad. I'm already here, couldn't I just finish up and leave?" the woman asked with urgency, shifting her body weight back and forth on her feet.

He looked forward to the woman, back at the door, and back again to the woman dancing in front of him. She was wearing normal Summer clothing consisting of a light blue T-shirt, faded jean shorts, and flip flops; Scott paused to think, and in a few seconds, he knew what he wanted to do. He nodded *yes* and turned to leave. She thanked him and walked straight into the closest stall. Turning around and sitting to do her business, she had already lowered her shorts to her ankles when she stretched forward to close the door.

The brunette was looking down at her feet when it stopped short of closing. Looking up to see why, she noticed the park official reaching in to grab her. She pulled back as far as she could go before stopping, leaving her back resting against the cold cinder block wall. She stared forward in disbelief at the CO pointing his service weapon directly at her face.

"Stand up!" he shouted, waiving his pistol from her to him.

She stood, and were it not for being interrupted, she would have been doing her pee-pee dance, or worse, spraying the area yellow. Handing her his phone with his pistol still trained on her, he told her to take some selfies.

"Just your face. Start smiling. Now frown. Pictures of your face only. Smile again. Show your breasts now; smile and show your breasts," he demanded.

Looking at him half frozen, she hesitated before she obliged and started taking pictures. More instructions came from the CO demanding more smiles, before asking her again to frown.

"Show me angry," he joked, grinning back at her.

Again, she found herself hesitating, and with a brief pause, she finished and handed the phone back before lowering her shirt.

Placing his cell phone in his pocket after a quick review, he grabbed a handful of her hair and guided her forward to the sink mounted to the opposite wall. When they were close, he stopped, and lowering his hand, he pushed her down to the floor.

"Get on your hands and knees, and for Christ's sake, pull up your shorts," he yelled.

The brunette was crying as she pulled them up and went to her knees. Leaning forward, she placed both palms flat on the floor. Staring at the tile on all fours she waited, thinking what she should do next. He held on tightly and started walking to the door.

"Follow me outside," he commanded.

Virginia was half crawling, half dragged out of the women's bathroom and positioned in front of the SUV's driver side rear door.

"Get in," he said, kicking her behind to motivate her.

She crawled in and sat opposite another. She did nothing except look forward, she thought it best not to anger this man. *This is going to be great*, Scott thought, as he closed her door and went inside to remove Joseph from the shower. Placing him in the back area, he ensured he was still out cold before closing the hatch. Scott checked the back seat before getting behind the wheel.

"Keep quiet and everything will be fine," he said over his shoulder as he drove away.

Obeying the posted campground speed limit, he looked at the sites that he passed. It was not a goal for him to remove all of Robin's friends from their equation, he just felt overwhelmed and angry when he saw one. Things were worse when he ran into them, especially with how awkward things were now with Robin. If he found a chance to hurt one, he wanted to do just that; but she was his focus, he needed to obtain his Robin. He saw her everywhere he looked, but upon closer examination, it usually turned out to be someone else; he grew tired of this revelation, he wanted the real thing.

Since the brunette was the only one of his three that was lucid, he opened her door and pulled her out first, tossing her out onto the ground. With his pistol ever present, he made sure she knew to keep quiet. Lowering his hand he pointed the way, and when she didn't move fast enough, he kicked her. Virginia took a step and slowly headed for the camper door.

"Back down to your hands and knees," he told her. She immediately began crying. Before she was back on all fours, she was already violently shaking and watering the ground with her warm, salty tears.

"Oh, come on. If I wanted to kill you, you would already be dead," he informed her.

Directing her to the steps, he opened the camper door and motioned for her to crawl inside. Moving in quickly behind her, he closed the door and then moved even closer. She crawled forward on all fours past the suitcase next to the door and looked around. Taking hold of her head, he chose to move her to the bedroom by again holding on to a fistful of her hair. Pulling her up to her feet, she understood to walk the rest of the way. When she was close enough, she climbed into bed. He slid in beside her and pushed her forward.

Virginia awaited her beating, her rape, her death; she wasn't sure of the order, or if she would make it out of this, but when the time came to escape, she would go for it. Scott secured his pistol on his waist and wrestled with her, asserting control. He positioned her this way and that, and every time he took hold of her, he forcefully removed a piece of her clothing. Her shirt was the first to go, followed by her shorts, her bra, then her underpants. She wasn't crying at this point, she did push back though, but he thought it playful, and meant to be so; again, she thought about what she could do to facilitate her escape.

With the woman totally naked now, it was time for some pics.

"Smile and give me some good ones. Try to impress me, OK?" he said smiling, and handed her his cell phone.

Virginia did her best, posing four or five times, she lost track, before the man snatched his phone away. He grabbed at her pubic hair. Taking a handful and pulling upward, he motioned for her to sit up. He let go and pushed her over, stretching her out flat on her stomach. Placing his hands between her thighs and the bed, he pulled her close.

Scott probed her willingness paying close attention to her arms, as they were not yet secured. Leaning forward, he lowered his pants and let them slide to the floor, safely out of her reach. Next, he placed himself against the slightly deviated crack of her ass. He took her arms and pulled them tightly behind her. When his handcuffs closed, Virginia felt her chances to escape as out of reach as the man's pistol that was now resting comfortably, just out of reach at the foot of the bed.

If her chances of escaping were lowered upon having her hands disabled, they were totally gone now when the man climbed on top. She was squirming to get free when a clear plastic mask was held tightly over her face. Virginia fought heavily against this, but her struggles were futile. Scott held on tightly until the woman he was sitting on learned that she had lost.

He watched her closely; the more she breathed, realizing she would eventually run out of air, the less she struggled. *Soon she would be relaxed enough*, he thought, *soon she would understand.* He removed the mask and looked at her briefly, before turning her onto her back. Climbing on top as he grew harder, he slid forward and took her breasts. Scott held on and enjoyed them as he looked at the woman beneath him. He could not know if she had been drinking tonight, or if she had taken drugs, so he leaned in close to find out.

"Have you been drinking or smoking pot?" he whispered into her ear.

The woman shook her head *no* and started to cry and shake uncontrollably; looks of confusion came and went over her face.

"Nothing at all?" he spoke to her, moving in closer.

Virginia felt the warmth of his breath on the side of her face, against her ear. Again, she shook her head no, adding more tears to her shaking and whimpering. Taking her ear into his mouth, he licked and sucked on it. Virginia cringed and shook even harder now; she couldn't' hide her fear, she jerked and jumped as she tried to get him to stop. She wanted this man off of her, she just wasn't sure how to do it.

Scott went back to her breasts. He massaged them roughly before letting go to gauge her sobriety. He believed her; n*ot quite there, not yet,* he thought, wondering what he could do to help.

"I'll be right back," he said, getting up and leaving the bedroom.

Bending down at the kitchen sink, he opened the door and moved some bottles and cans around until he found what he was looking for. He stood and held the can under the light and read the warning.

"Yes. Alright. Uh huh. I understand," he said, speaking loud enough for the woman in the other room to hear.

After saying those words, he grabbed a trash bag and closed the cabinet. Scott walked back into the bedroom with a large smile on his face. He quickly lost that smile when he stood in the doorway looking directly into the woman's eyes. She had turned all the way around in the bed and was now on her stomach, facing him.

"Looking for something, Precious?" he said, producing his pistol from behind his back; "I hardly go anywhere without it anymore," he finished.

Virginia's heart sank. Deep back in her mind, she doubted if she could have even used it effectively with her hands secured behind her back, but she had to try. Scott approached her, twisted her around, and flipped her over. She found herself exactly how she was moments ago when he had left the room.

"Please don't kill me," Virginia begged.

He stared at her, not saying a word.

"I'll do anything you ask. Please let me go," she continued.

Climbing up on the bed holding a spray can, he stretched to open the cabinet above her head. Scott swapped the can for the Duct tape. He took his knife and cut a piece large enough to cover her mouth. Moving higher up on the bed, he pulled her head backward uncomfortably, and wrestled with her chin until he could tape her mouth shut.

She found herself unable to scream or shout; *nails in my coffin,* she thought, as she concentrated on breathing through her nose. Tossing the tape to her right on the table beside them, he reached for the spray can. Scott slid over her back and sat on her; she wasn't going anywhere, anytime soon.

Virginia was worried. She had experienced rough sex before. She had been sequestered, man-handled, and held in uncomfortable positions before, but it was with someone that she loved, or thought she cared about. She had never been beaten or raped. She had never been abused. Virginia experienced familiar emotions, or at least they started off that way, she thought, as the man sitting on top grabbed a handful of hair and tried to pull off her head.

He reached for the can of clear finish spray paint. Turning her head to the right and again pulling it backwards sharply, he showed it to Virginia through her squinting eyes. She didn't fight or struggle to stop him from forcing her head to the side. She had to relax her body and bend the way he wanted her to, because if she didn't, Virginia was sure he would break her in two. Through all her pain, she really didn't get a good look at what he was showing her. From the way he was holding the can, the writing was too small. *Probably the back, or the warning label*, she thought, as she read what words she could. *Avoid prolonged exposure. DANGER. Vapor is harmful. May affect the brain or nervous system.*

Virginia's takeaway was that he was holding a very menacing looking spray can, and that she was fucked. Rotating it in his hand to tease her, he began shaking it violently. She heard what sounded like several metal balls trying to escape their metallic prison. *Right there with yah,* she thought. *They were obviously mixing the contents inside the spray can but mixing what?* Letting go of her head, Virginia's face fell onto the pillow. Turning to breathe, she saw the CO place her T-shirt on the bed beside her.

Her eyes darted around the room, betraying her calm. Her mind raced. She thought about her mom and dad back in Detroit, her sister back in their camper, and her schedule next week at the office; all of those things came and went as quickly as her eyes scoured the room for something to help her escape. She knew she was being held in a camper, and that it wasn't too far from the bathroom where she had parked her car; those two things didn't help to calm her though, not in the slightest.

Virginia's breathing quickened, taking in oxygen as best she could with her mouth taped. Breathing through her nose faster now, she watched as the CO folded it a few times to thicken it. Virginia was almost at the point of hyperventilating when he sprayed her T-shirt, soaking it heavily. She smelled paint fumes, pure and simple. That smell was strong in the small bedroom, and although raising her head up as far as it would go did seem to help, she could not hold it there for long.

Scott was watching the woman's concern as he slid his hand underneath the T-shirt and picked it up. Pressing it against her face, he took several minutes to ensure she had breathed in enough fumes. Virginia threw her head around trying to escape the chemically laden T-shirt, but his hand held it loosely over her mouth. She thought about moving her head backwards to breathe in clean air, but it only seemed to make him press harder. He was now bending her neck back as far as it would go, holding her head tightly against him.

There was nothing she could do, she thought. Lying with her stomach flat on the bed she felt helpless. Her arms were handcuffed behind her back. Virginia was facing forward, with the doorway and her attacker behind her. Off to her right was the outside bedroom door, but she doubted she would be using that today, not willingly anyway. Her eyes darted around wildly, but they were slower than the thoughts that raced inside her mind. Trying to calm herself and regain what little composure she had, Virginia closed her eyes as hard as she could, opening them slowly after several seconds passed, and began to cough.

With her head held motionless and uncomfortably pulled backward, and all of the weight of her attacker pressing her down onto the bed, all she could effectively do was wait. Virginia breathed in the same, normal healthy volume of air she usually did, she just did it through her nose. She could not hope to get out of this unscathed, but it wasn't for a lack of trying. She stayed calm, she tried to cooperate so she could get time off for good behavior, and she even thought about giving her mashed potatoes to the lunchroom bully for payment; Virginia wasn't sure where those thoughts came from, but nothing else today made sense, so she didn't worry too much about them.

More coughing came as the air she tried to breathe filled her lungs with oily and acrid fumes. The foul air assaulted her nostrils on the way in, and her lungs when it arrived. It made her insides feel heavy and weighted. Breathing in and exhaling only through her nose was unnatural, laborious, and inefficient, at best; it was a game she was going to lose. Her body required fresh air full of oxygen, but what she was allowed to breathe was ripe with chemicals. It was spoiled, carrying with it more pollutants than oxygen. Along with everything else were the painful drawbacks from the chemicals that took the place of what she needed; Virginia wasn't getting enough pure, clean air.

There was nothing she could do, she thought. Had she thought that before? Virginia couldn't be sure. She coughed and gagged, both of which should have resulted in exhaling forcibly through her mouth, but instead everything came out her nose. She tasted paint? she had never tasted paint before, or if she had it had been in passing, such as a strong smell that one notices and then immediately walks to another area. *I don't recommend it,* she continued, trying to stop coughing. Scott held on tightly to the woman as she continued coughing and trying to get free. He thought he heard her laughing, as he kept her shiny T-shirt pressed over her taped mouth.

Painful breath after painful breath stung her nose, her throat, her insides, as she took in several strong lungsful of chemicals. Between coughing, her body jerked; the more she inhaled, the more it bothered her, and the more she coughed. Scott mistook this as her trying to get free and leaned forward. Placing more weight on her further complicated things, and although Virginia didn't recognize why he was doing it, she did know it was now even harder to breathe through her nose.

She had no idea what she was being forced to inhale, for all she knew, it was common spray paint. Virginia had used ant and roach killer before; she would easily know that smell. She was happy that he wasn't using any of those, or peanut butter. *Peanut butter*, she questioned that thought. What she meant to say was fruit juice. Her high was coming on strong, but neither of them knew it. Virginia would take her victories as they came, it was a small one, but if she recognized her high, she would think it better than dying outright, possibly. Taking her T-shirt off her face, he placed it into a trash bag and left it on the bed beside her. Stepping out to bring in the boys, he left her to enjoy her high.

Now was her time, she thought. *Now! Go! Move!* Virginia didn't budge. It appeared to her that she could only lie still and enjoy the way she felt. She was aware of the man dragging something in, placing it in the dining area, and then leaving to do it again, but only barely. She didn't know what he was doing specifically and could not understand why he kept leaving and coming back. She turned her head to the side and continued watching and wondering what he would bring in next.

Virginia managed to move slightly to the left side of the

bed, but that's as far as she made it. Scott climbed up next to her, removed her handcuffs and took off her tape. He watched the woman's face light up when he moved over and called to her. She rolled on to her side, turned away, and bounced backwards as best she could, placing her body against his, and giggled. Scott stayed still and let her move around until she found the proper angle and pushed onto him. He stayed still, while she found out what would work, and what would not. *Just get on your back. Help a girl out,* Virginia thought; pulling away she looked over at him and paused, trying to smile.

Scott turned over and waited. Virginia started sliding closer and fell on top of him. She circled around to place her mouth on his maleness, taking him all the way. Her lips pressed against him tightly, moving slightly up and down, keeping him inside the whole time. He had never experienced this before. *I should have come three times over by now,* he thought, but nope. She went slowly, very slowly, and although she teased him with her tongue, pressing firmly whenever she wanted to, in total control of this man, he still felt he was in charge. That was her skill, her superpower, and she was good at it. Virginia couldn't draw upon much in the moment, but that was so natural to her, so familiar, that she was able to execute it without thinking.

A few times she pulled upwards to the tip, only to slam her head back down against his groin, again taking him in all the way. This she did as a means to control him, it was how she enjoyed her sex, it was how she liked it; Virginia hoped it was also how she could escape. Once she felt the man was in control, she felt herself losing what she loved the most about sex, *her* control. If Scott had understood this, he would know that he had finally found the one. Scott stayed put, motionless, until it was time for her to allow him to come. When he came, he came hard.

Virginia kissed and sucked and licked him to just shy of his goals, and by doing so, she achieved hers. Sliding all the way out, she turned to look at him. With a smirk, she puckered her lips, before opening them again wide. Closing her eyes, she turned away from him. Sliding herself around, she kissed his chest. Moving over him, she thrust downwards as he entered her, sealing the deal. Multiple times she thrusted, with her doing all the work. There was no pattern or series of steps that she did to keep him aroused, she just forcefully pushed him down into the bed, before raising up to do it all over again.

Kissing him from time to time, she travelled up to his face. Never stopping her thrusting, she loosed herself upon him. *Scott was still hard.* He cleared his mind, his thoughts. *Scott was still having sex. What was wrong with Scott,* he wondered. He began to over think things. Scott had the *I'm ready to come, right now* look on his face, Virginia let out a small smile, she loved it! Moving faster, and with her looking directly at him with slightly parted lips, Scott understood. Taking her by the waist, he pulled her in close, and began to reclaim control. Taking a handful of her hair, he pulled her back to the side, and rolled her over to exert himself. It was his turn to be on top, it was his turn to be the one.

"Fuck. What's with all the hair pulling," she complained.

Virginia didn't actually mind too much, she felt wonderful, light, full of life; she had given up some control, although those thoughts came randomly into her mind. For her to achieve her goals, for her to get what she wanted, she had to give a little herself, whether she understood that properly or not.

Raising her up to an almost uncomfortable angle, he pounded away. Quicker and quicker, harder, and harder he went. Letting go of her hair, he reached for the bag. Taking her T-shirt out, he held it over her face, pushing her neck back to his chest. Virginia didn't like that, and although she thought it somewhat painful, that thought didn't last long. The last thing she remembered was wondering how she would get free, how she was to escape, and where was the damn peanut butter?

Scott knew it was too good to be true. He could not trust his feelings, and he sure as hell could not trust hers. He held on tightly until they both became limp; then, he held on longer. Virginia struggled for one last attempt at freedom before losing consciousness. *Good thing I waited*, he smiled, as he removed the shirt from her face, letting it fall to the side of the bed.

"Well played, brunette, well played," he said to her as he secured her hands, her feet, and again taped her mouth shut.

By placing some pillows between the woman and the edge of her side of the bed, he ensured she would not fall off. Scott kept her on her back as he liked looking at her breasts. Over her face he placed her T-shirt so she could continue her high. Laying down beside her, he closed his eyes, hoping for the best night of sleep he'd had in years. If Virginia had been allowed the benefit of the doubt, allowed to relax beside him, she would have thought the same.

Scott woke up not one hour later with an urge to urinate. A small yawn escaped him as he stood to stretch. Taking a piece of pizza from the fridge, he went to use the bathroom. While sitting on the toilet, chewing a large bite of cheese and sausage pizza, he heard a moan. He stopped chewing and looked through the doorway, continuing to listen. Another moan drew his eyes down to the floor and looking below the dinette table he saw Brian and Joseph. *Their faces were fucked up*, he thought. Flushing the toilet, he swallowed the last bite of pizza before finishing his business, and then flushed again. Standing, he slid his underpants back up and stood in the doorway. Washing his hands, he looked out the door at the two men handcuffed to the dinette.

"Shut up," Scott said to them.

"Shut up, or I'll kill you both."

Walking out the door and closing it, he kicked Joseph just because he was closer. Joseph didn't respond. Brian recoiled more than he did, Scott noted. Laughing and shaking his head, he walked back to his bed. Sitting on it he yawned again, checked the time on his phone, and then crawled back under the blankets. Pulling them to fully cover his shoulder, he flipped the brunette over into a cuddling position. She lie almost perfectly on the half of his body that was exposed to her. *It wasn't a dream,* he thought, *this was really happening!*

Scott tried to go back to sleep, but he couldn't, he was too excited; all he could think about were the two men handcuffed to his dinette! Stretched out on the bed beside a beautiful woman, somewhat relaxed, and still trying to fall asleep, he thought of them. Without hesitating a moment further, he picked up the brunette and placed her on the floor by her side of the bed. Again, he put her wet T-shirt over her face and left her there.

Scott walked out of the bedroom to remove Joseph from the dinette. He carried him to the bed and sat him against the back wall. Thinking on what to do next, Scott handcuffed his arms behind him, and then gagged him by taping his mouth shut. He stared at the lifeless body on his bed, before going back to the dinette. Scott walked straight up to Brian, kicking him repeatedly several times, landing blows to his chest, his thighs, his back, whatever part that faced him. Every time Brian turned one way or the other struggling to get free and protect himself, Scott kicked him. Brian already had his mouth taped, so he made no discernable noises other than unrecognizable words and muffled moans when Scott kicked him again.

Kicking him one more time so Brian fully understood, Scott reached down and removed the handcuffs, pulling him out from under the dinette. He dragged him to the bed by his closest arm and positioned him to the left of Joseph. Brian looked at his lover with great concern. Scott took hold of Joseph's shorts and pulled them down to his ankles. Brian looked away, he already knew what Joseph looked like. Scott turned Brian's head back and pushed him closer to Joseph's groin, before ripping off his tape.

"Take him," Scott shouted.

"I don't understand it, so help me," he shouted again, pushing him closer to Joseph.

Scott took a few pictures of Brian's lips in close proximity to Joseph's groin, focusing on the penis positioned dangerously close to Brian's face.

"Make him hard, kiss him, suck him, lick it, do what you do," Scott demanded.

Brian did nothing but look away. Scott pulled his service weapon and brought it down hard on Joseph's shin.

"You might as well just do it, Brian. Or I'll hurt him, real bad. I promise," Scott stated.

Brian did nothing but look away. Scott backhanded Joseph across his face with his pistol. Looking at Brian not doing what he was asked, he slapped Joseph again.

"OK. Alright!" Brian said desperately.

He pressed his face over Joseph's groin. Brian tried to arouse Joseph by kissing, by licking, but he was still unconscious. Several attempts to arouse him failed, each like the one before. Brian didn't stop, but he did slow his efforts. A few more pics, and Scott took hold of Brian through his shorts. Squeezing and stroking, he moved Brian around the bed like an animal. At one point, all he did was squeeze harder until Brian was forced to look directly at him.

"Don't you dare get hard. Don't you dare come," Scott told him.

Releasing his death grip, he again started stroking. He made it a point to stare and watched as Brian did what he could to avoid him. After a while, he felt Brian getting turned on, *he was growing harder!*

"Don't do it," Scott stated, "don't you fucking do it," Scott raised his voice.

Scott quickened his pace, he wasn't enjoying this, it was done purely for torture... *He was doing it for control, pure and simple control;* that's what he told himself, and that's what he would tell the jury to stay his guilty verdict. Scott would squeeze when pulling, and when pushing his hand back down to his groin, he slightly loosened his grip, as he imagined milking a cow would be done. Repeating what seemed to be working, he did it several more times. *So that's how they do it,* he murmured. Scott stopped when he had his answer; Brian was definitely turned on, he was a basic male at heart. Scott did not know if it was due to him, or the process. There was one thing he could do, as a test; it would help him to understand if it was the process, or the person.

Scott let go of Brian and slapped his face. He took Joseph's feet and pulled him off the bed. His head hit the register with a thud. Keeping him moving, he dragged Joseph towards the living room's main camper door, stopping at the dinette. Scott secured him to it and pulled on his arms a few times to check his work. Upon leaving, for good measure he kicked him again in the chest. Hurrying back to the bedroom, he exploded inside; he was dying to announce his intentions to all present.

"I have to know Brian, are you the way you are right now because of the process, or the person?" Scott asked.

Brian was lost before, now he was totally confused. Scott taped his hands to his thighs. He wrapped Duct tape around Brian's chest, over his nipples, around his neck. He even taped his mouth shut, again. Scott took his pistol out and hit Brian several times about his chest, his face, his neck. After causing him great harm and pain, he positioned him on the center of the bed. Reaching down to the brunette, he lifted her by her waist, pulling her up beside Brian. He placed her facing his groin. She was half on, half off the bed. Her feet were on the ground, her breasts rested on the foot of the bed, her face higher still.

Brian's mind raced; he had no idea what to expect now. He wasn't sure if Joseph was alive or dead. He didn't know if the woman by his feet, her face only inches from his privates, was unconscious or dead. *I need to get ahold of myself, I need to get it together,* he thought. Thinking back to their day at the beach, and further to when they had entered the campground, he didn't remember having seen her. Brian squinted his eyes out of pain. He hurt all over; inside he was crying, but he was too busy processing what was happening, what had happened, and what was going to happen, to shed any tears.

Scott cupped her breasts and loved on them. He pressed against her, he pulled her nipples, he caressed her body. He pulled off the tape from the woman's mouth. He rubbed her face, her shoulders, he grabbed her ass, he tried everything he could to wake her. Taking a couple of fingers, he inserted them inside and pushed against her, moving them in and out. Virginia was awake the entire time, faking her unconsciousness. She could not fake this for much longer though, she was getting turned on. When she could no longer hide her ruse, she began to writhe in response to his probing.

Virginia opened her eyes slowly to whispers in her ear.

"I need you to get this man hard, to get him close to coming, and then cause him pain, do you understand?" Scott spoke barely loud enough for her to hear.

Virginia nodded *yes*, between his thrusting. Scott pulled out and stuck his thumb, along with his fingers inside her. He moved them together at the same time, in synchronized, double penetration. *It wasn't as powerful as having two men, or two toys at the same time, but it would do,* Virginia mused. Pulling out after completing the last of three sets, he slapped her across her ass.

"Let's go," Scott said, as he positioned Virginia where he needed her to be.

Brian looked on as the woman pressed down on him. He struggled against her efforts to swallow him whole. Once Virginia locked on, Virginia locked on; Scott knew it was all over. He took several pics, in which most Virginia saw what he was doing and posed before he asked her to, Brian inside her mouth an' all. Virginia pulled all the way off and sat her face down on Brian's thigh.

"Look, if you don't give me what I want, I'll smash my face down on you over and over and over, until you are so bloody and bruised that no one will ever need nor want you again. Got it, buddy?" Virginia asked with her smile fading.

She looked on at him before speaking again. Sticking her tongue out as far as she could, she licked him several times before stopping and smiling again.

"Nod if you understand, or I'm going to start to hurt you," Virginia told him.

Her demands might have been taken more seriously had she not blinked a few times and raised her eyebrows, as if trying to wake up or clear her vision. Virginia did everything she could to maintain her bluff, her poker face, but her high was still ever present.

Brian nodded. Virginia continued sucking. He grew harder in her mouth, against all his efforts to think of anything he could to ruin his erection. Virginia pulled off, announcing it wouldn't be much longer now.

"Who's my big boy?" Virginia asked as she continued with the man handcuffed and taped in front of her.

Placing her mouth back over him, she used her lips, her tongue, with more force than before. It was a change that was noticed immediately by Brian, he almost came right there. Scott took more pics, as if documenting what he already knew to be true.

Scott sat on the floor and put his back towards hers. He lowered his head and pushed in close to the bed frame. Moving underneath, he raised himself, pushing his open lips and tongue over her as he went, taking her into his mouth. Virginia felt him sucking on her clitoris which both pleased and upset her. Pulling her inside and letting it snap back, he took it again and again. Holding on to it, he sucked on her hard; again, he pulled her into his mouth before letting her go, before doing it all over again.

"Finish him now. Make him come. Ensure you do this, or you'll experience true discomfort," Scott sounded a little muffled, using his teeth harder than she liked, but she was paying attention; Virginia heard him loud and clear.

Brian shook uncontrollably. Virginia shook uncontrollably. Scott let go, stood up and entered her from behind. Virginia kept sucking Brian dry, and from the looks of things, Brian kept coming. Scott placed his hands around Virginia's waist and held on tightly. Her muscles locked down, all she was doing at this point was sucking, she would never willingly let go, not with Scott threatening her with more pain, not with the pleasure she was experiencing.

Scott finished inside Virginia. Brian finished inside Virginia. Virginia also finished, and having done so, went limp from behind, Scott noticed she stopped sucking; she no longer moved her body, Virginia was exhausted. Scott pulled her off the bed and onto the floor, kicking her twice. He expressed his dissatisfaction; after explaining it to her a third time, he picked her up and placed her fully on the bed beside Brian. Virginia looked at the CO, somewhat apologizing, and then glanced over at Brian, before returning to him. Scott pushed the woman's mouth over Brian. Virginia licked and sucked him until he again became hard. This took longer than Scott liked, but it was an interesting way to begin his day. Scott took more pictures.

When Brian was fully erect, he swung the woman around and let her get hers. Virginia found him easily enough, and with little effort, she enveloped him. Brian was horrified, embarrassed, ashamed. he would not tell anyone he grew hard in response to her, and then she had sex with him. Virginia moved faster and faster, she was already close, and honestly, this was all about her, not him. Brian thought of things that would not have, should not have kept him hard, but Virginia would not have it. Virginia used her lovemaking skills to keep him how he was, to make him harder, to make him hers.

Virginia leaned backwards, clasping her breasts, looking over her shoulder towards the CO. Scott took them, mashing them firmly within his grasp. At this point, Brian could not take it anymore. He could no longer fight it, he had to let go. Virginia was the first to notice, and rightfully so, he was fully hard inside her.

Scott entered her balls deep, all at once, on one of Brian's thrusts. Brian was pushing up when Virginia slid down, and unknown to Scott, he was pressing Virginia back towards Brian, allowing the process to perpetuate.

Virginia had never had such incredibly timed penetration before, she almost lost it all together. *It was going to happen, it had to*, Virginia thought, as she was having the most pleasurable, most forceful sex she had ever experienced. Closing her eyes, she enjoyed her Scott, she enjoyed her Brian, she enjoyed her high; in that exact order. She had those thoughts one after the other while her men struggled to please her. She was able to think more clearly now, she was regaining her composure. Virginia was losing her high, and she was recognizing it! She cried out in ecstasy, and then in pain, as Brian and Scott went deeper still and continued their thrusting in unison.

Scott kept going until he came. Taking her hair, he began pulling her neck backwards, ever slightly. When he was close to finishing, he pulled her backwards, and off of Brian. Turning her around to face the rear of the camper, he leaned forward and fell on her. Virginia's body landed on the cold floor. The blow was softened by her breasts, but she still hit the side of her face. Virginia felt continued pleasure with the sudden shock of pain, slightly dazing her, causing her to reset her vision. Scott never left her, continuing to finish, he kept thrusting from behind.

Scott pulled out and turned her over. Moving forward to sit on her breasts, he pulled her head up to him and inserted himself inside her mouth. Virginia looked up and her eyes agreed to finish him. Scott was coming even before she said yes. He held her head to him and stopped thrusting when she took over. Pushing harder against her, she found it even more difficult to move on her own. He spasmed inside her, she sucked and licked where and what she could, but she could no longer slide upwards the way she enjoyed it. Scott finished the way he wanted to, not the way she wanted him to; *I win*, he thought, as the last of his warmth emptied into her moist mouth. Virginia shook her head wildly over him, causing him to start spasming all over again, literally, and figuratively; restarting what he thought had already finished. Moments later, he realized *he had lost.*

Scott pulled out and held her close. Picking her up, he carried her over to the bed, kissing her cheek as he laid her down. Making her comfortable, he again slid onto the bed beside her. Brian was still taped up and positioned slightly off center on the bed. He was left with a mixture of confusing emotions; satisfaction, emptiness, disappointment were all words he would use to describe his feelings and his hard on. On one hand, he was filled with anger and rage that he was raped by Scott, by the woman. On the other, he was equally full of rage and anger as he was robbed of coming after all that happened to him, after all of that had been done to him; he received nothing in the form of closure. Had Scott known Brian's feelings, his thoughts, he would have come to a clear determination that he was, after all, deep down, just a man.

Leaning over to him, Scott pulled back, short of grabbing him, and pulled Virginia's head sharply to the left. While looking at Brian, he held her tightly, crushing her body against his, and then held the woman's T-shirt back over her face. *Not again, fuck,* were Virginia's thoughts, *she wanted off this fucked-up rollercoaster, once and for all.* Brian watched as Scott held the woman until she stopped struggling, and then let her fall lifeless to the floor.

"Your turn," Scott said to Brian.

Brian's eyes widened as he shook his head back and forth; *no*, he thought.

"Don't do it. No!" he shouted, but only muffled words escaped his taped mouth.

He took hold of Brian's legs and pulled his body closer to the foot of the bed. Letting go, he ran his hand over Brian's groin to looks of horror on the taped man's face. Scott wondered what he would sound like when presented with life and death, or mind and body-altering situations. Taking hold of his still hard penis he started squeezing, he started caressing; Brian's eyes attempted to pop out of his head when Scott took hold and started pulling Brian to him, by his balls!

"You better help, or I'm ripping them off," Scott said, continuing to squeeze angrily.

Brian flailed, hopped, and even attempted to jump closer, but for the most part, he wound up being dragged. When Brian was close enough, Scott climbed on top, and brought his thumb and forefinger to his nose. Scott pinched his nostrils, cutting off his oxygen, until Brian ceased to jerk and jump, until his eyes became lifeless, until Brian's chest stopped raising and lowering; all the while squeezing harder and moving his hand up and down him.

Towards the end, Brian had started to come as his body spasmed and jerked and he tried to breathe, or his body jerked and spasmed while trying to breathe, and then he came. Scott wasn't so sure on the timing, but either way, Brian was dead, he hoped. *Not a minute too soon*, he thought, and he was glad, Scott was tired of 'torturing him.'

    Leaving him on the bed, Scott went to dispatch Joseph. Kicking him one last time, he called his name before reaching down and moving him out from the dinette. Having regained consciousness, Joseph struggled and fought back as he could, but there was no progress that would change Joseph's situation, there was nothing he could do to get free.

    Scott mumbled some words Joseph could not hear as he hovered over him to take a closer look. The man was sickly thin and hungry after last night's run in. One of his eyes was shut. He sported fresh bruises about his face and displayed the remnants of a hangover; he was in no shape to put up a fight or make an attempt at gaining his freedom. The way he faced he could not tell if his partner, the love of his life, was breathing, though he didn't seem to be moving or trying to escape. Joseph closed his one good eye and kept it tightly shut, before trying to reopen it, but nothing changed; his eye remained effectively closed, his nightmare was ongoing.

    Lowering himself to the floor, Scott placed him into a headlock and squeezed his arm against the sides of Joseph's face. After a few minutes of struggling to get free, he released his limp body and leaned him against the couch to check for a pulse.

    Today was turning out rather nicely, Scott thought, as the man's body fell over onto the floor, but he still didn't have his Robin. Scott took enough time to refresh his coffee, before leaving to continue his search. *With any luck, the group would be together, or close bye, anyway; he would start looking there*, he thought, letting out a long yawn and petting the suitcase by the door before he left.

J ames and Lynn left their new friend's campsite and looked both ways before crossing the road, out of habit. Each carried a small flashlight, which they frequently shone on the ground to help them safely navigate the uneven surface. *It was awesome having them this close, where they could party and walk home, without needing to drive a vehicle,* he smiled.

When he was close enough to the front of the camper, he checked out the sides of the truck, the bed, the wheels, and then switched his eyes to the front of the camper. He made sure everything was where he left it, no damage, no thefts, such as missing propane tanks or half-eaten bags of fishing bait, all was well. They moved down the side of the camper, past the picnic tables, their coolers, nothing looked out of place.

Lynn was growing impatient, and wanted to go to bed, but James had to check the sides and the rest of the camper. Shining the light around the tree line he heard something, and just as he heard it, he saw it. Demon eyes! He saw red demon eyes!

"HB! Look over here," he whispered, motioning to the object he had illuminated.

They had two picnic tables, like most sites did. James had one in front of the camper, close to the secondary door, and when Lynn came down, he moved the other off to the side of the fire pit, to the edge of the tree line and directly opposite the one by the camper. On that second table sat the raccoon. It was holding their bag of Oreo double stuff cookies hostage. Those cookies were meant to be taken to Thomas and Shanelle's tonight for dessert, but they grabbed more important items first, such as beer, and forgot them.

Lynn thought it cute and named it Bandit. James saw the raccoon for what it was, a demon who continued to torment him. It was the demon who had jumped into the back of his truck bed and made the bloody murder scene. Splashing the bed and the outside of the truck on the passenger side blood-red by eating all of his catfish bait, scattering leftover bites of bait here and there, and exploding strawberry juice all over his white truck. Now it had taken an entire bag of cookies from the picnic table by the camper and drug it through their site to the other picnic table, where it proceeded to eat everything.

With a couple high pitched squeaks meant to antagonize him, James watched as the demon stood up on two legs, and turned away, flashing its backside. It jumped off the table and headed off into the woods dragging what remained of the bag of cookies in its mouth. It was at this point that Lynn looked over at James and burst out laughing. He knew now that nothing could be left outside anymore; everything had to be secured, food, trash, bait, everything. They Bandit-proofed their campsite, went inside, locked their door, and went to bed early.

Across the street Thomas and Shanelle neither heard nor saw anything of their friend's recent encounter with Mother Nature's four- legged living trash can. They brought their remaining snacks and empty cups into the camper and refreshed their drinks. Thomas and Shanelle then went back outside with their last refills, pushed the logs to one side to put out their fire, and sat beside it to enjoy the peace and quiet of the night as the warmth from their fire faded. Facing the road and looking at the campground sites between them and the lake, they talked about their recent fishing trip, their new friends, their dinner, and the fact that James only caught one fish.

"What are you doing over there on your phone this late?" Thomas asked, enjoying his bourbon.

"Well, first off, it's not late, it's early. Secondly, what do you think about getting James and Lynn T-shirts?" Shanelle questioned, sipping her gin.

"T-shirts? Well, by God. What for?"

"I thought it would be hilarious to get them for the day we first met," she giggled; "Rattler, and I'm with Rattler," she smiled, scrolling through screens on her phone.

Thomas smiled at Shanelle and turned back to the fire. Shanelle didn't need approval from him, she knew he thought it was funny. Clicking submit, she sat her phone down and returned her attention to her drink and the nature around her. With large smiles, they relaxed to the point where they almost fell asleep. The crackling sounds of an occasional pop of wood from their nearly spent fire and the warm glow of fading red embers helped them to finish their drinks, and then they too went to bed earlier than normal.

SUNDAY

The unwritten rules of psychological horror

Robin came out of the camper holding three double cast iron mountain pie makers, and a plastic bag of goodies.

"Cherry pies for dessert, anyone?" Robin said excitedly.

Christy cheered, and Linda threw her hands in the air, thumbs up, as she finished swallowing another mouthful of her drink. *That sounds wonderful,* Linda thought as she hurriedly walked over to Robin to help. Setting everything on the nearby cooler, the girls sorted their ingredients.

"There's something to be said for making your own food from scratch," Robin smiled as she mixed everything together in a small bowl, staying as close to the recipe as she could.

While she stirred, Christy placed more wood on the fire, and Linda went to make another pitcher of margaritas and to grab herself another beer.

"The water helped," Linda said as she hit the stairs; "helped me to drink more!" she exclaimed.

The rest of the directions were pretty simple. *Preheat the irons over open flames for ten minutes, spray the insides with non-stick cooking spray, put a piece of bread inside each half and press it down in the center to make a depression for your filling. Add the mixture and then connect the sides together. Heat over red-hot coals for about three minutes then pull it out to allow it to cool a couple more before eating. Easy peasy,* Robin thought. Filling the pies and closing the irons, she placed them on the hot coals.

"You have perfect timing, Linda," Robin said as she took her drink from her.

Christy got up from her chair and took hers, too.

"To the rest of the night with wonderful friends and homemade campfire cherry pies!" Christy toasted.

"Girl power!" Linda added.

They sipped on their drinks before taking their pies off the coals, walking to the camper, and leaning them over a stack of wood to cool. Robin and Christy went to sit back by the fire, and moments later Linda joined them. It wasn't long before they were sipping their drinks and thinking about their pies.

"I'll go and check on them," Robin said, placing her drink in the cup holder.

The girls watched the flames dance over and around the wood, enjoying their drinks and the lovely nighttime air.

"And on that note," Christy said facing Linda; "I'm going to grab a blanket from inside, I'll be right back."

Linda looked over at the camper and saw Robin fussing with their desserts, and Christy disappearing through the door before turning back to the fire. This turned Linda around long enough to allow the shadow behind her time to move to the adjacent campground without being seen. Slowly, the figure removed the string of lights from the awning, folding them back and forth. Not missing a beat, it started walking towards the woman in the chair, keeping to the shadows.

Scott was coming from the road and from behind the girl that sat at the campfire in her pink chair. Walking ever closer now, he was nearly there when he stepped on a twig. That was the classic telltale of impending doom, the warning of all warnings, except that to Christy, it sounded just like a pop of wood being consumed by their fire. Had she not been drinking, she might have realized what it was, a notification of imminent danger.

Taking another sip of her drink, she emptied her glass. With a sigh, she placed it on her tray to free up her hands and used them to push herself up. She stood stretching her arms into the air and took a step forward to the camper, except she didn't move forward, she was moving backwards. Scott had placed the string of lights over her head against her neck and tightened his grip, pulling back with all his strength. Linda was off her feet at times, half walking, half dragged on the ground backwards. She had been picked up into the air and held against someone's body. She was walked backwards through the tree line as she continued struggling, unable to scream or shout, until her view of the campsite slowly disappeared.

Linda's eyes widened. Once she understood what was happening, her hands went immediately to her throat in an attempt to free herself. She tried to scream but she could not. She kicked through the air, she clawed at the arms that held her in place, none of that seemed to work, Linda was still held tight against her will. She was growing dizzy, she was panicking.

Holding her against his chest and up into the air, he turned to the left to check out the surrounding campsites, all the while squeezing her harder. He threw her to the ground and pulled back, keeping the string of lights pressed firmly against her throat. Moments ago, Linda had panicked while being dragged backwards into the woods; now, she panicked because she could not breathe. Through several attempts to take breaths, nothing came. Her hands tugged at the rope around her neck, but she made no progress in loosening her attacker's grip.

Scott flipped her over on her back, sat on top, and switched from pulling the rope backwards around her neck to trying to push her head into the ground. Linda's eyes grew large when they focused on the man attacking her. They grew even larger when she recognized who it was.

"Scott! Oh, fuck no! Fuck no! Stop this. Get off me!" Linda tried to speak all those words, but nothing came out.

She told him again, but Scott kept going, he didn't even try to understand what she was saying. Linda was telling him one last time when she heard more twigs breaking and she stopped moving. Scott looked down at her. *Had he broken her neck before she had stopped breathing*, he wondered; *only the coroner could determine that, if there was a body to be found, that was*; Scott smiled at those thoughts.

He stopped strangling her and removed the string of lights, placing them to the side of her head. Taking her chin in his hand, he turned her face to the right to look away, as he removed her T-shirt. *Waste not, want not*, he smiled. Next, he pulled down her shorts, exposing her dark panties. Taking those off too, he placed them in his pocket, and reached to undo her bra.

Linda awoke to Scott inside her. He had just inserted himself and started thrusting, when Linda bounced upwards into the air, throwing him off. The realization of her still being alive after he thought he had killed her shocked him to his core; deep down he was horrified. Scott was caught off guard and found himself lacking in response, as he quickly thought of what to do.

A single, brief scream announced itself to the campground before it was silenced. Scott jammed her underpants into her mouth and slammed her head against the ground several times until she stopped moving, this time for good. The blood that was spilling out beside her head was proof that Linda was now silenced, once and for all. Climbing back on top, he finished what he started, and a minute later he was done. Leaning forward, he took hold of her breasts and pushed himself off of her to a standing position. He took her underpants and wiped himself off, placing them back into his pocket, as he listened to the campground around him. There were normal sounds in the distance, radios, an occasional car engine; he was sure no alarm would come from Linda's brief, interrupted scream.

A camp site away, Robin returned to their chairs around the campfire with three cherry pies on a plate. Looking at Christy sitting by herself, and noticing Linda was missing, she glanced at the campers across from them, back to Christy, and then again over to Linda's empty chair.

"I dunno. She was gone when I came back," Christy said, buried deep below her blanket.

Taking a pie, Christy claimed her large bite and smiled, shaking her head in approval. *She probably walked her drunk ass to the comfort station to use the restroom, or the side of a nearby camper, more likely. Don't be concerned*, Robin thought.

Robin sat down and took a large bite of hers, raised her eyebrows twice in excitement and confirmed to Christy that the pies were indeed remarkable. Scott watched the two women through the darkness, awaiting another chance to grab Robin.

"Since we started off with the hard stuff, we should be fine switching to wine. I'm going to get some, it would go well with our pies," Robin said as she stood and searched again for Linda.

"Bring three glasses, just in case," Christy said.

Nodding, Robin left for the camper, and again ascended the stairs.

"Excuse me ma'am," the man said quietly, as he stepped out of the darkness to her left.

Christy was startled but calmed a little when she saw the man wearing a park official uniform walk into the light.

"I'm sorry to bother, but we have just received word that

there's an escaped prisoner on the loose. We are systematically searching campers. It's for your safety, do you mind?" he asked pointing to the camper.

"Oh. Yes. I'll take you inside. It's Robin's camper; we've been in and out of it all evening, I'm sure he's not here," Christy said, leading the park official to the camper.

"Who said it was a 'he'?" the CO shot back defensively.

The park official's tone and response made Christy think. She lowered her eyebrows and looked over her shoulder at the green uniformed man who was rapidly approaching.

"That's far enough, Christy," Scott said, pulling his service weapon.

Christy was stopped with her left foot on the first metal step when he struck her from behind. She was falling forward when he reached to grab hold of her. Managing to catch Christy before she faceplanted into the camper door, he held her upright and continued opening it. Walking past her, he dragged Christy inside, closing it behind them. He quickly scanned the camper for Robin before locking the door.

Scott Tied her hands behind her back with Linda's bra and pushed her moist panties inside Christy's mouth. Scott cut a six-inch piece of Duct tape to gag her, then looked around again to lay eyes on Robin.

"I'm in the bathroom," he heard Robin say with impeccable timing.

She must have heard them come in or felt the camper rock when they had entered; either way, he was in, and she would be surprised. Soon he would once again have Robin within his grasp. Walking over to the electronics, he turned the radio on and increased the volume. Robin heard sad country music, and assumed the girls were in for the night.

"I hope you pulled the logs out to the edge of the pit. We don't want the fire to go all Lionel Richie." Robin said playfully. *Lionel Richie*? Seriously? *All night long*? Robin sounded her disappointment.

Scott did not answer, nor did anyone else, but he did find her statement amusing; *and smart too,* he remarked. Robin flushed the toilet and ran the water to wash her hands. Wiping them on her shorts to dry, she opened the bathroom door and stepped out to see

Scott standing menacingly over Christy.

Robin stood motionless and did not speak. Looking at him, and then down to Christy, she looked back at Scott.

"Did you kill them? Did you kill them all?" Robin asked cautiously.

"Sit. Move your ass to the dinette, and sit," he said sternly.

Robin moved slowly and sat on the right side, trying not to stare at the gun in his hand. Scott was making a point to block her exit. The way Robin saw things, she had a chance to run for the bedroom door, but she wasn't sure she could make it.

She looked away from him. Scott was still holding his pistol in his right hand, as he rummaged through her cabinets. Taking a box of Girl Scout cookies, he threw them on the table. They slid from one end to the other and stopped in front of her. Robin didn't move. He opened the refrigerator door and pulled out the last three beers they had. He sat them down in front of her.

Scott was erratic, talking quickly and moving his pistol around through the air as one would their hands, while he paced and talked.

"Open those cookies and start eating," he told her.

Robin looked on without doing or saying anything. He walked over to Christy and kicked her in the stomach. This raised her body upward and slightly backwards, moving her further underneath the dinette. Looking back at Robin, he told her again.

"Start eating," Scott demanded.

Robin reached for the caramel cookies and quickly opened the box. He watched her closely before reaching for the beer and opening them all, one after the other. He walked over to Christy and kicked her again.

"You like to party. You like to drink. You can't have that much alcohol without food. Quickly. Eat quickly," he shouted.

"Well? Go on," *if you won't take care of yourself, I will,* he mumbled.

Robin didn't hear what he said, and although confused, she jammed two cookies in her mouth and started chewing. This she did once, before slowing down. *She was in no way making quick work of them,* she thought, *she could barely eat two, how was she going to eat an entire box?* Sliding a beer to her, he nodded when she looked down at it and back to him. Robin was on her second sip when he slammed his fist down on the table and motioned to the cookies.

"I'm disappointed in you, I really am," he said, pointing back at them, demanding she eat quicker.

Robin took a cookie and after finishing it, she took another.

"There you go. Now pick up the pace," he said.

When Robin wasn't eating fast enough for his liking, he walked over to Christy and kicked her a third time. He looked at Robin and waited. He didn't say anything, he didn't have to. She seemed to eat her cookies faster when he hovered over Christy. Soon the entire box was gone. She was thankful for the beer, it seemed to be the only thing that helped her get those damn things down.

Robin looked up at him with a full stomach, and eyes oozing tears.

"Get up," he said calmly.

Robin knew if she didn't listen, he would hurt Christy again. She stood up and waited for him to approach. He pushed the pistol in her direction, poking her a couple of times in the ribs.

"Turn around."

Scott watched as Robin did what he wanted. He leaned in against her, pushing her forward onto the table. To the front of her face, and just off to the side, Scott's pistol lay out of reach; all Robin did was stare at it. Pulling her hands behind her, he taped them, then moved to the floor and did the same to her feet. Wrapping things up, he secured his pistol in his lower back.

"Stand up straight," he told her.

Reaching forward, Scott placed both hands around her waist and squeezed. Moving them up and down, he pushed inwards, massaging her stomach before moving to her breasts. Those too, he massaged before letting go. Robin recoiled when he touched her, as much as she could with being taped, which did not go unnoticed by Scott.

Placing a hand on her shoulder, he pushed her to the floor and sat her next to Christy. He turned around to the stove and took the small hand towel from the door. Reaching into the sink, he wiped it around the sides, soaking up any liquids present. Turning to Robin, he jammed as much of it as he could into her mouth before taping it shut. Having not cooked all weekend, Robin tasted the soap from when she last washed her hands, and vodka. *Vodka?* she pondered on who she was going to kill after all this was said and done. S*he knew she never wasted any alcohol; her bet was on Linda!*

"Very disappointed," he said again, as he pushed her under the dinette alongside Christy.

"You try to escape, and I'll kill her first. I'll find you next, and you'll wish you were dead, too," he threatened.

"I'll be right back," he said, walking out the camper and closing the door, leaving Christy and Robin under the dinette.

He had been hiking for almost two hours before the building came into view. Moving slower than normal due to exhaustion, he continued putting one foot in front of the other. The muscles in his legs hurt, his body ached, the bottoms of his feet were bloody from walking barefoot; The CO was miserable, but he had survived, he had persevered. Each step hurt more than the last, but he was almost there.

Walking straight up to the keypad to the left side of the rear door, he punched in the six-digit number and entered the ranger station. It was after hours, and nobody was inside-which was good for him, it meant he wouldn't have to explain why he was naked. He quickly made his way into his office and turned on his coffee maker. A step away from where he stood, the CO opened his desk drawer and pulled out a bottle of water and drank it all down; he was starving, but he needed water above everything. Looking around, he thought of what he needed.

Pulling back the rug to expose the floor safe, he put in the measurements of the most perfect woman to have ever walked the face of the earth, Ms. Monroe herself. Spinning left he stopped at 36. Passing the second number up, he stopped at 24. He finished by spinning right to 34. He pulled the handle and reached for his things. Taking his backup pistol, his spare wallet, and a set of keys, he placed everything on his desk. The CO started a cup of coffee and went to get dressed. With great attention to detail, he tucked in his shirt, shored up his tie, and stretched his arms above his head. The wonderful aroma of hazelnut coffee quickly filled the room; *perfect timing*, he thought. He placed his pistol in his holster, grabbed the rest of his things, and headed for the door.

Taking vehicle 23, he drove to the main gate. He was nearly there when he had finished his coffee; *damn, I should have made two*, he complained. Seeing no one present didn't worry him, there were lots of reasons why someone would step away, or why it wouldn't be staffed for a short period of time. Glancing over at the window and door as he passed, he saw nothing out of the ordinary. Taking the first right, he kept going until he reached the camp gate. He parked and got out. Walking past the building for one more check, he started off Northeast to run into the Honeysuckle trail.

The CO left the trail and started walking through the campground searching for the man who had tied him up and left him to die. Kevin didn't dwell on the thoughts that he was trying to block from his memory. Making him get naked, taking his clothes, and stealing his vehicle and service weapons; those memories were as painful to him now as when they first occurred. He had passed through several sites finding nothing, when he noticed a woman's naked body stuffed into the bushes at the edge of a campsite.

He approached quietly and shone his light on her. She had been strangled, and probably raped. She was definitely dead. Looking closer, he found the woman's clothing in a nearby bush only a few feet away. He was still investigating the scene when a camper door flew open, and a man came out. He was dressed just like him! He sank back into the darkness, past the tree line and watched him approach.

The imposter walked straight up to the woman and taking a fistful of hair, dragged her to the fire pit. It was obvious the man knew exactly where she was, and therefore the fact that she was already dead. *He was the one who had probably killed her in the first place,* the CO thought, as he continued watching the man. The man made sure nobody was looking before positioning her sitting in the chair and walked back to the road to check out how it looked. Scott returned to the woman and looked at her. He pulled her upward a little, making more of her body visible, and turned her head slightly to the right. Leaving her there, he started walking back to the camper.

The CO took this time to call for backup. He radioed in his position and gave a brief description of what was happening, along with the campground site number. He silenced his radio and went back to watch the camper and wait. He looked on in disbelief as a golf cart pulled up and Carmen got out.

"Hey there! I saw you out and about; hope I caught you at a good time," she paused.

Scott tensed up, waiting to spring into action; he was barely breathing as the woman looked past him to the camper and then back at the woman sitting in the chair.

"I'm following up on a missing dog. Have you seen him?" Carmen asked a little louder.

There was no response from the woman sitting by the campfire. Scott didn't move either, he continued listening though.

"Hey you. You by the fire. Have you seen a stray dog? His name is Parker and he's a Golden Retriever?" she asked again.

There was still no response from the person warming themself at the campfire. Unnoticed by Carmen, there was still no movement from Scott, who stood motionless facing her direction not two feet from the camper door. Carmen took a few steps towards the campfire before she noticed the man standing nearby in the shadows.

"Tom. George. Is that you? Kevin?" Carmen asked, recognizing the uniform.

Scott knew the whereabouts of the dog, but he wasn't telling. Kevin knew the whereabouts of the killer, but he couldn't reveal his position, not yet.

"Shhh. You'll scare him. I found the dog here, they have him inside and are giving him some food and water before they bring Parker out," he said quietly.

"How wonderful!" Carmen smiled, still trying to figure out who she was talking to.

"Can you come over and get him? He won't come to me. You'll have to go inside for him though, I'm afraid," the CO told her.

"Sure, I'll be happy to," Carmen said as she walked straight at him.

The CO hiding in the bushes watched as the volunteer

walked up to the imposter, who waited until she was close enough before pistol-whipping her, knocking Carmen senseless down to the ground. Although her vision was blurred, and her hand-eye coordination was off, she still flailed her arms trying to protect herself. Gone was her ability to articulate, to speak; to passersby, she looked drunk, or hung over, at least. Scott took the struggling woman and dragged her inside the camper by her feet. Her head hit every metal step that led to the door. She made a small moan of pain each time she hit her head.

Scott closed the door and dropped her just inside the entryway, before looking over at Robin and Christy. The women were still underneath the dinette. Both had tape over their mouths, with Robin's hands and ankles taped as well; everything looked as it should have, Scott was seeing everything come together.

Outside, the CO couldn't help feeling some level of despair, after all, he knew Carmen personally. *There were at least two people inside that camper, possibly three,* he thought, as he tried to come up with a plan. *If there was no one inside before Carmen had arrived, why didn't he just make up a story and leave? Why didn't he kill her and then leave, instead of taking her hostage?* His mind raced to come up with answers. Staring out through the darkness, his thoughts trailed away before he again focused. He didn't want the re-enforcements arriving without a plan, he had to think.

Scott found it somewhat easier to manipulate Robin when a friend or a total stranger was involved. Robin acted and responded differently when it wasn't herself she was risking. He could tell that she loved her friends, that she loved everyone, everyone except him. Case in point: reaching down beside Robin to grab Christy, he saw her flinch and close her eyes, pretending to be unconscious. That didn't surprise him, he was expecting her to be awake by now. Pulling her out into the main walkway, he let go of her, and Christy hit the floor with a loud uncomfortable thud. She landed flat on her back, immediately closing her eyes again. Robin recoiled and looked on, trying to hide her concern.

Scott walked backwards to the volunteer and scooped her up into his arms. Carrying her over to the kitchen sink, he propped her up against it. The woman's stomach and breasts were helping to keep her upright, leaning forward and resting her body against the sink. Her head was turned sideways, with her ear against a few dirty plates, leaving her short bright red hair hanging slightly over the edge, the tips floating in dirty water.

"Pick one," Scott told her.

When Robin didn't respond with anything except a whimper, he reached down and took Christy, raising her into as much of a standing position as he could; with her still feigning asleep, she was dead weight. Turning her to face Robin, he held Christy against his body and to the right of the volunteer, before asking again.

"Pick one to save," he yelled.

The CO outside heard two words: *pick* and *save*. *Things were going from bad to worse*, he thought as he crept closer to the camper door. He had reached the outside power receptacle when he felt the urge to hide. The CO quickly crawled under the camper and turned around facing the stairs and held his breath. Scott placed Christy headfirst into the captain's chair and stuck his head out the door to investigate.

The door swung open wide, and the CO saw the man's left boot step down and pause. Scott scanned the campground, thinking he had heard something. Looking again to his left, he stood quietly listening to the nature around him-there was none, it was deathly quiet. Scott knew that sound, he was all too familiar with it, or the lack of it. He went back into the camper and closed the door. The CO continued hiding underneath the stairs and out of sight. *I won't miss you again,* the CO thought as he heard the camper door lock.

Picking Christy back up, he walked over to Robin and let her go. This time Christy hit the floor face-first and bounced slightly toward the refrigerator. She opened her eyes to check her surroundings and quickly closed them again. *By not telling me, you've made my decision,* he thought. Looking over at Robin, he reached behind and grabbed Carmen by the arm and pulled her toward him. She fell forward down to her knees, with Scott holding her upright only by her left arm. Taking his Allagash from his belt, he opened it and pushed it deep into Carmen's stomach, all the way in, twisting his wrist to the right before stopping.

Robin started violently shaking and began dry heaving or throwing up, Scott couldn't be sure. He acted quickly. He pushed Carmen off his knife and onto the bedroom side of the camper and reached for Robin's face. He pulled her toward him to get her closer on the laminate and removed her gag. *His timing was perfect,* he thought sarcastically, as Robin emptied the contents of her stomach, literally tossing her cookies all over his shoes. He wiped his knife clean on her shirt and placed it back in his pocket. Moving to Christy, he pushed his boots under her body, raised her slightly up into the air, and cleaned them off as best he could.

"Her bloods on your hands," Scott said with exaggerated strength.

Robin had finished throwing up and was leaning forward on her knees when Scott looked back down at Christy, catching her closing her eyes yet again. Pulling out his service weapon he lowered it to her shoulder and pulled the trigger twice. Christy flailed and bounced around in pain, screaming as loud as she could through her taped mouth. Blood poured out all over the camper floor, spraying the refrigerator and the wall beside it.

Scott noticed that the camper was not levelled properly; his first clue was the torrent of blood quickly painting the floor red, making its way for the carpet in the bedroom. The red river flowing through the camper distracted him for a moment, but Scott quickly focused.

Outside the camper and below the steps, the CO prepared himself for the takedown. He gathered his resolve, drew in a few quick breaths, and then waited for the man to try to escape. A few feet above and behind the CO, Robin felt sick. Off to her left, Carmen lie unconscious bleeding slowly from her stomach, and to her right, Christy was rapidly draining her life onto the floor around her, writhing in pain.

"Hang in there Christy!" Robin managed, before Scott kicked her.

He pulled Robin up by her neck and forced her toward the kitchen sink. She struggled to get free, jerking hard enough to surprise him. This was quickly ended when he slammed her head against the bloody refrigerator once, then again. Robin grew limp in his arms. He held on tightly, raised her back up to her feet, and slammed her against it one more time, before stepping over Christy's body, dragging Robin along with him.

"I'm coming out," Scott yelled as he opened the door.

Pausing before moving down the steps, Scott looked out

into the darkness, but saw nothing. *How I wish I brought those damn goggles,* he thought, pulling Robin in front of him. Holding her tightly against his chest, he slowly took the steps, one rung at a time. The woman's feet were taped together at the ankles and rested on the man's left boot; the CO knew exactly how this was going to go down. As the imposter took another step, with poor timing came the sirens. Scott heard them in the distance, and guessed he had several minutes to escape before he would be seen driving away; *make haste,* he thought as he took more steps.

The CO watched him from beneath the camper, without making a sound. He waited until both feet were on the lowest step. Again, the CO watched as the imposter paused to cautiously check his surroundings; the suspense was killing him, but for him to have a chance at being successful, he had to delay his action. He waited longer, telling himself to be patient. *Wait for it. Wait for it,* the CO thought. Scott started down to the ground with his left foot first. Finally, the CO had what he was waiting for.

Behind Scott in the camper, Christy would never know what happened to Robin. She was in great pain when one moment Scott and Robin were there, and after closing her eyes and opening them, the next moment they were gone. Christy walked her good hand forward on the floor and out above her head, grabbing the edge of the couch to pull herself closer to the door. If she could make it to the truck, she could get her cell phone and call for help. Pulling herself forward until her elbow was bent, Christy lost consciousness.

Scott's left foot had just touched the ground when the CO took hold of his ankles and started to pull him backwards under the steps. Scott fell forward on top of Robin, choosing not to let go of her. He grew enraged and kicked his feet backwards, striking the CO and the stairs several times, but the CO did not let go. Scott continued kicking, grunted a few times, and finally decided to let go of Robin to pull away. Leverage was with him, and after a few more tries, he broke free. Scott crawled forward on his hands and knees, almost leapfrogging, until he was out of reach. He jumped to his feet and turned to grab Robin, *he wasn't leaving without her*, he thought, as he grabbed again and came up empty.

The CO had rolled out from the camper steps and grabbed the woman, throwing her backwards to the dying campfire. He too went to his feet and when the imposter turned to see where Robin was, the CO tackled him, throwing his shoulder into Scott's chest. Scott lost his air and struggled to breathe as the CO moved closer and hit him with his pistol. With as much damage as Scott had dealt out to others, it appeared he could not take it himself. The CO hit him several times before he watched the imposter stop moving and his eyes close shut.

Onlookers from adjacent campsites awakened from gunshots watched from a distance as one CO turned over another, placed his hands behind his back and handcuffed him.

"Two in one night, hot damn!" Audrey said excitedly as the old couple looked through their camper window at the scene unfolding in front of their very eyes.

"Where's the commotion coming from, is it James and Lynn?" Shanelle asked.

"No, it's not their camper. I don't know what's going on," Thomas replied between sips of his bourbon.

"I think everything's all wrapped up now," James told Lynn, as he went outside to get a closer look.

The sirens grew louder, and it was obvious to him that his backup had already entered the park and passed the main gate; *time to get going,* Kevin thought.

Turning on his radio, he prepared to call in an update and give further instruction to his team. Looking at the girl, she was breathing but seemed unconscious. Leaving her where she was, he slowly stepped into the camper and viewed the crime scene with the eyes of a detective.

"I'm off into the woods on this guy's trail. There are two women who need medical attention inside the camper located just west of site 123. Get an ambulance and rope everything off as a crime scene; follow the usual," Kevin told them.

"Alright. Understood," Kevin heard in reply as he climbed down from the camper and took everything in one last time.

Moving over to the imposter sprawled out to his left, he

dragged him to the SUV, pushed him into the back seat and closed the door. Walking toward the fire pit, he reached for the woman, who recoiled; she was now awake, and she was still trying to escape her nightmare.

"It's OK. You are safe now. Can you stand?" the CO asked as he reached again for her.

Robin nodded and this time accepted his help. Leaning over, the CO cut the tape from her feet and stood back up. Kevin took hold of her arm to help her stand and led her over to his vehicle. They slowly walked, until Robin started to pull away.

"My friends. What about my friends?" Robin asked painfully.

"They are going to be fine; they'll make it. The ambulance is on the way," the CO told her, opening the front door and moving her closer.

"You're not going to untie me?" Robin asked, as he slid her inside.

"Now what do you think? Why did you have to be such a tease? Why didn't you just leave when you could have," he paused before closing the door and quieting Robin's screams.

James watched from the side of the road in front of his truck, while Lynn struggled to get a better view through the bedroom window. Thomas and Shanelle watched from the side of their RV with drinks in hand. Audrey and Jimmy finished their beer, microwaved a bag of popcorn, and peeked through their main cabin window, hoping for more. Everyone watched as one CO picked up the other and dragged him to the back of the SUV before turning around to check on the woman. Helping her into the vehicle brought closure to the onlookers, and with little or no chance for a fight or additional gunshots, they turned their lights off and went to bed.

Thomas and Shanelle's exterior lighting turned off first, followed closely by James turning off his as he went to check on Lynn. All the lights on the nearby campers were off now, and everyone was settling in for much needed sleep, all except Audrey and Jimmy. Their outside lights were already off before things went down, and of the three couples witnessing tonight's drama, they had the best view of the woman being put into the front seat.

"Was she tied up?" Audrey asked him.

"I don't know. It sort of looked like she had on gray handcuffs?" Jimmy replied.

None of the nearby campers cared about the approaching sirens, they had already seen the good stuff. They didn't care to watch a few police men come and tidy up the crime scene, nor did they want to be bothered by answering questions clear into daylight; they needed sleep, they had their excitement for the night.

Kevin walked around to his side and got in, started the vehicle, and took off in the opposite direction of the approaching sirens. He would be leaving from the left side of the main road, which would circle back around to the main gate, effectively missing his team. There would be no questions asked when he reported back in that he didn't catch him. He'll give a description of the attacker, of the car, he'll document how he was detained in the woods for days; everything he will share with them, everything except the details on how he escaped being tied to a tree and left for dead, except how things turned out tonight.

Robin had stopped screaming at this point and just sat there, looking through her passenger side window. She felt total despair and grief overtaking her; she didn't want to live anymore, not with everything that had transpired this weekend, not with what had happened to her friends. Some of them she had not seen in days. Robin wondered what Scott had done to Teena and her husband. Kevin looked over his shoulder at his brother Scott in the back seat who was still unconscious. He glanced over at Robin as he drove away, wondering what Scott had ever seen in her. Although both Kevin and Robin thought about various things in their heads, they didn't talk to each other, they didn't speak out loud, everything was quiet as he drove away.

Back at the camper, nobody was present as the shadow gingerly moved along the edge of the campsite against the trees, staying just within the darkness. It cared nothing for hiding behind trees or along the ground, basically, it moved as it wanted to. He knew that secrecy was important. He also knew that he could easily dispatch anyone who noticed him approach, well, almost anyone. Pausing from time to time to keep an eye on his surroundings, he took unusually large steps, covering the distance between the road and the camper door quicker than a normal man could.

      Standing motionless behind the camper, he watched as they drove off before heading inside. He had taken but a single step when the ambulance pulled up. Their sirens had been announcing the arrival of the first responders for miles now, and they had beaten the police, or the DNR as they were called; it was unfortunate for them, but such was the life of the first responder. Moving back into the shadows behind the camper, he paused cautiously. The sirens shut off, and shortly after that, a person got out. *There was only one*, he thought, as the woman jumped out holding her trauma kit and bolted for the camper.

      The dark figure waited for her to get closer before stepping into her path and taking hold of her uniform, throwing the EMT backwards out of the light of the campers and deep into the darkness. Before she had hit the ground a man was comfortably resting on top of her. He added his weight to hers, knocking the wind from Martina as they landed. On her back, and nearly ten feet behind the camper, she found herself looking up through the trees at a long cloud that was backlit by tonight's full moon. Struggling to understand how she got there, Martina now fought to breathe. She found it impossible to scream when her lungs demanded oxygen. Making matters worse was the man who sat on top of her, placing his hand over her mouth to silence her, or to stop her from breathing outright.

      Second to the initial shock of being thrown into the air and having someone land on top of her before she hit the ground was the fact that she could not breathe. It was that feeling that crushed her, that disturbed her the most. The EMT tried to dislodge her attacker by flailing wildly and jumping into the air; she pressed her hands against the ground for extra leverage and again pushed her body upwards, but he was too strong. She thrust with her lower body; using her legs she bounced several times up into the air, this did not work, either. Martina was caught and slammed down onto the ground.

    She found herself now on her back, with the dark figure pressing down against her. She resorted to attacking the face; using her palms to push him away, she extended her arms. When that didn't work, she used her fingers; she bent them forward, digging them into the flesh on his cheeks.

    All those things she tried while gasping for air through the narrow spaces between the man's fingers that pressed down hard against her face; she grew desperate, realizing that very little oxygen came her way.

    He was unusually pale in the diminished light of the moon, yes, unusually pale, and cold. Most of the moonlight was blocked from them and hidden by the camper, but he still had a light complexion about him. Her body spasmed and jerked as she tried again to take in air. She panicked as her attacker gathered up her hands, stretching them out above her head. He held them in one hand, and his other stayed firmly over her face. *He was very cold,* she thought, as she continued to struggle to get free, as she struggled to breathe. She felt herself losing consciousness, or worse, dying. It became harder to keep her eyes open, and as it started to get darker around her, she lost all hope.

    He shook her a few times and watched her respond, before letting go of her wrists. Taking his free hand, he placed his thin index finger over his lips, telling her to be quiet, then removed his hand from her face. The only noise heard if one was close enough, was that of air continuing to be drawn into her lungs. He slid his right hand over her breasts and kept going lower. Pressing against her, he caressed and rubbed her thighs. She looked at the man as she continued to catch her breath but didn't struggle or overly protest. Martina did everything she could to breathe, she wanted to live.

    Moving his hand to the center, he pressed inward and upward with his thumb, he was as sloppy as a six-year-old. *Damn, I really need to date more, I'm out of practice,* he thought, continuing to try. *Ah screw it,* he grew frustrated. *Look away from me,* she heard in her head. *Smile and look away from me.* His eyes were looking through her as Martina turned her head to the left, offering herself and ceasing to struggle; a smile passed briefly over his face when she stopped protesting, although he somewhat preferred the challenges of a struggle. He kissed her chin, the side of her face, her neck, while his left hand strayed once again onto her breasts, his thumb moving rhythmically faster, harder. A small jerk from the woman in acknowledgement and he went from mashing a breast in his hand to pressing down on her. That was followed by a small gasp when he sunk his teeth deep into her throat.

For him, feeding wasn't just a basic need for survival, for nutrients, for blood, it was sensual. The entire time he partook of her blood, he was reliving that fateful day when the same was done to him. He knew how it felt, what she was thinking, the pleasure, the pain. He pushed harder against her, keeping her in place as she tried to struggle free. Then it was over, the woman lie beneath him as if in a dormant state. He had taken his fill, and then some. Removing his right hand, he pushed off with his left and stood up. Looking at the lovely Hispanic woman, he pondered; it had been years, literally years since he'd enjoyed one, and with a smile he turned away.

The vampire looked at the trees, at the camper, enjoying it all again for the first time, and then craned his neck up towards the night sky before he knelt back down beside her to bury his head into her neck one last time. With a single kiss he pulled away. His eyes had never left his surroundings, he never ceased listening to the night around him. He remarked how he had remained ever vigilant, alert; it was one of the most important strengths of a vampire, and one that he had mastered over the years.

Off to the side of the EMT, he looked at her closely, taking in her beauty. *She wasn't Karen, or Amalie, but she had qualities; if he hadn't needed to feed, if things were different, if he had met her out in public, who knows,* he thought, *who knows*. He picked her up and quickly walked to the ambulance. He tossed her inside and climbed in after her, closing the door behind them. It was then he heard more sirens off in the distance. He didn't care anymore about the potentially dead bodies inside the camper, it was better to feed off the living; it was preferred, no, necessary. His thoughts went now to survival and escaping unnoticed for what he was; keeping to the shadows of the mortal's lifetimes around him was paramount.

His train of thought was interrupted by the sirens that had just arrived outside the ambulance. Like earlier, they were turned off, and then he heard a door close, and then another; *two doors closed, he wouldn't be so lucky this time,* he thought.

"Think. Think," he said quietly, followed by *a hurry, hurry* in his head.

The vampire, or Dr. Stevens, as he was known to humans in this lifetime, opened the ambulance door and jumped out. Smiling briefly at the two men in uniform, he read their name tags and then turned to close the door, shaking his head sadly.

George and Thomas looked at him, with their weapons drawn. The two were obviously surprised by the man jumping out of the back of an ambulance only feet away from them.

"You know, you shouldn't do that," Tom said.

"Yeah. That could have been bad," George added.

"Sorry guys," the EMT replied.

There was something about him that felt calming. He was short, unusually short one would say, probably standing barely five feet tall. He was an older man with blonde hair mixed with gray. It was long enough to be pulled back in a ponytail, but not too long where it landed all about his shoulders. He wore a loose fitting blue EMT uniform. A pocket protector that must have held at least six different pens and pencils distracted anyone unfortunate enough to lay eyes on it. Underneath, and slightly off to the side was his ID badge held in place with a small metal alligator clip. Overall, he was a gaunt and frail looking man. George and Thomas were staring at the EMT with peaceful expressions on their faces, thinking the exact same thing-*the uniform that he wore looked like it was at least two sizes too big; he looked thin, and frail.* After a short second passed, the men both turned to face the camper.

"Stay focused guys," George said as he opened the door and Tom's eyes darted around to cover him.

Half a mile down the road, Kevin slowed to yield the right of way.

"Glowing eyes, those were red glowing eyes," Kevin said without thinking, as he checked his rear-view mirror.

Drawing a blank expression from Robin, he looked over his shoulder before stomping on the gas and throwing gravel behind them. She couldn't see anything through her tears, and by the time she had squeezed off as many as she could to clear them, it was obvious to her that the man driving the car had lost sight of whatever it was. She whimpered and sniffled, her mind racing, before she found herself again looking out her window for a way to escape. Moments later she went back to hanging her head and looking down to her knees.

Hours later, back at the campground, James turned on the TV in the bedroom and cuddled into Lynn to enjoy his morning coffee and the latest news. She was still sleeping and would probably remain that way for a several hours more. It had been a late night, and with the recent events keeping them up, they were exhausted. Although he had coffee to help him, he was fighting the urge to fall back asleep. Pushing the channel down button, he waited for the TV to honor his request.

"Good morning, I'm reporting live from Hearty Lake Campground, where a shocking and tragic incident unfolded sometime last night. Authorities have confirmed a double murder that has sent shockwaves through this otherwise serene campground," the woman stated.

The camera that was zoomed in for a closeup of the reporter against a camper flanked by a few trees panned out and moved to the right, leaving her behind and focusing on the vehicle. It was cordoned off with yellow caution tape and several uniformed men walking around with clip boards and black plastic trash bags.

"Details are still emerging, but what we know so far is that two individuals were found deceased in this campsite earlier this morning. DNR enforcement officials have cordoned off the area as they conduct a thorough investigation into this gruesome crime.

Witnesses in the vicinity reported hearing disturbances and raised voices from the direction of the victims' campsite earlier in the evening. Shortly after, the sounds abruptly ceased, prompting concern among nearby campers. Upon investigation, the grim discovery was made, leading to an immediate call to emergency services.

Authorities have not released the identities of the victims, pending notification of their immediate families. The motive behind this tragic incident remains unclear, leaving both campers and law enforcement officials deeply unsettled," the woman's voice said confidently.

The camera now moved sideways across the caution tape and centered on the camper front door. The reporter walked into the shot and turned to face the metal stairs, continuing her story.

"The campground, typically a haven for nature enthusiasts and families seeking a peaceful retreat, now bears the weight of an unsettling crime scene. Shock and disbelief ripple through the community as campers are evacuated and law enforcement officers work tirelessly to gather evidence and piece together what transpired.

Investigators are urging anyone who may have information or witnessed anything unusual in the area to come forward and assist in the ongoing investigation. At this time, there's no indication of a suspect in custody, heightening concerns among campers and prompting reminders about safety and vigilance."

James looked away to the ceiling and thought about those last statements. They had all witnessed a man and a woman being taken away. The vehicle left and ambulances came afterward to assist with the injured. With two murders reported earlier, and having seen two people taken away prior, he wondered what else had occurred.

"As the sun rises over the campground, a somber atmosphere pervades as authorities continue their efforts to bring clarity to this tragic event. We will obtain further updates as this story develops. Carrie Jones reporting live from Site 123, Hearty

Lake Campground; back to you in the studio," Carrie concluded.

James finished his coffee and stretched over Lynn to look through the bedroom window. The area did indeed look like a crime scene, although he didn't fully understand why. The ambulances were gone. In their stead were a few police cruisers, a DNR vehicle, and a few unmarked cars. At least a dozen men in various enforcement uniforms scampered around investigating and collecting this and that. Continuing to stare out the window, his attention was drawn back to the TV.

He watched as they switched to a commercial. When the news returned, gone were the references to the events unfolding outside his bedroom window. With his coffee now gone, and Lynn still sleeping beside him, he thought about his chances of waking her when he got out of bed to get another cup. He chose to let her sleep.

"We now switch back to our scheduled programming," he heard the announcer's voice say, before turning over and falling back asleep.

Miles away, and much later in the evening, two men were sitting in large recliners eating fast food and watching the nightly news. The normal headlines of inclement weather, corrupt politics, the latest mass shooting, and today's update about the war overseas had just finished. The picture changed to a familiar building nestled against the backdrop of heavily forested trees, and then a local story came on.

"The recent vandalism at the raptor rehab center has left a trail of destruction and raised significant concerns within both the wildlife conservation and local communities. The deliberate act of defacing property and disturbing the rehabilitation efforts aimed at nurturing injured or endangered raptors is not only disheartening but also raises questions about the motives behind such an egregious act," the reporter said.

Switching camera views and panning slowly, the camera walked up to the door and filmed into the building showing only part of the destruction that was being described.

"Authorities arrived at the scene to find enclosures damaged, equipment destroyed, and some of the resident birds agitated, distressed, or missing all together. This disruption not only poses an immediate threat to the well-being of these rehabilitated raptors but also disrupts the crucial conservation efforts being undertaken by the center," she continued.

Switching to a DNR vehicle in the background, the camera moved into the forest, past the trees and up into the sky in search of wildlife, stressing that no nature was present.

"The incident has sparked outrage among wildlife enthusiasts and advocates, who see this as an attack not just on property but on the broader mission of protecting and rehabilitating endangered bird species. Calls for increased security measures and stricter surveillance around such facilities have gained traction in the wake of this incident.

Interviews with center staff reveal a mix of emotions—shock, dismay, and a deepened resolve to continue their vital work despite the setback. The collaborative effort between law enforcement and the center's management is in full swing, with a joint investigation underway to identify the perpetrators and ascertain the motive behind this senseless act.

This disturbing incident underscores the vulnerability of wildlife sanctuaries and the pressing need for heightened security measures to safeguard these crucial facilities. It serves as a stark reminder of the challenges faced by those dedicated to preserving our natural world and the imperative to protect these vital spaces from vandalism and harm; Connie Kondun, Channel Six News."

The first man looked over at the second, slightly shaking his head, before taking another bite of his burger and turning back to the TV.

"The world we live in today, I tell you."

The second man looked down to the floor in deep thought. *There was no mention of a murder there. Nothing about Luna or Mary.* He waited for the reporter to bring up the camper abandoned down by the amphitheater, and its contents. *His camper, the suitcase by the door, nothing else was mentioned.* Reaching for another bite of his burger, he fought to remember, and reminisced…

"I know, right?"

Not the end.

EPILOGUE

      I met my camping friends Thomas and Shanelle, whose names were changed to protect their innocence, close to how the story portrayed. Camping, hiking, cornhole with Redds, boating, fishing, lighting a fatty*, roaring campfires, a fish fry in near total darkness, and good times spent with wonderful friends; those are just some of the memories I'll never forget. Yes, I did receive that T-shirt as a remembrance of that dirty day where I first met my camping friends.

      Loose ends; inevitably, there are always loose ends. If you find any that you are curious about, message me directly on social media (no spoilers for others), and I'll clue you in to why they exist. I'll give you a hint. Other than the obvious one from the ending, the magical number three rears its majestic head once again.

---

* "A fatty is a section of pine tree root heavy with sap. It burns hard and ignites quickly with little effort. You can use one and if conditions are right, you won't need kindling or tinder," Thomas informed me, sharing one of his many camping secrets.

AUTHOR BIOGRAPHY

James H. Summers was born in a suburb of Chicago, Illinois, back in the 1960s. His family moved to Kentucky in the 1970s, and James has called Kentuckiana home ever since. He enjoys all things horror, particularly B movies. Some of his favorite authors are Edgar Allen Poe, Clive Barker, J. K. Rowling, Stephen King, J. R. R. Tolkien, Anne Rice, and R. A. Salvatore. Several of his favorite directors are Quentin Tarantino, Guillermo del Toro, Ron Howard, Robert Zemeckis, Peter Jackson, Zack Snyder, Chad Stahelski, and someone who would love to make his dreams come true and get him on the big screen!

Seeing darkness in all things good and knowing all too well there is good and evil within us all, James describes the horror around us that is ever-present in our daily life. It was there yesterday though no one noticed. It is there now, although it will not make tonight's news. It will be there tomorrow, just out of sight, if you are lucky. This horror has been occurring from the dawn of time, year after year, ever since the first man picked up a rock as a means to an end.

Loose your mind and allow it to race as James clues you in to what your neighbors, your friends, your family, what total strangers do in the dark, just outside the edge of comprehension, of reality. It's bad enough to make you turn away. It's bad enough to plead ignorance and hide from. It's bad enough to make you wonder why, or how it could happen. Deep down inside you want to know; deep down inside you don't.

OTHER WORKS BY JAMES H. SUMMERS

Bereft Reality is a psychological horror thriller. It takes place in the slums around Lincoln Park, Detroit, and touches on the human aspects of self-worth and self-esteem. It stresses the good and evil inside us all, making you question what you would do in certain social situations. Heavy in pop culture references, shock and awe, and dream sequences to boot! Beware of Jake! This is the first book in the Fine Lines trilogy and was published 4/16/15.

Picking Murphys is a supernatural psychological horror thriller. It takes place around the wonderful vacation town of Murphys, California. Follow a family of four as they are set upon by an evil spirit on the way to the trip of their lifetime. A pair of good spirits are never far behind; but seem to fall short when attempting to determine why the evil has centered on that family. The vengeful, evil spirit will stop at nothing to achieve its goals. Detailed dreams and nightmares convolute reality, shocking you to your core. This book was published 2/15/16.

First Responder is a dark romance psychological horror thriller. It takes place near a college in southern California. The main characters are a vampire who holds down a job as a psychologist, an EMT, and a college student. Delving into psychiatric disorders, along with the difficulty of being a vampire in today's society, James explores the need to survive and the desire to do good. This is the first book in an unnamed trilogy and was published 2/21/17.

www.ingramcontent.com/pod-product-compliance
Lightning Source LLC
LaVergne TN
LVHW021808060526
838201LV00058B/3280